"HA...
T...
GILM... ...URED.

"Nay," Isobel whispered.

"Or kissed?" He knew he shouldn't move closer. He knew he shouldn't touch her. And when he leaned in, he knew beyond a shadow of a doubt that he shouldn't kiss her.

But he did, softly, upon the cheek. And once that bridge was crossed, he could not seem to stop, for he kissed her jaw, then moved lower, down the smooth length of her neck.

Her skin was warm, her breathing shallow, and when he forced himself to lift his head, he saw that her eyes were closed.

"Mayhap being loved would not be so hideous," he suggested.

She opened her eyes slowly. "Methinks," she said, "that you are mistaking love for lust."

He couldn't help but smile, for desire shone like a fire in her eyes. "Either way, lass, I am well flattered."

Other AVON ROMANCES

BEFORE THE DAWN *by Beverly Jenkins*
BELOVED PROTECTOR *by Linda O'Brien*
AN INNOCENT MISTRESS: FOUR BRIDES
FOR FOUR BROTHERS *by Rebecca Wade*
THE MAIDEN AND HER KNIGHT
by Margaret Moore
A MATTER OF SCANDAL: WITH THIS RING
by Suzanne Enoch
SECRET VOWS *by Mary Reed McCall*
AN UNLIKELY LADY *by Rachelle Morgan*

Coming Soon

HEART OF NIGHT *by Taylor Chase*
HIS UNEXPECTED WIFE *by Maureen McKade*

And Don't Miss These
ROMANTIC TREASURES
from Avon Books

A NOTORIOUS LOVE *by Sabrina Jeffries*
THE OUTLAW AND THE LADY *by Lorraine Heath*
THE SEDUCTION OF SARA *by Karen Hawkins*

LOIS GREIMAN

HIGHLAND ROGUES

THE MacGOWAN BETROTHAL

AVON BOOKS
An Imprint of HarperCollinsPublishers

AVON BOOKS
An Imprint of HarperCollins *Publishers*
10 East 53rd Street
New York, New York 10022-5299

Copyright © 2001 by Lois Greiman
ISBN: 0-380-81541-9
www.avonromance.com

First Avon Books paperback printing: November 2001

Avon Trademark Reg. U.S. Pat Off. and in Other Countries, Marca Registrada, Hecho en U.S.A.
HarperCollins ® is a trademark of HarperCollins Publishers Inc.

Printed in the U.S.A.

10 9 8 7 6 5 4 3 2 1

To Micki Nuding,
the best editor in the universe.
Thanks for laughing and crying
in all the right places.

The Prophecy

He who would take a Fraser bride,
these few rules he must abide.

Peaceable yet powerful he must be,
cunning but kind to me and thee.

The last rule but not of less import,
he'll be the loving and beloved sort.

If a Fraser bride he longs to take,
he'll remember these rules for his life's sake.

For the swain who forgets the things I've said,
will find himself amongst the dead.

Meara of the Fold

Prologue

Isobel scanned the great hall, making certain all was prepared for the feast.

'Twas the eve of Christmas at lofty Evermyst. The Yule log, as large around as a destrier's barrel, burned bright and merry in the great hall's giant hearth. Red berried holly gaily adorned the walls in sprigs of twelve while the scent of roast boar and ginger dolls wafted dreamily throughout the keep.

Thronged with Frasers and MacGowans and assorted guests, the high castle had never been merrier. Near the broad wooden stairs, a group of brightly dressed children laughed over their game of hot cockles, while their elders continued their jubilant wassailing, toasting every nonsensical thing that came to mind. And beneath an arched doorway, where fresh cut mistletoe was hung by a scarlet string, Ramsay MacGowan pulled his young bride into his embrace.

"You cannot escape me so quickly, love," he murmured, "for you still owe me a good dozen kisses."

"A dozen?" Anora's tone was breathy. And though she glanced at her husband as if horrified, Isobel could not help but notice her sister's cheeks were flushed and her eyes bright with happiness.

"Aye," Ramsay murmured, bending closer to his wife's upturned face. "One for each day of Christmas. 'Tis tradition, is it not?"

"Mayhap 'tis tradition by your father's hearth, Rogue," Anora chided. "But here at Evermyst, we find better things to occupy our time."

"Do you now?" Ramsay asked, his tone hopeful, and Anora laughed in that sweet, silvery tone Isobel had come to love so well.

"I but meant I must see where our Mary has got off to."

"Ahh," said Ramsay, and glancing past Isobel, spied the babe crawling toward a bevy of giggling women who played hoodman's bluff nearby. Resignation crossed his handsome features, but happiness still shone in his soulful eyes. "Mour," he said, but when there was no response, he raised his voice and tried again. "Gilmour."

From the midst of the happy crowd, Gilmour Mac-Gowan, the rogue of the rogues, straightened. A white sleeve was tied securely about his eyes, but his slanted grin was evident as he reached blindly toward the maids who danced about him. "Is it not clear that I am busy, brother?"

"Aye, and 'tis that very thing that worries me. Make yourself useful now and see to wee Mary."

"Mary?" Gilmour said, turning his head. "Ahh, Mary, me love!" he declared and without removing the blindfold, strode rapidly through the crowd to snatch the babe from the rushes. Tossing her into the air, he caught her above his head and kissed her apple bright cheek. The baby's squeals of joy were mixed with the young women's cries of dismay, for vowing blindness, he had patted more than a few in quite inappropriate places.

"Whatever is amiss?" Gilmour asked as he pulled the cloth from his eyes. "Surely you do not think I could see through me hood."

There was a general gasp of dismay and Gilmour laughed, flashing that crooked smile that made wise fathers blanch from London to Lisbon. "Blindfold me with the cloth of your choosing, then," he challenged, "and we can begin anew."

Laughter mixed with a dozen voices, and in the melee, Gilmour settled wee Mary against his chest and turned his attention to Isobel.

Their gazes met, and in that moment his expression turned almost somber, almost devoid of that devilish spark that was his alone. "And what of you, wee Bel of the feast?" he asked. "Will you be joining us in our merriment?"

For a moment the entire world seemed to still. She could hear naught but her own heartbeat as she stared at him above the pitchers she carried.

"Laird Gilmour, we be ready for you," a maid called and giggled as she held up metal gauntlets and an ancient visor.

Isobel broke free of her trance. "Nay," she said and lifted the pitchers as proof of her duties. "I am needed elsewhere."

"Aye," he murmured, and grinning, brushed her hand with his own. "And badly."

A shiver coursed through Isobel, but she lifted her chin and refused to acknowledge the feelings, for she knew precisely what his words meant. The rogue of the rogues was on the prowl again. But despite that knowledge, despite the maids giggling inanely in the background, despite the months she'd spent learning to fend off his advances, not a single scathing rejoinder came to her lips.

Laughter swelled around her and suddenly it seemed too warm in this place, too warm and merry and smothering. She could not breathe, could not think. Then an epiphany presented itself, shining on her like a single ray of sunlight.

Her days at Evermyst had come to an end. It was time for her to leave.

Chapter 1

Henshaw, Scotland
The month of May, in the year of our Lord 1535

"**E**ffie lass, your hair is as lovely as me stallion's. And like me destrier . . ." The Munro leaned closer to the maid. She stepped warily backward, eyes wide, for even seated, he towered over her. "The very sight of such a bonny filly makes me long to bree—"

"You have our thanks, Elga!" Gilmour interrupted hastily. Straightening, he drew the maid's attention to him with the full force of his renowned smile.

The Red Lion's young serving maid pulled her gaze from Innes Munro and let it fall on Gilmour. He noticed with some satisfaction that for a fraction of a second she forgot to inhale, but it was her breathy sigh that did his heart the most good.

"The meal was a rare treat," he continued and found that he was able to relax somewhat now that the Munro had ceased his horrendous attempt to be charming. "And your kind attention has been much appreciated."

"I am happy I have pleased you, me laird," she said and curtsied. She had not yet reached eight and ten years, but she knew how to flirt using nothing more than her eyes. Of course, her breasts, prettily displayed above the kindly bodice of her gown, did nothing to detract from her charms. Ahh . . . women.

"Shall I fetch you a bit more ale?" she asked, dimpling coquettishly.

"I am tempted, Elga," he said and knew immediately that she realized he was thinking of more than the ale, for she blushed and dimpled all the more. "But nay, I'd best not."

"More of Issa's manchet bread?" she suggested. "Or another wedge of crowdie, perhaps?"

"Nay. Naught. I am well sated."

"Well, I am not sated atall," rumbled Innes Munro, scowling, first at Mour, then at the maid. "But I think you might be up to the task of seeing the job done if you've a mind to, lass. You've but to show me to your chamber and I'll—"

"What's that?" Gilmour rose abruptly to his feet, grasping the maid's arm as he did so. "I believe I hear your master calling."

Elga stared at him with wide, dreamy eyes. "Nay," she breathed. "Master Gibbs is not—"

"Mayhap it was the cook, then. You'd best go, wee Elga," Mour insisted and dropping his hand to hers, bent to kiss her knuckles. " 'Twould wound me grievously if you came to trouble on me own account."

"Oh. I . . ." She floundered for words as he caressed her fingers with his thumb. "You will return?" she asked.

"I'll be back this very night if you'll promise me a

tumble—" began the Munro, but Gilmour interrupted again.

"Certainly," he said. "We shall return. But you must go now."

She left with a troubled glance for Innes and a smile for Mour, but it was really the sway of her skirts that was the most intriguing.

"What the hell be you doing?" Innes rumbled, snatching Gilmour's attention from the girl with the grating of his voice. "She was just now warming up to me."

Gilmour found his seat and nodded casually to Russell Grier, Baron of Winbourne, who was nursing a horn of spirits some tables away.

The baron raised his drink. "Laird Gilmour of Evermyst," he called. "Where one can see forever and even the goat herder is bonny."

"To your health," greeted Mour and raised his ale. It would have been better if no one knew of the Munro's sojourn at the Red Lion, but rumor said Winbourne had troubles of his own to worry on, and by the looks of things, he was a goodly way into his cups. So Gilmour turned his attention back to his giant companion. "Warming up to her," he said, keeping his tone level. "She was about to crack you on the pate with your own goblet. What the devil did you think you were about?"

The Munro's heavy brow lowered dangerously. "I was wooing her, I was."

"Wooing! If you were wooing, I was birthing—" Gilmour began, but in that instant he noticed the other man's right hand. It was as big as a battering ram and wrapped rather suggestively about a short bladed dagger. Raising his brows, Gilmour tilted a slow grin from the knife to the bearer. "In truth," he said, nodding thoughtfully, "I've seen worse attempts." Though the chieftain of the notorious Munros couldn't flirt worth sparrow droppings, he was the devil himself when it came to knife play. "Still, if I am to help you I think you may need a wee bit more practice."

"I have practiced," grumbled the other.

"Aye. Well, these things take time." The word "forever" came to mind.

"I tire of this game," said the Munro. "Playing cat to these scrawny kitchen mice."

Tire of flirting? Was it possible? Gilmour wondered, then brought his attention rapidly back to the matter at hand: Innes Munro, his lack of charm, and his knife.

"It but takes time to understand a woman's mind," Gilmour said.

Munro deepened his scowl. "And how did you learn, MacGowan?"

Mour mulled over the giant lord's question. After all, there was no need to teach an eagle to soar. "Some are simply better suited for certain tasks than others," he began diplomatically. "In truth, I'm not particularly gifted at . . ." But now that he thought about it, he couldn't name a single task he wasn't particularly gifted at. He smiled at that realization and began to announce his findings, but at that second Munro shifted his knife with suggestive malevolence.

"How are you at dying?" he rumbled and Gilmour laughed out loud.

Time with the Munro had its merry moments after all.

"Easy now, Innes," he said. "How would it look if you attempted to kill me right here in the Red Lion?"

"Attempted?" Munro's brows lowered even more, all but hiding his porcine eyes.

"Aye," agreed Gilmour. "Losing a battle rarely makes a man appealing. Thus I would suggest that you have a try at the lassies again before—"

"Are you challenging me, MacGowan?"

Gilmour knew it would be unwise to answer such a question with a grin, but some said a mischievous imp resided in his soul and though Mour would have liked to deny it, he feared it would be less than honest to do so.

"Nay, not challenging you," he said, trying, against the odds, to keep his expression perfectly somber. "Merely attempting to fulfill me end of—" he began, but just then two women exited the kitchen, drawing Munro's attention abruptly away.

Gilmour glanced in that direction and raised his brows. They stood with their backs to the tables, and although one was broad from stem to stern, the other was as shapely and delicate as a summer blossom.

"Now there's a likely looking maid," Gilmour mused, his own interest roused already. "You've but to recall what I've told you."

Munro said nothing. Neither did his attention shift from the women.

"Remember," Gilmour said, his voice low, "best not to compare them to beasts of any sort. Never refer to lovemaking as breeding. In fact," he added, glancing at Munro's lax jaw, " 'twould be best to refrain from mentioning lovemaking atall and . . . are you listening?"

"Lovemaking," Munro intoned.

"Aye," Gilmour agreed and glanced once more at the women. "Show an interest in her," he added. "Not just in bedding her, and for the sake of heaven, learn her name. Can you do that?"

The great bull of a man turned mutinously toward him. "Do you think me daft?"

Gilmour might be a good many things, but he wasn't fool enough to answer such an inflammatory question outright. Neither was he cautious enough to ignore it altogether. "What was her name then, Munro?"

"Whose?"

"The lass who just left."

"That bit of a thing what served us?"

"Aye. What was her name?"

Munro glared as his thick lips pursed inside his unkempt, bushy red beard. "Effie."

"Nay."

"Edrea."

"Nay."

"Damnation," growled Laird Munro. " 'Tis Edrea if I say 'tis Edrea."

Gilmour leaned his shoulder against the wall and stared across the table at the giant. " 'Tis Edrea if she is an entirely different maid who happened to be christened Edrea."

"Are you challenging—shh!" Munro hissed, darting his eyes sideways and back. "She's coming."

"Who is—"

"Don't look," Munro warned, slipping his dirk back into its boot sheath and wiping a hand on his plaid. "What shall I do?"

Gilmour raised his brows in surprise, but the huge man's expression of abject panic was difficult to ignore.

"Greet her," he said, "but don't growl. Compliment the inn. She must be employed here."

From the corner of his eye, Gilmour saw the women part company. The larger of the two exited through the door while the slim maid turned back toward the kitchens. But just then her wrist was grasped by a patron at a table across the room. She turned abruptly toward him.

"Marry me, Issa," slurred the man.

His drunken companion slipped an arm about the girl's willowy waist and pulled her closer. "Nay. The lass is mine," he argued and murmured something unheard.

Gilmour rose silently to his feet. He was a good natured fellow by all accounts, but it went against his grain to see a maid handled against her will. Thus, he meandered across the stretch of floor between them.

"Is there trouble afoot?" he asked.

The girl didn't look up, but addressed the men who restrained her. "I am flattered, Regan of Longwater, but I fear your proposition may be humanly impossible. At least in your present state," she added and slipped easily from the men's grasps as they chuckled.

"No trouble," she said and lifted her gaze to Gilmour. "And a good thing, for you, MacGowan . . ." she added, "for you will forever be more the sort to cause trouble than to cure it."

Gilmour stared for a moment. "Damn me."

"A mite late for that, I fear," she countered and strode toward the kitchen.

He followed. "What be you doing here, Isobel?"

"I work here, MacGowan. And you?" She turned in the mortared doorway, her shapely form framed by the arch, her golden curls limned by the fire behind her.

"Work—"

"Aye," she interrupted and smiled as if he were a wee lad questioning his elders. "Work. Mayhap you have heard the word before."

Gilmour remembered instantly and poignantly why he disliked this woman. It wasn't because she had wounded his brother in battle at their first meeting, or even because she had attempted to have his other brother abducted before his marriage to her sister. It was because she had a wicked tongue and truly lacked any sort of appropriate appreciation for his God-given charms. She was wholly unlike the other women at Evermyst. Even Ailsa, the bonny, dark-haired widow who forever yearned after Ramsay, had a softness for him.

"I believe I *have* heard of work," he said. "I but failed to realize it involved pricking the paying customers."

"Only if those customers be me kin by marriage." She said the words softly so that none other would hear of their bond and motioned toward a slim maid child even as she turned away. "Plums, mind the eel sauce."

"I thought you had traveled to Edinburgh," Mour said.

Isobel glanced up from swinging a metal arm away from the fire. Uncovering the hanging pot, she tasted the contents, then swept the entire thing back over the flame. "Whyever would you think so, MacGowan?"

He leaned a shoulder against a rough timber set into the doorway and watched her work. The sight was disturbing. Not because she labored, for though her veins flowed with noble blood, there was none he'd rather see toil. What disturbed him was the fact that she had shed the dowdy garments she had forever worn at Evermyst and now stood dressed in a bright and simple gown that seemed to accentuate every feminine curve. "Mayhap 'tis because that is where you said you were going," he suggested.

"Ahhh yes," she agreed. "Well, there is a likely explanation."

"Which is?"

"I lied."

Rounding the corner into the kitchen, Mour bent a leg, placing a foot upon the wall behind him. The thin lass called Plums glanced timidly toward him. A reddish purple birthmark covered her left ear lobe and part of her jaw. He gave her a quick grin, but she glanced rapidly away. "Any particular reason?" he asked, turning his attention back to Bel.

She shrugged. "So you would no longer bother me."

It happened then: his little finger twitched. He had first noticed it over a year ago when he'd just met her. There was something about her that made him twitch. He'd never quite ascertained when it had ceased, but he now assumed that it was immediately upon her exodus from Evermyst. It had been blessedly sedate at the high keep since then—so sedate, in fact, that he had considered returning to his parents' castle to the south.

Once upon a time he had asked old Meara of Evermyst how she could be certain Isobel was Anora's kin. After all, they had been separated at birth, and Iso-

bel had been lost. Still, the question had been somewhat facetious, for they looked to be nearly identical.
But where Anora was charming and refined, Isobel
was cool and harsh. At least to him. Old Meara, however, had explained that before giving up the babe, a
wee shell-shaped pendant had been placed about her
neck. He had mentioned at the time that the girl wore
no such pendant, but Meara was dismissive. It seemed
that Isobel had described it perfectly and declared it
lost. So he supposed he would not get away with calling her an impostor, regardless of her caustic temperament. "I did not *bother* you," he corrected.

"A pinch more mint, Plums," Isobel said, tasting another concoction before turning briefly toward him.
"Aye, you did, MacGowan. But I can hardly blame
you. Love is like that, I suppose."

"Love." With the sternest of control, Mour kept
himself from jerking like a mishandled marionette.
Even his voice remained even. Only his pinkie moved.

She shrugged. "Infatuation, then," she corrected.

"Are you suggesting that I am infatuated with you,
lass?"

She did nothing but stare at him, her eyes wide and
innocent in her elfish face.

"Me apologies if I have given you the wrong im-
pression, Bel, but I fear I have no interest in you other
than a brotherly—"

She laughed and turned away. "The tarts are ready,
Birtle, me lad. Have a care not to burn yourself."

"Aye, mistress."

"Then why are you here, MacGowan?" she asked,
facing him suddenly.

Gilmour stared at her. He had much preferred the

subservient kitchen maid she had pretended to be when in the company of others at Evermyst. Indeed, she had once believed she was naught but a servant, for upon her humble entrance into the world, her lady mother had sent her away lest some superstitious fool believe that twins were the devil's own. Even in these modern times there were those who were eager to cry, "Witch." But there was no need for that subterfuge here at the Red Lion; there was no one to guess the truth. And indeed, perhaps none to care if they did. None but Gilmour himself, and unfortunately, he had vowed to keep his knowledge a secret.

"MacGowan," she repeated, arms akimbo. "I asked why you are here."

The smile had faded from her lips, and it dawned on him quite suddenly that a good lie was in order—for if he began spouting the truth, there could well be sobering consequences for both himself and his kin.

"I heard that the spirits here are quite exceptional." He had intended to praise the meals, but she was obviously in charge of that front and he had no wish to enhance her obviously inflated concept of herself.

"So you rode ten leagues from Evermyst for a draught?"

"I was quite parched."

"And Stout Helena's brews could not satisfy you?"

He smiled. "I am not an easy man to sate."

"Actually," she said. "I have heard the opposite, that you are quite an easy man."

"Why is it that I think you mean to insult me, Bel?"

"Perhaps because I do," she said and smiled before beginning to chop a pile of green herbage set upon a wooden board.

"Tell me something, Isobel," he said, and strode across the kitchen to stand beside her. "Why do you constantly barb me?"

"Is it the truth you want, MacGowan?" she asked, glancing up.

"Might it be complimentary?"

She stared at him for an instant, then raised her fair brows and laughed.

"What is so amusing?" rumbled a voice from behind.

Gilmour swore in silence.

"Me laird." Isobel's voice was suddenly soft.

The Munro stepped even with Gilmour and stared. "Lady Anora?"

"Nay, me laird," she said, " 'tis Isobel. Me lady's maid some months past."

"Nay. You look—"

"Much like me lady. I know. 'Twas the similarity that first caused her to take me in, and 'tis said that familiarity only sharpens those attributes."

"Isobel?" His tone was still harsh with suspicion.

"Aye. See," she said. Pulling a gray cloth from a nearby table, she covered her hair. It was then that Mour noticed that she had once again begun to slouch.

The Munro's scowl deepened. "What be you doing here, lass?"

"Me lady had no further use of me, so I went abroad to make me fortune. And what of you, me laird, why do you honor us with your presence here?"

Innes shifted his gaze to Gilmour and away. "I was hungry."

"Ahhh." The word sounded perfectly innocent, but there was something in her eyes that spoke volumes. "I hope you found the meal to your liking."

Munro glanced about the kitchen. "You do the cooking here?"

"Aye. 'Tis fortunate that I've been able to find a place that would take me on."

"Mayhap they are the fortunate ones."

She curtsied shyly. "You flatter me, me laird."

"I do not," Munro denied, then brightened slightly as he realized this was not an accusation. Still, his brows remained scrunched over his narrow eyes "You look quite bonny in those bright colors, lass."

Hands fluttering, Isobel giggled and dropped her gaze to the cutting board.

Gilmour stared agog at the rapid change in her demeanor.

"Aye, you don't look half so scrawny as I recall. In truth, the sight of you such makes me wish to . . ." The Munro paused, shifting his gaze toward Mour. "Invite you for a draught."

"Oh." Isobel's voice was breathy. "I am honored, me laird. But I cannot. Me duties here keep me quite busy."

"Could you not—"

"Well, we'd best be off, then," Gilmour interrupted as he grasped the Munro's thick elbow. "Good eventide to you, Isobel."

"Good eventide."

"What the devil be you doing?" Munro gritted, trying to hang back.

"Leaving the maid to her duties," Gilmour said. " 'Tis what a gentle man would do."

"I am not a gentle man."

Gilmour glanced over his shoulder at a bemused Isobel and hustled the giant into the dining area. "That is what I am to help you change," he said and slid back onto his stool as half a dozen curious faces turned toward him.

The Munro stared down at him. "Me plan was just about to take shape," he said, his tone a bit too smooth for Gilmour's peace of mind. "And it will take a bit more than the likes of you to change me course now, lad."

Gilmour lifted his goblet and shrugged. "Then by all means, have at it . . . if you don't care that all of Scotland will know your reasons for coming here."

The Munro stood before him as stiff as a lance. "Might you be threatening me, MacGowan?"

From a distant table, the baron of Winbourne stopped his dialogue in mid sentence, while beside the hearth a clean shaven young man dressed in dark leather watched with grim, almost familiar eyes.

"Nay," Gilmour said softly, "no threats." His muscles were coiled as tight as wagon springs. "And mayhap I am entirely wrong. Even if the maid spent the night with the great laird of the Munros, perhaps she would feel no need to tell her friends at Evermyst of your time here."

The Munro's scowl was black enough to burn a hole through Gilmour's forehead, but Mour ignored it as he sipped his ale.

"There *would* be much to talk about," rumbled Innes.

"I can only assume," Gilmour agreed dryly.

"The Munro of the Munro's gifting a simple serving wench with his attentions."

"I'm certain it would be difficult for her to keep the news to herself."

"Aye," rumbled Innes, glancing toward the kitchen. "Aye. Mayhap I had best find me bed before I am tempted beyond me own resolve and ruin her for all other men, huh?" he said and banged Gilmour on the shoulder with his fist.

"Aye," Mour agreed sourly.

Later, as Mour opened the stable door to check on his steed, he wondered what the devil Isobel was doing here, so far from the comforts of her sister's keep. Might she be concocting some evil scheme against his brother Ramsay?

And more important, why the devil was she flirting with the Munro like he was some damned princeling? The man could barely pronounce his own name. And as for looks . . . there was no point even considering the possibility that she might be attracted to him. Was there?

Questions washed through Gilmour's mind as he made certain Francois was secure. The stallion had something of a roving eye and was wont to find trouble for himself if the possibility presented itself. But all seemed well, so Mour closed the door and made his way back toward the inn. In his mind, Isobel's willowy image danced with subconscious seductiveness from table to table as she laughed huskily with her inebriated customers.

Gilmour scowled as he made his way up the narrow stairs toward his bedchamber. Why would she choose to remain a servant when she had every opportunity to live nobly high above the crashing tide at Evermyst?

He didn't know the answer, but it certainly would be interesting to find out.

Chapter 2

~~~❦~~~

Fatigue weighed heavily on Gilmour as he entered
the rented room. Memories of the day just past
flitted through his mind in a dreamlike haze as he
slipped his leather sporran over his head and readied
for bed. He did not wear the leather bag around his
waist to lie against the front of his body, for he found
that it impeded movement . . . of all sorts. Instead, it
generally hung from his shoulder, crossing his chest
just below the pewter tipped lace at the neck of his tunic and residing at his right hip.

Tossing it upon his mattress, he pulled his dirk from
beneath his belt. Crafted of Spanish steel, the Maiden
was as sharp as sin with the handle molded in the
shape of a buxom woman. When it was grasped,
Mour's hand settled intimately between her hips and
her bosom, but he ignored her voluptuous figure just
now and tossed her beside his sporran on the bed. He
then reached for his buckle and wondered with idle curiosity where Isobel slept. Did she reside here in the
inn? Was she close at hand? Was she alone?

The wide belt cut into the muscles of his abdomen

before he loosened the tension and let it drop to the floor.

Why was she so cool to him? He had done naught to her.

In fact, he had been nothing but complimentary, he thought, as he unwound the shortened length of green tartan from about his waist. He saw little use for the many yards of wool most Scotsmen wore. His own plaid left a good deal of muscular thigh showing beneath it and did not bunch and fold like most, but wound just twice about his body.

The fairer sex had always found him alluring, yet Isobel merely seemed amused by him. What a strange lass she was. Not once had she sighed when she looked at him. Not once had she glanced up at him through her lashes as maids were wont to do. There must be something amiss with her. After all, her sister Anora had been quite genteel where he was concerned. Not fawning in that lovely way that women did, but she'd been suitably impressed. Of course, by all accounts, she'd given his brother Ramsay a devil of a chase before marrying him, and—

Gilmour's hands stilled for a moment, then absently folded the plaid and set it aside.

That was it, then—the reason Isobel tormented him so. She was in love with him. There could be no other explanation. After all, she couldn't dislike him. Women simply didn't. Therefore it must be that she was hiding her true feelings behind her contempt.

The poor thing! How obvious it was now, and how difficult it must be for her. She probably felt as though she were far beneath him. But there was no need, really. Even though her noble blood had never been acknowledged by the world at large, he knew she was high born. But in actuality, he cared little about a woman's station in life. If she was female, he appreciated her. And if she was *bonny* and female, he *adored* her. Which put Isobel in a fine position, for she was decidedly female. And as for physical attributes, well . . .

Reaching for the hem of his tunic, Gilmour snatched it over his head and folded it away. Flexing his shoulders, he set his downy wren feather to fluttering in his braid before it settled restlessly back against his neck.

In a matter of seconds, he was bare naked and threw back the blankets of his bed with a grin. Aye, the lass must feel somewhat awestruck by him, but if the truth be known, she almost made *him* feel insecure. And all the while she had been feeling inferior to—

A whisper of noise sounded from the hallway and he turned, scowling through the candlelit dimness toward the door. Had he imagined it, or—

It came again, slightly louder. Reaching for his plaid, he wrapped it about his waist and gathered it at one lean hip.

Who could it be? he wondered, but suddenly he knew. As if he could see her standing before him, he knew. It was Isobel, come to admit her true feelings, that she could think of naught but him. That she had loved him from the very first.

He opened the door without delay, and she was there, small and lovely, with her robin's egg eyes glowing in the candlelight.

"MacGowan," she said, her expression inscrutable

as she took in his near nudity. "You look like hell itself. Is something amiss?"

The smile dropped from Gilmour's lips, and he bunched the woolen tighter against his middle as his happy dream dissipated like silvery fog.

"Did you want something, Bel?" he asked, steadying his equilibrium. "Or did you just come to ogle?"

Her fair brows rose in sharp surprise. "I take it you've not met Smitty."

The woman had a tendency to change the subject without warning. 'Twas one of the many things he disliked about her. "Nay," he said, tucking the plaid under itself and leaning with studied casualness against the rough door jamb. "I don't believe I've had the pleasure."

"Ahh, well, that would explain a bit of your conceit, unjustified though it be."

He grinned, lifting just one corner of his mouth. "I am many things, lass, and conceited may indeed be amongst them. But 'tis not unjustified, of that I assure you."

"Well . . ." She pressed past him as if he were a somewhat moldy side of beef. "You'd not be so cocksure should you dare compare yourself with the Smitty."

He turned, wondering if Anora would take offense if he throttled her wee sister. "A man among men, I'm certain," he said.

She glanced up at him and in her eyes was that bedazzled light he had seen a hundred times—only on those other occasions, the expression had been reserved for him. "Each day at eventide, after he shoes his last steed, he removes his tunic and goes to the river to wash the sweat from his manly form."

Gilmour's finger twitched. "I'm certain 'tis quite exciting for you."

She stared at him for a moment, then drew herself from her trance and laughed.

"MacGowan," she said, her tone filled with surprise, "you're not jealous, are you?"

"Jealous?" he said, his tone bland.

"Of Smitty."

"Aye, in fact I am, lass," he said, closing the door and pacing closer, "for I am thinking mayhap you do not offend his ears by speaking to him, but only watch as he lumbers down to the river."

She laughed again. "Gilmour MacGowan," she said, "the rogue of the rogues. Jealous of a simple blacksmith. Who would have thought it possible?"

"No one in her right mind, but that would not include you, would it, Bel? So feel free to enjoy your delusions if they brighten your day."

"Me thanks," she said, and he nodded.

"Are you getting near to telling me why you have come by, then?" he asked.

She fiddled with the bedpost for an instant, looking more like the hesitant lass all had known at Evermyst and less the harpy who had revealed herself to him alone. "I but wished for some word of me sister."

"Anora is well."

"You have spoken to her recently?"

"Aye. Just before leaving. She and Ram were about to challenge the firth for a visit to Levenlair."

"And leave Evermyst unprotected?"

"Lachlan shall remain behind."

"Then your brothers are well, also?"

"Lachlan is . . ." Mour shrugged. "Well, Lachlan is Lachlan. Cantankerous and bedeviled. But Ramsay is content. In truth, I have never seen him happier."

Though she smiled, there was a shadow of unidentified emotion in her eyes. Sadness, perhaps. Or loneliness. Maybe he should have been ashamed that the expression intrigued him, but Gilmour had oft found that shame was overrated.

" 'Tis glad I am of course to know that marriage agrees with him," she said.

"But?"

She glanced at him, surprise in her eyes. "What?"

"You are glad of course, but . . ."

"I am glad that me sister and her laird are happy. That is all."

"Then you care not that me brother has taken the love of the sister so long lost to you? You care not that your dearest and nearest kinswoman adores Ram so devoutly that she has all but forgotten *your* bond with her?"

A dozen emotions flashed through her eyes before she lowered her gaze to her hands, twisted against her pinned up overskirt. "Mayhap . . ." Her voice was very soft suddenly. "Mayhap 'twould be easier if I had never found her."

Guilt speared him at the honest regret in her voice. Never had she revealed so much of herself to him. She looked small and helpless against the backdrop of his bed. Her elfish face was lowered, her sapphire eyes hidden by downcast lids.

"How could it be better to never have known her?" he asked.

"I've heard it said . . ." She glanced up through her lashes at him. "That 'tis better to have lost your love than never to know love atall."

He nodded, urging her to go on.

"But I think 'tis not true. I think mayhap 'twould have been better to have gone forever thinking meself alone in the world."

Her sadness was all but palpable now. "You are not alone, lass," he said simply. "I should not have said the things I did."

"Nay." She shook her head slowly. Firelight danced across the golden waves of her hair and one lone diamond-bright tear traced down her alabaster cheek. "You were right. Me sister prefers to spend her days with her husband. And 'tis as it should be, of course," she added quickly. "It is simply that I . . ." She paused, seeming to fight for the proper words while Gilmour struggled to remain where he was, removed from her.

"You are lonely," he said, completing her sentence.

She raised her gaze. Against her milky complexion, her lips looked as bright and succulent as wild berries and he swallowed hard, using every bit of little-used self control at his disposal.

"You understand," she murmured.

A second tear followed its mate's course, slipping more rapidly down her cheek to fall past the point of her peaked chin and onto the high rise of her breast. Gone was the modest gown she had worn below-stairs, replaced by this garment of white linen. Strange that he hadn't noticed that earlier, he thought, for now he couldn't take his eyes off her—her loveliness, her loneliness, her breasts, so pale and full and tempting, with that single tear slipping down the dramatic curve into darkness—soft, tantalizing darkness.

"You know how I feel, then," she said.

"Aye, lass," he agreed and still remained unmoving, though it was difficult to raise his gaze from the tear's descent. " 'Tis only natural that you would miss the only one with whom you share blood."

"So you would miss your brothers?"

"Nay." He grinned. "But I would miss your sister."

She laughed, but the sound was unnatural, hiccuping slightly at the end before she raised her hands to her face. "I am sorry," she murmured. " 'Tis simply that I . . . I . . ." All other words were lost. There was nothing Gilmour could do but go to her. No choice but to slip his arms gently about her minuscule waist.

No corset stiffened her torso. Beneath her simple, virginal garment there was nothing but flesh—soft, lovely flesh.

"There now, sweet lass," he said, calming his breathing. "There be no need to cry, for you can return to Evermyst on the morrow, if you wish."

She shook her head, but even as she did so, she slid her arms hungrily about his neck as if starved for his strength, his compassion. " 'Tis not true." She whispered the words, brushing the sound with tender sweetness against his ear lobe. It shivered titilatingly down his neck.

"Aye, lass. I will take you there on me own steed in the morn, if you like."

"You do not understand."

Her hair felt like satin beneath his fingertips. He closed his eyes, breathing in her scent, a heady mix of sweet herbs and something deeper, something that was only Isobel. He remembered smelling it before, catching a whiff of it when she passed him at Evermyst. Smelling that sweet, unique aroma and feeling himself harden with the scent. Aye, he had forever wanted her, ever since the very first.

"I cannot go back," she whispered. The sliver of sound quivered over his bare shoulder, and against his chest her breasts felt as soft and enticing as heaven. "For I cannot bear the truth."

He stroked her hair again, feeling her emotion in his very soul. "And what truth is that, lassie?"

"You do not know what it was like, for you have always . . ." She paused, clearing her throat and laughing a little. "You have always been adored. But I had no one. Not until Nora. And then 'twas as if the world blossomed. I was everything to her, and she to me. 'Twas as if we shared one mind."

Her body felt as firm and supple as a bending reed in his arms with her hips pressed against his and her thighs, so sweet and strong, spread ever so slightly to encompass one of his own.

"Do not be sad, lass," he whispered, finding it suddenly hard to speak for the need that rushed through him. "Me earlier words were cruel. I am certain your sister misses you as surely as you miss her."

She whimpered softly against his neck as if such a thought evoked too much emotion to contain. "Do you think so?" she asked, lifting her face a bit to look into his eyes.

He smiled, for truly, her beauty was unsurpassed, with her heaven-wide eyes brimming with unshed tears. "Aye, lass, I know it. Her love for me brother has not diminished her adoration for you."

"You think not?"

"Nay," he said and swept her hair gently from her face. Dampened by her tears, it curled intimately about his fingers. "Come back with me and judge for yourself."

She managed a tremulous smile, but shook her head at the same time. "I cannot. Evermyst is not me place in the world."

"Where then do you belong, Bel?"

She shrugged. The movement caused her breasts to lift lovingly against his naked chest. A thousand wanton desires sprinted like devils through his overheated system, but she was lonely and hurting, and he would not take advantage of those raw feelings. Never let it be said that Gilmour MacGowan, the rogue of the rogues, could not tempt a maid without such emotions to aid his cause.

"Mayhap this be me place," she whispered.

"Here?" His heart pounded against her bosom. "In me arms?"

She smiled and lowered her eyes. "In Henshaw," she said. "At the Red Lion."

His desire throbbed insistently, and he could not help but wonder if she felt it. "Surely not, lass, for you were gently born."

Looking down at her delicate face, he could just see the slight tilt of her lips as she smiled sadly. "Gently born, mayhap, but not gently reared. Do you forget? I am naught but a commoner."

" 'Tis not true. You are the daughter of the laird and

lady of Evermyst and therefore it is only proper that you have all that the title entails."

"Nay," she said. "Me mother was right to send me away at birth, for there are many who would pit one sister against the other for the sake of her inheritance, and even more who would believe that both siblings are evil for the circumstances of their birth."

"Thus you would spend your life as a commoner, even though you know 'tis not true?"

"In truth, I am far more comfortable with the bare feet of a laborer than with the satin slippers of a lady."

"But surely you cannot plan to go on like this, lass, for you are far too delicate to spend your days in hard labor."

"Delicate?" She laughed a little and canted her head so that her gaze rested with feline softness on him and her hips pressed ever so gently against his. Gilmour tightened his jaw against the delectable onslaught. "Mayhap you do not know me so well as you think, MacGowan," she whispered.

He remained unmoving against her, lest the slightest motion send him over the edge of desire. "Do not fear, lass, me brother Ramsay will . . ." he began, but just then her lips touched his neck. A thousand errant sensations sizzled through him like living sparks. "Will . . ." He tried to catch the lashing tail of his displaced thoughts, but they had been burnt beyond recognition.

"Will what?" Her whisper shivered against his throat.

"Will find you a suitable husband," he said, but she had tilted her head downward now and kissed his collarbone. His head fell back of its own accord.

"And what if I do not want some stodgy but suitable husband?" she asked.

Her hand slid with slow warmth down his arm. He should stop her now, but somehow his muscles failed to do so, for her touch was like magic, unreal, beyond hope, and as it slid from his arm to his belly, he felt the flames of desire dance like demons in his aching nether parts.

"What if I want a lover instead?" she whispered, and suddenly her hand dipped beneath the weight of his plaid. The tartan unfurled like spring bracken, falling hopelessly to the floor at their feet. "What if I want you?"

"Lass . . ." It was difficult to breathe, impossible to move. "I do not think—"

" 'Tis best. Do not think," she murmured and slipped her hand lower. It closed with velvet warmth around him and suddenly all thought was gone, burned to ashes by the satin strength of her touch.

Inhibition was laid waste. Good sense flew like autumn leaves. There was nothing he could do but lift her into his arms. Nothing to do but bear her to the bed behind her and there he laid her upon the mattress. She did not resist, did not hesitate. Instead, she curved her slim fingers about his neck and drew him closer. Their lips touched like a dream, but she was impatient, eager— nay, *hot* for him—and suddenly he could not wait another moment to gaze at her beauty. He pressed her gown upward, revealing the ivory smoothness of her thighs, but he could not rush here where perfection lay. He dropped to his knees beside the mattress. Sliding his hands up one delicate calf, he kissed the inner curve of her knee. She gasped and he smiled against her flesh, loving her reaction and then kissing higher, over the sweet length of her thigh, drawing ever nearer utopia.

"Mour!" He heard her gasp of pleasure, but refused to be rushed, for he had waited long for such a moment.

Thus he slid his fingers over the arch of her hip and upward, feeling the luscious curve of her waist, loving every intimate detail of her and kissing each one in turn, her hip, her belly, her navel.

She jerked at the sensation and he lingered there a moment, sliding both palms beneath her buttocks to lift her upward and lave his tongue across the dent of her birthing scar.

"MacGowan!" Her fingers tangled in his hair with some force.

"Aye, me love?" he whispered, lifting his head enough to gaze into her frantic face. "What is it you would have me do?"

Her body was taut with desire, her knees bent in a supplication of unhidden need. "Touch me," she whispered.

They were the sweetest words ever spoken, so sweet, in fact, that he longed to hear them again.

"What's that you say, lass?" he asked.

But suddenly the dulcet melody of her voice roughened into an ungodly deep timbre. "I said, touch me again and I'll kill you here and now!"

Gilmour wrenched his eyes open even as he jerked backward. Sleep fled like frightened lambkins, leaving him to stare dumbfounded into the narrowed eyes of Innes Munro.

Chapter 3

❦❦❦

"**M**unro! What the devil are you doing here?" Gilmour rasped, but memories of the night before were already rushing back. Not enough room at the inn. They'd been forced to share, and somewhere in his desire maddened dreams, he'd made a foul mistake.

"I'll tell you what I'm doing lad, I'm preparing to kill me first MacGowan," growled the giant, and in that moment Mour realized that the man's right hand was well out of sight. "One more move and the rogue of the rogues will trouble maids no more."

Gilmour lowered his gaze ever so slowly. It was no great surprise to find the Munro's fist wrapped about his much favored dirk.

"I preferred the dream," Mour said, watching the knife.

"You were dreaming?" Munro's tone sounded doubtful.

Gilmour raised his brows. "You thought me awake?"

No answer was forthcoming.

"I've no wish to offend you, Munro, but you're not me usual type."

33

"If I thought otherwise you'd be propositioning the devil this very minute!" snarled the Munro.

"That seems more than just," Gilmour said and found that his ardor could cool quite quickly when in the proper company. The last golden memory of Isobel fled his misty brain, and he backed out of bed, fully dressed and immensely happy to realize it. "In fact, methinks it would be preferable to die by your hand than to have others learn of me mistake."

The Munro scowled, still holding his knife at the ready as though not quite certain Gilmour could control his passion for his oversized and somewhat aromatic bed mate. "So you'll be telling no one?"

Gilmour wondered vaguely who he would *ever* want to share such news with. He cleared his throat. "No one comes to mind."

Munro's scowl deepened as he too backed from bed. "I'll have your vow."

"You have me word of honor." And that was the truth.

The Munro glared one more instant, then nodded and slipped his dirk grouchily into his boot sheath. It was then that Mour realized the giant had worn his boots to bed, but truly—the more clothing available in their present situation, the better, he thought, and turned gratefully away.

"Who did you dream of?"

Gratitude fled, for events had been humiliating enough without admitting his lurid dreams for a maid who did naught but barb him. "What's that?" he asked, pretending confusion as he dipped his hands into the wooden basin set on a stool near the door. The scent of rosemary filled his nostrils as he splashed the washing water onto his face. What he needed was a good cold lochan and never to set eyes on Isobel of the Frasers again.

"Who was it you were dreaming of? Was it the cheese maker?"

"Ailsa?" Gilmour asked, remembering Evermyst's buxom goat herder with some relief.

"Aye. I think that be her name. 'Tis said she be a lively tumble."

" 'Tis said," Gilmour replied, preoccupied.

Munro laughed. "For such a frolicking dream, the rogue sounds none too happy. Could it be you chose the wrong maid?"

Gilmour sent the giant a peeved expression. "Aye, he was hairier than I prefer. And ungodly large."

"And a bit more vengeful than most lassies, though . . ." The Munro stopped suddenly, his mouth remaining open. " 'Twasn't your brother's bride you dreamt of, was it?"

Gilmour scowled. "I fear me bid for Anora is already past. She chose another. Poorly, but 'tis too late to change her mind now, I suspect."

"Ummm," Munro agreed, which made Mour wonder for a moment about the giant's own feelings for Ramsay's lovely wife. After all, there was a time he had hoped to have her for his own. But whether he'd wanted her for her own delectable self or for her unbreachable keep, no one knew for certain. "Who then do you . . ." Munro began, but suddenly his heavy brows dipped dangerously. " 'Tis not the Red Lion wench you covet, is it?"

Gilmour's stomach clamped as he remembered Munro's words from the night before. How could he have forgotten that this Goliath had his eye on Isobel? Bugger it! He should have never agreed to help Innes. Even though he dearly needed assistance, it could only lead to trouble.

"Let me say this." Gilmour set his plaid straight, then opened the door. "The sooner I return to Evermyst, the better I'll like it."

Munro followed him down the stairs, and the wooden steps groaned beneath his heavy weight. "So the Red Lion maid does not interest you?"

Gilmour prepared to shake his head as he stepped into the common room, but just at that instant, as if called from hell itself, Isobel came into view. She wore a gown of dusky blue, pinned up at the sides to show a pale underskirt. Her sleeves were the color of a midnight sky and one tiny braid entwined with scarlet ribbon encircled her golden head like a crown. For one brief moment, Mour could not speak.

"MacGowan!" Munro growled. "Does the Red Lion's maid interest you?"

Isobel turned away, whisking like a wind-blown petal into the kitchen.

"Nay," he managed. "No interest atall."

" 'Tis good," Innes said, seating himself at the nearest table, "for I'd hate to have yet another reason to kill you before our task is finished here."

"Aye, 'twould indeed be a shame."

Their plan was to break the fast and leave Henshaw, but the ale was well to the Munro's liking, and by the time the broad maid called Martha returned with more, he was only too happy to sample another few mugs and proclaim each better than the last.

By mid morn the Munro was well into his cups, by

noon he was sloshing like a beer wagon, and Isobel still had not reappeared from the kitchen. Not that Gilmour cared. After all, he had had time to consider his dream and deduced it meant naught. It was merely Isobel's aloof demeanor that threw him off the mark. The sooner he saw other maids—normal maids, maids who fawned over him—the better off he would be. He would return to Evermyst post haste, and soon the lassies would be flattering him with outrageous remarks while he bounced a wee, giggling Mary on his knee and forgot all about Isobel's unnatural ability to ignore his charms.

"It would be wise to reach our destination before the light fails us," Gilmour said.

"What's your hurry, lad?" Munro asked and beamed across the room at Martha, the stout brew mistress. "We've more ale to finish off. And I've barely tasted her honey meads."

"If you're determined to drink Martha's entire supply, mayhap 'twould be wiser to hire a wagon to carry it back to your keep."

"What a clever idea!" Munro roared. His voice had grown louder by the minute. "But at me own keep . . ." He leaned closer to the stout maid who had concocted the stuff. She was by no means a great beauty, but mayhap size and brewing skill covered a host of flaws for a man of Innes Munro's ilk. "There will be no clever ale mistress to sweeten the brew. Aye?"

The big woman laughed. The sound was low, her words lower still, or perhaps the Munro's roaring had simply dulled Gilmour's hearing. Whatever the case, Munro chuckled in return, his face red with drink.

"What say you?" Munro asked, his voice finally

hushed somewhat, "would you return to me keep with me, sweet Martha?"

"I am flattered, me laird, but me place is here with me son at the Red Lion."

"It's a son you have, is it?" Munro asked.

Martha began to answer, but just at that moment, the door opened. Silvery laughter entered the room, heralding Isobel's arrival. Something stirred in Gilmour's gut like a waking dragon.

"You cannot stay all the day through," Isobel said, her gaze on her companion. Her *male* companion. "Eventually Master Gibbs will toss you out on your pate."

"It may well be worth the bruising if you would see to my wounds. What say you, Maid Isobel?" asked the man at her side.

"I say . . ." She smiled at him, her eyes alight. "Enjoy the meal, Regan of Longwater. It may be the best you get from me."

"May be?" He sounded breathlessly hopeful.

"And what of me, Isobel?" asked the baron of Winbourne, who again sat beside the hearth. "If I am bruised will you see to me?"

"That depends what part is bruised, me laird."

The balding baron grinned. "Name the part, lass, I'll see what can be done."

She laughed as she swept past the tables. "I cook, lads. Naught else. Unless . . ." Her gaze skimmed the crowd, then settled for an instant on the aging baron. "One of those parts be irresistible."

Laughter followed her into the kitchen. Gilmour rose abruptly, his finger twitching. "I go to prepare the horses," he said. "Be ready, Munro, if you wish to ride with me."

"Nay, MacGowan," argued the Munro. "Ready a wagon, for I like your suggestion. If I cannot have the bonny brew-mistress, I shall make do with her brew."

Gilmour saddled his own steed first. Francois was cooperative enough, though he was wont to tilt his golden head toward the left in an attempt to gaze fondly at the bay mare in the adjacent stall.

"She'll only cause you trouble," Mour growled as he pulled up the girth, but Francois tossed his heavy mane and sidled sideways, and in the end Gilmour was convinced to allow him to roam loose in his box so as to spend a few more minutes flirting with the bay.

Although it took a good deal of time to locate a draught horse and suitable dray, the Munro was still not prepared to leave when Gilmour returned to the inn for him. In fact, very little had changed. Regan of Longwater still nursed a brew at a table beside the door and the Munro was still deep in his cups, speaking to Isobel.

"I don't believe a word of it, Laird Munro," she was saying.

" 'Tis true," he argued, glancing boyishly toward his mug. "There was not a hog to be found when I awoke in the morning. Turns out they cared no more for the smell of me than I for them."

She laughed. "You smell just fine to me, me laird."

Did he blush? Gilmour stared agog at the sight.

"You're over-kind, lassie."

Charming? A charming drunk? Innes Munro?

"Come smell *me*, Isobel," said a man near the kitchen. He was grotesquely fat and wore a yellow cloth cap that drooped over his head much as his extra chins drooped over his collar. "You'll like it."

She laughed again. The sound curled huskily in Gilmour's gut.

"I know how you smell, Redmont. Like me gyngerbread. 'Tis the same everyday."

"Ahhh but you must like the smell of me, then," said the fat man.

"Not so well as your wife does," another man chimed in. The occupants laughed, but near the door one young man remained silent, watching. Dressed in a leather jerkin and dark calf skin hose, he rarely shifted his gaze from the maid.

Gilmour scowled. Who was he? What was he doing here watching Isobel so intently, and why did he look vaguely familiar?

"And what of you, Laird Winbourne?" she asked. Was there a breathlessness to her voice when she looked at him? "Did you enjoy me hotchpot this day?"

"Aye." The baron nodded. He wore a beard, cropped short and perfectly groomed, perhaps to compensate for the lack of hair on his head, Gilmour thought, and felt a mite better for his own shoulder length locks. " 'Twas delectable as always." He rose, proving to be taller than he'd first appeared. "But I would gladly trade it for the briefest touch of your skin against mine."

Oohs of appreciation accompanied the compliment. Only the slim man dressed in leather jerkin and dark hose was silent as Winbourne strode across the room toward her.

She curtsied impishly. "Then 'tis your lucky day, me laird," she said.

The crowd fell into watchful silence.

"For you get the meal and . . . me hand." She raised her arm, and though he scowled as if disappointed, he took her fingers in his own and kissed them.

"You have my thanks, Maid Isobel," he said, then grinned, still holding her fingers. "And should you tire of serving this motley lot you are once again invited to work your magic at Winbourne."

"Indeed, me laird, I fear you would tire of me simple meals."

"I was not speaking of cooking," he said.

She pulled her hand from his with a shy smile. "You'd best watch your tongue, lest I take offense."

"Aye," said the one called Regan. "Insult Isobel and you'll find your meals seasoned with hemlock instead of saffron."

"Being near her may well be worth the poisoning, aye, lads?" someone said.

"Aye, and . . ." another began.

Gilmour turned toward Munro. " 'Tis time to leave," he growled.

"So soon?" asked the Munro, looking surprised, as if he hadn't been drinking for half an eternity. "The place is just becoming lively."

Lively! Damned irritating, was what it was. "The day grows old."

"I've not known you to be the one to spoil the fun, MacGowan."

From his left, Isobel laughed again. Gilmour's little finger jerked spasmodically, but he shrugged casually. "You are right. There is no reason to hurry. Surely no one will suspect your true reasons for visiting Henshaw."

Even in his inebriated state, the Munro seemed to understand Gilmour's implications, for worry settled like sundown over the man's heavy brow.

"We'd best be off," he rumbled.

"If you insist," Gilmour said, and turned toward the door with the Munro behind him.

"Surely you do not plan to return to your home today?" Isobel's voice stopped him.

The Munro turned. Mour ground his teeth and did the same even as she came toward them.

"Aye, lass," rumbled the giant. "But I will forget neither your fine inn nor the splendid company." His gaze skimmed toward the kitchen.

She smiled. "Me thanks. But 'twill be past dark by the time you reach your beds. Surely you could remain here one more night."

"I fear we cannot," said the Munro, regret heavy in his tone.

"So you will be leaving too?" she asked, shifting her attention to Gilmour. Her gaze smote his, as blue as sunlit sapphire, and for one tremulous moment he saw something unsaid in her eyes. Something almost hidden, but just discernible, if one knew women well.

"Aye, I fear I must," he said.

"Oh." She murmured, and for a moment her berry bright lips seemed to tremble.

Mour's heart did a daring capriole in his chest, and he stepped forward. "Will you miss me, lass?" he asked, his voice low.

She took a minuscule step nearer, as though she dare not come too close. Their gazes melded, then she glanced rapidly over his shoulder, not quite able to look him in the eye lest he see the truth in hers.

"You've but to say the word and I'll remain here," he whispered.

"Hey now! Not a word of that is true, Longwater," she scolded, and Mour realized suddenly that she had been watching the man by the door the whole while. "I'm sorry." She turned back with a brusque smile. "What's that you say, MacGowan?"

His finger twitched. "Good day, Isobel," he said, and turned stiffly away.

"Godspeed," she chirped.

Gilmour left the inn door open and stormed toward the stables. Godspeed, indeed! Godforsaken was more likely. He couldn't get out of this bedeviled village fast enough. What the hell was wrong with her? One moment she caressed him with her eyes and the next she dismissed him like an evil smelling hound.

A tease was what she was. He hated teases. Of course, there had been a few lassies who had called *him* a tease, and it was true that there were times when he had an ungodly amount of fun with outrageous flirts. But not with her. Isobel Fraser was not a fun kind of lass. At least, not with him.

And why *not* with him?

It didn't matter, he assured himself. Not atall, he decided, and slammed open Francois's stall door. The stallion jerked, but remained where he was, his tail toward him and his . . .

"Bugger it!" Gilmour stormed, realizing suddenly that the animal's front legs were stuck unceremoniously atop the wall that separated his stall from the mare's. "What the devil have you been up to?"

Francois turned his head, looking sheepishly toward his master, but just then the mare on the opposite side whickered invitingly, calling his attention elsewhere. He pricked his lively ears over the fence and answered in a deep throated equivalent of a lewd joke.

"Hell's apples, horse, you'd slice off your legs for a bit of arse," Mour gritted, scowling between the timbers at the bay on the far side.

A chuckle sounded behind him. "Like steed, like master, aye?" said Munro.

"Shut the hell up and give me a hand."

In the end it took a bit more than a hand, for not only had the stallion gotten his broken rope caught fast on a splintered board, he had become wedged tight as a cork between the ceiling and the fence and cut his front cannon in the process.

"Damned foul luck!" Gilmour steamed.

"Ahh, there now, 'tain't so bad as all that," Munro placated him, reminding Mour that he was more pleasant drunk than sober. After all, it had been some hours since he'd threatened to kill anyone. "Your bonny steed will be right as rain in a fortnight or so. Ride in the wagon with me. You can return later to fetch him."

Gilmour scowled and glanced down the road toward Evermyst. There was nothing he wanted more than to return to that quiet haven. The lassies there had fine taste in men, unlike here, where . . . His finger twitched again.

Francois shifted his weight to his left side, looking miserable. The bay mare stuck her head over her door, whickering demurely.

"Don't you answer," Gilmour warned, pulling the stallion's head to the side.

Francois gazed at Mour with large, limpid eyes, employing his most innocent expression.

"I'll have to stay," Gilmour grunted.

"What's that?"

"I'll have to stay, until the morn, at least." Gilmour ran a hand down the stallion's golden foreleg. The muscles twitched beneath his fingers. The wound was messy, but it would heal well, given time. For that he should be grateful.

The towering Munro scowled. "It couldn't be that you planned this just so you could have one more chance at her, could it?"

"What the devil are you muttering about?" Gilmour asked.

The Munro jerked his head toward the inn. "She's not interested in you, MacGowan. Leave her be."

Gilmour straightened in outrage. "Are you suggesting that I hoisted me steed upon the stall like a side of beef just so I could have a go at propositioning the barmaid?"

"She's more than a barmaid."

"I'm not sure she's even a woman," Gilmour gritted.

"What's that?" Munro steamed, stepping closer. "Do you slander the lady's name?"

"And what if I—" Gilmour began, then realized how he sounded. Jealous! Like a damned jilted suitor. He didn't get jealous, and he didn't get jilted. What the devil was wrong with him? Raising his hand to his face, he scrubbed his forehead miserably. "You have me vow, Munro," he said, "I've no more wish to remain in this village than to cut off me *own* leg." He glanced irritably at Francois's wound. The stallion pushed him gently with his nose, adding a wide eyed stare of adoration. "He's a daft, randy bugger is what he is," Mour said, straightening the flaxen forelock.

The stallion sighed and rested his broad brow against his master's shoulder. "But Mother would have my liver for breakfast if I left the beast behind." Absently stroking the heavy ivory mane, Mour lowered his voice. "I'll stay with you, lad," he added, but when he glanced down at the stallion's head, he noticed that Francois was just dragging a longing gaze away from the mare and back to his master. Even his damned horse didn't have any honest feelings for him.

"I don't trust you, MacGowan," Munro said. "You'll be returning with me."

Gilmour considered arguing, but that would do little more than cause a battle, and he so much preferred making love to making war. Unless it was a battle between others, of course. Instigating trouble between his brothers was a particular favorite pastime of his. But as for battling the Munro himself . . . it would cost far less to outwit him.

Shrugging, Mour gave the Munro a bored glance. "If you're nervous, I'll accompany you home."

"Nervous?" The big man stiffened like a Highland pine. "What the devil be you talking about?"

"It is a long journey back to the north, and you without a single guard. It may well be dangerous."

"You think I'm afraid, lad?"

"Nay." Gilmour paused. "Of course not."

"You think the Munro of the Munros needs some scrawny arsed MacGowan to keep him safe on the few leagues between here and Windemoor?"

Apparently the mellowing ale was wearing off.

"I never said as much."

"And you'd damned well better not," Munro growled and pushed past him toward the dray that waited in the street as Gilmour trailed behind. "I'll be traveling alone, I will."

Even the giant's irritable tone couldn't raise Gilmour's spirits much, for he would still have to spend another night or so at the Red Lion. Still, it was something. "If you're sure you'll be safe . . ." Mour said, resting a hand on the seat of the dray.

"What's that?" Munro growled, looking down at him.

"I said, I'm sure you'll be safe." Mour added a shrug. "After all, who would dare challenge the Munro?"

"No one," growled the other.

"Exactly," agreed Gilmour, feeling somewhat better. "And you needn't worry about Isobel. I've no interest in her."

"Isobel? There ain't enough of her to clean me teeth on. But if you lay a hand on sweet Martha . . ." The Munro leaned close, his breath fragrant, "You'll rue the day, lad."

Chapter 4

~~~∽✦∽~~~

It didn't take Gilmour long to tend to Francois's wounds. Soon he was bandaged and secured a few stalls down the row from the tempting bay. And though Mour tried to draw out the procedure, eventually there was nothing to do but secure a room for another night. Morose and irritable, he made his way down the rutted village streets in the opposite direction of the Red Lion. At the far end of Henshaw near the listing palisade, he found an old wattle and daub building that dared call itself the Duke's Inn. Stepping inside, Mour nodded to Laird Grier, who was just exiting the common room.

Only two patrons remained. They were a rough looking pair. One large and brutish, the other effeminate and twitchy, they sat hunched over their mead. Gilmour found a seat and tried to believe it wasn't too bad a place to spend the night, but after one sip of ale, he realized the drink was as sour as the company and somehow he could not stay.

It was almost dark when he found himself in the Red Lion once again. Taking a seat not far from the cozy fire, he noticed a new maid delivering drinks and decided that all would be well. Perhaps there would not even be a reason for him to see Isobel. Requesting a meal from the bright eyed lass, he settled in to drink his ale and listen to the gossip. It was a mixed group that gathered at the Red Lion. Fishers and crofters rubbed elbows with merchants and lords, and though Gilmour was loath to believe it, he had to admit that his meal was extraordinary. Although he generally favored the earthy taste of ale, he requested a goblet of wine and steadfastly kept his gaze from the kitchen door.

Patrons came and went. Laughter swelled and lulled and the hour grew late.

To his left, a gnarled gaffer leaned his bony back against a wall and spun a yarn to his audience. Gilmour listened with half an ear until the old man's tale came to a breathless ending. A moment of silence followed before a red-nosed miller shook his head and quaffed his ale.

"It cannot be true. No livin' horse could jump so high."

"Nay," agreed another. "You dream, old man."

Gilmour took a swig of his drink and shrugged. "Just because your own mounts cannot soar, does not mean all steeds are bound to the earth."

A half dozen faces turned toward him. He met their eyes with an easy smile. "Methinks we MacGowans must raise a different type of mount if you do not think the gaffer's tale possible."

"MacGowan, you say?" asked the nearest man. He was as lean as a lance, with a sallow complexion and a decided lack of teeth.

"Aye. I am Gilmour of the MacGowan."

"Lady Flame's lad?" asked the old man, cocking his head as if able to hear from one ear alone.

Mour gave the gaffer a smile. "You know me mother, do you?"

A sigh left the grizzled lips. "Once upon a summer's eve I had the good fortune of delivering a steed to Dun Ard."

"Then you know the tales be true," Mour said.

"That she is the most bonny maid of all time?"

Gilmour raised his brows. "I meant the tales of her ability with horses."

"Oh. Aye," agreed the old man, but his eyes still looked dreamy and a nearby patron laughed.

"I have indeed heard that the Flame of the Mac-Gowans is a rare jewel. 'Tis said, in fact, that one of the Duke of Nairnon's statues were modeled after her. And you know his statues are all bare—"

Gilmour cleared his throat. "Let us not forget that we speak of me mother here. I've no wish to have a need to defend her honor."

"Aye," someone murmured. " 'Tis said the Flame is best at doing that herself."

"Are you suggesting that me mother is less than the epitome of femininity?" Mour asked, his voice low and steady as he eyed the crowd.

A quiver of nervousness ran through the group.

"I only meant that I heard it is wise to keep a dirk out of her . . . that is to say, there are tales—"

"And they all be true." Gilmour shook his head as though resigned to his fate and contemplated his wine. "I tell you, lads, 'tis difficult indeed for a boy to prove his mettle when his mother is forever battling any who would challenge him."

"Say you that her laird did not keep her from inter-fering?"

Gilmour gave the speaker a dry glance. "Me father is many things. But a fool he is not."

"So Roderic the Rogue has his hands full," mused someone.

"Aye," agreed another, "and judging by the king's statue, me own hands should be so lucky."

Laughter followed the statement. Gilmour tried to scowl, but his mother would be the last to be offended by such a statement, while his father would be down-right jolly. So he lifted his mug in a sort of salute and said, "Careful what you wish for, laddies."

"What say you?"

Mour took a sip. There was a delicate taste of laven-der in the wine. He mused over that for a second as his audience waited. "Me sister is much like me lady mother."

"And is she wed?"

A few chuckles sounded from Gilmour's listeners.

"Indeed, she is," Mour admitted. "Though Da de-spaired for a time of ever finding her a spouse."

"If she looks like the Lady Flame, why was it a worry?"

"Might you know of a Laird Halwart of Down-shire?"

"Aye. I've heard of him."

"He courted me sister for a time."

The man called Redmont shrugged. "He seems un-scathed by the experience."

Mour sipped again. "Aye, he does indeed, but have you ever wondered why he has no heirs?"

"There's a tale here, lads," said the gaffer, and Gilmour grinned.

"Aye, there is," he agreed and launched happily into

the story. One tale led to another, and that to another, but still not a soul interrupted, for Gilmour was not one to let a simple thing like truth stand in the way of a good yarn. His only pauses were made for dramatic effect or to thank the barmaid, who finally pulled up a seat nearby.

Not a soul left and only one more entered—the young man with the leather jerkin who took a chair and sat quietly near the fire. Minutes slipped into hours before Gilmour began to wind up his final yarn.

"So there I was," Gilmour said, "with naught but a scrap of cloth about me loins and a wood ax to defend meself against her five towering brothers."

"Should we be expecting an heir from *you* anytime soon, MacGowan?" asked Redmont.

Mour joined in the chuckles even as he shook his head. "It looked bad for me, that it did, so I told them God's own truth. Lads, I said, you can reap vengeance if you like, but this I swear—I did naught that the lass did not beg me to do with her own lips."

"And that quieted her kinsmen?"

Gilmour shook his head sadly. "In truth, it had quite the opposite effect. They came at me in a rush, so I raised me ax to defend meself, but just as I did . . . me only meager garment abandoned me. I was bare naked to the world. Sure as sunrise I thought they would kill me, but sudden as the wind they stopped, took one long glance at the whole of me, and bolted in the opposite direction." He took another sip of wine. "I never set me eyes on them again."

"And why is that?"

Gilmour shrugged, "I can only assume they were intimidated by the size of my"—he glanced at the bar-maid and grinned—"ax."

Laughter broke out like a wild torrent.

The barmaid rose, swishing her skirts about her ankles as she did so. "I'd like to stay," she said, "but I fear the lies be getting a bit thick hereabouts."

"Lies!" Mour gave her a wounded expression. "Surely you do not doubt me story, Fleta."

"And what if I did, MacGowan?" she asked, glancing down at him, her legs slightly spread as if prepared to do battle.

"That depends," he said and grinned up at her, "whether you doubt the outcome . . . or the size."

Wild hoots of approval followed, but the maid was not to be outdone.

Raising her brows, she crossed her arms against her buxom chest. "They say seeing is believing, Mac-Gowan."

Gilmour rose slowly, doing nothing to contain his grin as he set his hands to his belt. "I am always happy to assist another's faith, but . . ." He tilted his head toward their onlookers. "I've no wish to belittle the lads here."

There were snorts from the men, but Fleta was grinning openly.

"A private showing, then?" she asked.

"I'm always—"

"Lads," Isobel interrupted. Gilmour turned toward her. She was standing not far from the kitchen door, eyeing his listeners. "I do so hate to interrupt your revelry, but if we do not lock up, we do not open again on the morrow."

There were boyish groans of disappointment, but she soon shooed them out the door until only the barmaid and Gilmour remained.

"I'm waiting for—" Fleta began, but Isobel interrupted again.

"Plums could use your help in the kitchen, if you're not too busy, Fleta."

The barmaid shrugged as she turned her gaze from Gilmour to Isobel. "Me imaginings are generally better than real life anyway."

Mour grinned. "I hope you have a large imagination then, lassie."

She laughed as she swayed her way into the kitchen.

Then only Isobel and Gilmour remained.

"So . . ." She lifted a trio of mugs from a table. "You are still here, MacGowan."

He watched her carefully and found that a belly full of ale was a kindly ally where she was concerned. Nonchalance was his friend.

"Aye, Bel, I am here. Me presence doesn't bother you, does it?"

She shrugged. Candlelight stroked her skin like a lover's slow caress. "Of course not. Why should it?"

"I believe you said you dislike me."

She smiled. "In truth, MacGowan, I am not overly fond of many of me patrons. That does not mean I refuse their coin."

"Should the coin not go to the owner, Bel?"

"Master Gibbs is getting on in years. 'Twas his idea that I take over the duties as well as collect the funds."

"After knowing you so short a time?"

"Mayhap he is more trusting than you."

"And mayhap you give him more than is good for his aging heart, aye?"

She stared at him. "Is that the ale talking, or is it the charming rogue himself?"

Gilmour just stopped himself from wincing. "Me apologies," he said. "I did not mean to impugn your virtue."

"Didn't you?"

"Nay. In fact, I have no wish for harsh feelings between us. I am simply out of sorts."

"I was sorry to hear of your steed's injuries."

"How did you know?"

"I spoke with Guthrie, the stable boy."

"You weren't checking up on me, were you Bel?" he asked, then chastised himself. Why in the name of all that was holy would he continue to try to flirt with her?

"I was checking on Wren."

He raised a brow.

"Me mare," she said. "Mayhap you saw her. I believe your steed was hanging over her wall when you found him."

Bugger it! He should have known the troublesome mare would be hers. "A wee bonny palfrey. Where did you get her?"

Gathering another trio of mugs, she glanced over her shoulder as she headed for the kitchen. "I would love to stay and chat the night through," she said, "but I have tasks to see to before I find me bed."

"Where is your bed?" Truly, there was something wrong with him.

"What's that?"

He refrained from knocking himself in the head as she turned back toward him. "I worry for your safety; you should not walk alone in the dark. 'Tis not wise."

Sharp humor shone in her azure eyes. "As long as you remain here, I am certain I will be untroubled. Henshaw is a peaceful place."

"And you imagine yourself safe here, without a protector?"

"I did not say I was without a protector."

His gut cramped. "So there is a man who looks after you?"

"I did not say that, either."

He tried not to grind his teeth. "He should take better care of you, Isobel."

Their gazes held tight.

"So that's it, then? The rogue of the rogues has stayed to protect me?" There was sarcasm in her tone.

Gilmour stared at her and realized quite suddenly that Francois would be fine on his own. Far better to leave the randy steed than wait for Isobel to make him insane.

"Perhaps I have," he said, and she watched him an instant before laughing.

He was mildly offended for a moment, but when the laughter showed no sign of lessening, he began to get truly peeved, and he was rarely peeved. Nevertheless, he waited until quiet entered the room before he spoke.

"Something amuses you, lass?"

"Aye." She was still smiling. "The idea of the rogue thinking of anyone but himself."

Settling a hip against a lengthy table, Mour watched her. "Whatever gave you such a low opinion of me?"

"I believe 'twas the few months I spent at Evermyst whilst you were there."

"You doubt that I could protect you?"

"Nay," she said. "I merely doubt that you would have time, considering your many interests."

"Such as?"

She shrugged. "Ailsa. Elga. Fleta. Shall I list them in order of time or size?"

" 'Tis no sin to enjoy women, Bel." He smiled. "Or to be enjoyed by them."

"And what of deflowering virtuous young maids?" Her tone was sharp and he raised his brows at her rancor.

"What of it?"

"Is that not a sin?"

"I suspect it is if they do not long to be deflowered, but once they have met me . . ." He let the sentence fall into silence and gave her a modest shrug.

She watched him very closely for an instant. "I truly do not think I have ever met a man who thinks so highly of himself."

His grin twisted up a mite, and he wondered if he was losing that innocent quality he was striving for. "I'm certain there are reasons, Bel."

"Meaning?"

"Most men have little reason to think highly of themselves."

"Not so much as you, at any rate."

"Exactly," he agreed.

"Well . . ." She took a deep breath and plunked the mugs back on the table. "On those words of wisdom, I shall wish you farewell."

"I thought you had tasks to finish here."

"I do," she admitted. "But suddenly I am feeling strangely nauseated."

He couldn't help but laugh, and stepped toward her as she turned to the door. "I have that effect on women sometimes."

She glanced up at him from a crooked angle. "I'm surprised you admit it."

"They usually get over their illness in a few months time."

She stumbled as his meaning came home to her, and he laughed harder.

"I jest, Bel," he said. "I have fathered no bairns."

"Oh? And how can you be certain?"

"Do you truly want to know, lass?" he asked, chuckling.

She scowled at him as she set a candle to the fire, then fitted it back into an iron bound lantern. "Nay, I do not. But such a magnificent lover as you think yourself—"

"*Magnificent*." He laughed. "Who have *you* been speaking to, lass?"

"None but you," she said. Then, "Fleta," she called, raising her voice. "I fear I must leave now. Can you finish up for the night?"

An affirmative answer issued from the kitchen and soon Isobel had stepped outside. Gilmour followed without comment.

Silence settled between them. Up ahead in the darkness, the light from her swaying lantern shone off the smooth face of a puddle. Slipping his hand around her upper arm, Mour urged her aside.

"Would you like me to carry you?"

"Mayhap at me funeral," she said and pulled her arm firmly from his grasp.

"Let us not get ahead of ourselves, shall we?"

She eyed him askance. "What do you mean by that?"

"Might you think I am planning your demise?"

"Are you?"

"I would hardly have time. What with all the virtuous maids yet to be deflowered."

She snorted, lifting her pale underskirt slightly, and pointedly ignoring him.

He gazed appreciatively at the trim turn of her ankles and grinned. "What possible reason could I have to wish you harm?" he asked.

"What reason could you have to be here atall?"

"You cannot believe that I wish to protect you?"

"If that is the case you can put your mind at ease," she said.

"You think you are capable of caring for yourself?"

Finding her way down a rough walkway of inlaid stones, she turned at the arched door of a thatched cottage. "More capable than you, MacGowan."

"You do not want me help?"

"The rumors are true then," she said. "You are indeed quick witted."

He bowed, making a show of his chivalry. "Your wish is granted then, me lady. I will bother you no more. Indeed, if I meet a score of slavering brigands, I vow to do naught but point them in your direction."

"Me thanks," she said and he nodded.

"Farewell to you," Mour said, and as he turned away a man smiled from the deep shadows of her cottage.

Chapter 5

On the following morning Gilmour visited the stables.

A nicker greeted him as he opened the door, but he realized in an instant that the warm welcome was not for him. Francois was pushing his powerful neck over his gate toward a scrawny lass in a washed-out gown that hung askew from her bony shoulders. She stood well out of reach and stretched one hand timidly toward the steed.

Frustrated by the smell of the turnip in the girl's cupped palm, Francois pressed forward and flapped his lips across the lassie's fingers.

Startled, she dropped the treat and lurched away, looking for all the world as if the steed might very well eat her alive. Gilmour could not help but laugh.

The girl jerked toward him, somber eyes wide in her too narrow face, lips pursed.

"Here then," said Gilmour, striding close to pick up the abandoned offering. The girl backed away, thin fingers spread across her ear. He recognized her then, for between her fingers he could see the discoloration that stained her lobe and jaw. It was both the color and the size of a well-ripened plum. He straightened, watching her. "You're the lass from the Lion's kitchen, are you not?" he asked.

There was a slight delay before her jerky nod. Her hair, mousy brown and stringy, fell over her fingers, and she drew her hand slowly away.

Mour turned the piece of turnip in his hand. "Does your mistress know you ferret away treats for the steeds?"

Her eyes widened even more and Gilmour laughed again. "You needn't worry. I'll not tell her, though Francois hardly deserves your attentions. Truth to tell he's a greedy beggar."

"He is wounded."

The words were spoken softly and solemnly, as if that was all that needed be said. The beast was wounded and so she had come to ease his pain. And though there were few creatures on earth that needed less easing than this one, Mour could not help but appreciate her kindness.

"Here," he said, lifting the turnip toward her.

She shook her head and backed away an additional step, and he saw now that she limped a bit on her right leg.

"Humph," he said and frowned. "I would not have thought it of a lass like you."

She stared at him a moment longer then spoke. "Thought what?"

"That you would tease a poor wounded beastie with a tasty morsel only to let him go hungry."

Her pink mouth fell open slightly, but she reached timidly for the turnip and he grinned.

"But beware," he added, as she lifted the treat back

toward the stallion who lipped it happily from her palm, "Francois has his pride. He does not accept charity. You're now committed to ride him."

It took some time for Mour to convince the girl to mount the steed, but finally she did and sat hunched on his back, clinging to his heavy mane as Mour led him out of the stable and up the rutted street toward the Lion. It was not a simple task to get her to tell him she was on her way to the inn, and it was downright impossible to convince her to share her given name.

"Plums," he said and scowled as he walked along. "A pleasant enough fruit, but said to be unwholesome when eaten fresh. They be best served in jellies and pastries." He glanced up. "You're not to be baked into a pie, are you, lass?"

She shook her head, and with that motion she gave him the slightest of smiles. Her teeth were crooked and she was missing a tiny premolar, but in that instant it seemed as if the sun shone on her face alone.

"Nay. No one with such a bonny smile should be called by the name of a pitted fruit," Mour said and spent the rest of the journey trying to guess her given name.

When he moved to lift her down near the Lion's door, she stiffened, but allowed his touch. Still, as she backed nervously away, her cheeks were as bright as her eyes, which she shifted toward a noise behind him.

"I shall have to call you something," Mour said, "for I fear I need your help. Francois will become as fat as a swine if he is not ridden, and with his wound, I fear I am a bit heavy for him. Mayhap you would agree to exercise him again on the morrow."

Her gaze flitted back to him. Her crooked smile

lifted for a fraction of a moment, and then, like a
wounded sparrow, she scampered into the inn.

Gilmour turned away. Isobel stood beside the wattle
and daub building, watching him. For a moment their
gazes held, but he had made a vow to leave her be and
he was not fool enough to break it. Nodding curtly, he
returned Francois to the stable, but despite his words
to the wee lassie, the horse was not grievously
wounded and required little attention. Therefore, there
was naught for him to do but return to the Red Lion
and while away his hours at one of the inn's well-
scrubbed tables.

It should have been a pleasant time. Indeed, there
were few things he enjoyed more than sipping spirits
in a cozy inn with an appreciative crowd to listen to his
tales and a bonny maid to give him a come-along
glance now and again.

In fact, he very much considered coming along a time
or two, but something always distracted him. It wasn't
Isobel. Nay, her entrances into the common room disturbed him not at all. Oddly, it was the other patrons
who irked him. The fellow in the leather jerkin, for instance. Seated at a table near the door every evening, he
watched Isobel with dark, brooding eyes whenever she
was in view. Dressed as a warrior, he wore a knotted
strip of leather about his neck. It hung down inside his
dark tunic, not showing whatever charm it might hold
on its end. He was no giant of a man, average in height
and girth really, but dour of expression.

In an attempt to draw him out, Gilmour had ordered
him an ale and engaged him in conversation, but the
smooth shaven fellow had given him little more than
his name, and that in a grunted soliloquy.

"Hunter," he had called himself. Hunter, and nothing else. 'Twas a strange name for a strange fellow. But what it was that irritated him about the man, Gilmour could not quite say. True, he watched Isobel with unwavering attention, but she was a bonny lass, and therefore drew the eye—until one got to know her. Still, the man's actions peeved him.

And what of the fellow called Redmont? He was as fat as a toad and undeniably irksome. Surely no lass could be interested in him. Still, Gilmour's finger began to twitch with unfailing regularity when the man joked with Isobel. But it was probably naught but the sight of his sister by law that made Gilmour irritable.

There were always others present, but perhaps it was Laird Grier who annoyed Mour most of all, and it had nothing to do with his endless flirtations. Gilmour barely noticed the attention he showered on Isobel. Like the Munro, he too had spent some time courting Anora, but that was well before Isobel's time there. Still, the two of them had become acquainted somehow and now seemed to share a camaraderie that never failed to raise the hair on the back of Gilmour's neck.

Bugger it, Mour thought, and steadfastly kept his gaze from falling in that man's direction. He had a tale to tell, and his audience, an eclectic group of labors and landowners, was enthralled. It made little difference that Isobel had decided against gracing them with her company, for he had no interest in her. Indeed, he had promised to leave her be, and he was always a man of his word. Well, he was usually a man of his word.

Sometimes he was a man of his word.

Actually, absolute honesty had always seemed somewhat overrated to Mour, and he wondered if he should accompany her home. She had not yet left the inn and already it was dusk. That meant she would be journeying home in the dark, which made his stomach curl into a hard ball in his gut.

"You say the lad was no lad atall?" The question drew Gilmour back to his story.

Happy to leave his present thoughts, he wound expertly through his yarn as time marched on. But still Isobel remained on his mind until the story's wild finale.

His listeners gasped or groaned, depending on their dispositions, and Gilmour rose leisurely to his feet. Stretching expansively, he gazed down at his audience and spared only the briefest of glances toward the kitchen. It was still bright and noisy. "Well," he said, "the hour grows late. I think I shall step outdoors for a bit before I find me bed."

Fleta straightened as she wiped her hands upon her apron. "Will you be wanting any company?"

"Outside or in his bed?" someone murmured. Sniggers followed the question.

"That remains to be seen," said Fleta huskily and Gilmour smiled as the crowd hooted.

Taking her hand in his, he kissed her reddened knuckles. "I prefer to walk alone. But the other . . ." He raised his brows at her and let the sentence fall into silence.

"We'll see then," Fleta cooed, then flitted a cool glare at the faces that surrounded them. "When we do not have a pack of ogling oafs round about."

"Mayhap later then," Mour said, and giving her a quick bow, left the inn.

Behind him, laughter wafted and voices rose and fell, but Gilmour's mind was roiling, for the truth was bedeviling; he had no desire for Fleta's company. And that very knowledge baffled him, for she was buxom, comely, and willing. Three of his favorite attributes, so why was his interest atypically downcast?

Perhaps he was coming down with a fever, he thought, but nay, there was nothing wrong with him. He was simply eager to return to Evermyst with its secret passageways and grandmotherly ghosts—where he had brothers to torment and a tiny niece to coddle. Indeed, wee Mary was growing by leaps and bounds and would soon be walking. 'Twas little wonder he felt such a strong need to leave Henshaw's dreary streets. Well, Francois would soon be healed and able to travel.

Mour remained where he was, loitering in the shadows of the inn and drinking in the stillness of the night. The moon was nearly full, with only a slim slice pared from its right edge. A lovers' moon it was. Bright as a polished livre, it smiled down at him.

He scowled in return and shifted his shoulders from the rough plaster of the inn, but just as he did so, a door opened on creaky hinges.

"I assure you, I do not need company, Regan of Longwater," Isobel said.

The man murmured something in return and she laughed, her eyes bright in the light of her iron-bound lantern.

"Nay," she insisted and pulled her fingers firmly from his grip, "but I am well flattered. Goodnight to you."

With that, she hurried down the path to the south. Longwater remained still for a moment watching her, then, pulling his gaze away, he paced off in the opposite direction at a goodly clip.

The hairs on Gilmour's neck stood upright. Why was the man leaving? It didn't seem right, for by the moonlight, one could still see the sway of Isobel's hips. Not that Mour cared, but if Longwater was so infatuated, why did he not stay to watch her out of sight?

Perhaps he had no intention of leaving her be? What if he doubled back to accost her? And what of the dour, hauntingly familiar fellow called Hunter? Where was he? He had left sometime before. Might he not be hidden away with ill intent? Indeed, there were any number of evil souls who might be lurking in the shadows, he thought, but the truth struck him suddenly: *he* was lurking in the shadows, and he certainly had no designs on her. Therefore, there was probably no one in Henshaw who thought of Isobel Fraser any differently than he did.

His feet moved of their own accord, carrying him hurriedly down the path behind her, but in a matter of moments he lost her. She had extinguished her light, he realized, and sensed more than saw her turn off the path to the right.

Curious now, he hurried after, keeping to the shadows. Where was she going so late at night? It was only a matter of minutes before he knew the truth.

"Rhone?"

He heard her voice in a whisper of sound, but the answer was softer still.

"Issa?" The response came from the deepest of shadows. Against the glow of the moon, Gilmour saw the high, stark skeleton of the old mill. "You came."

"Oh course," she murmured and disappeared into the darkness of the shrubbery that surrounded the grain mill.

Gilmour's breath stopped in his throat. A tryst! She had come here at this late hour to meet a lover when she blatantly turned him aside at every opportunity? Who the devil was this Rhone, and why would he not come to the inn, or meet her in her own house? What did they have to hide? Was he a married man, or . . .

Laird Winbourne!

The image of Isobel in the arms of the stodgy laird struck him like a blow to the side of his head. But why would that grand noble not court her openly?

It was none of his concern, of course, but curiosity and something less agreeable drew him deeper into the shadows until finally he could hear an irregular smattering of their murmured words.

". . . I would . . . for you, Issa."

Her voice was softer, almost impossible to discern, but after a moment, Mour could hear the man's again.

Barely breathing, Mour shifted carefully through the brush that surrounded the mill.

". . . Trouble," said the man, and then on an errant wisp of wind, Gilmour heard, ". . . Anora."

He froze where he was, grasping a branch in one hand and straining to hear. Why had the unseen fellow spoken of Ramsay's wife? What did they plan together here in the darkness? But just then leaves rustled beneath the two, and the truth was obvious. A lass did not often traipse through the village darkness to meet a man unless she planned to give herself to him. To that he could attest.

Emotions smoked in Gilmour's gut, but surely those emotions did not involve jealousy. Nay, he was only concerned about his kinswoman's welfare. What would Bel get in return for her favors? It must be something substantial. Certainly it was not simply for lust's sake, else she surely would have shown interest in . . .

The branch broke in Mour's hand. In the dark silence it sounded like the blast of a cannon. He jerked, glancing up just in time to see Isobel step from the bushes. In the moonlight, her face looked as pale and perfect as a newly minted coin, and for a moment he was held mesmerized, but she did not delay. Instead, she turned and hurried away, leaving Gilmour to squint after her in silent surprise. No tryst? No moans of pleasure? His mood soared, but he stifled the feelings. After all, there was no way of knowing what had transpired or what she planned. Where was she off to now? Had he scared her away from her intended pleasure, or had she only planned to speak to the man? And was her lover even now sneaking through the brush to accost him? Gilmour straightened and narrowed his eyes at the thought. Let the bastard come. He'd be happy to . . .

A shadowy image exited the bushes and hurried off in the opposite direction.

Humph. What an odd thing. What kind of man would meet with Isobel of the Frasers and be content to leave in a matter of minutes? Gilmour had no answers. It seemed wise to follow the man and find out, but instead he found himself following Bel's course through the darkness.

Isobel jumped as laughter burst forth from the common room, but there was nothing to fear. Probably just another of MacGowan's far flung tales.

Ladling the last of the mutton stew into a wooden

bowl, she kneaded her temples for a moment. She was tired. Even though all had gone well during the meeting with Rhone the night before, her sleep had been fitful. Had she imaged the noise in the bushes, or had someone been watching her from the shadows? Nay, she was simply growing skittish, for on several occasions lately it had seemed that someone watched her, and yet no harm had befallen her. All was well, or it would be if MacGowan would leave Henshaw. Why had he come here? And why was he with Innes Munro? It could bode no good. Even though the Munros had formed a cautious alliance with the Frasers since Anora's wedding, Isobel didn't trust them. Their clan had coveted Evermyst for many years, and it was unlikely that would have been altered by the exchange of a few vows. So why was Ramsay's brother with the giant laird of that troublesome tribe? And why had the bedeviling rogue remained behind? Could it be that he knew the truth?

"Is that—"

Isobel jumped at the sound of Fleta's voice, then jerked about to see the smile drop from the other woman's face.

"Issa love, what's ailing *you*?" Fleta asked as she retrieved the stew. Although she was only a few years older than Isobel, she treated all with a motherly concern. So surely there was no reason to be irritated by the woman.

" 'Tis naught," Isobel breathed, but found herself wondering why Fleta looked so happy. In truth, though, she knew the answer. 'Twas MacGowan's shameless flirtations that had brought a smile to the maid's lips. Flitting her eyes downward, Isobel cleared her throat. "I am fatigued is all."

"Then why not go home?"

"I must clean up afore—"

"Nonsense." Fleta took her arm firmly, drawing her toward the back door. "Elga and I will tidy up. Birtle and Plums will help. You find your bed."

Bed. She stared aghast into Fleta's dark eyes. Was that what she was thinking about? Did she plan even now how best to coax everyone out of the inn so that she could sneak into MacGowan's bed?

"Are you well, love?" Fleta asked, her tone concerned.

"Aye." She almost jumped again, guilty at her thoughts. After all, Fleta's affairs were none of her business, for she'd been naught but kind to Isobel since the day she'd arrived some months before. "Aye. I am fine. Still, I could do with some rest. Perhaps I shall go home," she said and within moments she found herself ushered out the door, lantern in hand.

She scowled as she walked along. Aye, she would sleep well tonight and by morn she would be quite herself again, she thought, and glanced past her swaying circle of light into the darkness beyond. All was well. MacGowan would soon be gone, and, in the meantime, if he entertained himself with Fleta it was no concern of hers. Still, they seemed a mismatched pair. For all of Fleta's pretty eyes and kindly nature, she did not seem the type to appeal to MacGowan. After all, he was vain and shallow and the thought of him holding her against the bare strength of his chest—

She stopped abruptly. Heaven's saints! What was

wrong with her? She didn't care a whit who he held
against his chest, bare or not. She had no interest in
him whatsoever, except to find out why he was with
the Munro.

Still, his bare chested image bedeviled her mind.
Though she tried to be rid of it, she was stiff with tension, and she no longer felt sleepy. She'd go to the
burn for a while and listen to the waves against the
shore. True, it didn't have the spellbinding appeal of
the sea, but the soughing sound had a way of easing
her mind, of freeing her soul. And just now she desperately needed to be free.

Where the devil was she going tonight? Gilmour
wondered as he stepped into the darkness. Luckily,
none suspected that he'd exited the inn to follow her,
for though she had left through the back door, he had
his ways of keeping track of her whereabouts. It had
been simple enough to make his excuses and leave
shortly after. But now he wondered about her destination. Did she go to meet another lover? Or hadn't the
man from the night before been her lover atall? Rhone,
she'd called him. A strange name. Might he have been
an informant of some kind? And if so, what kind of information did he carry?

Thoughts milled like wild ewes through Gilmour's
mind. The moon was hidden just now, but even so, he
thought he saw Isobel glance back and held his breath
as he froze in the darkness beside the path. For a moment it seemed as if the whole world held its breath,
but finally she turned and continued on, over the rick-
ety bridge by the mill and on to the wooden palisade
that contained the village. There she stopped and

glanced about once again. No sound interrupted the silence, and with one furtive glance behind her, she turned and disappeared from sight.

Gilmour waited where he was, watching the black space where she had disappeared and realizing in a moment that she had slipped through the wooden enclosure to the rustling burn beyond.

Gilmour left his hiding place to creep silently forward, careful not to disturb the quiet. It took him a moment to shimmy over the wooden wall, and once on the opposite side, he paused to search for her. But he could see little.

A gnarled rowan leaned its deep shadow over the burbling stream that ran beside the village. The moon had escaped from the bondage of the clouds and shone with cool brilliance on the face of the water, but beneath the rowan branches, it was as dark as sin. Gilmour stopped there, letting his eyes adjust, but there was nothing that could have prepared him, for suddenly, in the blink of an eye, Isobel appeared on the bank of the stream.

Gilmour's breath caught hard in his throat, for she was naked.

Moonlight, saintly in its timing, skimmed past scattered branches and flooded like a beacon from the sky. It glimmered off her hair, casting it in a hundred silver hues as it flowed to her shoulders and caressed the tops of her ivory breasts. Shadows lay below, parted only by the magical movement of her thighs as she stepped into the water. It lapped in hungry, glistening waves about her delicate calves, reaching ever higher. She bent, scattering light across the lawn of her back and spilling it in kindly glory over the splendid twin curves of her buttocks.

Though she remained on the bank for only a matter of moments, every detail was chiseled indelibly in Gilmour's mind, freezing his limbs and hardening him with instant, aching appreciation.

She slipped into the water, and her hair, bright as candlelight, spread across the waves like lily petals. His heart hammered heavily in his chest, and lower, where he was stiffened and aching, it beat again, like the rhythm of a slow drum, building tension, promising action.

But there would be no action.

Loosening his fists at his sides, Mour exhaled carefully, then searched madly for reasons why there should be no action. She was, after all, of age. They were comparable in station and . . . but nay. He shook his head in a sad attempt to clear it. He didn't like her. She was cool and aloof to him. And yet . . .

She glided through the waves like a water sprite bent on enchanting him. And he was enthralled, unmoving, unspeaking, barely daring to breathe, lest he break this spell and find that she was naught but a dream.

Mist rose in ghostly fingers along the edges of the pond and curled sleepily toward the dark, reaching branches above. It was into this mist that she finally rose, her ivory shoulders seeming to lift the rest of her spectacular body from the loving embrace of the waves.

Gilmour exhaled quietly. He had never seen her equal. Every line of her was as fluid and graceful as a swan. Every inch was as beautiful and refined as a work of art.

She lifted her hand to grasp a branch as she stepped

into the shadows, and as she did so light glimmered down the length of her wet arm. Moonlight glistened in silver splendor across her lovely breasts, then fanned over her belly and fell in softened waves upon her thighs.

Gilmour stared at her unearthly beauty, and then she was gone, her perfection hidden by darkness and distance.

Something ached in his soul. He moved to follow her, but with his very first step, reality seized him.

What the devil was he thinking? She wasn't perfection. She was snooty and aloof to him while being blatantly flirtatious with others. But her face was as perfect as . . .

Nay!'Twas not so different than a thousand other faces. And as for her form . . . for a moment his mind froze, seeming absolutely unable to compare her with others. But he forced himself.

Her form, he told himself silently, was neither so buxom as Fleta's nor so youthful as Elga's. In fact, there were a host of other maids just as appealing, and yet she seemed magi—

And yet nothing. There were no "and yets," he thought, and madly reined in his skittering thoughts. She was no water sprite. No fairy folk. No enchanted being of any sort. She was simply a woman of flesh and bone, imperfect in a hundred ways. And once his erection eased enough to allow him to move, he would remember those imperfections and put her forever from his mind.

Chapter 6

Gilmour swore in silence as he slipped through the darkness. Three days had passed since he'd seen Isobel by the stream. Three days since she'd disrobed in the darkness. Three days since she'd stepped like a pixie princess into the misty waters. Three days since he'd had a moment's relief from the hard ache of his desire.

He had vowed to find her physical flaws, and he had. Above her left eye was a scar the size and shape of a winter pea. He had concentrated on it for some hours and deduced, after several ales, that it was quite hideous. Her hair, though fair and long, had a crimped sort of wave to it and was wont to creep from bondage down the back of her too narrow neck. And her face . . . it was rather oddly shaped, really, almost triangular, with a tiny peaked chin like an impish elvish maid's, and slanted azure eyes that laughed at him at every turn. Laughed. At him. Which pointed to a host of emotional flaws. Aye, she was not normal, and though her waist might be minuscule and her breasts . . .

Mour realized suddenly that he wasn't breathing and forced himself to do so. In and out. In and out, as if everything was normal. Her breasts, after all, were nothing special.

In and out. In and out.

He liked buxom women, always had. And she was not buxom. In fact, her bosom was like the rest of her, small. And soft and fair and . . .

Bugger it! In and out. In and out, he reminded himself.

Nay, she was hardly perfect. Which meant that he must be following her because he did not trust her, not because he was enamored.

Aye, that was it. She was not a natural sort of maid, but did strange things in strange manners. Late night visits to darkened burns, clandestine meetings with unknown men. Nay, he did not trust her, and so he feared she might be planning a plot against his brother and his wife.

Relief splashed through him as he remembered his reasoning. They were perfectly sound, after all. He had heard Anora's name whispered in the dead of the night, and 'twas his duty to make certain there was no plot planned against his kinswoman.

But Isobel had almost reached her home, so apparently the maid had no secret meetings planned for this night, which meant that Mour was almost free of his duty and could . . .

But in that moment she glanced behind her and turned to the left.

Gilmour's heart lurched as he froze in the shadows. Was she going to the burn again? Dared he hope—

Not that he cared, he reminded himself, but when she stepped toward the palisade and disappeared from view, his lips chanted a silent prayer of thanksgiving.

He waited outside the line of rowan trees as long as he could, then stepped quietly into the blackness toward the water.

Aye, there was a God, for the moon was bright once again. And aye, He was kindly, for she was naked and shown to perfection in the silvery light. For a moment he saw the glimmer of her body and then, like a mythical nymph, she slipped into the blessed water. It flowed over her silken shoulders, and then, because he was straining to see, he realized that she had dived beneath the surface. For a moment her legs flipped upward, just visible above the lapping waves, and then she was gone.

He held his breath in surprise. How was it that she could swim beneath the surface like a spotted eel? And why would she do such a thing? He had known others who could stay afloat in the water, but none who delighted in the depths, none who disappeared beneath the waves.

He shifted, searching the surface for sight of her, but she didn't appear. Might she be in trouble? Could there be some sort of ravenous beast in the water? Or—a man! The thought came to him suddenly. Surely someone had been lying in wait for her and had pulled her under. He was suddenly certain of it and took a quick step toward the burn, but in that instant she appeared, launching from the depths to shoot above the surface like a bobbing cork. Water sprayed bright as quicksilver into the air. He heard her harsh rasp for breath and then she was rushing wildly toward shore.

Fear! He could feel it. Snatching his dirk from his belt, Mour raced toward her.

"Nay!" she gasped as she scrambled onto the sand.

"Isobel." He reached for her with his free hand. His other was wrapped about his dirk and threatened the darkness around them, but no brigands attacked.

"Anora!" Isobel rasped.

Mour closed his hand around her arm, drawing her to him, to safety, but she screamed and struck him.

Pain reverberated in his skull. He staggered backward, still holding the knife in an dazed attempt to protect her.

"Nay!" She lunged toward him. "You'll not . . ." she began, but the remainder of her statement dropped into silence. She blinked as if waking from a frightful dream, and a rock fell unnoticed from her fingers. Only her ragged gasps could be heard for a moment, then, "Anora?" she murmured.

"What the devil!" Gilmour rasped, still staggering.

Her breath stopped for a moment. Her arm dropped. "MacGowan?"

"Aye." He steadied his stance and felt his skull, but whether the dampness he felt was water or blood was uncertain. Still gripping the Maiden, he glanced about again. He thought he heard a faint sound in the underbrush, but no evil was forthcoming. None but the two of them stood upon the shore. "Can I ask you something, lass?" he asked and felt his skull again.

She didn't answer, only stood like one transfixed, her wide eyes gleaming in the darkness.

"Might you be possessed by a demon?"

"I . . ." She glanced around as if uncertain where she was. "I'm not . . ." she began, then paused and drew a slow breath. "What are you doing here?"

"I am saving you from whatever brigand tried to ravage you." He too glanced about. "But it seems there is—"

She crossed her arms against her breasts. "What are you doing *here*?"

"I . . ." He scowled, then glanced down to replace his weapon and think for a hard-pressed moment, but when he looked up, all he saw was the back of one leg flicking into the trees. He tried to see into the brush, but there was little hope, for the darkness beneath the rowans was complete. Still, he was certain she was already dressing. A man's good fortune could only stretch so far, and he seemed to be fresh out. Perhaps that was best, for it gave him a few moments to organize a decent reason for his presence there. "I discovered this bonny spot some days hence," he said, raising his voice and peering into the underbrush. " 'Tis a lovely place. Peaceful, and I find I most enjoy—"

"You followed me." Her voice came unbidden through the darkness.

"Followed you!" He forced a laugh. "Hardly that." He heard her walking away and followed tenaciously, pressing the branches aside in an attempt to see through the trees. A flash of her hair was all that caught his eye, and he realized she had already shimmied through a hole in the palisade. One glance told him it was too narrow for him to squeeze through, so he vaulted over the top and continued after her.

"Where do you go?" he asked, for she was dressed in a gown so dark it was all but impossible to see her in the night. She was carrying the lighter-colored gown that she oft kept pinned up at the sides. It must be the very devil getting those garments on over all that glorious wet skin in the . . .

She stopped abruptly. "Why did you follow me?"

She had dropped the rock sometime before, but he well remembered that she was the very devil with a sling shot and he had known women, his mother included, who were quite handy with a knife. His sister Shona was rather deadly with a bow, so there was no way of knowing what the maid was capable of. Indeed, her behavior of late was beyond strange. Might she be mentally deranged? he wondered, but she was still watching him with catlike intensity.

"Tell me, MacGowan," she said. "Have you run short of virtuous maids to deflower?"

"Are you saying you are not virtuous or that you wish to be deflowered?" he asked.

She gazed at him for one long moment, then turned and paced away into the darkness.

He followed. "What frightened you in the burn?"

No response was forthcoming.

He glanced behind, remembering her fear, her words. *Anora,* she had said. Why?

She kept walking.

"Did a beast frighten you? An animal of some sort?"

The silence was broken only by the muffled sound of her feet against the dirt path. He realized at that moment that she carried her shoes, and found that disturbingly fascinating for some time. It was only when her footfalls sounded against her own rock pathway that he came to his senses.

"Isobel!" he said, and grabbed her arm just before she reached her door. "You should not leave the inn alone."

She raised her chin slightly. Damnation, she was stunning . . . except for the hideously disfiguring scar, of course.

"Tell me, MacGowan," she said. "How do you know that I leave the inn alone?"

Oh hell, he thought, but soon found a way to leave wee Plums' collusion out of the conversation. After all, she had seen enough troubles in her short life without repaying her fierce loyalty with betrayal. "Either you left alone or you planned to swim naked with another," he reasoned.

She said nothing, and his gut twisted. Then good sense broke through his foolishness, reminding him that he had seen her there before. Alone.

He relaxed a smidgen, dropping her arm. "Tell me," he said. "Are you the kind to invite another into the burn with you?"

"Tell *me*," she said, "are *you* the kind to lie at every juncture?"

He opened his mouth to answer, but she turned and slipped like a fairy through the doorway. He thrust his foot into the opening without cognizant thought, then winced as the heavy timber slammed against his calf-skin shoe.

"Get out," she ordered.

"When you tell me the truth," he said, and pressed into the opening. She thumped her palm against his chest and leaned against the door, but she was a frail thing. Either that, or she wasn't trying very hard, he thought, and almost smiled.

"The truth!" She laughed, sounding breathless. "You are the last man to deserve the truth, Mac-Gowan."

"Nevertheless," he said, then paused to touch his wound with careful pathos. "Pity oft opens doors otherwise closed, and I have been sorely wounded while trying to defend—"

Pain stabbed his hand. He yanked it out of harm's way and in the same moment felt her heel slam against his knee. Even as he stumbled back, the door thudded shut.

Rubbing his wounded knuckles, he glowered at the offensive wood. Blast the maid and her devilish gown pins. "Bel," he called, more miffed by her trickery than her pin pricks, "let me enter."

"Go away, MacGowan."

"I will do so when you tell me what happened at the burn."

"I was followed by a deceitful lout who spied on my few private moments."

He smiled wistfully at the memory, but unfortunately there was more afoot here than a naked fairy woman in the moonlight.

"Open the door," he insisted.

"And why would I be doing that?"

He put his fingers to his skull. Aye, it was blood. "Because I am wounded by your own hand."

"If you do not like the treatment, you should not have followed me."

"And if you do not like me hanging about your door, you should not have struck me."

"You admit the truth then? That you slunk through the darkness to spy on me?"

There seemed little reason to deny it. After all, the lass may be piteously scarred, but she was not a fool. "Would me confession gain me entry?" he asked.

"Nay, but 'twould give me a reason to report your churlish behavior to your brother."

"Believe me, lassie . . ." His fingers felt sticky as he rubbed them together. "Ramsay would be the last man to be surprised by me behavior."

"Leave me be, MacGowan. Now and forever."

He scowled at the door. " 'Tis clear you do not know the rules to this game, lass."

"We play a game do we?"

"Aye. 'Tis the game where the hero saves the damsel in distress."

"I was not in distress."

"Then, in gratitude," he continued, ignoring her denial, "she sees to his wounds and coos over his bravery."

He could hear her snort clearly through the door. It was distinctly unladylike. Yet another flaw.

"But if the damsel fails to do her part, the rules change," he added.

"Do they now?"

"Aye," he said and leaned a shoulder against the cottage wall. "Then the hero goes to the inn and tells all he knows about how the damsel likes to disrobe before swimming naked as a bairn in the burn. Generally, it causes quite a stir amongst the village folk and—"

The door opened with a snap. "I am trying to believe that even you would not do such a thing."

He grinned. "Any luck thus far, lassie?"

She opened the door the rest of the way and nodded toward the interior. He stepped inside. A single tallow candle glowed in the room, spilling light across the rough table where it sat.

"What do you want?" she asked and closed the door behind him.

Light flickered across her face, shading her eyes an unearthly blue and glimmering along the crimped waves of her honey toned hair.

It was certainly a shame about that hideous scar. Where the hell was it, again?

"You are supposed to see to me wound," he said, "sustained in a grand attempt to protect you."

"Protect me from what?"

"That was me very next question."

She didn't respond.

He glanced about. "You live here alone?"

"Who were you expecting, MacGowan?"

He quelled any relief that might try to well up inside him.

"You have no protector, then?" he asked.

She turned away. "And what would he protect me from? Men who might try to force their way into me home?"

"Those who would mean you harm."

"No one means me harm," she said. "Leastways, not until you."

"Truly? Then what frightened you?"

She glanced away, and for an instant a flicker of worry crossed her elvish features. " 'Twas naught but me imagination."

"Truly? I would not have thought you the skittish sort."

"And I would not have thought you the shallow sort . . . until I met you."

He propped a booted foot upon a nearby trunk. "You spoke your sister's name."

She caught his gaze for one nervous moment. "You are mistaken."

"Rarely."

"And astonishingly vain."

"Always. What did you fear?"

Her scowl deepened for an instant, but finally she flipped her palm upward and spoke as if the incident was of little import. "I remained beneath the water too long and became frightened, is all."

"Truly?" he asked, not believing a word. "And you seem so at home in the water."

"Meara tells me I was born to Evermyst and therefore the waves will forever call to me."

"I meself have a new found appreciation of water," he said. "What frightened you, lass?"

" 'Twas nothing."

"Were you caught in the plants? Wedged between sunken branches?"

"As I said, 'twas merely me imagination. I panicked and—"

"Panicked." He watched her carefully. He had first met her some months ago on a wildling night in a battle with the fierce Munros. Not a flicker of fear had crossed her ethereal features then. He touched the wound on his skull again. "Tell me, lass, do you always attack your protector when you panic?"

"You are not me protector," she said, then scowled at his wound, looking peeved. But he wondered if her hands shook just a mite. " 'Tis just like you to get yourself injured, MacGowan," she said. "Sit down. I'll have a look at it."

He shrugged and took a seat on a three-legged stool

that threatened to spill him onto the swept dirt of her floor. "Since you are so gracious."

The room fell silent for a moment. She probed at his skull, none to gently, and he gave her a sidelong glance of discontent.

"It should be stitched."

"I think not."

"It will scar."

"Truly?" he said and couldn't quite contain the enthusiasm in his voice.

"Is that good news, then?"

He shrugged, not controlling his grin. "Maids like scars."

"Do they, now?" She crossed her arms against her breasts, and they pressed upward slightly. He concentrated hard on *her* scar. Unfortunately, it was difficult to see in the dim light.

"Ramsay has several. Scars, that is."

"How fortunate for him," she said but there was little conviction in his voice.

"He won Anora."

"And you think 'tis because of his scars?"

He widened his grin. "If the truth be told, lass, I am superior in every other way."

"So that's your hope, to gain a few scars and win me sister's adoration?"

"What's that?" he asked, tilting his gaze up to hers in surprise.

"You're not about to deny that you are attracted to her, are you?"

He snorted. "Saint Michael himself would be attracted to her."

"She will not leave her husband."

It took a moment for her meaning to become clear. "Is that what you think?" He swiftly rose from the stool. "That I would cuckold me own brother?"

She shrugged as if unconcerned and moved casually away. "I've seen you look at her."

"And I've heard you speak her name in the dark, then strike out with a rock. Why?"

She turned away, but he grabbed her arm, pulling her back.

"Why?" he repeated.

"I was afraid and confused. Me sister and I spent much time beside the water at Evermyst. I thought for a moment that she was with me, and I feared I could not save—" Her eyes were enormously wide as she paused for breath.

"What?"

"I feared I could not save meself. That I was about to drown."

"You were already on shore."

"As I said, I was confused."

He narrowed his eyes, trying to decipher the truth. "What threatened you, Isobel?"

She shrugged, pushing aside the emotion he had almost been able to read in her face. "I struck out blindly."

"Hoping to save . . ." He remembered how she had gasped her sister's name. But what were the emotions behind it? ". . . Yourself."

"Let me go," she said, but her voice was soft, her eyes wide in her delicate face. 'Twas a face that was meant to be cherished, a body meant to be worshipped.

And yet, here she was, alone in a poor village, with not a soul to care for her. Why, when she harbored such strong emotion for her sister?

"Cannot you admit your feelings, Isobel?"

Her breath stopped short in her throat. "I have no feelings for you, MacGowan."

He was honestly startled. "I meant your feelings for your sister."

"Oh." She darted her gaze sideways. "Anora has been good to me. I have not denied that."

"And you cherish her?"

She shrugged. "It makes little difference, for I was not meant for life at Evermyst."

"Then what were you meant for?"

She glanced about dismissively. "Cooking in Henshaw. Weaving in Glenshire. I am at home where ever I travel."

"And you do not long for a place of your own? A family?"

"In truth, I would not know what to do with a family."

"Surely you remember your own childhood."

"Aye," she said simply. "I do."

He watched her closely, trying to read her thoughts, but she showed little in her expression. "And you do not miss being coddled and cherished?"

She pulled her arm stiffly from his grasp. "You should not judge others' lives by your own, Mac-Gowan."

"Old Meara said she gave you to a woman who longed for children but was blessed with none of her own." He could imagine her as a child, a tiny cherub, as round and bright as a bauble. She would giggle like wee Mary, her tiny cheeks rosy as her mother beamed and her father chuckled.

"Perhaps," she said, and in that fleeting moment he saw the truth revealed in her face.

"Your foster parents were not kind to you."

"It doesn't matter."

"Aye, it does," he said, and something grew hard and cold in his belly. "It matters a good deal."

She didn't respond, but set her shoes beside the misshapen straw mattress that was her bed.

"I wish to know the truth, Bel," he said and she turned toward him, her tilted eyes bright in the tallow light.

"You want to drink fine ale by the fire side and tell outlandish tales to women who bat their eyelashes and flatter your vanity. But the truth, MacGowan? I think not."

"Did they harm you?" he asked, his voice low.

"Why do you ask?"

He said nothing, but his gut was knotted like twisted hemp.

"Because I have noble blood? Is that why you care?"

"Meara gave you to them in good faith. They were to cherish you, Bel. Did they not?"

Her face was sober, her slanted eyes intent, but she said nothing.

"Tell me, lass," he said, stepping rapidly forward, "have you never been cherished, adored, coddled?"

She backed abruptly away. "You'd best go, Mac-Gowan. Master Gibbs has given me this cottage to use, if he learns you were here I may well lose me place at the inn."

"Are you afraid?" he asked and took another step toward her.

"What?"

"Of being cherished," he said. "Are you afraid?"

She breathed a laugh. "Aye," she admitted. "I have no fear of hunger or brigands or evil, but kindness . . ." She faked a shiver. "I cannot abide it."

He was close enough now to touch her, and he reached up slowly. Her face felt indecently soft against his palm. "At Dun Ard, me home . . ." He paused to skim his thumb across her cheek. "Every lassie is treated like a princess."

She seemed to have ceased breathing, but she managed to speak. "Are they?"

"Aye. Me father thought me sister could do no wrong. Spoiled her shameless, he did. Just as Ramsay will spoil his wee fosterling."

"Spare the whipping, burn the sauce," Bel said. "I do not like burned sauce."

Slipping his hand backward, Mour brushed her hair behind her ear. It was as delicate as a unfurled rose. He followed its upward curve with his fingertip. "You have no desire to be spoiled?"

"It seems to me that if one is spoiled she is also owned."

"Owned?" he said and carefully curled his hand around the back of her neck. "Mayhap she is only loved."

"I would not know." Her tone sounded breathless as she pressed her back against the wall behind her.

"Because you were not loved?"

"The past is past," she said, "and of no interest to me."

"And what of the present?" he murmured. "Have you no wish to be loved today?"

"Nay," she whispered.

"Or kissed?" He knew he shouldn't move closer. He knew he shouldn't touch her. And when he leaned in, he knew beyond a shadow of a doubt that he shouldn't kiss her.

But he did, softly, upon the cheek. And once that bridge was crossed, he could not seem to stop, for he kissed her jaw, then moved lower, down the smooth, endless track of her neck.

Her skin was warm and supple, her breathing shallow, and when he forced himself to lift his head, he saw that her eyes were closed.

"Mayhap being loved would not be so hideous," he suggested.

She opened her eyes and turned them slowly to his. "Methinks," she said, "that you are mistaking love for lust."

He could not help but smile, for desire shone like a gemstone fire in the depths of her eyes. "Either way, lass," he said, "I am well flattered."

Chapter 7

Reality struck Isobel like a cold wave. She pressed her hands against the wall behind her and straightened abruptly. "Get out!" she ordered.

"I did not mean to anger you, Bel," MacGowan said. "I merely wished to prove—"

"Out," she repeated.

He raised a hand between them, palm outward, as if he were soothing a fractious mare. "I'll do naught to harm—" he began, but somehow she managed to wrench the door open and prod him through it. Snatching a timber from its resting place against the wall, she shoved it home with a vengeance.

For a moment all the world was silent, then, "Hmm." She could hear his voice easily through the solid portal. "Such a wee skittish thing, you are. Tell me, Bel, why is it that you fear me so?"

She said nothing. Quiet drew out again. Not until she heard him leave did she turn away. She wasn't afraid of him. In fact, he was the one who should fear her, for she knew the truth. Aye, she knew he was up to no good and he would not get away with it, no matter how charming he was. No matter how his eyes danced

93

when he smiled. No matter how it seemed that his laughter could dispel any worry, or that his hands could . . .

Clasping her own hands, she paced to the far wall.

Nay, she neither longed for him nor feared him, and yet she must be cautious, for she had been warned.

She shivered as the memory of the burn burst over her. All had been peaceful and soothing. Water had surrounded her, cradled her. And then it had happened. Something, *someone*, had seized her and held her under the waves. And yet there had been no one there, and it was not herself that was threatened atall, but Anora!

Isobel shivered and clasped her hands around her arms, trying to warm herself. It was confusing, baffling. She was herself, yet for a terrifying span of time she was not. She had been Anora, and she had been in danger. Pacing again, she tried to find her calm, to think. What did it mean? Was Anora in danger even now? Taking a deep breath, she paused for a moment, setting her mind free, and there it was, at the back of her consciousness, a moment of peace.

Anora was well. Isobel was certain of that. And yet, something had happened. Something or someone had threatened her. But who would—

"MacGowan." She spoke the name aloud, unbidden, unwilling. And yet the word lay in the darkness, feeling right. Somehow MacGowan was involved. She knew it, felt it in her soul. But how? He had been here with her, watching her from the bank of the burn. Gooseflesh rose eerily along her forearms. Aye, he had watched her, had seen her enter the water, had followed her home, and there he had kissed her, had touched her, not as if she were someone of no conse-quence, but as if she were precious and perfect.

But why? Did he merely hope to distract her? Did he realize she could feel Anora's emotions? Did he know she had sensed her sister's panic? Was that the reason he was so concerned about her fear? But if he had somehow caused Anora's unknown troubles, how could he be here at the same time? And why would he wish to harm Anora? He liked her, or at least he ad-mired her. But mayhap he would sacrifice her for a greater gain. Mayhap he had set his sights on Evermyst. But in order to gain that citadel he would have to be rid of his brother, too. Was he that evil? He was vain and he was shallow, but evil . . .

She shook her head, trying to scatter the confusing thoughts that milled like wild bullocks in her head.

Anora was safe for now. Isobel could sense that much, and as for MacGowan, she would watch him, learn about him, and if he plotted any evil against her sister, he would surely live to regret it.

The night passed and morning began. Gilmour saw to Francois, but there was no need, for the wee lass was already there, stroking his heavy mane and feed-ing him bits of dark bread crusts. Once again, Mour boosted the tiny lass aboard the stallion's broad back, trying not to touch her any longer than necessary, for she seemed so frightened beneath his hands. Once again he tried to guess her name, and once again, she refused to tell him, though for a moment she gave him that crooked grin when he suggested she might be King James himself, since the young monarch was well known for his disguises.

Stopping Francois before the Red Lion's door, Mour glanced up at the girl and tried one more wild guess. Hunched over the stallion's withers, she shook her head, and he could not help but notice the flash of fear and exhilaration she felt upon her high perch.

"Very well then," he said. "Since I am certain you will see to Francois's well being should any ill befall me, I shall forgive your reticence and wait for the truth on the morrow. Hop down here now, before your mistress wonders where you've gone."

She glanced frightfully toward the earth far below and he motioned as if impatient.

"Come along now," he urged, but in that moment the Red Lion's door opened and Isobel stepped out. She was drying her hands and the scents of ginger and cinnamon wafted out with her.

"I need Plums' assistance in the kitchen. Lift her down, if you please." Her tone was brusque and yet there was something odd about her demeanor. Could it be that she was protecting the lass? From him? Could it be she saw some similarities between herself and the girl?

"Her name is not Plums," he said, intrigued against his will.

"What's that?'

"Her Christian name, 'tis not Plums," he repeated.

Isobel blinked at him. "Nevertheless—" she began.

"Thus I think she should be made to sit upon Francois until she tells me her given name." He spoke in jest, yet when he glanced up at the lass, he saw that she was pale with some unspoken shame and that her fingers were wrapped white and tight into the steed's flaxen mane.

"Let her be, MacGowan," Bel ordered. Her voice

was low and when he turned toward her, he saw the truth in her somber eyes. The girl had never been given a name, or if she had, it had long ago been forgotten in deference to her birthmark. He winced at his foolishness, but he was not called the rogue of the rogues for nothing, and shrugged in the same motion as he turned back toward the girl. "Very well, then, lassie," he said. "Keep your secrets to yourself. But as for me I shall call you. . . . Claude."

"Claude?" The girl whispered the name and Mour raised his brows as if she had protested.

" 'Tis the queen of France's given name. But if it is not good enough for you, I could call you. . . ."

She was already shaking her head.

"Very well then, me bonny Claude, come down from your perch."

Isobel stepped rapidly forward. "She cannot—"

"The queen of France is a wonder on a steed, and needs no man to help her dismount. Hold on to the mane, lass, and swing your leg over."

"MacGowan," Bel warned, but the girl was already sliding down the horse's barrel.

Her skinny arms stretched and shook, but her toes were yet inches from the ground.

"Let go," said Mour.

"MacGowan!" Isobel's voice sounded panicked, but he stood between her and the girl and in that moment the child's grip gave out.

She dropped with a small gasp of dismay, landed on her feet and wobbled sideways, but Gilmour shifted his weight ever so slightly, so that she bumped and steadied against his legs. He didn't reach out to aid her but nodded once as she gained her balance.

"Just like the princess herself on her first try," he said and bowed slightly from the waist. "Do not worry, Maid Claude," he whispered. "Your royal secret is safe with me."

Her eyes widened and then, like a startled lambkin, she pivoted and hurried toward the inn.

Gilmour turned back to Francois, but the look on Isobel's face stopped him. For a moment she stared at him with eyes as wide as the child's, and then she too turned and disappeared into the Red Lion.

It was the last he saw of her for some hours and the day seemed to drag away interminably, until, on the following morning, he stood in the stable and ran his hand down Francois's injured cannon once again. The stallion picked unflinching at his barley hay and stared moodily down the aisle toward the unseen mare.

Aye, the steed was ready for the journey to Evermyst. There was no longer anything holding Mour in Henshaw. Except Isobel. Why had she stared at him with such solemnity after Claude's departure? Not that he cared, for it surely wasn't her charms that kept him there. Hardly that. Aye, he remembered how her eyes had fallen closed when he kissed her, remembered how her breath had locked in her ivory throat. But with fear or with pleasure? And if it was fear, what did she have to be afraid of? Was she planning some evil that she longed to keep from him?

Who had she met with in the dark of the night? Did she hold some grudge against her sister? Might it be that she resented the circumstances of her past so vehemently that she now sought revenge against those she perceived to be at fault? Did she hope to gain revenge only or was there a deeper plan? Might she intend to be rid of Anora in the wild hope of gaining Evermyst for her own?

Surely no one with eyes like hers could be evil. But worse atrocities had been done for smaller gain, and she had nothing to call her own. But even if Anora were gone, Evermyst would not be Isobel's, for her heritage was not common knowledge. And although Scotland's king himself had decreed that Evermyst would be passed down through matriarchal lines, she would have a difficult time proving kinship.

The possibilities spun through Gilmour's mind like swirling autumn leaves. Replacing Francois's foot on the ground, he swept his hand down the stallion's neck and tightened his girth.

If he had interpreted Isobel's conversation with Laird Grier correctly, she should be here any moment. It seemed the good baron had a weakness for mushrooms and it was clear enough that Isobel wished to please him. A few words with Martha had told Mour that Isobel gathered her ingredients for the day's meals in the morning. A passing conversation with Elga had informed him that the Red Lion's kitchen was devoid of mushrooms, thus he waited in Francois's stall, for a bit of dialogue with Fleta had informed him that Isobel was wont to ride her mare when she went gathering.

It was only a matter of minutes before the stable door opened and closed. Light footfalls hurried down the hard-packed aisle and soon he heard Isobel crooning to her steed. It was then that Mour stepped out into the aisle with Francois following eagerly behind. Walking toward the door, Gilmour stopped abruptly as he glanced into the mare's stall.

"Isobel?" He made certain he sounded surprised and

couldn't help but grin a little when she jumped at the sound of his voice. "And what might you be doing here? Dare I hope that you've come to meet me?"

She scowled at him. Her gown was woven of a simple gray plaid, yet its hue seemed to make her eyes as bright and wide as the morning sky. "Are you leaving us so soon, MacGowan?"

"Nay," he said. "Wee Claude has done a fine job with him, but I fear he needs more exercise."

For a moment her eyes clouded, but then she smoothed her expression and glanced haughtily at the golden stallion. "He looks quite hale to me."

"Aye, well . . ." Mour tugged at the reins, trying to calm the animal's restive motion. "He is very brave. Much like his master."

"Deflowering virtuous maids takes some nerve, does it?"

"You'd be surprised," he said and watched as she led the mare over to a slight outcropping of rock that protruded from the stable wall. Stepping onto it, she tugged the mare over, but just as she was about to jump onto the animal's back, Francois nickered, and the mare, pricking her ears forward and back, sidled away.

Isobel tried again, but Francois, encouraged by the mare's interest, arched his golden neck and pranced in place. The mare all but batted her eyes at such a manly display and flatly refused to cooperate with her mistress' urgings.

"Here, let me assist you," Gilmour said, and stepped forward, but Isobel backed quickly away.

"Nay, I am fine."

Not a stride separated them, making it possible for Gilmour to examine her upturned face at close quarters—

her bowed mouth, her feline eyes. If she didn't have that hideously disfiguring scar, he might almost be tempted to kiss her . . . again. And she might be tempted to pin-prick him . . . again. "Still stirred up from our time together in your cottage?" he asked.

She narrowed those impishly slanted eyes. "I was not *stirred up*."

"Excited, then."

"Have you nothing better to do than torment me?"

"One can only deflower virtuous maids for so long before . . ." He sighed with studied drama. "I fear even that loses its appeal."

"Your life is indeed difficult."

" 'Tis true," he agreed. "Let me give you a leg up."

She began to argue, but he bent and cupped his palms near her left knee. "Step on me hands."

"I was thinking of other regions."

"You'd best mount up before Francois becomes amorous."

She glanced at the flirting stallion, frowned, then, seeming to think it wise to remove herself from between the two beasts, stepped into his palms.

It was simple enough to boost her onto the mare's back, but her skirts, misplaced by the procedure, bunched irregularly under her legs. It seemed only courtly that he smooth them out, tugging them gently over her knee to skim them down the delicate muscles of her calves. It was a simple process. Innocent really, and yet he hardened immediately, making it difficult to pull his hands away.

Isobel, on the other hand, was already urging her mount toward the door. His hand fell reluctantly away even as other parts reached for her.

"And where are you off to this fine morn?" he asked, following behind on foot.

Isobel snatched her basket from the door top where she'd left it as the bay cast a sidelong glance at Francois. "Please do not concern yourself with me, MacGowan," she said. "See to your mount. 'Tis quite obvious he needs your care."

But his mount was now prancing in place, thumping his shod feet with cadenced impatience against the hard-packed earth in an attempt to catch the mare. Gilmour tightened the reins a tad.

"Francois but needs to stretch his legs a bit," he said, ignoring the steed's ridiculous display of burgeoning good health, "to ascertain whether he is fit for the journey home. Mayhap we could ride together."

"Pray, do not put yourself out," she said, and ducked as she passed beneath the stone arch of the stable door.

Gilmour followed, then mounted as Francois kept up a mincing piaffe.

" 'Tis no trouble," he insisted, riding behind. "After all, 'tis me duty as a man of honor to see to your safety."

She raised one dubious brow at him but said nothing, and the sun, just past the edge of the nearby woods, sparkled with golden optimism on the shabby village below. Beside the tanner's cottage two sows faced off in apparent disagreement, and farther down the lane, an old man ambled along pushing a wooden barrow.

"Good morningtide to you, Issa," he rasped in a voice that comes with old age and wood smoke. Stopping jerkily, he gazed up at her. "I had a mind to bring these fine eel to the inn lest you're in need of a bit of fresh meat."

"I am indeed," said Isobel. "Talk to Fleta. She'll see to it."

"Me thanks," said the old man and leaning his bent back over the cart, pushed off again.

Gilmour let Francois ease into a high stepping trot. "So, Bel, where are we off to?"

"Good morning to you," called a woman who was just opening the cobbler's shop for the day.

Isobel answered, but kept riding.

"A mystery, is it?" Gilmour asked, allowing his stallion to reach the mare's side. The steed canted his golden nose in that direction, snuffling her scent in greedy wafts as he nickered in deep-throated appreciation.

"There's no need to pretend, MacGowan," Isobel said, then, "Good day to you, Birtle." The lad had not yet reached his twelfth birthday, little more than wee Claude's age, and yet Gilmour could have sworn he saw a spark of adoration in the boy's upturned face. "Would you hurry on to the inn, lad, and tell Fleta that I said to give old Flynn an extra copper for his eels?"

The boy took off at a gallop, his knees bony beneath his flying plaid.

"And what am I pretending?" Gilmour asked, happy to have her attention to himself for a moment again.

"That you do not know where I'm going."

"I'm flattered."

She glanced at him, her question written on her face.

"I did not know you thought me gifted enough to read your mind."

"Not gifted," she corrected. "Meddlesome. You are following me, just as you did some nights back. Just as you most probably have every night since that time."

Although she was irritatingly correct, he just laughed and leaned closer. "Lass, it's only just morning."

Again she scowled at him.

"I'm hardly expecting you to go bathing in the bold light of day."

She turned her face away and steadied her mare, who arched her long black tail and eyed Francois askance. Silence settled in for a long stretch of time. Enough time, in fact, for Gilmour to wish he could see her hideously disfiguring scar from this angle. Because from where he sat, perfection seemed unavoidable.

"I wish to know why you are following me," she said finally.

"*Is* it too early to consider bathing?"

It was possible that she was blushing, but maybe it was just the rosy hue of the morning light that colored her cheeks. "Why?"

They rode side by side through Henshaw's slanting gate, and although Gilmour was uncertain why such an idea would enter his head, he couldn't help but think that such an ancient fence was not enough to protect a woman like Isobel from the evils of the world at large.

"You are me brother's wife's sister," he said finally, "and the only person I know in this village. Surely it doesn't seem strange that I spend a few minutes in your company when I happen to see you pass by."

"What of Fleta? She seems willing to share her time with you."

He couldn't help but smile. "Jealous, Isobel?"

"Daft, MacGowan?" she countered and nudged her mare into a canter.

Francois needed no encouragement to follow. Beneath the robin's egg sky, the road curled like a russet ribbon over a rock-strewn hillock and beyond. Isobel reined the bay to the east, leaving the path and making her way through gorsebushes and heather until they reached a quiet stand of crack willows.

Dismounting quickly, she let her mare roam and carried her basket into the woods.

Gilmour threw his leg over Francois's high pommel and jumped to the ground also, but deemed it wise to keep his stallion close to hand, for no matter what was said of *him*, he was still more trustworthy than his stallion.

The steed took a few willing steps, then tugged on the reins and glanced longingly back at the mare.

"Best not to think about it," Gilmour said and remembered that it was difficult to walk in a state of arousal. Apparently, hideously disfiguring scars didn't bother him as much as he had hoped.

Tying Francois to a willow that grew near a boggy stretch of moor, Gilmour entered the woods and found Isobel easily. Bending forward from the waist, she was apparently gathering mushrooms, but it was difficult to tell, for in that position, the high pale tops of her breasts were just visible, and suddenly he found it absolutely necessary to concentrate on breathing.

Sensing his nearness, she raised her gaze.

Gilmour shifted his attention and cleared his throat. "All this way for mushrooms?"

"The baron favors pigeon pie."

He knew that, of course, and yet he felt tension creep up his spine at her words. "And you favor the baron?" he asked.

"Laird Grier is quite generous."

Gilmour's little finger twitched once, but he crossed his arms casually and leaned back against a lone maple. "In exchange for what?"

She widened her eyes and gave him a pinched smile. "For whatever he wishes."

Gilmour MacGowan, the rogue of the rogues, did not feel jealousy, so what was it that ate at his gut? He didn't know, but he didn't like it, and pushed it aside as he turned the subject. "You should not come out here alone, Bel."

"Oh, and why is that?" she asked as she shifted around a moldering log for more mushrooms. The sunlight, bright in its early morning glow, fell through the branches and illumined her in a circle of golden light. Her hair glimmered like a thousand candles and her skin looked as pure and perfect as a blessed child's. Of course, he couldn't see "the scar."

"Surely you know what some unscrupulous knaves might do if they found you here alone."

"I'm certain you could tell me."

He tilted his head in concession to the insult.

"Unless you are offering, you should be more careful," he said.

"Unless I am offering what?" she asked and batted her ridiculously slanted eyes at him.

"I think you know what I speak of, lass."

"Men?" she guessed, "and how they can't be trusted?"

"Just so."

"Mayhap you are simply judging them by your own behavior."

"Nay," he argued. "I assure you, I know what they are thinking when they look at you."

"Truly?" She turned toward him so that he could see the delicate curves of her breasts, the more dramatic sweep of her waist, and the delectable flare of her hips. "And pray, what are they thinking?"

His nostrils flared, his finger twitched, and his desire pulsed to attention. "They are thinking they would like to have you," he said.

"As in own me?" she asked.

"As in, have their way with you," he said, and found that his tone was harsher than he had planned.

She stared at him for a moment, then turned rapidly away. "And they are different than you, MacGowan?"

His erection nudged against his plaid. Whoever thought a Scotsman should spend his days in course wool and no undergarments, had not spent time with Isobel Fraser. "Aye, I am different," he said and tried to will away his desire. It had never worked before and it didn't work now, so he rethought the idea of wearing his sporran around his waist instead of slanted across his chest. But then, 'twas surely a sin to hide one's light under a bushel. "I fear you shall never know the difference, Bel, for I only wish to keep you safe."

"Then go home, MacGowan, and I am certain I will be perfectly safe."

"You think me a threat?"

A glimmer of confusion crossed her face, but it was replaced so quickly with an expression of confidence that it seemed almost to never have been. "I think you are bored and you are wealthy, MacGowan, and in me own experience those attributes can cause naught but trouble."

"Truly?"

"Aye." She shrugged. "You want what you cannot have."

"And what might that be?" he asked and stepped closer.

She looked directly into his eyes, her own as steady as the earth. "Me."

Something flipped in his chest, but he calmed it. "But the baron can?"

"If I say he can."

"So you give yourself to that dull . . ." He smoothed his tone, took a careful breath and tried again. "So the laird of Winbourne is your lover?"

"Truly, MacGowan, 'tis none of your concern."

"You are me kinswoman, and therefore 'tis me responsibility to see that you are treated well."

"And you think he does not treat me well enough?"

Sweet heaven! Had she truly slept with the man? Something knotted in his stomach, but he kept his tone neutral and his expression calm. "He is only the fourth son of an aging drunkard, but methinks he could do better than allowing you to work like a slave in yonder inn."

"I shall keep that in mind," she said and turned away, but something gnawed at his soul, making him push up behind her.

"Then you have done it?"

"Done what?" she asked, as if not quite able to focus on his question.

He struggled for calm, but his hand reached out of its own accord and swung her toward him. "Have you given yourself to him or nay?" he asked, his voice low.

"In truth, I do not think I should divulge such delicate information. For despite what you say, I think you are jealous, MacGowan, and I have no wish to endure your wrath should me answer displease you."

Surprise made him loosen his grip a mite. "You think I would harm you?"

"You are vain and spoiled, and little have you desired that was denied you." She nodded, still holding his gaze. "Aye, if you were thwarted you would retaliate with vengeance."

He stepped up close, not because he meant to, but because he was drawn against his will. "What do you think I would do to you, lass?"

She had to raise her chin to look into his face now, but she did so, though she didn't answer for a moment.

"Do you fear that I would take you against your will?" he asked, and pressed closer, so close, in fact, that he could feel the heat of her willowy body against his. "Tell me, Isobel, what do you fear?"

Still she did not answer, and so, with aching slowness, he cupped her cheek in his palm. "Do you fear me touch?" he asked.

Her eyes were wide and intense, her mouth pursed in silence and though he told himself to pull away, he did not. Instead, against his better judgment, he skimmed his thumb with slow deliberation across her ruby bright lips. He felt the impact of that simple movement sizzle down his spine like summer lightning. *Pull back,* his mind commanded, but his body was on another course entirely.

"Or is it this?" he asked, and bending forward, touched his lips to hers.

Her mouth was soft and full beneath his. Fire smote him, burning on contact. He slipped his fingers into her hair, and when she did not pull away, he opened his mouth and tasted her with a slow touch of his tongue.

For an instant he felt her quiver, and then she pulled away.

"Leave me be, MacGowan." Her eyes were cool and steady, her voice perfectly modulated, unruffled.

'Twas a sad thing, really, because he was quite certain that if he dared speak, his own voice would come forth in naught but a mewling whine. So he took a moment, watching her in silence and waiting for his desire to abate enough to allow him some semblance of pride.

"I wish you no harm, Isobel," he said finally. Truth be told, he suddenly felt she was the one with the power. Power to punish, and power to please.

"Don't you?"

"Nay," he said, and though he told himself to leave off, he could not seem to keep from stepping forward. When he slipped his arm around her waist she felt as slim and willowy as the trees that graced the moor. His hand slid over the curve of her hip, and with that simple movement, he felt his composure crack a smidgen more. "I may pleasure you," he whispered, "but I shall never harm you."

Her head was tilted back, her eyes half closed. "Do I have your vow?" she whispered. Her lips were parted the barest amount. He felt her breath on his cheek and perhaps that was the most erotic touch of all.

"Where I am, you are safe," he promised.

"Good. Then you will not object when I take the baron to me bed," she said, and pressing her palm against his chest, pushed herself away.

Chapter 8

W hy in heaven's name did he still follow her? Isobel wondered. She had done everything possible to be rid of him. Indeed, in the woods, Isobel had thought he might strike her or force her. Instead, he had done nothing but drop his hand and allow her to leave, and though he had followed her back to Henshaw, he had stayed some distance behind.

The following morning he had again spent time with Plums. Isobel had watched from the window of the inn as he'd taught her to climb the stone wall, then scramble onto the stallion's muscular withers. It had taken her several attempts to squirm into place, but when she'd achieved that feat, Isobel could see her tiny glimmer of a smile even from that distance. Claude, he called her, and already the kitchen help had begun to follow suit. Strange it was, and though Bel was certain it could not be true, the girl seemed changed somehow, as if a different name had given her a different spirit. She stood straighter, moved easier, and made Bel's heart leap with hope.

Why had he done it? What did he care about a mousy lass with a purple birthmark and a limp?

Nothing. He was bored. Surely that was all there was to it, yet when the girl glanced at Mour, her eyes glowed and Isobel was uncertain whether to weep or rejoice for her newfound interest in life. Soon he would tire of Henshaw, that much was certain. And though Isobel herself looked forward to that day with anticipation, wee Claude could well be crushed. After all, she was only a child, alone in the world and easily bedazzled by MacGowan's charm. One could hardly blame her for being enchanted by the roguish twist of his smile or the shivery roughness of his laughter. But soon he would be gone. What would happen to the girl then? Already, he was ignoring Isobel. It was a relief, of course, for it seemed that he barely knew she was alive, as if he were unmoved by her admiration for the laird of Winbourne.

But still when she had left the inn only minutes before, MacGowan had followed her. She could hear his footsteps off to the side, and the knowledge that he was there made her heart quicken, which made her feet quicken. After all, she was not some foolish maid ready to reel at the sight of his tilted grin, she thought, and tightened her hand on her lantern. It shook the slightest bit.

He was there, just a breath away, watching her. All she need do was ask, and he would come. Fortunately for her, she had no intention of asking.

It wasn't far now, just a few more rods to her cottage, and the solid strength of her door would stand guard between them. But her feet stopped, as if with a will of their own and she listened. The footfalls were close now, just a short distance behind her and continued for a moment after she paused. He was losing his gift of stealth.

"I know you're there," she began, but suddenly he rose up behind her and slapped a hand across her mouth. She jerked and twisted about, but he held her tight to his chest, barely allowing her to breathe. Panic rose like bile in her throat and she tried to scream. It was no use. She struggled violently, but he was ungodly strong and suddenly someone grabbed her feet, lifting them into the air.

So he had hired a brigand to help him. But what were his plans? And why? The answer came in a flash of panic. He hoped to take her against her will, but he dare not show his face lest his family learn the truth.

He planned to rape her without repercussions, she thought, and jerking her head to the side, managed to sink her teeth into his palm.

He cursed out loud and yanked away. She slipped downward, shrieking, her mouth free, but in an instant she was grabbed again and clasped hard, his arm banded like iron across her chest.

She tried to scream again, but he hissed a curse and slapped his hand across her nose and mouth. The air ceased immediately. She couldn't breathe and wrestled violently, but it was no use. No hope! Perhaps she had been wrong. It wasn't rape he planned at all. But murder! Why? Her mind reeled, but there was no time for questions or panic. She had not survived so long only to die beneath the hand of a spoiled rogue. She would not give him the satisfaction, she vowed, and so, after one last violent jerk, she went limp in their arms.

A chuckle of satisfaction issued from the man at her feet, but she remained still, unbreathing. Her lungs screamed for air, but she waited, struggling for patience. A moment longer. Just a moment, though her ears were ringing and her head spun.

"She'll do us no good dead," her captor whispered and eased his grip. Air washed into her lungs.

Isobel screamed and struck out at the same time, flailing with her hands and feet. Thrown off balance, her captors scrambled to hold her, but she was already slipping sideways. Her shoulder hit the ground with a jolt, but her legs were still caught. She kicked madly. Her heel struck something solid and she heard a grunt of pain, but hands were already reaching for her, drawing her back under control.

"Nay!" she shrieked, and felt a fist cuff the side of her skull.

Her head reeled, sounds dimmed, and it seemed for a moment as if all movement ceased. There was nothing she could do now. She had lost. Her mind drifted. Memories washed over her—the soothing sound of restless waves, a gentle touch, the sweet scents of earth and grass.

"Bel!"

Isobel blinked, finding with some surprise that she was free and lay on the turf upon her back. She could breathe and filled her lungs, just to be sure.

"Are you well?"

She turned her head. Gilmour MacGowan crouched on one knee beside her.

"You!" The word croaked from her lips. "Why—" she began, but in that instant confusion swamped her. The voice whispered in the darkness had not sounded like his. And if he were the brigand, why did he yet remain?

"Bel," he murmured and touched his fingers to her cheek. Did they tremble just a bit? "You are safe now."

"Safe?" She could not seem to think, to pull together one single truth as she stared into his moon-shadowed eyes.

Footsteps rushed up from behind them. Isobel jerked her attention in that direction, but in the darkness she could see naught but a shadow among shadows.

"What happened?" asked a gruff voice.

"Who goes there?" asked MacGowan, and even though he no longer touched her, Isobel could feel his tension.

"Who attacked you?" asked the newcomer again, and now Bel recognized the voice. 'Twas Hunter, the warrior from the inn, and in his hand was a sword. It gleamed dully in the moonlight.

"I do not know," she breathed, eyeing the blade.

"Come." His tone was brusque and husky as he motioned with his sword. "I will see you home."

MacGowan rose with cat-like caution from her side. Absolute silence filled the night for several seconds, then Gilmour turned to peer into the darkness where the brigands had disappeared. Silently pulling the dirk from his belt, he twisted back toward the warrior. "I would object," he growled, "but someone had best follow the bastards and learn what they were about."

The warrior paused, his eyes seeming to pierce the blackness. " 'Tis dark."

"Aye," MacGowan agreed and turned his blade. Its edge glimmered a silent threat in the moonlight. "But it has been a long while since I was afeared of the night. Care for the lass while I am—"

"Do you suggest that I am afraid?" asked the warrior and took a step forward.

"We waste time," snarled Mour, impatience in his voice.

"Aye." The warrior nodded once. "See to the maid. I shall return when I find the answers."

"Nay," said Bel. "Don't go." But he was already turning away. For a moment there was a sparkle of silver from the charm hung about his neck, and then he was gone, swallowed by the darkness.

"Where do you hurt?" MacGowan asked, and Isobel turned toward him in surprise, for already he knelt beside her, his tone calm, his dirk sheathed.

She lay in silence for a moment, then drew a careful breath and assured herself she was still free, still safe. "Tell me, MacGowan," she said softly, "did you ever intend to pursue me tormentors?"

He shifted slightly, skimming one arm beneath her shoulders and the other under her thighs. "There's something odd about that Hunter," he said. "If you insist on getting yourself ravaged, at least it should be by someone with a sense of humor."

"You tricked him."

"He's eager enough to do battle. He but needed a bit of encouragement. Put your arm about me neck."

"I can walk."

" 'Tis a good thing to know," he said and lifting her against the hard strength of his chest, carried her down the path to her cottage.

Somehow he managed the latch with one hand and

finally they were inside. In a moment he laid her gently on her mattress and moved to bar the door.

"Are you well?" he asked.

She watched his shadow cross the floor. "Aye. I am fine."

"Do you know who they were?"

She heard him fumble with a steel and flint. Light flared up like hope, illuminating his face. It was as beautiful as ever, but he turned, and in that light, she saw the wound above his ear. It had been reopened and oozed a droplet of blood down the flat plane of his chiseled cheek.

Her breathing ceased as she stared at him.

Setting the lantern aside, he turned and stopped. "What is it?"

"Your wound," she said. " 'Tis bleeding."

Absently, he set his fingers against the cut. " 'Tis naught," he assured her. "Just . . ." But he paused suddenly, catching her gaze with his own. "Why do you mention it?"

"I struggled against the brigands," she said, holding her breath for a moment and feeling the stiffness of her suspicions. "I kicked one of them in the head."

His expression was solemn, his eyes intent, and in the flickering dimness he looked not like the pampered son of a wealthy laird but like an ancient warrior sent to do battle. But battle with what? Good? Or evil?

A dozen possibilities flooded her head. "Was it you?" she asked.

"Do you ask if I attacked you?"

She nodded once.

"If I'd meant to harm you, would I then save you?"

"Mayhap you had no intention of saving me, but heard the warrior's approach and pretended you meant me no harm."

He nodded as if in concession. "And what vile crime do you think I planned against you, Bel?"

She shrugged. The pain in her head was receding, and in the flare of the lantern's light he looked like a golden god of war, with his hair bound in its usual braid, and the blessed wren's feather at ease against the masculine slant of his jaw. Perhaps it was there for luck, to keep him safe from drowning, as some fools believed, but at this moment he didn't look as if he needed any safekeeping, for he seemed suddenly to be a man who could fight the demons of hell for naught more than the satisfaction of the battle.

"How would I know your intent?" she asked, pulling her mind back to his words.

"You seem to have a sprightly imagination."

"Are you saying you were not the brigand?"

"I am asking what kind of crime you imagined I planned." His tone was noncommittal, but his gaze was deadly steady and she shrugged, made nervous under his uncommon sobriety.

"Mayhap you hoped to be rid of me."

"Murder?" He raised his brows as if surprised. "Any idea why?"

"Not out of hand, but me head hurts."

"Else you would have the answer."

"Aye," she said, but her voice sounded uncertain even to herself.

"Then let us assume that was not me plan. Do any other possibilities present themselves?"

She winced, perhaps more from his sardonic tone

than the pain, although her ankles hurt where they had been twisted in someone's hard grasp. "Theft?"

"I believe you yourself said I was wealthy, Isobel. Were you carrying something that might be worth me time?" He tilted his head and even now at this darkest of times, she saw his lips tilt ever so slightly into that notorious grin. 'Twas perhaps that expression more than anything else that made him irresistible to women. But she was not so easily manipulated.

"Mayhap your plans were even more hideous then," she said.

He stared at her, and to her satisfaction, she saw that his grin was gone, replaced by an expression of interest and more. "Rape," he said finally. She didn't respond, and he stepped closer so that his nearness filled her in a flood of feelings. He was not a huge man, but beneath his well-groomed elegance there was something in his carriage that suggested he was made of sterner stuff than she had formerly believed. Every line of him seemed taut just now. Aye, it might well be that he would be a demon in a battle if he chose to fight. But how much more dangerous would he be in bed!

Every movement he made, every word he uttered, seemed to elicit feelings best left unawakened.

"And tell me, wee Bel," he said, approaching her with the smooth strides of a wild cat. "Do I seem like the sort to have to force meself on a woman?"

Taking the last few steps between them, he sat upon the bed beside her. Their arms brushed as light as a whispered promise. Anticipation shivered up her spine, shaking both her confidence and her hands, but she dare not acknowledge such weakness.

Still, she could find no answer. Indeed, she couldn't find her voice atall, and in a moment he raised his fingers to the spot where a fist had struck her cheek. His touch was feather light against her skin, and without thinking, she let her eyes fall closed. He skimmed his fingers over the bruise, but there was no pain in the soothing touch.

"What happened here?" he asked and let his thumb play along the edge of her jaw. She was held strangely immobile, and his fingers slipped lower, following the course of his thumb before spreading across the width of her throat. For a moment she remembered the fear of being unable to breathe, of being held powerless in another's grasp, but soon his hand moved. As if he could read her thoughts, he slipped his fingers beneath her hair, caressing gently. "Did you fall?" he asked and massaged softly, waiting for her answer as he eased his magical hand onto her shoulder. The tension there gave way like dry sand beneath his touch. Still, she tried to marshal her senses, to hold firm to her memories. Despite everything, it still might have been MacGowan who had attacked her.

"I tried to escape," she said, and found that her voice was wonderfully cool.

"They struck you?" he asked, and she opened her eyes in an effort to ascertain his emotions, for his tone was as dark as the night, filled with a depth and intensity that she was certain he did not possess.

"And you believe I was involved?" he asked.

Their gazes held. "Why are you here?" she whispered.

"Not to hurt you," he murmured, and touched her cheek again, but with his other hand now, so that it seemed she was surrounded by him. "The sight of you wounded . . ." His words stopped as though he couldn't go on. Was he angry on her behalf? Was he merely acting? A dozen possibilities sped through her mind, but in a moment each one was swept away, for he kissed her not on the mouth, but on her cheek where she had been struck, and then lower, at the corner of her lips. She swallowed hard, knowing she should move away, yet not moving at all, only closing her eyes again to the piquant feelings.

"You did not recognize your assailants?" The words whispered against her cheek.

"Nay."

He kissed her top lip. "How many were there?"

She realized somewhat belatedly that she was breathing through her parted lips, and heavily, as if she'd been running for some time. Still, she tried to remain lucid, to catch her wind. "Two. There were two."

He kissed the left corner of her mouth and then her jaw, but in a moment he moved lower, forcing her to drop her head back against the pillow. "Did they speak?"

He kissed her neck, down the length of it, and then in the tiny dell at the base of her throat. "Isobel," he murmured.

"What?" Things seemed strangely foggy.

"Did you recognize a voice?" he asked, but in that instant she felt the warm lap of his tongue in the hollow of her throat and shivered at the contact. Sensations flowed through her like well-mulled wine. Somewhere in the back of her mind she remembered that she could not trust him, yet her body did not seem to care in the least.

"Bel," he said, massaging her shoulder and lifting his head slightly to look into her eyes.

She opened her own. "Nay," she said. "Nay. I did not know the voices."

"And yet you assumed it was me." His left hand was stroking her hair back from her face, absently skimming her ear as he did so, while his lips, as tempting as fine wine, were the merest breath from her face. "Why do you distrust me so?" he whispered, and leaning slowly down, kissed the pulse in her throat.

Her heart raced, bumping against the warmth of his lips, and begging her, nay, commanding her to wrap her arms about him and draw him close. She resisted with all her might.

"Bel," he said, and she realized distractedly that he was watching her again. "What have I done to make you distrust me?"

"This." The word escaped of its own accord, stopping his fingers against her skin.

"What?"

She exhaled softly, knowing she shouldn't have spoken. "Life is too easy for you, MacGowan."

"Is it?" he asked, and for a moment the corner of his mouth lifted in that devilish hint of a smile. She watched the expression and found that try as she might, she couldn't breathe, not until he leaned down to kiss the corner of her mouth again. And then she exhaled in a small sigh of sound. "And why is that, wee Isobel?"

"Because you are spoiled."

He kissed her nose.

"And wealthy."

He kissed the corner of her eye.

"And privileged."

"Am I?"

Without looking she could sense his smile, and then he skimmed his tongue soft as a butterfly's passing along the curl of her ear. She trembled and wished she hadn't.

"Aye."

"Because I get what I want?" He whispered the words against her lobe, sending the shiver deep into her soul.

"Aye." She could bearly force out the word.

"But I want you, Isobel," he said, finding her eyes with his own. "Right now. This very minute."

He was leaning over her, ungodly close, pinning her to the bed, yet she had no desire to escape.

His thumb caressed her lips. His kiss followed, slow and hot, steaming her thoughts to nothingness.

"But I would not take you against your will. On that you can depend. Indeed, I would mend the wounds caused by others if I could." He kissed her again, just as slowly, just as hot until she ached with an odd longing that she could neither explain nor defend. "I would take the wounds and let you fall unencumbered into sleep. Where do you hurt, Bel?"

She panted for air, trying to think, but it was no use.

"Here?" he asked, and kissed her bruised lips with careful, aching tenderness. "Here?" he asked, and rising slightly, kissed the bruise on her skull. She had no idea how he knew of its existence, and yet he did, and with that light contact the ache diminished a hundredfold.

"Where did they touch you?" he whispered.

She opened her mouth to answer, though in truth she

had no idea what she planned to say, but he kissed her to silence.

"Do not speak. I will find it," he said, and skimmed his fingers over her lips and down her throat. His kisses followed the same hot course. "Did they touch your shoulders?" he asked. Vaguely, like one in a dream, she felt her gown ease downward, felt his lips on her skin. "Your arms?" Were they bare? She wasn't really sure, yet she could feel his kisses, hot and heavenly against her skin. "Your elbow?" He held her arm in his hands and pressed a kiss to the inside bend. A moan whispered through the room. Surely it was not hers. "Your wrist?" he asked, and traced an aching course down her arm to her hand. It quivered in his grasp. But he was without mercy. Lifting it to his lips, he licked the hollow of her palm. She jerked, but he held her firm, kissing every finger in turn until he reached the pinkie. That tiny digit he pulled into his mouth and suckled. She opened her eyes to watch him in breathless silence, feeling her mouth go dry as if every ounce of bodily fluid was needed elsewhere.

But he was already moving on, lifting her opposite hand, kissing its heel, its knuckles, its thumb, before traveling languidly up her arm to her shoulder. His fingers skimmed a course along her collarbone.

"Did they hurt you here?" he asked, and kissed the high regions of her chest above her gown. Only, it seemed suddenly and rather dimly, that her gown was no longer there. "Or here?"

She jumped at the heat of his lips against her breast and realized with breathy confusion that she was clothed in naught but her chemise. It lay molded against her skin, outlining every curve.

"Or here?" he murmured and pressed his lips to her nipple.

She cried out, and found suddenly that her fingers were caught in his hair. He paused for a moment and then he lapped her with his tongue.

She bucked against him, and it was then and only then that he eased fully onto the mattress. Her knees parted like the petals of a rose and suddenly he was cradled between them. Against her thigh, she could feel the hard length of his desire. It pulsed a hot, slow beat.

"Did they touch you there, lass?" he rasped.

"Nay." Her voice was hoarse and she trembled as she spoke.

" 'Tis good," he murmured, and slowly, ever so slowly, worked his way down to her belly.

Her fingers fell weakly away from his hair, only to wrap once again in the blankets.

Through the sheer cloth of her undergown, he kissed her navel, her hip, her thigh, and then, easing his hands down one leg, he took her foot in his palm while her chemise flowed wantonly upward.

"What of your foot? Did they hurt that?" he asked and kissed the sole.

She all but screamed at the feelings that slammed through her and jerked her leg with all her might, tearing it from his grasp.

"Isobel?" His voice was a mere feather of sound in the candlelight. "Did I hurt you?"

She licked her lips, fighting for sanity, but it was obviously long gone since she seemed to be losing her senses over nothing more than the feel of his caress against her sole.

"Nay."

"Then give it back," he said and gently took her foot again into his hands to ease his fingers around her instep and kiss her toes. She trembled, but he did not stop. Instead, he worked his way upward, and when she winced, he paused.

"Your ankles?" he said softly, and she nodded, barely able to manage that much. Smoothing his hands over them, he kissed one side, then the other. Her shin was next, and then, when she thought she could bear no more, he trailed his tongue, light as sunshine, over the inside of her knee and up her thigh.

"MacGowan!" His name came to her lips in a low hiss of sound as she gripped his tunic in fretful fingers.

"Aye, lass, it is I," he said, but not for an instant did his fingers cease their delicious dance upon her flesh. "Never fear."

But she did fear. She feared that she would be consumed. Would burn up beneath his hands and never care that she was gone. She feared that she would be just one in a hundred to him, while to her he would . . .

Her thoughts stopped as he reached higher to cup her buttocks. Squeezing gently, he bore her upward. His mouth touched the sensitive inside of her thigh and she ceased to breathe, dared not move. But he had no such inhibitions. Indeed, the fire moved with his mouth, skimming along until he reached her apex.

She jumped and froze. He kissed her again. His mouth was hot and firm against her, sucking, soothing, toying.

Her breathing came in short gasps now and though she did not mean to, her body had begun a rhythm of its own, rocking against his mouth. Beneath her, his hands flexed and relaxed, bearing her up on every stroke, prodding her gently and irrevocably into the deep waves of pleasure.

Her breathing was harsh and some inner voice warned her to cease such foolishness, but the warning was drowned in the roar of feelings that welled around her. She was rising, bumping higher and higher, lifted by his hands, enlightened by his touch, until her body exploded in a rush of hot feelings.

She shivered as he kissed her again, and then, as he smoothed her chemise over her knees, he stretched out beside her. Her right hand, still curled tight in his tunic, traveled with him. Against her hip, his hard proof of desire pulsed with life, but he did nothing to relieve the pressure. Instead, he gently grasped one of her wrists. Her fingers fell away from his crushed tunic and he kissed the palm before placing it across her body.

"Isobel." Her name was the softest caress. She opened her eyes, finding his with breathless speed. "Did I hurt you?"

She managed no more than a weak shake of her head.

"Nor will I," he said and kissed her lips. There was passion there, hot as a skillet, trembling on the edge of control, yet held in check by a firm discipline she had failed to recognize. And in a moment he stood, pulling himself from her side. "Bar the door." His voice was low with feeling, but when she managed to lift her gaze to his face, she saw the shadow of a grin lift his lips. "When you find the strength."

Chapter 9

Isobel awoke blearily. She felt strangely limp, but when she rolled over, a hundred vivid memories crashed home in her brain.

She sat up with a start and noticed with surprise that her chemise was twisted about her waist like a traitor's noose. Heat rushed up her neck to her cheeks, and she closed her eyes, hoping against hope that what she remembered was not a memory at all, but only a wild outcropping of her imagination.

But the images were as real as life. She launched from bed in a frenzied attempt to escape them, to rush back to life as she knew it.

Hurrying to her basin, she washed with strained chamomile water and tried to ignore the heated memories that reared their swollen heads. But most of all, she tried to fend off the sweep of soft feelings that threatened to drown her. She had no place for such feelings. She could afford softness for no one, and certainty not for MacGowan. Like a swan and a brown sparrow they were, and while the sparrow wove a nest for her young, the swan paddled at leisure in the laird's placid lochan. But the sparrow would bear no young, she reminded herself. That much she knew, for in her lowly state there was no room for naïveté. Nay, naïve maids had a tendency to lie alone in painful childbirth. Naïve she was not.

And yet she couldn't forget the feel of his mouth against her, couldn't shut out the hot downward rush of blood, threatening to drown her in ecs—

Nay! Not ecstasy. Confusion, she corrected, and snatching a gown from a peg on the wall, dragged it over her head. In a moment she was dressed and cinched. Pulling a snood from a trunk, she tried to capture her hair, but her hands shook and she finally shoved her wayward locks from her face and rushed from the cottage, feet bare and breath coming hard.

"What a bold lass you are."

Isobel jumped, spinning toward the voice.

Gilmour MacGowan rose, languidly brushing dirt from his plaid.

"What are you doing here?" She meant to sound accusatory, but somehow she only managed breathy, as if she'd run too far, or perhaps waited too long to see him. God help her.

"You neglected to bar the door," he explained and nodded toward the portal. "I thought I'd best stay and make certain no one took advantage of that failing." He gave her a wisp of a grin and glanced at the ground beneath them. "Your feet are bare."

"I was . . ." He stood very close. She swallowed and tried to disavow the rush of feelings that threatened to drown her. "In a hurry."

"A bit of a risk, don't you think?"

She blinked, trying to find her bearing.

"In light of our discovery." Lifting a hand, he brushed a sprig of crimped hair from her face.

She considered bolting, but like an adder held entranced, she remained where she was, feeling his fingers skim like liquid magic across her cheek. "Discovery?" she whispered.

"Your feet," he said and leaned closer as if unwilling to let others hear. "One kiss to your sole and you are driven past the brink of control."

She stepped back so hastily she stumbled. Quick as a cat, he grabbed her arm and pulled her with lithe grace to his chest. "Are you well, lassie?"

"Aye. Aye." She was having trouble breathing, staying on her feet, thinking. "But I must be off."

"To the inn?"

She managed a nod and wondered dimly what had happened to her tongue.

"I will accompany you," he said and took her elbow.

Feelings snapped from his fingertips and shot along her arm like sparks from the smithy's hammer. "You mustn't," she said, staring at his hand, but seeming entirely unable to move away.

"Why not?"

"If they see us together this early they will surely believe that we . . ." She ran out of words.

"What will they believe?" he asked and grinned like a satyr as he reached up to run his thumb along the lower ridge of her lips. She trembled. "Bel?"

Jerking out of her idiot's trance, she snatched her elbow from his hand. "Methinks you know what they will believe, MacGowan."

"That I am the luckiest man in Henshaw?"

"Is that your plan? To let them think that we. . . ." Again, she lost her words, though she did her best to find them.

"What did we do exactly, Bel?" he murmured, and for one wild second she was tempted almost beyond control to kiss him. She leaned closer, drawn against her will, but just before their lips met, her good sense awoke with a start.

Spinning on her heel, she rushed away, not stopping until she flew through the Red Lion's door and almost collided with Martha.

"Hold up," said the big woman, nearly spinning off her feet as Isobel rushed by. "What's the hurry, lassie?"

"Nothing." She glanced wildly through the open door behind her, licked her lips, and tried again. " 'Tis naught." She calmed her breathing with an effort. "I simply have much to do."

"You look . . ." Martha eyed her narrowly. "Changed somehow. Is something amiss?"

"Nay—"

"The MacGowan lad, the one they call the rogue," she said, frowning. "Does he still rent a room here?"

"Aye." Isobel felt decidedly faint and a little sick to her stomach. "Aye." She slowed her speech to sound off-hand and airy. "As far as I know, he does."

"Ahh."

"What do you mean, ahh? Whyever do you ask?"

"No reason," said Martha and laughed a little. "But you're a lucky lass, aren't you now Issa."

Isobel meant to retort or deny or expound or whatever was necessary, but Martha was already gone, giving orders to Birtle as she went.

And so Isobel's morning began. It was a busy day. A cloth merchant on his way to Glasgow stopped to dine, and a young marquess, complete with extensive entourage, declared his need for a meal and a bed.

It was already nearing dusk when Isobel made her usual visit into the dining hall to make sure all was well.

MacGowan sat near the far wall. She kept her eyes carefully averted as she spoke to a few regulars, then moved on.

"And how was your meal this night, me lairds?" she asked.

The marquess looked up. He was plump and youthful, with an appealing smile and a nice voice. "And who might you be, lassie?"

She gave him a bit of a smile. "I am Isobel, the cook here at the Red Lion."

"Ahh." He glanced leisurely up and down, seeming to take in everything from her loose hair to her bare feet. "I thought the meal unsurpassed in its sumptuousness," he said. "But I see that I was wrong."

Three men beside him chuckled as if on cue. He gave them a grin before glancing back up at her and lifting his mug in a sort of salute. She realized a bit belatedly that he had imbibed a good deal of Stout Martha's heather ale.

"And will you have a draught with us, wee Isobel?" he asked.

"Me apologies," she said, "but I have duties to attend to before night falls."

"Dare I hope that those duties include keeping a young lord happy?" he asked.

She smiled, for she had seen her share of drunken

nobility. They were generally slow, both of foot and of wit, while thinking themselves the most clever of men.

"Again, me apologies. But I must go," she said and turned to leave, but in that instant, he grabbed her wrist, restraining her.

"I am not asking so much," he said and rose beside her, pulling her arm between them. "Just a bit of your time, and mayhap a bit of pleasure for you, too. Aye?"

"Lass."

She turned with a start and found that MacGowan stood directly beside her.

"I do hate to disrupt you, but you are wanted in the kitchen."

"Oh." She tried to pull her arm from the marquess' grip, but he held tight. "Me apologies, me laird, but I must go."

The marquess turned his heavy lidded eyes to Gilmour. "Tell them she will be along shortly," he said and smiled as he pulled her closer. "Me room is just yonder. This will take only a few minutes."

"I am certain it would," Gilmour said and returned the smile, "but I fear she is needed immediately."

"Mayhap," said the marquess and dropped Bel's arm as his three companions rose noisily to their feet beside him. "But I need her more."

Gilmour frowned. "I could tell her cousin that, but the Munro is not always as patient as some might think."

"The Munro?" asked the chubby laird. Gilmour smiled. Apparently the Munro's name was powerful enough to clear the haze even from this fool's lumbering mind, for he straightened slightly.

"She is the cousin of the Munro of the Munros?"

"Aye. Innes by name. Might you know him?"

"Aye, I have . . ." The marquess swallowed and glanced toward his companions. "I have heard of him."

"How fortunate," said Gilmour. "And mayhap he has heard of you. What be your name?"

The marquess shrugged. "Truly, 'tis of little consequence and the hour is late. Indeed, I think I will find my bed." Turning slightly, he made an awkward bow to Isobel and left with his minions following behind like whipped curs.

Gilmour watched them depart, then took a quaff of his own brew. " 'Tis a fine batch. Give me compliments to Martha," he said and placing the mug on a nearby table, left the inn.

It didn't take Isobel long to finish her duties in the kitchens. Soon she was tripping down the stone steps beneath the inn's back door. It took her a moment to realize she was holding her breath as she walked along.

The slightest scrape of a noise sounded beside her and her heart bumped. "MacGowan?"

He stepped out of the shadows. "Aye, lass?"

Relief washed through her like elderberry wine, but in a moment she chided herself for the feeling. He was not, after all, her savior. Indeed, it was very possible that he was the exact opposite.

"You do not have to follow me home," she said.

"Nay. But I wish to," he said and fell in beside her.

"Why?"

He shrugged. "You seem to have a penchant for finding trouble."

"I do not."

"So you like to be propositioned by plump lairds with girlie hands?"

"I could have—"

"You deserve more than girlie hands." He grinned as he leaned so close to her that she could see the dazzling curve of each dimple. An errant wisp of breeze sent his wren feather in a light caress against her cheek with the gentleness of his fingertips.

She felt the air leave her lungs as memories assailed her, but she struggled to keep her head. "And what is it you think I deserve, MacGowan?" she breathed.

He watched her for a moment, then, "Pleasure," he said.

Hot sensations tingled low in her gut. "I'm afraid I have no need for your kind of pleasure."

"Truly?"

Dear God, he had the devil's own smile. It steamed at her through the darkness.

"That did not seem to be the way of it last night."

Memories smote her again, but she struck back, driving them from her mind. "Regardless of how it seemed, I have no need of your . . ." What didn't she need? "Company."

"And what of me hands?" he asked, the devilish grin still in place.

"Nay." She choked out the word. "Not them, either." She was nearly to her cottage, nearly safe from his ungodly allure. She reached the rocky pathway and turned like a cornered hare near her door, but he blocked her escape with one arm across the entrance.

"And what of me mouth, wee Isobel?" He leaned in. There was a scent to him, something smoky and raw. She could only assume it was how a satyr would smell. His fingers touched her cheek and suddenly her neck felt strangely unable to support her head. His lips caressed the corner of her mouth. "Can you live without that?"

"Aye." Her voice shook, actually shook, like a damned leaf in a gale.

His tongue touched the crease of her lips with the softness of a dream. "But do you want to?" he murmured.

"MacGowan, I—" she began, but in that moment he kissed her, full force with all the power of a dream and all the mind numbing appeal of a god. Her knees went weak, so that he braced an arm across her back, keeping her upright. Desire roared in her ears. Her head spun and her nether parts insisted that she act now before it was too late and she deny them the heaven they surely deserved.

But suddenly the kiss ceased, and she opened her eyes to find his, so close she could feel the steam rising from his soul.

"Well, love?" he whispered. "What were you saying?"

She had no idea. Not a clue, but in that instant his fingers touched hers. Energy sparked through her, jolting her upright with the horrid knowledge that the simple touch of his hand could scatter her wits.

She would not have it. Could not afford it. Bracing her legs against the storm, she licked her lips and gathered her wits like tiny bits of wool on the wind.

"I am sure you are much coveted as a lover, Mac-Gowan." Her knees trembled. She locked them hard and continued. "But I have . . . other plans." What those plans were she could not imagine, but they did not include this man. Of that she was certain.

"Oh?" His tone was perfectly level, as if the kiss had never happened, as if it mattered not at all.

"Aye," she said. "And I feel it would be best if you left Henshaw and did not return."

He was silent for a moment as his fingers played across her wrist, like a master upon a lute. Her very tendons strummed beneath his touch. "You would not miss me?"

"Nay." Too high, too squeaky, too great a lie! She cleared her throat to try something a tad more believable.

"Tell me, Isobel," he said and skimmed his fingers over the crease of her elbow. "Is there another you have set your sights on?"

Her knees wobbled. "Another what?"

He chuckled and she tightened every muscle and pushed away from him.

"Aye!" she said, taking charge of her wits with a vengeance. "There is."

He was silent for a moment. "Is it the good baron?"

She almost asked what baron he referred to, but clarity rang in her head for a moment and she nodded. "Aye. 'Tis Laird Grier."

Nothing seemed to move in the entire universe. She held her breath.

"Does he pleasure you?"

"What?"

"In bed."

She could barely hear him, but she dared not lean closer, lest the maelstrom of his charisma drag her under.

"Have you taken him to your bed?"

Her head swam. She had to be rid of him before it was too late. Be rid. Be gone. Be safe. "Aye. I have."

"And did you find pleasure there?"

"Of . . . of course."

"And yet last night you responded to me touch like a virgin."

"Well, I am not one of those virtuous few whom you delight in—"

"I think you are," he said and slipped his arm about her waist. His eyes were like midnight stars, boring into hers. "In your soul. For you had not felt such feelings before." His lips drew nearer. Her heart stopped. His mouth touched the hollow at the base of her throat and then all hell broke loose. He kissed her neck, her jaw, her mouth, swiping his tongue with liquid slowness across hers.

"MacGowan!" She pushed with all her might against his chest. It was as hard as an oaken table, and he moved not a smidgen. "I must not."

"Because of the baron?"

"Aye." Lord save her! She was breathing like a running mule. "Laird . . ." What the hell was his name? "Grier . . . is very jealous."

"But he does not make you tremble," he said, and skimmed his fingers beneath the weight of her hair.

Her body jerked in concert, and he grinned.

She pushed again at his chest. "I do not want you, MacGowan! Not this night. Not ever."

The world went silent. He watched her.

"You are certain, Isobel?"

"Aye," she said and her body screamed in silent protest. "I do not want you."

"If I leave now, I leave for good, Bel."

"Go."

"I fear you will regret the results."

"Nay," she panted. "I will not."

"Very well then," he said and kissed her hard. Passion seared her, melting her will and whetting her appetite, but he stepped back.

Her knees threatened to spill her face first unto the earth, but she locked them tight and watched him turn away. Something inside her screamed his name, but she remained silent. 'Twas best he leave, of course. 'Twas good.

She turned toward her door, but in an instant she heard a sound behind her. Her heart stopped, awaiting him, and against her better judgment, she turned with a breathless smile.

For the briefest second she saw a shadow, a movement, a lift of something, and then, without warning, pain exploded in her head and darkness descended.

Chapter 10

⌒⌒○○⌒⌒

Isobel woke slowly. Her head ached. She tried to lift her hand to her brow, but found that her wrists were immobilized behind her. She lay on her side in the darkness. Her hands were bound and she was alone. But nay, wait. She heard a rumble of male voices, and in the same instant she realized that a fire burned near the men, not ten rods away. Who were they? Why had they taken her?

Panic struck her as scattered shards of memories rushed in. She'd been near her cottage when she'd heard a movement. There was little to remember since then—only muffled images of dark upon dark as she'd awakened and slept and wakened. She had no way of knowing how long she had been unconscious, no way of knowing anything, so she concentrated on her last lucid moments.

MacGowan had been beside her, walking her home. Keeping her safe. Surely he couldn't be involved with this. He may be spoiled and vain, but he had been kind to Claude, and—

It was then that she heard another voice.

"Damnable weather."

It was almost familiar. Changed somehow, but almost . . .

MacGowan! She jerked toward the sound, craning her neck to see, and he was there. From her position on the ground, she could just see a portion of his face, but it was he, seated before the fire. Seated with her captors, and suddenly she knew the truth.

Every word he had spoken had been a lie. She didn't know why, but one thing was certain: she had to escape before it was too late. If not for herself, for Anora—for even in her groggy state, she was certain that this plot did not revolve around a simple peasant girl like her. Nay, somehow the snare was set for the lady of Evermyst.

Rage coursed through her and she trembled. She should never have allowed him to touch her, to—

But she would not dwell on that. Instead, she would focus all her energy on foiling his plans. So she listened, not moving, barely breathing. Still, she could hear no one nearby. Footfalls moved away from her, easily heard against her lower ear. It was dark, and she lay stretched on her side. Her ankles were tied, as were her wrists, but as far as she could tell, no one guarded her.

Ever so carefully, she moved her head, tilting it upward. A shadow moved away toward the fire, and for a moment she wondered if that shadow had carried her there. Her hip and one shoulder hurt, as if she'd been suddenly dropped beyond the light of the fire. Was that what had awakened her?

If she craned her neck carefully and slowly, she could see the men by the fire without being noticed. MacGowan sat facing the blaze. Anger brewed like venom in her soul. He would pay, but not just now. Not yet. For now she would keep her head, gain her feet, and find a way to escape.

But how? She winced at the pain in her shoulder, then realized it was not soft turf that she lay on, but something hard and ungiving. Shifting her arm a fraction of an inch, she felt it scrape against a rock.

Perhaps if she eased her wrists over that stone she could sever her bonds. Perhaps . . . if they didn't check on her. She glanced carefully toward the fire again. MacGowan faced her, pouring himself a draught from a bottle. Isobel held her breath, terror rattling her lungs, but if he saw her move, he gave no indication. Indeed, he acted as if he did not see her at all, and perhaps he couldn't against the glare of the fire, for he turned casually away, still speaking to his companions.

"You've had no trouble, then . . . ?"

His words flowed away. There were murmurs from the men who surrounded him, but she didn't hear the words, for every bit of her attention was focused on the bastard she would make pay.

Drawing a steadying breath, she eased herself slowly across the ground, squirming silently along until she felt the rock against her wrists. She began sawing methodically at her bonds.

A voice swelled up and she froze, but all seemed well, and in a moment she continued on. Time ground away. Her arms cramped and she paused. It was that pause that saved her, for when she stopped, she heard footsteps.

Bel froze, not daring to turn toward the noise. Shutting her eyes, she prayed the man would pass her by.

But he didn't. Instead, he stopped near her. He nudged her with his foot, and she sensed that he squatted beside her. It was then that she realized she had ceased to breathe. He leaned down. Panic splashed over her. He pressed his face against her breast, and it took all her will to remain still, to refrain from screaming, but soon he straightened.

"Lazy slut," he said and rose, prodding her again with his boot.

She lay immobilized with fear, but the truth finally came to her: he'd been listening for a heartbeat and believed her still to be unconscious. She was safe for a while, but there was no way of knowing when they would check again. Indeed, she could not even guess what time of night it was or when they would be on the move again.

Fear held her paralyzed, but the murmur of Mac-Gowan's voice broke her free. His listeners laughed and she jerked, rasping her wrists against the sharp edge of the rock beneath her. She winced at the pain but refused to stop her sawing.

When the rope first gave way, she didn't immediately realize it, but when she tugged, her hands moved the slightest amount. Hope flooded through her. It didn't take long to sever the remaining threads. She waited, listening, before she drew her arms forward, and then, when she was certain no one watched, she pulled her knees to her chest and worked at the knots that tied her ankles. Her fingers tingled with pain and she couldn't quite manage to grasp the rope. So she waited again, listening hard and fighting the sharp edge of terror. In her immobility she could feel her heart pound against her arm and prayed in silent desperation for strength. It returned finally, and when next she set her fingers to her bonds, the knot came free.

Slowly straightening her legs, she paused to listen before carefully rolling onto her chest. No untoward sound penetrated the quiet, only the murmur of voices from the campfire. She rolled slowly onto her opposite side, until she could see the men clearly.

There were seven of them by the fire. Was that the total count, or were there others lurking in the shadows?

Laughter echoed through the woods again and Mac-Gowan raised a hand as if setting aside their appreciation.

Isobel's hair rose on the back of her neck. The bastard! "*I will not hurt you, Bel.*" Anger surged through her, stiffening her muscles, strengthening her resolve.

He was a liar and a traitor, for here he sat with her captors—so secure, so certain of himself that he felt no need to hurry them on their way. After all, no one would suspect the charming rogue of any crime, and she was of such unimportance that none would come to save her.

But he had made a dire mistake, for she would save herself. Drawing her feet up under her, she rose to a crouch. Her heart boomed in her chest, squeezing it tight, but she crept forward. A voice rose from the fire. She jerked toward the noise. Her toe caught in the hem of her skirt, and she tripped, pitching wildly forward. Terror ripped through her, but she found her balance, and in the same instant, she turned toward the flame again. Seven pairs of eyes were watching her.

Isobel froze like a cornered hare, and then someone

spoke, his voice barely rising above the boom of her heart.

"Get her!"

She didn't consciously move, yet she found herself running, racing through the woods, her fist wrapped in her skirt. Branches whipped past her face, snagging her clothes, frightening gasps from her throat, raw now from fear and exertion.

Where were they? How far behind? She turned, straining her eyes through the darkness. Nothing. She could see no one. Perhaps—

"There you be."

She bolted sideways, but it was already too late. A fist tangled in her hair, yanking her backward, and she shrieked in raw terror.

"Shut yer mouth, girlie or I'll give you something to scream about, aye?" The tip of a knife pressed against her throat. She whimpered in fear and rolled her eyes toward the blade, but it was too close to see. Instead, she felt the heat of her captor pressed against her back. She remained as still as death, her breath coming in hard gasps, which pulled his gaze toward her heaving chest.

Meaty fingers shifted in her hair, and then he eased his arm around her, crushing against her breasts. "Mayhap we can take us a few minutes, aye? I got me an urge." His arm loosened and the knife left her throat, disappearing somewhere below before his other hand shoved at her back.

"What are you about, Roy?"

Isobel was yanked to a halt even as she whipped her gaze to the newcomer.

"I got me a little business," Roy said.

" 'Is Lordship don't want 'er touched, y'knows." The lad twitched like a weasel. " 'E don't want 'er touched."

"Well now, that seems mighty selfish, don't it? Flirting her up, then keeping her for himself whilst we take all the risks?"

Keeping her for himself! The words rang through her head.

"Seems to me he's got enough already without this little scheme."

Isobel's mind raced. What were they planning? Something against Anora. Isobel had not thought she could be a threat to her sister's security, for so few knew of her kinship with the lady of Evermyst. But MacGowan knew, and now he planned some evil. What was it? Somehow to use her to overthrow Evermyst? To hold her for ransom until Anora paid?

"If'n you don't take 'er in, you're going ta 'ave to share," said the second man, shifting from foot to foot.

Roy cursed, then urged her back in the direction from whence she had come. She went willingly, for although she had been caught, she had not completely failed. Not yet, for one thing was clear: these men were only pawns.

She had but to be rid of MacGowan and the plot would crumble.

She stumbled. Her captor prodded her back onto her feet and she continued forward, her mind reeling. The man called Roy wore a knife. Where? She shifted her gaze sideways without turning her head. It was there. She could see the handle gleam dully in the firelight.

Firelight! They had almost reached their destination! Where was he? Where—

MacGowan stepped out of the woods only a short distance to her right. "What's this, then?" he asked, and smiled. Rage boiled in her soul. Already he was close, and coming closer still.

The man by the campfire swore, and Roy pushed her forward. She stumbled, but there was no time for failure, no room for defeat. She spun toward her captor, scrambling for his knife. It came away in her hand, and in the same instant she lunged.

MacGowan jerked sideways, but not fast enough. The tip of her blade skimmed along his chest, tearing open his tunic, and then, like a pack of wolves, the others dragged her down.

She went with a snarl. "Damn you!"

MacGowan stood, mouth opened, staring down at her.

"What the hell's this?" A man raced into the campsite, then slowed, his eyes darting.

"I snagged her," said Roy, "brought her back to camp. Then she sees him there and she goes mad."

"Why?" The one near the woods flicked his eyes to MacGowan.

Gilmour raised his hands as if innocent. "I meant her no harm. I've not even—"

"No harm?" She snarled the words. "Harm me sister and you harm me! You're a bastard, MacGowan! A bastard and a—"

"MacGowan?" The speaker was dark and lean as a scavenging wolf. "You said you were a Barclay."

"Aye," said Mour. "The lass is deluded, she is. Might that be why you keep her bound?"

"Deluded?" Facts melded with fiction in Isobel's battered mind. "Have you lied to them too, Mac-

Gowan?" So she had not been the only one he'd duped. Nay, he had fooled the lot of them with his oily ways, but she would tell them the truth. She turned her gaze to the lean wolf. "He plans evil against his own brother as well as against the lady of Evermyst." She rushed her gaze to the faces that surrounded her, but recognized none. Could it be that he had also lied to the gigantic laird he drank with at the Lion? "And what of the Munros? Did he tell you that they have made an alliance with the Frasers?" Not a soul spoke. "Aye, 'tis true. If you fight me kinsmen, you will have a battle with the Munros as well."

"He is a MacGowan—"

"Aye!" She spat the word, for they were weakening. She could see it in their skittering eyes. "You may think him powerful, but what good will that do you against scores of Munros?"

"MacGowan—" the wolf began, but in that instant Gilmour whipped the Maiden from his belt.

"That's enough now, lads," he warned. "I want no trouble here."

"No trouble?" Roy stepped toward him, huge hands clenching.

Another man leapt from the woods, eyes wild. "What happened to Dell . . ." He slowed, his eyes taking in the scene. "What goes on here?"

"MacGowan has come to visit us."

"MacGowan! Then 'twas he who murdered Dell!"

"Dell is dead?"

"Aye, and—"

Gilmour lifted a passive palm toward the crowd. " 'Twould be best not to leap to—"

But in that moment Roy leapt. MacGowan swept his

knife in an arc and Roy stumbled back, blood spurting from his arm.

Another man lunged forward. MacGowan struck again, but out of the shadows a man stepped up behind, swinging a branch like a club.

It crashed against MacGowan's skull, and he fell, dropping like a rock beside Isobel.

Chapter 11

Gilmour groaned as he came to. His ribs ached, his chest burned, and his leg throbbed from the hip down, but it was his head that made him wish for death. He opened his eyes and found that the sky was only nominally lighter than when he had ventured into this hellish campsite.

And speaking of hell, where was Isobel?

"So you're awake, are you, MacGowan?" Perhaps it was said in a normal tone, but it felt like the blast from a furnace, all but rattling Mour's eyeballs with the vibrations of sound. "And a lucky thing." The man who rose beside the fire was as thin as a reed. "The lads were all for doing you in if you didn't come to before dawn."

Gilmour squinted at the glimmer of light that invaded his world, then shut his eyes.

"But I think one of the MacGowan rogues can do us naught but good. Aye?"

Gilmour tried to think. He had seen the man called Roy before, but he couldn't quite remember where it had been. "I'll say as I've said before, me name be Russell of the Barclays," he croaked, no longer having to change his voice, for his throat was too parched for him to speak normally. "I was but passing through on me way to—"

He heard someone approach only moments before something struck his gut with the force of a battering ram. Pulling his knees to his chest, he expelled the contents of his stomach onto the hard earth.

And that was the best part of his day.

By nightfall, Mour figured he was two minutes from death and rather wished the grim reaper were not such a lazy bastard and would see the job done good and proper. He'd flitted in and out of consciousness like a visiting honeybee, and although he would have been happy enough to remain asleep, the jostling of the horse he was tied to awakened him more than once. At some point he realized his mount was Francois, and at another he'd been lucid enough to recognize that Isobel rode beside him, looking grim and weary.

Damn. He slept again, but eventually the cobwebs cleared a little, leaving him cramped and morose.

"Are you awake?" Isobel's voice was only a murmur in the darkness. He was no longer astride. That much he was sure of, but he had no way of knowing how long he'd been unconscious. One day? A lifetime? "MacGowan?"

He opened an eye. She sat only a short distance away, and although her hands were probably bound behind her back, she sat upright. He felt immensely jealous, not to mention impressed. Gilmour stared at her with one eye and wondered if he had the strength to kick her in the shin.

"Tell me, lass," he said, and found that he cared not

a whit if their captors heard him. In truth, he didn't believe he could hurt more than he already did—though he rather disliked the idea of having to prove his theory. "Have I wronged you in some way that I know nothing about?"

There was a moment of silence, or perhaps he lost consciousness. Either way it didn't matter much, for eventually he heard her again. "You said I'd regret—"

"What's this, then?" The coarse voice from above sounded like a boom of thunder. Gilmour winced even before the boot met his ribs. "Shut your trap, Mac-Gowan, or I'll let the lass do what she will with you."

Gilmour remained mute, lying in silent agony and thinking. Who were these bastards? Why did they want Isobel? Could they possibly have mistaken her for Anora? Did he have the strength to crawl away and die in peace? And if he did, what would happen to Isobel? Not that he cared. After all, she *had* tried to kill him.

"And what of the MacGowan?"

Gilmour awoke with a start as a medley of voices argued near the fire behind him.

Damn it! Mour thought groggily. He'd regained consciousness.

"He travels with us."

"I don't like it, Finn. Not one bit, I don't."

Gilmour winced. He didn't mind women fighting over him, but when a bunch of barbarian ball beaters found occasion to bash heads over him, it was generally not a good thing.

Glancing up, he saw that Bel was seated beside him. Her eyes were wide, but it was impossible to guess what she was thinking.

"How long have they been arguing?" he asked.

She didn't answer and he couldn't tell if she was afraid to speak, or if, by some patent foolishness, she still believed he was to blame for this predicament.

"Bel," he said. " 'Tis not . . ."

Then he heard the footsteps. Two pairs, one quick and light, one heavy and slow. Gilmour closed his eyes, feigning unconsciousness.

"Is he awake, then?"

"Nay. But he has been moaning," Bel said.

"Do you admit that he is a MacGowan?" It was the lean, wolfish fellow that spoke, the one called Finn.

"As I told you, I was turned about in me mind. In the darkness I mistook him for someone else."

"Then . . ." The words ceased, accented by a metallic scraping. Gilmour had heard a knife unsheathed enough times to recognize the noise in the dark. "There be no reason not to kill him."

A hand grasped his hair, yanking his head back.

"Nay!" Isobel shrieked.

"Nay?" The hand loosened slightly. Gilmour forced himself to breathe. "Do you say that you know him?" asked the brigand.

"Aye. You are right. He is of the MacGowans."

"Which one?" Finn's voice was smooth, well modulated.

"He is called Gilmour."

There was a slight intake of breath from the twitchy fellow. "The rogue of the rogues?"

"I believe some call him that."

"What interest does he have in you?" asked Finn.

"I know not."

A crack of sound broke the night. Gilmour jerked,

coming up off his shoulder with a start and immediately seeing the red imprint on Isobel's cheek.

"So you are awake, aye, MacGowan?" Finn smiled. Lean as a starved wolf, his teeth gleamed crookedly in the moonlight. "I wondered. Get on your feet."

Gilmour rose unsteadily before turning back to memorize the features of Isobel's abuser. Tolerance, after all, could be stretched only so far.

"Untie his legs," Finn ordered.

Roy did so. Hemp scraped against Gilmour's ankles, and then blood rushed painfully back.

In a matter of minutes they were by the fire, and Mour took a seat on a log without being told.

"So you are the rogue of the rogues."

"I . . ." Mour began, but his voice crackled from disuse. He cleared his throat, hoping Isobel could hear his words, for it might be handy if their stories matched. "I could use a drink."

Finn nodded and one of the others grudgingly handed him a horn mug. The contents tasted dull and brackish but the liquid felt soothing against his throat. Setting the mug aside, he glanced back at Finn, who seemed to be the leader of this moth-eaten pack.

"I am the rogue."

"Then you lied earlier."

"Aye."

"Mayhap you recall that I do not like to be lied to."

Gilmour kept his tone carefully casual. "I have some recollection, aye."

Finn smiled. The hairs on the back of Mour's neck rose eerily. "Why did you present yourself as a Barclay, then?"

"Is it the truth you want?"

"Why not try that?" crooned Finn.

"I thought it wise to use another name for a time, after leaving Henshaw."

"Oh? And why is that?"

Gilmour remained mute for several beats. "Some fathers would seek revenge for naught more than a few minutes of harmless . . . entertainment."

"So you swived some maid you shouldn't have?" guessed the closest fellow, but another was already glancing into the darkness toward Isobel and rubbing his crotch.

" 'Twas that one. You laid her and left her, aye?"

Gilmour memorized the fellow's face. "I am not called the rogue for naught."

"Indeed," Finn said and filled his mug from a bottle near the fire. "And how does your own father feel about your . . . entertainments?"

Gilmour drank again. "I try not to burden him with too many facts."

"Will he pay for your safe return?"

Mour shrugged. A plan was forming in his mind. It might well work, or it might get him killed. "We have had our differences over the years."

"Truly?" The lean brigand had been carving roasted flesh from a mutton bone and glanced up like a wolf over a fresh kill. "Then why should I keep you alive?"

Gilmour smiled. "Because I am me mum's favorite."

"And she has the coin to pay?" asked the hulking man called Roy.

"I see you have not heard of the notorious Flame of the MacGowans." Mour glanced from the hulk to the wolf.

"Enlighten me," said Finn.

"May I?" Mour motioned to a hunk of dark bread that sat on a log nearby.

Finn tossed Gilmour the loaf and waited in silence.

"The Flame will do what she will. You've but to name the price and she will pay the cost for me safe return, unless . . ." Gilmour scowled and turned his gaze briefly toward Isobel again. "It may well be that if I present her with one more bastard even she will tire of me."

"The girl's breeding?" asked Roy.

Finn turned his knife, causing the firelight to play along its edge. "Surely the rogue knows there are cures for that."

Mour's stomach twisted. "Me kin will pay well for me safe return," he said, fighting to keep his tone even. "And we could travel the faster without the girl. She is naught but a cook at a moldering inn. Why not let her go?"

"It might be that she is worth a good deal more than you know."

Mour snorted. "To whom?" he asked, and waited breathlessly for a response.

"You've no need to worry on that."

Gilmour shrugged and ate as if unconcerned. "Let her go and I'll cause you no trouble."

"So you have feelings for her, do you?"

Wincing ever so slightly, Mour rolled his shoulder back, easing the wound she'd left on his chest, and glancing surreptitiously toward Bel. 'Twas a fine line he walked. He must make them believe his life was worth a great ransom, but he dare not let them believe he was over-fond of Isobel, lest they think to have some hold on him with her presence. "Aye. Who would not?" he asked and winced again. "She's a bonny lass."

Finn laughed. "You're not afraid of her, are you, MacGowan?"

He glanced up as if surprised by their wild assumptions. "Of course not, but me kin will be most unhappy if I turn up dead, and you do not want the clan Mac-Gowan against you."

"Nay," laughed the brigand leader. "I can tell they be a fierce lot. Baron, take the bonny lad here back to the maid and bind his feet."

The one called Baron was slim and small and fidgety. He had not yet seen a score of years, but when he pushed Gilmour down beside Isobel, he did so with rough bravado.

Bel jumped and Gilmour jerked away.

From behind, Roy laughed. "You be gentle with him now, lassie." Taking his knife from its sheath, he made a show of cleaning his nails with it. "We would not want you maiming the poor wee lad."

Gilmour ignored him. "I meant no harm, lass. 'Twas just a bit of pleasure I was after," he said, making certain his tone was ingratiating, and Roy chuckled.

Baron knelt, but as he wound the hemp about Gilmour's ankles, his hands seemed to dally strangely on Mour's legs.

"Enjoying yourself, lad?" Roy asked and Baron tied the knot and jerked away.

As for Gilmour, he was never so happy to be securely tied in his life, and turned on his side as if to sleep. He could feel Isobel's gaze on him, but there was no way to explain his strange words with their captors so near. Indeed, there was nothing to do but plan in silence and hope they believed his lies.

They rode throughout the following day, keeping to the woods and making little time. Wherever they were going, they were in no hurry to get there.

That night they sat near a fire again, surrounded by elderberry trees and darkness. Gilmour's head felt fairly normal, and though the food was abysmal, he had eaten his fill.

"So you do not mind a good fucking, huh, lass?" Roy asked and brushed his knuckles across Isobel's as he handed her a mug. Gilmour stiffened, but Bel didn't even blanch. Instead, she took the offered drink between her tied hands and sipped immediately.

"What lies has he been spewing about me?" she asked.

"Lies?" The big man grinned. He was bearded and broad, with a chest like a wine barrel and hands like meat hooks. "Surely the MacGowan here wouldn't lie."

Isobel coughed over her drink, and Gilmour raised his brows. If her angry expression was an act, it was a shame and a pity women weren't allowed on the stage.

"What did he tell you?" Her voice was cool now, and as she lifted her chin, Gilmour saw the flash of her eyes in the firelight.

Bear man grinned. Apparently dental hygiene wasn't his fetish. "Not much atall. Only that you wasn't bad in bed . . . for a scrawny bit of a whore."

For a moment Gilmour was certain she wouldn't believe such lies, but suddenly she flung her mug with fierce strength. He ducked. Still, it missed his head by less than an inch. Stunned, he straightened slowly. Did she realize his ploy? Did she know he hoped to make them believe that her presence was not worth the trouble? That his ransom alone would be enough for all?

"You bastard!" she screamed and lunged.

MacGowan tripped backward. If she knew, she was a damned fine actress.

Roy caught her about the waist like a bawling calf. "Hold on now, you wee wild cat," he said and chuckled. "So you still got some of that vinegar left, aye?" She wriggled in his arms, glaring at Gilmour, but her captor turned her easily and grated one hand down her waist. "Mayhap you should save some for old Roy here, huh?"

She stilled in his arms, her eyes seeming to dull the light of the fire behind her. "Cut me loose," she ordered, her voice low and hard.

"What's that?"

"Let me at him," she said, "and you'll not regret it."

Roy licked his lips and shifted his eyes sideways. "Finn wouldn't be none too happy."

She straightened, pulling regally out of his grip. "Does Finn cut up your food for you, too?"

"Don't get uppity, missy, or—"

"Hey!" Baron was suddenly behind him, shuffling about like a high strung hound. "If anybody's going to do her I get a share."

"Shut yer trap!" Roy said and swinging his arm back, knocked the boy away with casual brutality. He stumbled and went down, but Roy failed to notice as he leaned close to Isobel.

"Are you—"

"What's this then?" Finn said, and stepped with casual grace into the firelight.

"The merry baron was trying to prove himself on the lass here," Roy said.

"Is that so?" Finn's eyes were as quick as light, sprinting from the boy to Isobel and back again.

"Aye. It—" Roy began, but Finn interrupted.

"I was talking to the maid."

She nodded, her lips pursed. "Aye," she said. "And I'm not that sort. No matter what MacGowan says."

Finn smiled. "Unfortunately, we'll not be finding out what sort you are," he said and pulled his dark blade from its hiding place in his sleeve. "Do you understand me lads?"

"Aye!" Baron nodded jerkily.

Roy only shrugged as if uninterested, and the others remained mute. Finn nodded toward Isobel. "Sit down," he ordered. "Over there."

She did as told, moving past the fire and sitting on the turf. Pulling her knees up to her chest, she tugged her gown over her ankles with her bound hands.

"Tie her feet," Finn said, and as Baron did as so, Isobel glared over his shoulder at Gilmour.

Well, thought Mour nervously, she could damn sure play a role.

Chapter 12

❧ ❧ ❧

They again rode through the next day, but stopped early for the night.

Why? Had they reached their destination? Gilmour glanced about, trying to get his bearings. Light had faded into darkness and Finn had not yet returned from wherever he had gone. It was not a good sign. Time was running out. That much he knew, but he shifted his eyes back to the fire, took a drink from his mug and tried to look relaxed. Bound hand and foot as he was, it was not a simple task, but it was Isobel's situation that made his nerves tangle up in hard-tied knots.

Her feet had been cut free so that she could go into the woods, but never was she allowed to go alone. Roy had accompanied her. Roy! The muscles in Gilmour's back cranked tighter, but he loosened them slowly, one by one, with a hard won effort. She would be safe. Roy was a barbarian and a bastard true enough, but he feared Finn, and Finn had insisted that she be left untouched. She would be safe. But the seconds ticked ruthlessly away, wearing at Mour's composure. Yet he dared not show concern if he wished to implement his plan. Still, he could wait no longer.

161

"So . . ." He glanced up at his captors. Three remained in camp. "How long have you known this Finn?"

Three heads turned toward him, blank eyes evil, expressions immobile.

Hmm.

"I take it Roy has known him longer, aye?"

Baron pushed himself from the tree where he'd been resting his back. If there was one to rise to the bait, it was likely to be him. Unfortunately, he was also the least able to prevent Roy from causing any mischief.

"What are you yammering about, MacGowan?" asked Baron.

He took another casual swig, though his stomach curled with nerves. "I was merely observing that Roy must be well trusted to take the girl into the woods for so long a time."

"It ain't your concern," rumbled the one closest to the fire, but Baron was twitching all over like a weasel on a scent.

" 'Ow long they been gone?"

"Roy'll be back when he's ready," said the first man and the second chuckled.

"Wouldn't take *me* long."

"What do ya mean it wouldn't take you long. What—" Baron began, but in that instant Isobel stepped into camp.

Relief flooded through Gilmour at the sight of her, even as he strained to make certain all was well, but not for an instant did she flicker her attention to him. Still, her head was high, and she seemed to be unscathed. If she looked nervous, who could blame her?

All was well, but Roy still stood close behind her. Too close.

"What's been takin' ya?" Baron's voice was whiny.

"I had me a leak," Roy said.

"You been 'umpin' 'er?" Baron asked.

"And why might you care, *Baroness*?"

The lad's hands crunched to fists. "You sayin' I'm a lily?"

"Me?" Roy chuckled. "Nay. I wouldn't say that, lassie. But MacGowan there seems to be bored if you're looking for some fun."

"Damn you!" Baron swore. "Give me ten minutes with 'er and I'll prove meself."

"I would," Roy said, "but Finn might take it poorly if we lost us another man."

The boy spread his legs as if for battle. "You thinking I couldn't 'andle 'er?"

Roy grinned. Evil exuded from him like a foul stench. "What do you think, MacGowan? You been with her. Do you think the wee Baron here can tame her?"

Tension cranked bile into Gilmour's gut as his mind spun for ideas. Things were coming to a head. That much was clear. "If you value your health, lad, you'll keep yourself to yourself."

"I don't need no advice from the likes of you," Baron snarled and Gilmour shrugged, every muscle tensed.

"Nay. But unless you know a good physic, you'll keep your wick in its candle."

"What the devil do you mean by that?" asked Baron.

Even the dull two had perked up.

"You saying she's diseased?"

"To look at her, she may seem worth the trouble," Gilmour said, "but after a fortnight or so of itching, you may think otherwise."

"You bastard!" Isobel growled. Her voice shook with emotion and Gilmour scowled. Holy apples, he was just trying to keep her safe. What the hell was *she* thinking? He caught her gaze, trying to press his thoughts into her mind.

"I did not have this trouble afore you," he said.

"I did nothing to you." Her voice rose and she took one shaky step backward. What was she doing? Did she have a plan? Might she hope to distract the men with their arguments, then lunge for the forest? But surely she hadn't forgotten about Roy. He stood right behind her.

"Aye," Gilmour agreed and drank again, though it was difficult to force the fluids down his throat. "You did, lassie. And here you were telling me that you were untried. It makes me wonder who you were—"

"Don't say it!" She took another unsteady step backward, all but bumping into Roy's immense force. But the hulk seemed relaxed, pleased even by their conversation, so perhaps she had a chance.

"Don't say what, lass?" he asked. "That you are a—"

"Nay!" She shrieked the word through the darkness, and suddenly she twisted wildly backward.

Gilmour lunged to his feet, ready to help her defeat Roy, to delay him an instant if he could, but in that second he realized that she had turned. A rope dangled from her loosed wrists and Roy's knife gleamed in her fist.

Like a maddened boar she barreled into Mour. He hit the ground with a shocked grunt. The knife slashed downward. He caught her hands between his palms, barely keeping it from his chest as he battled for his life.

"Are you daft?" he rasped.

"Scream," she hissed.

"What?" He stared at her, and in that moment he realized that her eyes were perfectly clear.

"Scream," she rasped and tilting the blade, wedged it between his bonds.

Reality dawned.

He shrieked like a baby and between their bodies, hidden from view, she swiped at his ropes. They sprang loose. He cried out again.

"Kill the bastard!" Roy roared.

"Help! Get her off me!" he shrieked.

Someone laughed. Gilmour clasped his hands together and pushed her away. She fell back, but in a second she was up, coming toward him on hands and knees.

Behind her, someone swore, but Gilmour had no time to assimilate who it might be, for in that instant she lunged again. He braced his heels against the turf and prayed.

Pain slashed his calf, but his legs burst free.

Springing to his feet, he grabbed her wrist. She stumbled, but he didn't wait. Dragging her to her feet, he bolted toward the woods, and she came, galloping madly behind.

Branches whizzed past his head, roots tangled about his boots. He almost fell. She snatched him back to his feet, pushing him on.

Curses and threats stormed through the darkness behind them, seeming to come from the very earth at their feet. Where were they? Where should they go? He stumbled again, his lungs aching.

"Hurry!" she gasped and turned to stare behind them, leading the way now as they scrambled on. But in that second she fell, sliding away into the darkness below them.

Gilmour's shoulders screamed as he hauled her back from the unseen abyss.

"Spread out!" The words were as clear as dawn and came from directly behind them. "The river's just ahead."

"We'll have them now." The voice came from their left. " 'Tis us or the fall."

Bel stepped to the side, searching for a way out. But there was none.

"Jump," she said.

"What?"

She glanced down into the unseen darkness below, then, "Jump!" she ordered.

"Where? H—"

" 'Ey!" The shout was nearly upon them.

"Go!" she screamed, and slammed her body against Mour's. He fell more than jumped, pummeling through the air for a timeless eternity. The water broke like glass beneath him, cracking against his chest, tearing at his shoulders, covering his nose, his eyes, pitching him into black death.

He tried to find the air, to reach the surface, but where was up?

Something struck him. He jerked away only to find air. It streamed into his lungs and he dragged it in.

Isobel! Where? It was then that he realized she was behind him, her arm across his chest as she pushed him downstream.

"Can't you . . ." She paused, breathing hard and bobbing under. He felt himself sink beneath the surface and paddled madly. "Swim?"

"Of course I . . ." he began and went under again.

She hauled him back up. "Hurry!" she hissed.

He tried, but if the truth was known, he swam like a rock. It took an eternity for her to propel them to shore. He crawled onto it, coughing, and she crept up behind.

From the far shore someone cursed again, but the following words softened. "If you return to us now we'll not harm you. You have me vow."

Gilmour almost laughed. Grasping Isobel's arm, he rose to his feet, but she lay where she was, face down on the coarse grasses.

"Go!" He heard the low order from the cliff top.

"Nay, I—" Baron said, but it was followed in an instant by a splash. Apparently Roy was no more patient than Isobel had been.

Bending rapidly, Gilmour snatched the girl into his arms. Upstream someone splashed wildly and he dared cross through the water, letting the sound cover the noise of his own retreat.

Some minutes later, he stumbled onto the opposite shore. One glance behind him told him nothing, so he rushed on.

"I can walk."

He almost dropped her in his surprise, then let her legs slide to the ground . . . and fold, and spill her like a sack of grain onto the earth.

"Aye," he said and lifting her back into his arms, took off at a trot. "You can walk like I can swim."

An eternity passed before he stopped again. His chest burned, his legs throbbed and he was pretty sure that his arms were about to be yanked out of their sockets. She wriggled out of his arms and found her feet. They lurched forward together, but their reserves were running low. A branch reached from the darkness, snagging his feet. And he fell hard onto his knees—and beneath a withering log, he found a large hole.

It was little wider than his chest, but they managed to wriggle into it and peer out into the darkness, legs cramping as they fought for breath.

Close at hand, a man swore. Gilmour held his breath. Isobel's fingers tightened in his tunic. Footsteps rushed toward them. Mour tried to reach his dirk, but the footfalls rustled past.

Gilmour let his eyes fall closed and pulled Bel tighter up against him. Minutes passed like hours. Noises crackled and moans threatened, but they remained unfound until fatigue took them finally and they slept, wrapped like frightened hedgehogs in their hole.

Sometime during the night they awoke. Something stirred outside their den, but they had no way of knowing what it was and no way to escape if they must, so they lay together, barely breathing until the moment passed and they slept again.

An eternity later, gray light filtered slowly into their lair. Isobel exited first, slithering her way out of the hole and pummeling Mour in the process. He creaked out next. They stood in silence, listening, before Mour turned toward her.

"You've a gift for acting," he said. "I thought you truly wished to kill me."

She said nothing, but stared silently into the dimness.

"Bel?"

She turned abruptly toward him. "Why?" she asked. "Why did they do it?"

He shook his head, as baffled as she. "I had nothing to do with it."

"I know that," she said and turning rapidly away, headed toward the north.

Gilmour followed her, for indeed, there was not much else to be done, and there seemed little point in staring at her with his mouth hanging open.

At midmorning, they found a bit of watercress growing in a trickling burn and as they walked they ate a bit. Sometime near noon they heard a sound and hid in the woods. But the noise passed and soon they were moving on. It was apparent, though, that they could not go much farther without food. Gilmour limped to a halt.

"What are you doing?" Isobel asked and turned toward him.

He glanced up. "Resting."

She peered into the woods, her expression strained. "We cannot stop here."

He almost laughed. "Then mayhap you should not have stabbed me in the leg," he said and turned down his stocking to examine the wound on his calf. It was swollen and red and throbbed like other appendages which were wont to grant him a good deal more pleasure.

She pushed his hands away. "I would not have stabbed you if you had not gotten yourself trussed up like a Michaelmas goose."

"And I would not have been trussed up," he said, "if you had the least bit of sense."

She was tearing a strip of cloth from her underskirt and raised her head, her eyes snapping. "So it is me own fault that I was attacked."

"Mayhap," he said, "but 'tis certainly your fault for attacking *me* at the very outset. What the devil were you thinking?"

She began bandaging his leg, and she was none too gentle. "I was thinking you were proving to be the scoundrel I always thought you to be."

"Scoundrel! If that were the case why would I bother to find you, ensconce meself by the brigands' fire, engage them in a lively tale, befriend—"

"You're an ass, MacGowan," she said and tied off the bandage with a vengeance. "Did you never think that it was those very things that made me believe you were in their league?"

"Surely not." He stared at her in utter astonishment.

She stared back. "What is it, MacGowan? Do you think yourself so charming that no matter what the circumstances, women will trust you and adore you and throw themselves into your arms?"

"Aye, that is exactly what I expect."

"Then you are sadly mistook," she said and tromped off through the woods.

He had little choice but to follow. And indeed,

though he tried to remain mute, he found it quite impossible.

"I assure you," he said, "women . . . *normal* women do find me charming."

"Hush." She raised a hand. "Someone comes."

He fell immediately silent, his head slightly cocked, then. "They're on the road, but are they friend or foe?"

"We dare not risk finding out."

"And neither can we walk all the way to Evermyst without sustenance." He hurried through the woods, then dropped to his belly and wriggled toward the road.

He heard the laughter long before he heard the voices. It was high and feminine and leisurely, accented between the neat clip clops of a cart horse, and in his wildest imaginings, he could not imagine either Roy or Baron sounding so delightful. Thus, after a moment's hesitation, he rose to his feet and stepped forward.

Isobel snatched desperately at his sleeve. "What are you doing?"

"Saving our lives," he said and pulled out of her grasp.

The cart came closer. He could see the horse now, a piebald cob with a steady trot and a regal curve to its well muscled crest. Behind it, perched a woman. She was a large, shapely maid and elegantly dressed.

"How do you plan to save us?" hissed Bel.

Gilmour grinned. "By being charming," he said and stepped onto the road.

The cob slowed to a walk, then halted, champing its bit.

"Good day me fair lady," Gilmour said and executed a bow that hurt his knee and sent daggers skittering through his chest. "What a pleasure it is to find you here on this day of days. I wonder if—"

"What do you want?" The question was said in a hard voice that brooked no quarter. Even the piebald seemed impatient, shaking his spotted head and glaring through blue cast eyes.

Still, Gilmour stepped closer. After all, the whole of Scotland couldn't suddenly be immune to his charms. Mayhap the woman couldn't see his roguish grin. "Have no fear, me—"

"One more step and it may well be your last," she said. "As you can see, me steed is eager to be off and would not be averse to crushing you to dust on his way to his stables."

Gilmour raised his hands. "I assure you, lass, I mean you no harm."

"And I assure you, it would be wise to worry about your own fate if you do not remove yourself from the road this—"

"Lady Madelaine?" Isobel said.

Gilmour shifted his gaze toward the rear as Bel stepped onto the road.

"Belva?"

"Me lady!" Bel stumbled forward, her damp, grubby skirt crumpled in one fist. "Is it you?"

"*Mon enfant! Mademoiselles!* 'Tis Belva," proclaimed the lady and suddenly there was a rush of women piling from the dray like an unfettered stream. They hurried past Gilmour, surrounding Isobel as if she were the duchess of York.

"Whatever brings you here?"

"Are you well?"

"Come. Let us not delay here." The large lady glanced down the road. "Hie yourselves into the cart. 'Tis not a long journey to Delshutt Manor."

And so Bel was ushered away, leaving Gilmour to stand in the road like yesterday's cabbage.

They seemed to remember him at the last moment.

"But what of him?" asked a wispy voice.

All eyes turned in his direction. "Is he accompanying you, Belva?" asked the woman ensconced behind the reins.

It took Isobel an inordinately long time to answer.

"Aye," she said finally, and with a wave of an imperious hand from the woman called Madelaine, he was urged to pile into the cart with the others.

It jostled beneath him, threatening to jerk his joints loose at every turn as the women cooed over Isobel.

Aye, he thought, and wished with fervent earnestness for unconsciousness. He was still charming.

Chapter 13

Gilmour awoke slowly. His aches had diminished, but his limbs felt heavy and slightly chilled. Still, he was absolutely content to remain where he was, for he was comfortable, and just now that seemed the most wondrous of things.

"So who is he?" The woman's voice was husky and smooth, like well-spiced cider, and he almost opened his eyes. But it was so sweet to just lay there, utterly still and unresponsive even though the voice sounded vaguely familiar.

"His name is Gilmour, of the Dun Ard Mac-Gowans." Isobel's voice, on the other hand, was unmistakable. Dulcet and quiet in the stillness of the candlelit room.

"Ahhh," said the other and her name seeped slowly into Gilmour's memory. Lady Madelaine, she had been called. Large, commanding, and unmistakably French. "And why is he with you?"

"I was . . . set upon."

"Attacked? *Non!* By whom?"

Isobel paced. Gilmour could hear her light footfalls against the floor, for although he kept his eyes closed,

he had leisurely discerned a few things. One was that
they were inside a room of some sort, most probably in
the chamber where he had fallen asleep the night before. A wizened little woman of indistinguishable heritage had jabbered something about dressing his
wounds, but fatigue had overwhelmed him, and he'd
been able to do nothing more than take a bit of food
and drink before falling into oblivion. They'd obviously decided rest was the best medicine, for here he
remained, perfectly content so long as no one was trying to kill him. It was interesting how one's standards
lowered so quickly.

"I recognized none of the men who took me," Isobel
was saying. "In truth, I know no one who might wish
me ill. Except—"

"Who?"

"Him."

Me? Gilmour thought.

"This MacGowan?" Lady Madelaine's tone evi-
denced her surprise. "What grievance does *he* have
against you?"

Aye, what grievance indeed? Gilmour wondered fog-
gily.

"I know not. I have done him no harm."

Gilmour's chest throbbed an argument, but it was so
wonderful to simply lie there in silence.

"Then why do you suppose he wishes you ill?"

"I first met him at Castle Evermyst where I stayed for
a spell. He is the brother by law of Anora—*Lady* Anora,
whom I served there. Even then we . . . had words."

Madelaine was quiet for several heartbeats, and
when she spoke it was as if she were musing. "So he is
the son of Roderic the Rogue, who is . . . let me

think . . . a duke now, I believe. And his lady mother, well honored at court and known by all as the Flame. You were a servant in his brother's castle and you . . . had words."

There was utter silence for a moment, then, "Just because I am beneath him in me station does not give him the right to . . ." She paused. "He thinks himself quite irresistible."

"Most men do, *ma chère*." There was a shrug in her voice.

"And most men are wrong," Isobel stated.

"But not this one?"

"Especially this one!"

Gilmour almost scowled. Madelaine laughed.

"So he wished to take you to his bed, *oui?*"

Isobel said nothing, but the elder woman continued nevertheless. "And why did you refuse? From all I hear he has the coin and the . . . gear . . . to make it well worth your effort."

"I was not interested in his proposal."

The older woman was silent for a moment, and it almost seemed in Gilmour's misty state that he could feel her gaze on him. "Ahh. Well, on with your tale then."

"Eventually I left Evermyst to—"

"Why?" Madelaine interrupted.

"I . . . 'Twas time, is all."

"Tell me, *mon petit enfant,* have you ever wondered why you run?"

"I did not run. I merely felt it was time to be off."

"So you left the comforts of the castle where they adored you. I am correct in assuming they adored you am I not, Belva?"

Madelaine obviously did not know that Evermyst's

lady was Isobel's sister, and yet she had guessed well. Evermyst's people *did* cherish her. Of course, she probably hadn't stabbed more than two or three of them—an action which had a tendency of cooling one's feelings toward another. Perhaps.

"I got on well there," Isobel admitted.

"I thought you would. Nevertheless, you ran—"

"I did not *run*."

"Ahhh, yes. You went to . . ." Lady Madelaine paused, waiting for Isobel to continue.

"I lived for some months in the village of Henshaw, where I prepared the meals at a inn called the Red Lion. All was—"

"You have such a talent with the spices. 'Tis like magic. I oft wondered if hunger made you gifted. Perhaps those of us who are forever well fed do not appreciate fine food as we should. But I prattle. Go on with your tale. Were you happy at the Red Lion?"

"Happy?" Was Isobel's tone a bit strained now? Was he awake? Or was he dreaming? "I suspect I was. Happy enough."

"But not filled with joy as you were at Evermyst?"

"What makes you say so?"

"No reason. Continue."

"I was content in what I did." She said it with some feeling. "Then one evening MacGowan turned up in the common room."

"And began where he left off with his propositions," suggested Madelaine. "But still you were not interested?"

"Nay."

" 'Tis strange. For even with the bruises he is quite fair to look upon."

Gilmour almost smiled. But he did not, for there were few times in his life when he had more enjoyed doing nothing. He felt strangely at peace, almost dreamlike, and ever so interested. It took him a moment to realize that Isobel had not answered.

"Belva?"

"What?"

"Do you not agree?"

"Regarding what, me lady?"

"Do you not agree that he is a bonny lad? Almost . . . sweet of face." Her tone was retrospective. "Yet deliciously wicked at the self same time."

Isobel cleared her throat. "He is bonny enough, I suppose."

"Ahhh," Madelaine said and laughed. "So he made his appeal yet again and you refused him . . . yet again. But I still do not know how you wound up here, so near Delshutt Manor, looking as if you'd been trampled by a maddened bull."

"I thought all would be well in Henshaw even after MacGowan's arrival. After all, the Munro was about to return to his home and—"

"The Munro?" asked Lady Madelaine, her interest piqued. "I have heard tales of him. Tell me, Belva love, is he as large as they say?"

"Aye . . ." Isobel sounded baffled and somewhat distracted. "I suspect he is. At any rate, I assumed MacGowan would accompany him on his journey north, but his mount became injured and so he continued to stay at—"

"Why did he not purchase a new steed?"

Looking at the situation from this new position, with his body battered like a wind-blown apple,

Gilmour had to admit that such an idea had a good deal of appeal.

"I do not know," Isobel said. "But it makes little difference. Whatever the reason, he stayed on at the inn."

"Ahh. So he remained at the Red Lion and continued to bedevil you."

The room was quiet for a moment. "Aye."

"And you did not enjoy his overtures?"

"Nay! Of course not."

"There is no need to become distraught, *chère*," Madelaine said.

"I have been abducted and threatened and chased down like a hunted hare. I think I have the right—"

"Poor *enfant*. But let us continue with the tale, shall we?" Lady Madelaine soothed. "So he was interested in you and you were not completely certain how you felt about his attentions. Thus—"

" 'Tis not true. I had no interest atall in his advances."

"Ahh. Well, let us forget that part for a spell. Now, what of the abduction? How did you end up in the company of the young rogue?"

Isobel sighed, then paced again. "He had taken to following me home."

"From the inn?"

"Aye."

"In the dark."

"Aye."

Gilmour could almost hear Lady Madelaine's cream-eating smile. "Continue."

"Aye, he would follow me home, and—"

"Tell me, Belva, do you still love the water so?"

Memories washed over Gilmour like mulled wine.

As for himself, he had never been comfortable in the water. It wasn't that he was afraid of it . . . exactly, he just appreciated the fact that land did not have a tendency to flow out from under his feet like water did. But seeing her by the river's edge with the moonlight stroking her ivory breasts and waves lapping her delicate ankles, had made him feel somewhat differently. Of course, he'd rather she didn't push him off a cliff again. In fact, now that he thought about it, there was no reason she couldn't simply disrobe for him and *pretend* she was by the river.

"Aye. I am ever at home in the water," Bel admitted. "Why do you ask?"

"Simple curiosity. Nothing more. So he followed you to your home but still you refused his advances."

"I . . ." Isobel's voice fell into silence like a pebble in a pond.

"Belva?"

"Of course I refused him."

"Ahhh. Go on."

"Then one night I was attacked, knocked unconscious and carried away. When I awoke I knew not where I was. All I knew was that I had been abducted and that he was at their campsite, laughing and conversing with them. 'Twas perfectly logical to assume—"

"That he was one of your captors."

"Aye."

"But . . ." Madelaine let the word lie there in the quiet.

"But I think I . . . may have been mistaken."

May have been! They'd beaten the living stuffing out of him.

"And why do you think so?" Madelaine asked.

"Well, when I said his name . . ."

And tried to kill him!

"They grabbed him and . . ." To her credit, Isobel seemed unable to go on.

"And?"

"In truth," Bel murmured, her voice feather soft. "I thought he was dead."

"And this distressed you?"

"Of course it distressed me. I never wished for him—"

"They beat him," Madelaine interrupted.

"Aye."

"And kicked him, by the looks of it."

"Aye."

"And stabbed him."

"Ay . . . well, in actuality . . . I do not think they . . . stabbed him."

"I was certain Liddie said there were stab wounds on his chest and leg."

Isobel cleared her throat. "Aye, well, it could be that those wounds were caused by . . . meself."

"You stabbed him?"

Damn right she did. And it hurt like the devil.

"When I saw him by the fire with the brigands I . . ."

"What?"

"I fear I lost control."

"Lost control, Belva? You?"

"I believed he had betrayed me."

The room went deadly quiet for a moment, then, "A man cannot betray a woman unless she trusts him to begin with, *chère*. Did you trust him?"

"Nay. But still I was . . . incensed."

"And so you flew at him and stabbed him." Lady Madelaine sounded a bit baffled, but not nearly as bloody baffled as Gilmour himself had been.

Isobel cleared her throat. "Aye."

"Ahh well, one scar upon that bonny chest will do him no harm, will it now? Indeed, mayhap 'twill make it only the more appealing for the lassies, *oui?* Still," Madelaine continued, "would it not have been more sensible to try to escape since the opportunity presented itself?"

What a fine idea! Too bad Isobel had not considered that at the time.

"I was not thinking straight. I had been struck on the head, if you recall."

"Aye. The brutal bastards. Fortunately, you have mended well. The rogue here has a bit more healing to do since they wounded him on both sides of his pate."

Isobel said nothing.

"There is an open wound on the left side. Did they strike him with something? A club, mayhap?"

"I think perhaps . . . that wound was caused by meself also."

"You struck him on the head?"

"Aye."

"With a club?"

"A rock."

"While the brigands looked on?"

"Actually, the incident happened somewhat earlier."

"Afore you left Henshaw?"

"Aye."

"Beside the burn?"

"What?"

"When he saw you unclothed in the water?"

"How did you know I—"

"I well remember the months you spent with us at Milford House, Belva. Perhaps you did not realize that I knew you made a habit of swimming in the pond."

"I—"

" 'Twas an intriguing habit of yours. And I made certain the lads did not disturb you, but mayhap it would have been wise to forestall it once you were no longer under my protection."

Nay, 'twould not have been wise atall, for of all the memories that drifted through Gilmour's hazy brain, that was his most favored. His mind wandered dreamily and below, his interest swelled.

"The lad here doesn't look the sort to miss that type of thing," Madelaine continued. "Go on with your story, *chère*. After you attacked him."

"I did not attack him . . . exactly."

"What would you prefer to call it?"

Yes. What?

"I was but protecting meself."

"From what?"

The silence was quite long now. Gilmour waited.

"I suspect it is possible that he was attempting to protect me," Isobel murmured.

"Ahh, so he followed you to the brigands' camp and when your captors realized his reason for being there, they beat the devil out of him."

"I'm willing to wager there is still a bit of devil in him," Isobel said and Madelaine laughed.

" 'Tis good to know you learned a bit about men while you were in my employ, Belva. What happened after they beat him?"

"We traveled, seemingly forever. MacGowan was unconscious much of the time."

"He seems to have a penchant for that," Madelaine said, but even in his odd, dreamlike state he could have sworn he heard a dram of humor in her tone.

"I planned and schemed, trying to think of a means of escape, but what could I do while he was unconscious?"

"Leave without him, mayhap?"

"But . . . I . . . he had planned to save me . . . I think."

"And so you hoped to do the same for him."

"I thought they had killed him." Isobel's voice broke.

"I believe you have already said that, lass."

Bel cleared her throat. "Then when he awoke . . . there was no time for apologies. I attempted to tell him of me plan, but when he spoke they . . ." She paused.

"They are evil." Madelaine's tone was softer than Gilmour would have thought possible, for it was clear she was not a women prone to foolish sentiment. "God shall deal with them if man does not get the opportunity, and the lad shall recover."

"Aye." Isobel went on, her voice brusque. "I had no chance to tell him me plan, but I convinced one of the brigands to untie me hands. I promised him . . ." She paused as if gathering strength. "I promised him meself if he would give me one chance at MacGowan."

"One chance?"

"I had, ahhh . . . tried to kill him you know. They believed I hated him."

"Didn't you?"

"I . . . aye, I did. I do."

"Except for that one time."

"What time?"

"I think you know, *chère*. 'Tis a strange thing; men can be bumbling bastards their entire lives and then they touch you . . . just that once and you wonder why you never knew they were magical."

It had been magical. Gilmour remembered the feel of her skin, the whisper of her sighs. Sweet heaven, she had moaned like a goddess under his fingertips. Even now he was hard with the memory.

"We did not . . . it was not what you think," Isobel said.

"Truly?"

"I did not . . . give meself to him."

"Ahhh. And yet you felt the magic?"

"Nay, I—"

"Go on with your tale."

It took Isobel several seconds to continued, and then there was pacing again, the steps faster now. "Only a few of the brigands wanted to keep MacGowan alive. The others thought him too risky. The guard knew I would go for his knife. That much he knew, but he thought I would kill MacGowan."

"Instead of free him."

"Aye."

Madelaine sighed. "And so here you are, with the very man who has bedeviled you for so long."

The footsteps halted. Again it seemed that he could feel gazes upon him.

" 'Tis said he has been with scores of women."

"A goodly number."

"I would be just one more."

"Would you?"

"If I gave meself to him. But I will not."

"So that he cannot wound your heart."

"He cannot wound me!"

"Indeed? So you have no feelings for him?"

There was the slightest of pauses. Gilmour held his breath.

"Nay, I do not," Isobel said, her voice soft. "He has done naught but plague me since first we met."

"What do you mean, 'plague,' exactly?"

"Have I not just told you? He followed me every-where. I could not be shed of him."

"Ahh." He felt the lady's hot gaze skim his body. "For shame."

" *'Tis* shameful! He would not give me a moment's peace."

"Except that one time."

"There was no one time! He followed me home, is what he did, and forced himself—"

"He forced himself on you!"

Gilmour waited, breath held, but Isobel didn't speak. The room seemed suddenly quite cold.

"I am a patient woman," Madelaine said, but her tone was no longer husky and smooth, but hard and chilled. "I am also forgiving, for I know that God will send justice on those who most deserve it. My first husband, for instance. But some things should not wait for the Lord's judgment. If he forced you, Belva then he shall pay the price this very day. Were you willing, lass?"

"Nay, I—"

"Then he shall dearly regret his actions." She was directly beside the bed now, and in that instant Gilmour felt the weight of fabric lifted from his hips. "Belva, fetch the knife," she said and Gilmour's eyes snapped open.

Chapter 14

Madelaine stood over him, one hand holding up a
strip of cloth while the other perused his lower
body.

Gilmour shot his gaze downward and found to his
wordless amazement that he was naked. Completely
and utterly naked but for a scrap of scarlet linen that
flowed over one hip and away.

"I did not say—" Isobel began, but the older woman
interrupted once again without shifting her gaze the
slightest degree.

"Although it does seem a bit of a shame considering
all," she admitted and tilting her head for a better view,
turned her brazen smile on Isobel. "If I am not mistaken, our young Scot has been thinking of you, Belva.
Tell me, *chère*, is he ever called 'Mour'? It would
seem quite appropriate."

Reaching out, Gilmour snatched the linen from
her hand, but Madelaine turned with elegant slowness, showing not the slightest surprise that he was
awake.

"Ahh, Laird MacGowan," she said. "So you have
finally decided to join the discussion, have you?"

"If it is not too much trouble, I would broach a question," he said.

She raised one eyebrow at him. It was as thin as the stroke of a quill on her high patrician forehead. " 'Tis no trouble. Ask away, lad."

"What the devil are you doing?"

"Ahh, that. I was just about to make you less troublesome to the maids. 'Tis the price to be paid when one forces himself on *m' enfant*."

Somehow he could not find a single word, but turned his perplexed gaze on Isobel and tugged the linen up toward his chest. Recalcitrant as an aging mule it snagged beneath his thigh and slid sideways, baring one of the few thing that had managed, thus far, to remain covered.

He tried to lift his thigh and found that the bruised muscles refused to budge the slightest inch. Thus, he raised his gaze with slow deliberation back to Madelaine and asked, "What have you done to me?"

"Saved you a great deal of pain, *monsieur*," she said and slowly lifted her gaze back to his face. "Liddie is a marvel with the herbs."

"She drugged me?"

"Oui."

"Hmmm," he said and philosophically relenting his hold on the linen, plumped the pillows with a painful twist of his arm before settling back against them. After all, if she was intent on staring, he might as well let her have her fill and give his legs a chance to rejuvenate lest it became necessary to make a wild dash for the door.

"You said he would remain asleep until dawn." Isobel's voice sounded none too strong.

"Did I?" Madelaine smiled. "I must have been mistaken. How is it that you feel after Liddie's ministrations, MacGowan?"

Well, he was naked and bandaged, and apparently not able to move the lower half of his body. "Not quite up for a gelding," he said and though he was determined to keep his expression impervious to their stares, he couldn't quite help wishing that the linen was just a hand's breadth to the right.

Madelaine laughed. "Mayhap it can keep, then. What think you, Belva? Were his sins against you so heinous that we must seek immediate justice?"

Gilmour realized in that moment that he had never seen Isobel at a loss for words, and although her chin was high, he noticed that her hands were clasped and her gaze locked firmly on his. She looked decidedly flushed.

"I never actually said he forced himself on me, me lady."

"Didn't you now? I was certain 'forced' was the word used."

"I was about to say that he forced his way into me *home*."

"Ahhh. My mistake. We might as well put that away then," she said and tugged the scarlet linen over his nether parts. Her knuckles brushed him just so, and she smiled. "You're well enough crafted, MacGowan, for a Scot."

"I'm thrilled that you approve, so long as you see no need to keep me better parts in a jar by your bedside."

"Of course not," she said and laughed. "After all, the situation has been well explained now, has it not? You but forced your way into her *house*. Is that correct?"

"Aye," he said and watched as she sat down on the mattress beside him. She was not a beautiful woman, but she was arresting, smooth skinned and commanding.

"How does your chest feel?" she asked and placed the palm of her right hand flat against his unwounded pectoral.

He raised his brows. Behind her, Isobel was scowling. "As if I'd been stabbed," he said.

"Our Belva has been rough on you." She tsked and smoothed her hand sideways. His nipple contracted. Hardly ever did women threaten to geld him and caress him in the same moment. "But that way you will not forget her, *oui?*"

"Where are we exactly?" he asked, but in actuality he wasn't certain if he truly cared just now or if it merely seemed wise to maintain some semblance of sanity.

"You are a guest at Delshutt Manor," she said and slid her hand downward, letting her fingers bump slowly, one at a time, over his nipple. "So you are the rogue of the rogues. I have heard tales."

"They are most probably exaggerated."

"Ahhh, modesty." She raised her brows in surprise as she slid her hand lower. Mour held his breath as it tripped down his abdomen and stopped just above the linen.

Gilmour raised his attention from her hand to Isobel. She stood frozen, her tilted eyes wide, and for a moment, for just one second he wondered if he saw a momentary flash of violence in her gaze.

"Tell me, *monsieur,* what is it you do that makes *scores* of women swoon with longing?"

He pulled his gaze from Isobel and met Madelaine's. "Perhaps 'tis naught more than me reputation that makes them sigh."

"But surely you have done something to gain that reputation."

He shrugged. The action still felt strangely disembodied. "Mayhap some find me charming."

She smiled her approval. "And what do you do that women find so enchanting? Or have I already witnessed the height of your charms?"

He canted his head, so that his feather, still firmly fixed in his braid, dropped against his shoulder. "That depends on one's point of view I suspect."

"I have the point of view of a widowed baroness who is oft bored," she said and lifting all but her ring finger from his skin, slid it sideways, so that it just skimmed the edge of the cloth. "What might you do for me?"

"I fear you are above me own humble station, me lady," he said and Lady Madelaine chuckled.

"Watch this one, Belva," she said, her voice smooth and husky again. "He may be neither as large nor as charming as some, but it could be he is craftier than all." Her finger trickled onto his arm and down his knuckles. "He is also filthy."

The change of verbal direction seemed to catch Isobel by surprise. "What's that?"

"Your lad," she said, turning her attention to Bel. "He is in dire need of a bath."

"He is *not* me lad."

"Ahhh. Then you would like someone else to assist him with the task?"

Isobel's lips moved for a second without sound,

then, "He is a man fully grown. Surely he can bathe himself."

"He has been wounded." Madelaine's hand tripped from his fingertips onto his thigh. "By you, I believe."

"I did not ask him to follow me. In truth, I insisted that he leave me be."

"Indeed." Madelaine rose slowly. "You are quite right. Tell Polly to draw a bath and prepare to wash our guest."

Isobel scowled. "Why Polly?"

"I think he'll enjoy her. Don't you?"

"He cannot even move."

Madelaine glanced with some surprise at Isobel. "What are you suggesting that they might be doing?"

"Nothing! That is to say, 'tis none of me own concern what he does."

"I only meant that she would be pleasant company," explained Lady Madelaine. "I find Polly to be quite a likable lass, don't you?"

"Aye, but he is still influenced by Liddie's herbs. Surely he will need someone stronger to assist him. One of your lads, perhaps or—"

"I've not known you to fret so over my guests in the past," Madelaine said.

"I am not fretting. I merely—" she began, but Madelaine was already hustling her out of the room.

"You've had a hard time of it, *chère*. Brigands, abductions, this rogue bedeviling you . . ." Glancing back, the corners of her subtly painted mouth quirked the tiniest amount. " 'Tis surely time for you to rest."

For a moment Isobel balked at the door. "Truly, I am feeling quite—"

"None of that now," Madelaine said and pressed her

into the hall. "Liddie will never forgive me if I allow you to become overtaxed."

Madelaine gave him one last glance as she closed the door. "You rest, lad," she said. "We'll have time together later."

Gilmour was still debating what that meant when a knock sounded on his door. To his surprise and relative delight, he found that he could move his legs enough to cover himself sufficiently, dragging the sadly inadequate linen up his legs and nearly to his chest.

"Who—" he began, but the door opened with a flourish before he'd managed the second word.

"Good eventide, love." The maid that bobbed in the doorway was short and bonny. She dimpled when she smiled and her breasts, carefully displayed above a lacy bodice, were possibly the largest he had ever seen. And he'd seen a few. Breasts, as it happened, were two of his favorite things in the entire world. "Come on in then, lads."

The lads came. Broad and tall, one fair and one dark, they carried a tall copper tub between them. Muscles swelled like giant bellows as they set it easily to the floor and straightened. They were both strikingly well favored and just past a score of years.

"Will there be anything else, Polly love?" the nearest one asked. Bending close, he slipped a brawny arm about her waist. Plump as she was, she could bend with surprising ease.

"As a matter of truth, there is," she murmured.

"What's that?" he asked, leaning in.

"Water," she said and danced away. "For the poor man's bath."

The lad smiled. "Later then," he said.

"Mayhap," she replied and giggled.

The door was closed in a second. Polly placed her fists on round hips and perused him. It wasn't the first time that day that he considered hiding under the bed.

"Now then, what of you, Gilmour of the Mac-Gowans?"

"What of me?"

" 'Tis time to get you cleaned up, it is. Madame doesn't like her lads soiled."

"Her lads?"

"Aye. You've just met two of them."

He tried not to let his brows shoot into his hairline. After all, he was worldly, he reminded himself. "And what exactly do her lads do?"

"Oh, some of this and some of that," she said and paced a bit closer. " 'Tis said you're exceptionally good at such things. I was thinking, in fact, that I might get a wee taste—ach! But here comes the water already." A "lad" entered, carrying a bucket the size of Manchester. "You've always been a bit quick on the draw haven't you, Boots?"

The dark-haired man grinned. "The better for a second go," he said and emptied his bucket into the tub. The fair-haired fellow followed on his heels, and in a moment the copper basin steamed at him from the far corner. The lads disappeared with a grin for Polly and a happy, conspiratorial sort of nod that made Gilmour feel a bit queasy. What the hell sort of situation had Isobel gotten him into?

"Well then . . ." Polly stood with arms akimbo, smiling broadly. She could, it seemed, smile while talking. "Out with you."

"What's that?"

Dropping her fists from her hips she paced toward him. "Get out of bed now and into the bath."

There had been a time, he realized, when he had thought he had seen a bit of the world. He had, it seemed, been as innocent as a swaddled babe. "I fear me legs don't work."

"Your legs don't . . . ach!" she exclaimed. "Liddie was after you was she not? Here then, the lads will carry—"

Lads! Nude!

"Nay!" The word escaped a bit faster than he had planned, but the thought of those two burly brutes lifting him naked into the tub was just a bit more than he could stomach just now. "I think I can manage."

"There's me scrappy lad."

The scrappy lad's legs cooperated quite nicely, actually. Apparently whatever Liddie had given him had worn off while leaving his legs intact. A soothing thought. But it was quite difficult, he noticed, to wrangle the linen about his hips as he shimmied toward the tub.

Polly took his arm, as if he was a decrepit old man who might lose his course on the way to the garderrobe, but in a moment they had reached their destination. She smiled and tugged at the linen.

"Here now," she chirped, happy as a green finch in spring. "There's no need for this now, is there?"

He wanted to argue, but he couldn't think of a reasonable excuse for dragging the linen in with him like a bairn with a favored blanket. It came away in her pale, dimpled hands.

"Ack!" Her eyebrows rose. "How nice. I was wondering why Madame called you More."

"What—"

"Into the tub with you."

It was, perhaps, the most embarrassing moment in his life to step into the water. His balls brushed the cool metal. The water steamed against his knees.

"There, now. Isn't that better? Just relax."

Relax?

"Here." Folding a huge loose woven cloth, she propped it behind his head. "Lie back, love. Little Polly ain't going to eat you up."

He leaned back with frank misgivings and rolled his eyes toward her.

"Let me think now. Where did I put that soap? Oh yes!" she exclaimed and dipped her hand into her bodice. "There it be."

He truly hadn't thought there would be room between her bosoms for so much as a hound's tail hair. But there you go. Wrong again.

"What needs washing first?" she asked and eyed him up before tsking. "Them poor ribs of yours. Whatever happened?"

"It seems there are those who do not care for the MacGowan clan."

"Jealous, were they?" she asked and laughed. "They must of seen you in the altogether aye?"

Again he tried to verbalize thoughts, but she bent to soak a rag in the water, which caused her bosom to pop out of her bodice. His eyeballs popped as well.

"Oops," she said and shaking her shoulders, settled them back into place.

"If I may ask a question," he ventured.

"Certainly," she agreed and wrapped the wet rag across his face.

He spoke through the only opening. "What manner of place is this?"

"This?"

He didn't bother to respond.

"This is Delshutt Manor. Madame's summer home."

"And Madame is . . ."

"Relax now. There's a good lad. I'm going to give you a shave. We don't want them nasty whiskers burning any tender flesh, do we now?"

She uncovered his face and lifting an oddly shaped bottle from a nearby trunk, poured out a few droplets of oil. Its scent, pungent and strangely sweet, filled the moist air. He breathed in and, despite everything, found himself relaxing. It was then that he realized she had produced a blade from somewhere. He stiffened as memories stormed back. Talk of castration tends to make one jumpy.

"Madam is Lord Fulton's widow. Before that she was wed to Sir Ludlow of Huxcliff and Lord de la Font."

"At the same time?" He eyed the blade as it drew nearer.

Polly giggled. The razor wobbled. "You're a wry one, ain't you, laddie?" she said and scraped the blade across his cheek, over his jaw and down his throat. He dared not swallow. Indeed, he may have stopped breathing. "Nay, o' course, not at the same time. The church frowns on that sort of thing, don't it now. Still . . ." She straightened and as she did so, her bosom pressed intimately against the back of his head. "Madame does what pleases her. But . . ." She drew out the word as she leaned over him to finish his right cheek and draw the blade down his left. "She's as generous as they come."

"Generous?"

"With her staff. We be more like family than—ach, now I'm dripping," she said, and sidling to the right, leaned over the tub to gather a droplet of oil from his chest onto her fingertip. With the cooper pressed against the underside of her bosoms, they swelled up like raised dough, pale and swollen and fragrant with the soap that had somehow been hidden between them. "Well now . . ." Her face was very close to his. "What needs me ministrations the most?" she asked and taking the soap from its place by the tub, ran a foamy track down his chest. "Very nice," she murmured, and dipped her hand beneath the water. It slid downward. He tensed.

"Polly!"

She jumped. He jumped. They turned in unison. Isobel stood in the doorway, dressed in a borrowed nightrail that billowed about her fragile frame. Only her pale, narrow feet were visible beneath the embroidered hem.

"Polly." Her voice had softened. " 'Tis so good to see you."

"Isobella!" The plump woman straightened with a smile, her arm wet past the elbow, suds dripping from her plump fingertips. "I was terrible worried for you. You've had yourself a time of it."

"Aye." Her gaze skittered to Gilmour and away. "Aye. But I am safe now."

Polly nodded happily and reached out to distractedly lather Gilmour's shoulder. " 'Tis glad I am to hear it."

"Aye!" The word was a little sharp.

"Were you in need of somemat afore you find your bed, Isobella?"

"Nay, I . . ." Her hands fidgeted. "Well, in truth, Lady Madelaine has asked me to fetch you."

"Madame? But 'twas she who set me to this task."

"Aye well . . ." Bel paused for a moment and licked her lips. "I suspect she found something more pressing."

"More pressing than this?" Polly asked and laughed. "I have me doubts. She wanted the lad bathed right quick. In any event I'll be finished here in a hop," she added and leaned forward to slip the soap merrily down Gilmour's chest again.

All eyes followed its descent.

"Polly!"

"Aye?" The soap stopped just below the water surface.

" 'Tis quite urgent, I believe."

For the first time in Mour's short acquaintance with her, Polly frowned. "Are you certain?"

"Aye." Isoble stood as straight as the king's royal guard. "Quite certain."

Chapter 15

❧ ❦ ❧

The room fell into silence as Polly closed the door behind her. Isobel stared at it, holding the soap the woman had handed her, and wondering why in heaven's name she had told such a lie.

The quiet stretched, growing increasingly uncomfortable.

"Well . . ." She cleared her throat and chanced a glance in MacGowan's direction. His hair was damp, slicked away from his face, allowing a glimpse of the bruise above his left ear. Other than that, he looked amazingly strong and hale, considering the ordeal they'd been through. But then, she couldn't see his lower body from where she stood. *Not* that she cared to. She scurried for something with which to fill the silence. "I suspect you can finish the job yourself."

His brows rose. It was amazing, but even after the nightmarish events of the past few days, his features seemed unchanged from their usual conviviality. He raised his arms from the water, casting them casually over the rim of the tub. They were golden in hue, sculpted with power and heavy with strength. For a pretty boy he had an unusual amount of muscle. Not that she thought he was pretty. But his chest was broad and firm, rising in smooth hillocks of power above the water's surface. Naked as he was, he had a certain primeval appeal. Not that she found him primevally appeal—

"What job is that, Bel?" he asked.

"What?" She jerked her gaze from his chest.

He grinned. The tendons in her knees went lax and she realized abruptly that she hadn't gotten nearly enough rest. Surely she was exhausted, thus the weakness in her legs.

"What job can I finish by meself?"

"Bathing."

"Oh." His grin widened. Always and forever he had reminded her of a satyr. Irritating, irresist—*irreverent.*

"Of course," she added and pursed her lips.

"Still," he said, " 'twas good of her to offer."

A boatload of words almost spilled from Isobel's mouth, but she held them back with an effort.

"After all . . ." He winced as he slipped a hand from the tub's rim and cradled his injured arm against his chest. "I have been badly wounded."

A boyish satyr, he was, with eyes the color of a cloudless sky and hands like—she stopped the thought, straightening her back and her frame of mind in one quick gesture.

"I did not ask you to follow me, MacGowan."

"So you have said. Still, I did and . . ." He sighed dramatically. "In the process of saving you, I fear I—"

"Saving me! 'Twas *I* who saved *you!"*

He shrugged. A bead of water slid languidly around the curve of his shoulder, then found a wayward course across his chest.

Isobel licked her lips.

"You are right, of course," he said. "Mayhap 'tis I who should be bathing you." He canted his head and lifted a palm toward his bath. "Would you care to join me?"

Her knees buckled again. She firmed them with a snap. "MacGowan," she said. "Polly is gone."

He gave her a quizzical glance.

"I am not so easily enamored."

"Ahhh," he said. "A challenge."

"Is that what I am? A challenge to you, yet another of the hundreds of maids to fall under your charms?"

"Hundreds?" A dimple etched itself into his cheek. "And just a short while ago it was mere scores of maids who adored me."

She shrugged and paced toward the bed, needing something to do to keep her mind from melting like bacon fat. "I am certain you've been busy since I saw you last."

He laughed. The sound filled the room like the essence of magic. "I am wounded, lass. Surely that would slow down even a rogue like meself."

"I doubt it."

"I am flattered."

"I meant it as an insult."

"What a pity. You never answered me question."

"I'm certain that is because it was foolish."

"On the contrary, I asked if you would like to share me bath."

"You're not a man for subtleties are you, Mac-Gowan?"

" 'Tis not true." He could smile with nothing more than his eyes, but at times his entire being joined in the assault. It was then that she must be most careful. "I can be quite subtle. Would you like a wee example?"

"Nay."

"I don't know why you continue to insist that you are not attracted to me."

"Have you ever considered the possibility that I am not?"

"Nay, I have not."

"In truth, MacGowan, I am surprised Polly went unmolested as long as she did."

"Are you impressed?"

"Not in the least."

He loosed his grin, threatening to turn her joints to pig jelly. "Then mayhap you did not see me in the altogether, as our Polly put it."

"Polly talks too much!" The words surprised Isobel herself. Her hands fidgeted and she found, when she glanced at them, that she still held the soap. "Here!" As she dropped it into the water, he reached out to snag her wrist.

"You would not leave me here alone, would you, Bel?"

"Aye." She leveled her gaze on his and lied to save her sinking soul. "Gladly."

"What if I grow faint and drown?"

"Mayhap you should summon one of those hundreds of adoring maids to assist you."

"Tell me, lass . . ." His fingers were gentle but firm. "Do you believe every word you hear?"

She could feel her pulse beating in her wrist, thrumming a tattoo against the hard pads of his fingers. "Are you saying there have not been hundreds?"

Tilting his head back slightly, he laughed. His throat was broad, corded with finely hewn muscle. "Aye," he said. "That is what I am saying."

She should pull away. Should leave. Immediately. "How many?" she asked.

He stared at her, and she met his gaze as evenly as she could, pretending that her heart wasn't galloping like a destrier in training, pretending that she always breathed like an overexerted bellows.

"Isobel . . ." he crooned and gently caressed the underside of her wrist with his thumb. "Are you asking how many lovers I've had?"

Her knees, damn them to hell, threatened to tilt her face first into his bath. But she straightened them with a jolt and a shrug even as she tried to pull her hand from his grip. She failed and scowled. "In truth, Mac-Gowan, I wouldn't care a whit if you spend your nights with three sheep and a doxy."

"Truly?" he asked and skimmed his thumb across her wrist again. "Then whyever did you ask?"

Dear heavens, his lashes were ungodly long, like a wee lad's. But there was nothing immature about the body that disappeared beneath the warmth of his bath water.

She gave him a shrug and hoped to God she looked neither as panicked nor as needy as she felt "I spent some months in the village of Callander," she said.

He waited for her to continue, seeming to feel no need to hurry her from the spot, even though she had but to tilt her head to the right to see to the bottom of the tub.

"Upon the hillock lived the laird of Unther."

Still he waited as his thumb played across the shivering tendons of her arm, but she studiously turned her mind away from the sensations.

"He had himself a son named William. At times the lad would journey down to the village to buy ralstons from the baker. He loved—"

Loosening his grip slightly, Gilmour stroked a circle into the center of her palm.

"Ralstons?" he asked.

"What?" Her tone seemed oddly breathy to her own ears.

"William . . . he loved ralstons?" MacGowan guessed.

"Oh. Aye. Certainly. Ralstons." She took a deep breath and found her stride with some difficulty. "One day the village was all agog at how many ralstons he had consumed."

He grinned ever so slightly as he watched her. "And?"

"And I was curious then, too, as to the number."

"Ahh," he said. "So you are saying 'tis only because of idle curiosity that you ask."

"Exactly."

" 'Twas an ungodly long story for so simple a moral. Perhaps . . ." he began and lifting her arm ever so gently, kissed her wrist.

Something akin to lightning bolted from her wrist to her belly in sizzling heat.

His grin widened, lifting the right side of his mouth and deepening one dimple to lethal depths. "Perhaps," he repeated, "you were looking for an excuse to stay."

"I was doing no—"

He kissed her again, halfway up her arm.

She found, to her numbed dismay, that she could not move.

"I would gladly bathe *you*," he murmured, "if you would but ask."

Images bloomed like hotbed flowers in her head, steaming through her mind and dizzying her thoughts.

"Isobel?" he murmured, pulling her closer.

"Nay!" she said and jerked her hand from his grip.

He gave her a wounded expression, but his grin never slipped. "I would be very gentle."

"Don't . . ." she took a few fortifying breaths. "That's ridiculous."

"Surely you need to bathe from time to time."

"I already bathed."

"And I missed it—such a pity. But I suspect I had best simply see to me own cleansing if I ever hope to win your . . ." he began, but when he reached for a cloth, he winced.

She took an involuntary step toward the tub. "What is it?"

"Oh, 'tis naught," he said and took the cloth from the tub's rim.

She scowled. "Is it your arm?"

"Nay, nay, lass. Worry not. Me arm will mend," he said, but when he lifted the rag to his chest, she saw the darkened bruise that spread across his lower ribs.

"Do they hurt?"

He lifted his gaze to her. His grin was sheepish now and entrancingly boyish. "I would tell you truth, lass, but I have found, through arduous study, that women are rarely impressed by a man's weaknesses."

"Liddie was to ease your pain."

"I am certain she did me naught but good."

Isobel scowled. "You are not to strain yourself."

"I do not think bathing can be considered a strain, lass," he said and lifted the cloth to his shoulder. Water streamed in warm rivulets down his arm and chest.

She followed its descent with her gaze and remembered to breathe. "Mayhap I should assist you for a spell."

"I did not mean to cause you guilt," he said.

She took a step closer. Tiny bubbles covered the surface of the water, obscuring all that was beneath. "Didn't you?"

"Well . . ." His grin lifted, showing teeth that were slightly crooked but ungodly white. "Mayhap I thought a bit of guilt would do no harm."

"Give me the cloth," she said, and though every ounce of good sense screamed in protest, she sunk to her knees beside the tub.

He handed over the rag, then retrieved the soap from the depths. She reached for it. Their fingers brushed. Lightning sizzled from tip to tip, but she refused to feel it.

"Your forehead is dirty."

"Is it?"

"Aye," she said and wringing out the cloth, washed away the grime.

"Better?"

She nodded jerkily. "Your hair needs washing."

" 'Twould not surprise me."

"There's . . ." She reached out to touch his wound, but drew carefully back in an instant. "Dried blood."

"They were not nice fellows, those men you traveled with."

She turned her mind away from the memories, away from the idea that she may well be dead now if he had not appeared. "I would have to remove your feather." She kept her tone firm, but found it oddly difficult to meet his gaze. "Why do you wear it?"

"Do you not know?" he asked. "'Tis to keep me safe from drowning. But you may have had a hand in that, as well," he said and grinned.

Isobel swallowed hard but kept her mind on her task. A narrow strip of leather held the feather in place, and in a moment she realized that a hole had been made in the plume's narrow shaft. She untied it and laid it aside before setting unsteady fingers to his braid. Her hand brushed the curl of his ear, the hard slope of his jaw, and still he watched her. His nostrils, she noticed, were slightly flared, and he was no longer smiling. In fact, there seemed to be a decided lack of air in the room.

She fumbled with his hair for a moment, then loosened the braid before smoothing it beside its straighter fellows, along his cheek and onto the corded strength of his throat.

He dropped his head back against the towel behind him, but she found, when she dared a glance, that he still watched her. Even under his gaze, it seemed impossible to keep from skimming her fingers along one taut tendon and onto his collarbone. A smudge of dirt was nestled in the dell beside it, and she lifted the cloth to wipe away the soil. It was only natural, then, to slip the rag lower over the swell of muscle that was his chest. His nipple was dark and small, erect and firm. She eased the rag over it, continued to breathe, and washed the other side.

It seemed only right that she wash the cloth down his shoulder, carefully cleansing his wound before moving downward. Veins, raised beneath the sun-darkened skin of his forearms, ran rampant at his wrist. She felt the pulse beneath her fingertips and silently marveled at the strength that was him. His hand lay palm up in hers, relaxed and open, and the sight of it brought back a warm flood of memories—of his kiss against her palm, her wrist, her . . .

She brought her mind sternly back to the task at hand, and bringing forth the scented soap, lathered him from nails to wrist. Then, abandoning the soap, she smoothed her thumbs from the hollow of his palm outward. It was fascinating somehow to see the soap spread away from the pressure, and when she turned his hand over, there was no doubt that every finger needed her ministrations. She washed each one with mind numbing dedication, fascinated by every joint, every turn, every movement until he grasped her hand in his own.

She glanced up, surprised from the absorption of her task.

"Isobel." Her name was no more than a whisper on his lips. "Join me."

"Nay," she breathed, and yet she had no idea how she found even that much strength, for she realized, to her abject amazement, that there was nothing she wanted more than to do exactly what he asked.

"Why?" he murmured.

His thumb was strumming her wrist again, causing her blood to course faster through her veins. "Do you not know the consequences of such acts, MacGowan?"

"Consequences?" He slipped his fingertips up her arm, and she shivered as a track of water was laid along her vein.

"Mayhap not for you," she said. He leaned forward, touching her cheek and inadvertently brushing the bare strength of his chest against her fingers. She swallowed. "But surely for the women who are left with your bairns."

"Bairns?" He moved back slightly. "Lass, surely you know how bairns are made."

She refused to blush, but if the truth were known, it could well be that her entire body was already flushed, for her blood felt as hot as a witch's cauldron. "Aye, MacGowan, I know."

He smiled a little. "Then you are thinking of other things than I suggested, Bel, for I only asked you to join me. Surely you know that one can taste the bounty without consuming the feast."

She laughed softly, unable to move away.

"Something amuses you?"

"Aye." Very well, she could admit the truth. He was beautiful as no man should be beautiful, and every weak fiber in her trembled with longing at the very sight of him. But when he was gone, she would still have to make her way in the world, and she was not such a fool as to make that way more difficult by the time they'd spent together. " 'Tis amusing that you think I would trust you to restrain yourself."

"Do you say that after all we have been through together, you still distrust me, Isobel?"

"Aye." She found the strength to nod. "That is exactly what I am saying, MacGowan."

He remained silent for a moment, watching her as he slipped his thumb over her lips. "And if I give you me vow?"

"Your vow?" Her mouth quivered over the words.

"Not to take you." He leaned closer, and in a moment she felt his lips touch hers. She closed her eyes and let the feelings shiver through her. "No matter how you beg."

It was somehow difficult to open her eyes, but she managed it. "You are vain beyond words, Mac-Gowan," she said and he smiled.

"Am I, lass?"

"Aye."

"Then you can withstand the temptation?" he asked.

"There is no . . ." He kissed the corner of her mouth. Her hands shook, but she braced them against the rim of the tub. "Temptation. I have no desire to join the host of fools before me."

"A host is it, now?" he asked and kissed her throat.

"I've no way of knowing the exact number, for you refuse to tell me."

"Then let us make a wager," he said. "If you join me here and do not beg for me to take you, I will tell the number."

She laughed, but the sound was breathy. "Then either way you win, for if I beg you you will oblige, and if I do not you will coerce."

"I will not couple with you this day," he said, "no matter what the circumstances. This I vow."

Say no, her good sense insisted, and while her body thrummed the opposite response, a tiny, conniving part of her brain whispered, *Why not do it? Why not do it and test his mettle?* After all, if the rogue of the rogues could resist a woman naked in his arms, surely he could be trusted in other things. And she must learn the truth about his intentions, after all, before it was too late and tragedy struck where she could not bear to see it.

His fingers skimmed beneath her hair. Her eyes fell closed.

Say no! logic screamed.

Say yes, her body shrieked.

She remained as she was, torn in every direction as his fingers massaged her scalp.

His lips touched her. Heat stroked her, searing her to her fingertips.

Aye, that's it, murmured her conniving mind. *Test him. 'Tis for your sister's sake and not your own.*

You're a fool, wailed logic.

"Bel?" Gilmour whispered. "What say you?"

"Aye," Isobel breathed.

Her body sighed. *It's about bloody time.*

Chapter 16

She didn't know how her nightrail disappeared. It was simply gone, slipped over her head or under her feet, or perhaps disintegrating like mist in the sunlight, but whatever the case, she was naked. Absolutely and totally naked with her senses still sending up a wailing litany about nonsense and need and . . .

She was in the water before she realized it. It rose up her thighs, touched her navel and swelled like magic over her breasts. Candlelight shimmered off the water's dark surface.

"Isobel." He breathed her name like a prayer and touching a finger to her lips, traced a wet trail over her chin and downward. She shivered. "You are beautiful beyond words."

"Am I?" she asked. She tried to sound distant, for of course he told every woman that, and yet she found that she longed to believe.

"Let us make this pact," he said. "For this short span of time, we shall tell each other naught but truth."

She watched him.

"No lies shall pass me own lips, and none shall pass yours. Can you do that?" he asked.

"I am not the one who tends to lie."

His hand smoothed over her shoulder and down her arm, pulling her closer. "So you will have no trouble telling the truth?"

"Nay," she lied.

"Then tell me this, lass, do you find me unappealing?"

They were close now, close enough for her to feel the warmth of his body. Somehow, his legs, bent at the knee, cradled one of her own, and slowly, like the sweep of the sun, he pressed his hand down her spine. She arched toward him, and he kissed her throat.

"Isobel?"

"Unappealing?" She licked her lips and tried to hear the voice of her good sense. It was damnably faint, but she thought she could just discern its wail of dismay, as if it came from a thousand leagues away.

"Aye, lass," he said and kissed her shoulder. "When you look at me, do you feel a longing to touch me?"

"I am not the type to—" she began, but he pulled back slightly so that he could look into her face. Her words faltered. "You are a bonny man, MacGowan," she admitted. "That you know."

To her surprise, he didn't smile. And indeed, it seemed almost that in this sober mood, he was more beautiful than ever.

"I know that some like the look of me," he said. "But that is not what I asked."

His fingers trickled down the curve of her spine, then cupped and smoothed ever so slowly over her buttocks.

"I asked *your* feelings Bel. Have you a desire to touch me?"

Although she listened, she could not even hear a whisper of caution.

"Aye," she murmured. "I am not beyond the effects of your charm."

"Then why do you hold yourself back?" he asked and smoothed his hand along the underside of her thigh. His other hand had joined the assault and gently stroked her hair back from her face.

"Is it still truth you want?" she asked.

"Aye."

"I hold back because you would do me no good. A moment of pleasure mayhap. No more."

"A moment?" He kissed her where his fingers had swept her hair away from her ear, then the corner of her mouth. "Methinks I have given you more than that already."

She raised a hand, but whether it was to fend him off, or pull him near, she was unsure. "You know just what I mean."

His fingers found her chin, and tilting his head slightly, he kissed her lips with agonizing softness. "You mean that I would use your tender body and leave you for another." His lips were so close, she could feel the brush of his words against her mouth.

"Aye," she said, barely able to force out that single word. "That is exactly what I mean."

"And yet I wonder; if I had you once could I ever let you go?" he asked and trailed his fingers with languid tenderness between her breasts.

"You have no choice," she breathed.

"Because you would not have me or because you would not let me go?"

"I would not—" she began, but his kisses had slipped down her chest, and in that moment his tongue touched her nipple.

"MacGowan!" she hissed.

He lifted his head with slow reverence. "What were you about to say, Bel?"

With one hand, he now held her astride his thigh, so that her bottom was pressed tight to that powerful muscle. When he shifted, the muscle danced, and she closed her eyes and pushed unconsciously against it. Pleasure swept through her and she realized with mind numbing surprise that he had begun a rhythmic stroking from the small of her back to the curve of her bottom.

He kissed her mouth. His tongue touched her lips and she opened for him, hungry, nay, starving for his kiss. There was nothing between them, not the merest space. His chest felt hard against her breasts. Beneath her, his thigh shifted with power, and along the flat of her belly, his cock stretched up like a ancient symbol of fertility, pulsing with power.

It was that portion of him wherein lay the danger. She pressed shakily against his chest, managing only to push herself a few scant inches from him.

"MacGowan . . ." she was breathing foolishly hard.

"Aye lass?" he said and kneaded her bottom.

She closed her eyes and quivered against him. "You made a vow."

"And I've done naught to break it," he said and kneaded again.

She writhed against him, seeming unable to stop the crush of her body against his.

"Have I now, lass?" he asked and slipping his hand sideways, skimmed a finger up the crease of her buttocks.

She gritted her teeth and bucked against him, but he had ceased all motion.

"Have I?" he repeated.

She groggily opened her eyes, then let her gaze skim down his torso. Her fingers were spread across his chest, and his nipple, peaked and dark, poked from between them. She licked her lips, and lowering her head, lapped her tongue across the summit. He gasped a sharp breath through his teeth and she raised her head to watch him before licking him again.

His erection spasmed with life against the heat of her flesh, and though she meant to tease, she found that she too could not help but grit her teeth and fight for control. It came after a shuddering moment and then she slipped her hand down the undulating length of his belly. He sucked in his breath, and glancing down she could not help but notice that her knee was lodged firmly against the apex of his body, cradling his balls like precious jewels against her leg.

Mesmerized, she slipped her hand lower. He was holding his breath, she noticed, and yet that did not seem so fascinating compared to other things. Another inch and her fingers closed around him and tightened.

He groaned, and glancing up, she noticed that his head had fallen back against the towel. She couldn't help but kiss his throat, couldn't help but stroke her fist up his hard length, couldn't help but feel a spasm of her own tight need. She stroked again, then found his nipple with her teeth.

His body jerked against hers and suddenly he was

atop her, pressing her back against the heavy metal. Water splashed about them as she braced her weight back upon her hands. His cock, hard and broad, bumped with heated urgency against her swollen bottom, and she remained still, breathlessly awaiting the thrust. Planted beside her torso, his arms quivered.

"Lass," he whispered. "I think mayhap I have overtaxed meself."

"Wh-what?" she panted.

For one quavering instant, she felt him thrust forward, but then he pulled back and lurched to his feet.

Water dripped from him, running in rivulets down his belly to fall like raindrops between his thighs. She watched their progress, then leaned impulsively forward.

He stumbled backward, nearly falling out of the tub.

Reality streamed abruptly into Isobel's brain. Snatching up a nearby towel, she pulled it to her chest and rose on shaky legs.

Retreating from the tub was ridiculously difficult, but she managed somehow and turned away with frantic haste, blindly searching for her nightgown, or possibly a hole in which to hide.

"Isobel." His voice traveled up her spine, quivering at the back of her neck. "I am sorry."

"Sorry?" She turned as one in a trance, still holding the towel before her, draped ineffectually between her breasts.

"I am recovered now."

"Recovered?" She was mimicking his words like a festival parrot, and yet she could do naught else, for when her gaze fell lower she could see every inch of his manhood. It stood like an impatient soldier against the hard packed muscle of his belly and throbbed as if in agony.

" 'Twas not me intent to be rude. But if I am to keep me vow . . ." He shrugged, making the muscles of his perfect body dance. Firelight flickered off every damp inch.

Isobel swallowed.

"Mayhap you should find your bed."

She raised her gaze to his face. "What?"

"I am usually quite controlled."

She nodded in mute agreement.

"Me apologies," he said and stepped forward.

She stumbled back as if just awakened. " 'Tis quite . . ." She had no idea what she was saying. " 'Tis quite all right."

"Here." Turning slightly, he bent. Firelight gleamed off the bunched muscle of his buttocks and between his thighs. His testicles bulged into view. "Isobel . . ."

She realized a bit belatedly that he was speaking and pulled her gaze to his face with hard won discipline.

His voice was hoarse. "Your gown."

She reached for it. Truly she did, but when their fingers touched, her body moved in and she kissed him.

Feelings sizzled like lightning across her lips, and suddenly she was pressed up against him, needy and wet. He kissed her back. There was no longer tenderness, but passion, fierce and wild, and suddenly she was on the bed, pinned beneath his weight.

She knew she should struggle. Should scream, for if she did, rescuers would come. But . . . damn the rescuers! His kisses left her lips, blazing a hot trail down her throat and stopping at her breast. She held her

breath as he cupped it in his hand, and then he took her
nipple in his mouth and suckled.

She did scream then, but softly as if she were dying.
His penis nudged between her thighs, slipping against
her wetness. Her moan echoed his, but in that moment
she felt his muscles harden with control. His hands
slipped to her waist and then he turned, rolling beneath
her until she was planted atop him, straddling his
thigh.

She groaned and contracted against his strength. He
bent his leg, aiding in her cause, and she bucked
against it as his mouth found her nipple again.

Feelings sizzled through her. Heat consumed her,
and her head dropped back as she pressed again and
again against him. There was nothing else in the universe now except the feeling, the crescendo of sensations that wracked her body until the world exploded
in a blaze of colors and she fell limp and sated atop
him.

She was sweating, breathing hard, lifeless, with her
hand lying against the firm skin of his chest.

Sated, she was sated, she reminded herself, but the
sight of his nipple drew her hand and she slipped her
fingers over it.

Gilmour jerked beneath her as he caught her wrist.

Blinking, she pulled her gaze to his.

"Lass." His voice was low, almost threatening. "I
have fulfilled me own part of the bargain. I would not
press on if I were you."

But he was beautiful, so bonny of face and form that
she could not help but smile. "It seems to me I have already pressed on, MacGowan," she said and turning
her face just so, kissed his opposite nipple.

He clenched his teeth and squeezed his eyes closed. Every lovely muscle hardened like granite beneath her, and between her legs she felt that now familiar ache. Shifting slightly, she felt the brush of his balls against her thigh.

"What are you about, lass?" His words were little more than a growl, and she raised her gaze to his once again.

"Whatever do you mean?"

Gone was his ever present smile. Indeed, his expression looked as hard as his lovely body.

"I mean, what is your intent?"

" 'Tis naught," she said and slipping her hand from bondage, skimmed it onto his chest again. " 'Twas it not you who said one can enjoy without consuming?" His was a phenomenally lovely chest. She trailed a finger across it, then lower, over the hillocks of his belly and onto his pulsing penis.

He sucked air between his teeth, and her wrist was caught again.

"What is it you want?" he growled.

She smiled into his strained expression. "What do *you* want?"

His muscles relaxed the merest degree. "I never thought you to have such a short memory."

"How so?" His lips were very full, his lashes ungodly long.

He growled, "Do you forget that you promised the truth?"

"Oh." In fact, she had forgotten most everything. "Nay, I remember," she said and tried to wriggle her wrist free.

"Then tell me truly, Bel, did I not satisfy you?"

Satisfy? She skimmed her gaze down his chest and lower. Between her legs she felt wet and warm and heavy and sated, but still, he was naked and . . .

"Bel!" He wrenched her attention back to his lips. Such nice lips. "Did you enjoy it or nay?"

"Aye." She said the word like a sigh.

"Then why . . ."

"Is it so unheard of to want to feel it again, Mac-Gowan?" she whispered.

"This quickly? Aye. 'Tis unheard of."

She raised herself on an elbow, relinquishing control of her wrist, which he still held in a steely clasp. "I do not believe you," she said. "Surely in all your experience you have found a woman who wants it more than once a night," she said and brushed her thigh, light as moon shadows over his crotch.

He dropped her wrist, but before she could take advantage of the situation, he had grabbed her about the waist and swung her to her feet. He was beside her in a moment and prodding her away from the bed, but she refused to budge, so he bent, and, throwing an arm behind her knees, he lifted her into his arms and bore her toward the door. Somehow he managed to wrench it open without dropping her, and suddenly she was in the hallway . . . stark naked.

Her jaw dropped. "I cannot go without me—"

Her nightrail appeared from nowhere and was snapped over her head, binding her arms by her sides.

His teeth were clenched, his body framed to perfection in the opening of the door as he spoke. "Fair warning. Next time you touch me, there will be no vows," he said and closed the door on her bemused expression.

Chapter 17

I sobel pivoted numbly toward her bedchamber.

"M' enfant."

Bel jumped, then turned, shoving her arms hastily through her sleeves as she did so. "Lady Madelaine."

"Belva, dear. Polly said I might find you here."

Her lips moved. Heat brushed her face as memories smote her. What the devil had gotten into her? Not MacGowan that was certain, no matter how big a fool she had made of herself. But then, it was certainly her duty to learn if his word could be trusted. 'Twas surely the only reason she had acted so—

"Belva?" Madelaine said.

"Oh! Aye. I thought I might . . . look in on Mac-Gowan."

"Ahhh. And how does he look this eve?"

"Fine."

Madelaine laughed. "I thought he might," she said, and slipping her arm beneath Isobel's, steered her down the hall. "And did you bed him?"

"What?" She reared back as if struck. "Nay, of course not."

They turned in tandem into a small sitting room.

"Mayhap I should make myself more clear," Madelaine said and dropping Isobel's arm, crossed the room to pour two draughts of wine from a round bottomed bottle. "I meant, did you make love to him."

Again Isobel's lips moved while her mind tried valiantly to race along behind. "N . . . nay." Technically, that may well be true. She had no way of knowing and no wish to find out.

Madelaine took a sip of her wine. "May I ask why?"

"Me lady." Was she panting? "You have been naught but good to me . . . those months I was in your household as well as now, and I have nothing but the highest respect for you, but I am not the sort to . . ." Hot memories bombarded her, heating her face. "That is to say—"

"Do you mean to tell me that you are still a virgin, Belva?"

Isobel winced. "Mayhap."

Madelaine laughed and urged the other to drink. "Whatever for?"

The wine soothed Isobel a bit. She exhaled gently and took another sip. "Surely I am not the first virgin you have met, me lady."

"Nay, if memory serves, even I was a virgin once upon a time. But the truth is, Belva, you are no babe any longer. Neither are you a great lady who is much in demand on the marriage mart. Indeed, besides your skills in the kitchen, which are admittedly vast, you have little to show for your life. So why deprive yourself of the pleasure a companion could give you?"

"Do you not believe fornication to be a sin?" *Please say no.*

Lady Madelaine shrugged. "Is your God the type to create something pleasurable only to punish you for enjoying it?"

Isobel might have answered if she'd been able to think, but her experience with MacGowan seemed to have driven any semblance of sense straight out of her head.

"I have known many folk who enjoy each other well but never marry. Then there are those who are wed at home, or in fields or even, and I can attest to this . . ." Madelaine said, slanting an uneven glance at Isobel. "Some are wed in the marriage bed itself. Some are virginal, some are not so, and some wait until well after the birth of their first *enfant* before their vows are spoken. Others barely meet before they are marched before their partners and wed while scores of grand folk look on. They are bound together in great cathedrals with bejeweled guests and fine wine.

"And yet it seems that the latter group is no more content than the first. Neither are they more blessed, for many who share a bed outside the bonds of wedlock truly cherish each other, while those bound before God and man spend their days detesting their spouses. Which couple, do you think, is the Lord more pleased with, the ones with vows truly spoken who despise one another, or the ones who did not exchange the vows yet honor each other in word and deed?"

Isobel blinked rather foolishly and wondered if there might be a better time to debate deep moral issues. "I do not know."

Perhaps she sounded as befuddled as she felt, for Madelaine smiled. "And yet you wait," she said. "I but wonder why."

"Mayhap I wait for the right man."

"The wrong ones are oft more tempting, *chère*, on that you can take my word."

"I am not tempted."

Madelaine took a sip of her wine. "Not even by the rogue?"

Isobel's face felt hot, but she forced herself to meet the other's eyes. "N—" she began, but the lie was a bit too large, for in the midst of the word, she felt her hands shake. "Mayhap a wee bit."

"Aye." Madelaine laughed again. "Mayhap. And yet you did not partake of what he could offer." The seconds ticked by. "Might it be, Belva, that you are afraid?"

"Begging your pardon, me lady," she said, "but living with you has given me the idea that there is no great pain involved with the act of joining."

"I did not mean that you are afraid of that which is physical, Belva. You were an orphan from birth, were you not?"

"Aye, but I fail to see what that has to do with the matter."

"So you are not afraid of finding love only to lose it?"

"Nay. Of course not. Whatever would make you think so?"

"And you are not afraid of the physical aspects of a couple uniting."

"Nay."

"And we have already discussed God's part in this, thus . . . There is no reason for you to deny yourself the pleasure any longer." She paced toward the door and opened it, as if everything had been decided.

Isobel followed her stiffly, her heart wild in her chest. "Have I not told you, MacGowan holds little temptation for me?"

Madelaine stared at her a second, then laughed. "Silly girl, I am not about to toss you into the bed of one you do not desire. Nay," Madelaine added, curling her arm about Isobel's back. "But I have others who will surely meet your standards."

"What?" Isobel reared back, but Madelaine prodded her forward.

"Come along, sweeting, 'tis late and you are surely tired. Go to your chamber and I will send by a couple of likely lads."

"I have no wish for a couple of likely lads."

"Then choose only one if you are so inclined. Although, as I've oft said, two are as good as one, only better."

"Me lady—"

"There now, no balking. 'Tis my gift to you for the trouble you have seen. You are so tense. 'Twill help you relax. And you needn't worry about the problem of an unwanted babe; my lads will take care of that too."

"But—"

"Meanwhile . . ." They were almost to Bel's chamber. "You do not mind if I pay your MacGowan a visit do you?"

Isobel's mind spun like a whirling dervish as she stumbled to a halt again. "What?"

"MacGowan," Madelaine repeated. "I know you do not find him particularly appealing, but I rather like the look of him. You have no objections do you, *chère?*"

Isobel was never sure if she nodded or shook her

head or squealed like a pig, but Madelaine leaned forward and kissed her cheek.

"Not to worry, *m' enfant*, I'll be gentle with him, and you'll be the same with my lads, *oui?*"

In a moment she was gone. The door closed. Isobel's mind whirled. What, she wondered, had just happened?

Someone rapped on Gilmour's door. He stopped his pacing and found to his chagrin that he had ceased to breathe again. But who could blame him? It may be Isobel, returned to relieve him of this terrible ache she had begun. He turned rapidly toward the door, but a question held him in place. Would he still be held to his vow to restrain himself or would this be considered an entirely different meeting? He couldn't afford to be found lacking where his vow of abstinence was concerned, for he feared Isobel may consider the entire ordeal some kind of horrid test.

He scowled at the portal, his stomach pitching and his loins pulled tight and high like a stallion kept too long alone.

"Who comes?" he asked, doing his best to keep his tone controlled.

" 'Tis me, Lady Madelaine," came the answer.

Something sank in Gilmour's belly. "How can I help you, me lady?"

"You could invite me in."

He was in no mood for companionship. Nevertheless, he could hardly refuse the lady in her own home. He glanced about, searching in vain for his plaid. "I fear I am not prepared for compan—" he began, but the door opened before he had finished the sentence.

Madelaine stepped inside, her gaze sliding down his naked body to his erection. Slowly, she closed the door behind her. "On the contrary," she said, "it looks to me as if you are quite ready for company."

Instinct told him to snatch up a blanket and dart behind the bed.

Gilmour MacGowan was not a man strong on cowardly instincts.

"Me lady," he said, folding his arms across his chest to keep them from a sad attempt to cover his nether parts, which had a life of their own. "How is it that you keep seeing me in the altogether?"

"Some might think it blind luck." She canted her head at him and took a step away from the door. "I would have to dissuade you from such nonsense."

He said nothing. What was there to say?

"I heard you and Belva did not couple."

His stomach churned as he swore in silence. But he raised one brow and kept his expression carefully impassive. "Mayhap this is not something to be discussed between the two of us."

"I but came to extend my condolences," she said and approached him.

"Regardless what you may think, me lady, I do not bed every woman I meet."

" 'Scores' wasn't it?" she asked and began walking around him. "And scores"—she smiled—"is a fairly large sum."

He turned in tandem. His father had taught him at a tender age not to turn his back to an adversary. "That depends on what one is referring to."

"I believe your sexual partners are the discussion at

hand," she said and continued to circle him. He, too moved. "Why do you keep turning?"

"This is me best side."

She laughed and came to a halt. "Is it now?"

"May I ask why you have come, me lady?"

Her chuckle was low and seductive. "I have had a few partners myself, Laird MacGowan."

"You are a handsome woman, me lady," he said. "You are most probably drowned in offers."

She smiled, but watched him carefully. "Mayhap you have met my lads?"

"Helpful fellows?" Mour guessed. "Goodly sized?"

"Aye. Very goodly sized and well proportioned, if you take my meaning. Might you guess their purpose here?"

"Your personal secretaries?"

The smile lifted slightly. "The fair haired lad is called Cheval. Do you speak *français*, MacGowan?"

"Are you trying to tell me that he's not called horse because of his skill with steeds?"

She laughed out loud. "I have long admired the equine species," she said and began to circle again. He gave up and retrieved his plaid from the floor. "Horses, after all, have such impressive . . ."

"Intelligence?"

"Girth," she corrected and lifted her gaze to his as he sloppily wrapped the woolen about his waist. "I wouldn't have suspected you for a modest man, Gilmour of the MacGowan."

"No one is more surprised than I," he said and she laughed again.

"Am I too bold for you?"

"I've not crawled under the bed yet."

"Nay, but you *have* just hidden away what are, apparently, your best assets."

"Would I be a fool to ask again why you have come, Lady Madelaìne?"

"You might well be shocked."

"A bit late for that, methinks."

"Then I'll tell you the truth. I've come to ask if you would like to make love to me."

Regardless of his reputation, he had never heard a sentence phrased quite like that. "What's that?"

"I can assure you I have learned a few things through the years."

"I do not doubt your skill," he said. "I but wonder why you offer since you have the horse man at your beck and call."

She shrugged and placed a hand on his arm. "As much as I admire his size, his technique is somewhat lacking. And from what I've heard of you . . ." She paused.

"In truth, me lady, it may be that me reputation exceeds me expertise."

"I suspected as much," she said and ran her hand down his arm and over his bent elbow, "until I saw Belva's expression."

Her hand slowed as she skimmed her fingers along one rib.

He held his breath. "Expression?"

"Aye. I've not seen anything quite like it. Euphoric," she said and dropped her finger to the next rib. "And yet still hungry."

She bumped over the last rib and traced a line between a pair of muscles stiffened with stress.

"Perhaps she should eat more," Gilmour said. "She is such a wee, small—"

"Why did you not make love to her?"

He drew a deep breath. "She refused me."

Her smile suggested that perhaps she knew a bit more about the situation than he did. It was disconcerting to say the least.

"Refused you?"

"Aye. 'Tis not unheard of, you know."

"Ahhh, then you must be frustrated indeed." Her fingers skimmed lower, along the edge of the plaid, and in that moment she raised on her toes so that her mouth was very close to his. "I could relieve that frustration."

"I've no doubt you could, me lady." And yet, in a manner that defied all logic, he did not want her to.

"Have we an agreement then, Scotsman?" she whispered.

"Me apologies." He said the words carefully. "I fear I cannot."

"I'm quite sure you can," she said and tickled her fingers across the rolling muscle of his abdomen.

He held his breath. "Mayhap I misspoke."

"Are you refusing me, MacGowan?" she asked.

" 'Tis not because you are unappealing, me lady."

"Then why, if I may be so bold?" she asked and continuing her trek, skimmed her fingers around his side.

He gritted his teeth. "The maid Isobel . . . interests me."

She lifted one brow. "The pope interests me," she said. "Thus far it has not prevented me from having my pleasure with others."

Her hand was already straying downward, and he caught her wrist just before it reached its destination. They stood inches apart, facing each other.

She smiled. "So you long for Belva?"

"Long? Nay. She is bonny. That is all."

"But she would be only one of the scores before her."

"As you said, that would be a goodly sum."

She watched him carefully as though reaching into his mind.

"Dozens, then?" she asked.

" 'Twould be unseemly for me to put a number to them."

"So you have not kept count?"

"Nay."

"Many do."

"I am not like many," he said.

"Aye," she agreed and tugged her wrist from his grip. "I almost begin to believe that, so I think I will share a secret with you if you would return a favor."

"What secret is that?"

" 'Tis something I believe you would like to know," she said.

"Indeed? And what is that?"

" 'Tis something about your Belva."

He should, of course, tell her that the girl was certainly not "his." "In exchange for what?" he asked.

She laughed. "There's no need to look so concerned, MacGowan. I am not about to bind you hand and foot and force myself on you . . . though the idea has merit."

"I doubt you'd ever have to use force, me lady," he said and she smiled.

"There is little question why you are desired. Still, I am curious," she said, "How many women *have* you had?"

"Never in me life has that been so oft discussed."

"So Belva asked you, too. And what was your answer?"

"I will tell you true if you share your secret with me first."

"Very well," she said and smiled. "At this very moment Belva is being visited by my lads."

"What!" His gut coiled, hard and cold.

"Not to worry. She will enjoy the experience. Indeed, this may yet prove be to your bene—"

"Where is she?"

Her brows rose toward her hairline. "Surely you do not resent the girl having some pleasure, MacGowan. After all, you've no abiding interest in—"

His hand shot out of its own volition, once again wrapping tight and hard around Madelaine's wrist. "Where is she?"

She raised her chin slightly. "You've no right to stop her. Not with your own vast experience behind you. Although I admit, the lads get a bit eager at times."

"I warn you, me lady, if they harm her in any way they will be of little use to you henceforth."

"Truly?" She look intrigued at most.

"Where are they?"

"First you must fulfill your part of our bargain."

"Less than scores," he said and she laughed.

"You will find her on the upper floor, at the end of the hall."

He turned away without a second's hesitation, but

she called him back and he turned, impatience thumping in his gut.

"Do not worry, lad. Your secret is safe with me."

"What secret is that?" he asked, and she grinned.

" 'Tis a secret."

Chapter 18

Isobel stood perfectly still in the doorway of her bedchamber, lest any movement be misconstrued for acceptance. "Me apologies," she said and turned her gaze from the big Irishman to the one called Cheval, "but I fear Lady Madelaine was mistaken. I have no wish for company this eventide."

"My lady said you might be shy," said Boots. "But once you see the size of me tools you'll not be so retiring."

He was big, huge, really, outweighing her by a good five stone, and every ounce seemed to be packed in tight muscle bound through his thighs and torso. Chances were good that he'd be able to beat her both in a foot race and in a battle of strength.

"I assure you," she said. "I am not shy. I simply have no need of company just now."

"You heard her, O'Banyon," said Cheval. "Good night to you, then. And I assure you, my lady, you've made the right choice, for if the truth be told, his tool is more the size of a hand trowel than a plow shear. If you take me meaning." She turned her attention to him. He was just slightly smaller than his companion, but where the booted fellow was dark, the horse was fair-haired and grinning.

"Believe this," she said and tried to push the door shut, "I've no interest whatsoever in the size of either. Now if you would be so kind as to—"

"Three hands," Cheval said and with seemingly no effort atall, pressed into the room.

She scowled at him. "What's that?"

"Me own tool," he said. "I measure it in hands like the height of a steed. 'Tis three hands if it's an inch."

"Then it's not an inch," said Boots and pushed in beside him. "Aren't you the wee bonny flower? And randy too, by what me lady says."

"Get out of me room or you shall surely regret it."

Boots grinned. "Lady Madelaine said you was lonely," he said and stepped toward her.

Isobel turned and snatched a lighted candle from a nearby candelabra. She held it waist high, where it would do the most damage. The flame flickered and wax dripped to the woolen tapestry beneath her feet, but she held it steady. "Did she also say you'd have to forfeit your beloved *tools*?" she asked.

"Nay." Boots scowled. "In truth, I do not think she would be pleased if she could not enjoy me—" he began, but suddenly he lunged, and though he was the size of a largish bullock, he could move with surprising speed. One instant the candle was in her hand, the next it was snuffed out beneath their feet and she was pressed up against him like grapes in a vat.

"Do you feel that, lassie?" he asked and smiled as he pressed his hips against hers. "I'm rearing for you already, but I can take me time if that be your preference."

"Let me go." She said the words carefully, but if the truth be known, panic was welling up like dark water around her.

"Now, lass, there be no need to fret. I only—"

"Boots, isn't it?" asked a voice.

"MacGowan!" Isobel turned her gaze frantically toward the door, and he was there, dressed in naught but an adequate plaid and looking disturbingly unconcerned.

"So laddie," said Boots, his tone congenial. "Finished with Polly already are you? 'Tis not surprising, I suppose. She's a quick one is our Polly. But soon enough beggin' for more."

"Aye, she was asking for you already," MacGowan said. "Were I you I'd go to her post haste."

"Aye, she's taken a likin' to me, she has. But I'm a wee bit busy just now. Cheval, why not go see to her?"

" 'Tis you she's wanting, O'Banyon. I'll take care of your duties here."

"Nay, I'll—"

"She wants the two of you," MacGowan interrupted. "Something about a friendly goat and a couple bottles of wine."

"You jest," said Cheval after a moment and laughed.

"What kind of goat?" asked Boots.

"A bonny one. What do you say?" asked Gilmour. "Isobel's not interested."

"You're sorely mistaken, MacGowan. And too, I work for the lady of the house, and she asked me to come."

"She made a mistake."

"The lady is never mistook," said Boots, his brows lowering.

MacGowan watched him for a moment, then smiled, but the expression was strangely grim. "Care to know what I've heard said of your Lady Madelaine of Delshutt?"

O'Banyon's dark brows lowered even more. Cheval was already turning toward him, hands formed to fists.

"You've something to say about the baroness?"

"Aye," Mour said. "Come into the hall and I'll share the news."

"You'll not want me out there if you've naught good to say of the lady."

MacGowan grinned. "You'd best come too, Irishman, unless you believe the rumors I've heard spread."

"Aye," O'Banyon agreed. "But it can wait. I've got me duties here first."

"Do you hear that?" Gilmour asked, turning to Cheval. "It seems your Irish friend has little desire to defend your lady's honor."

"Aye, and he'll pay his due," said the horse and stepped into the hall after MacGowan. "But I'll see to you—"

The words came to an abrupt halt. There was a brief moment of silence, and then the sound of something solid striking the floor.

MacGowan appeared in a second. His smile was gone and a bright light sparked in his azure eyes. "I am a peaceable fellow, Irishman," he said, "but if you don't loose the lass, you'll regret it for as long as you can recall—which, judging by your intellect, may not last till the morn."

Boots smiled as he stroked his knuckles down Isobel's cheek. "Spoilin' for a fight already, MacGowan?"

"Not atall," he said and turned his hands palms up. "I've no wish for trouble."

"Truly?" O'Banyon said and slipped one huge hand down Isobel's shoulder.

"Truly," Gilmour agreed affably. "But if you don't take your hands off her I'll have your liver for me breakfast."

O'Banyon laughed. "You think you can take me, lad?"

"I think the lass could take an Irishman. I am simply here to save her the trouble."

"So it's the Irish you don't like, is it?"

"Aye, that and moldy gruel and—"

O'Banyon launched toward Gilmour. Isobel screamed an instant before they made contact.

Boots struck his adversary just below the ribs. MacGowan flew backward and slammed against the wall behind him. There was an audible grunt of pain before he sagged against the plaster, but when Boots tried to scoop him into his arms, he came to life like a corpse from the grave, thumping his feet against the wall and driving Boots wildly backward. They landed in a pile with MacGowan on top.

O'Banyon pulled a knife from the high tops of his boots. Gilmour rolled to his feet. The Irishman rose more slowly, but lunged immediately.

Isobel screamed again, but it was Lady Madelaine's voice that seemed to reverberate in the room.

"What goes on here?" she asked in a dark voice, and O'Banyon skidded to a hand, skimming his gaze from MacGowan to his lady and back.

Breathing hard, he wiped his knuckles against his nose. Blood smeared from his fingers to his wrist. "I was just doing me job, me lady."

"I do not recall telling you to kill the Scotsman."

"Aye, but you told me to see to the lassie's needs."

"And you thought she needed MacGowan dead?"

O'Banyon shifted his gaze and shuffled his feet. They were, Gilmour realized, the size of Highland sheep. "Mayhap I got me blood up and forgot—"

"Well, get your blood back down," Madelaine ordered, "and go to your chambers."

"He insulted—" Boots began, but the baroness interrupted him.

"To your chambers," she repeated.

O'Banyon bobbed his agreement and shuffled sheepishly toward the door. "Me apologies, me lady."

"Aye well, on second thought," Madelaine said and sighed, "hie yourself to my solar . . . and take Cheval with you."

Boots chanced a grin, then ducked his head and hurried from the room. In a moment they heard him grunt as he hoisted his friend to his feet. Cheval's voice sounded groggily disoriented as they made their staggering way down the hall.

Isobel's bed chamber fell silent.

"Well," said Madelaine finally. "Are the two of you always so amusing?"

"I would appreciate it if you would keep your playthings to yourself henceforth, me lady," MacGowan said and snatched his plaid back to his waist before it abandoned him completely.

"But Polly would be ever so disappointed if I did not share," Madelaine said, spearing MacGowan with an arch gaze. "And what of you, *chère?* Did you find my *playthings* diverting?"

Mind spinning, Isobel pulled her gaze from Mac-Gowan's face to Lady Madelaine's. "They are certainly . . . large."

Madelaine smiled. "Aye, that they are and quite tractable normally. I can send them back to you when they're a bit more . . . patient if you like."

"Me thanks," Isobel said shakily, "but I think not."

The lady raised a brow and shifted her gaze to Gilmour. "And what of you, MacGowan? Shall I send Polly to see to your wounds?"

"Nay."

"You are right, of course. 'Tis Belva's place to see to you since you were her so gallant champ—"

"I'll be fine," Gilmour said and stepped toward the door, but Madelaine blocked his way.

"You're bleeding," she said and nodded to his arm.

" 'Tis naught. I'll see to it meself."

"My carpets have no fondness for blood. Sit down."

"Nay, I—"

"Such a difficult one you've found for yourself, Belva," Madelaine said. "Sit down, MacGowan, or I'll change my mind about tethering you hand and foot."

He bristled. "Truth to tell, I do not think your lads are up to the task, me lady."

"I was thinking of my maid servants," she said. "They would enjoy it more and mayhap you would enjoy watching, Belva. What say you?"

Somehow all the oxygen seemed to have been sucked out of the room. "I'll . . ." Isobel's voice was breathy. "I'll see to him meself."

Madelaine looked at her as if surprised, then smiled.

"Very well then," she said and turned with regal coolness toward the door. "But don't be too noisy about it will you? We don't want the girls to get jealous."

She closed the door with a smile. The room fell silent.

Isobel cleared her throat. Gilmour turned toward her, and despite everything, he felt his desire tighten restlessly beneath his haphazard plaid.

Isobel kept her gaze resolutely on Gilmour's face.

Bugger it!

"Me wounds be fine," he said.

She nodded. "Nevertheless, you'd best stay for a spell, lest she . . ." She cleared her throat again. "Lady Madelaine has her own way of doing things."

"So I noticed," he said, and scowled at the door. He was not a temperamental sort, neither did he rise easily to anger, but he felt that emotion now, swelling strong in his veins.

"So she . . ." Isobel wrung her hands and took a few faltering steps across the floor. "Did you speak to her?"

"Aye."

"In your chamber?"

Her tone sounded strange. He turned toward her. "What's that?"

"I was just curious whether she came to your chamber."

"Why do you ask, Bel?"

"No reason. She just said she might."

"Why would she do that?"

"I have no idea."

"Truly?" he said. "Might you think she finds me appealing?"

"I would not know."

"But you're a woman. You must have some idea what she's thinking," he said and took a step toward her. "Indeed—"

"Halt!" Her voice was shrill, close to panic.

He stopped where he stood.

"Listen, MacGowan, I've taken about all I care to take, what with Madelaine and Polly and those two giant clods. I am sick to death of playing games, so if you wish for the truth, here it be. You are handsome and you are charming and when I am with you I want nothing more than to rip the clothes from your . . ." Her gaze fell down his body, reminding him with some clarity that he wore very little. "You are bonny," she said, soothing her tone. "Polly seems to think so. As does Madelaine. Mayhap even Cheval covets you. Whatever the case, I'll not stand in your way." She seemed breathless and agitated.

Gilmour grinned. " 'Tis actually O'Banyon I have me eye on."

"What?" The air seemed to leave her lungs in a whoosh of sound.

He laughed, then sobered and approached her slowly. "You think me bonny, Isobel?" he asked and reached for her hand.

She let him take it, though she closed her eyes at the first touch of flesh against flesh. "My, but you're a needy one, MacGowan."

"You've no idea," he said and leaning down, brushed his lips against hers. She trembled beneath him and he straightened. "Good night, Bel," he said and turned away, but she held his hand.

"You cannot go."

His breath caught hopefully in his throat. "Why's that?"

She didn't meet his eyes. "You need rest."

"I go to seek me bed even now."

"There will be someone in it."

"What?"

"Either Polly or Dena or . . ." Her voice dropped off. She cleared her throat. "If you've a mind for their company, I've no wish to keep you from them."

"Don't you?" he asked and shifted toward her.

She almost winced. "I am tired, MacGowan. Too tired for sparring."

" 'Tis not sparring I had on me mind."

"I see that," she said, then dragged her gaze away from his plaid.

He laughed. "What would you have me do, Bel? Return to me chambers and fend off all comers so you can sleep soundly in your virginal bed?"

She stiffened. "Do whatever you like."

He raised his brows and moved closer. "Truly?"

"I meant—"

"I know what you meant," he said. "You meant that though you are not willing to give yourself to me, you'd like to know that I am forever longing for you. Is it not so?"

She said nothing.

He smoothed his fingertips across her cheek. "For one who confesses to be lowly reared, you have a good deal of arrogance, Bel."

"I think it may have been bred into me."

He laughed softly, relaxing a smidgen. "However did you come to this household?"

"It seemed a safer place than that which I left behind."

"Safer?"

"I was two and ten," she said. "And I did not care for the smell of the man I was to be given to."

"Nay!" His hand tightened in her hair.

"Aye," she said.

"I am sorry."

She caught his gaze with her own. "Have you ever taken a lass of twelve, MacGowan?"

He gritted his teeth and for a moment she thought he would not answer. "Nay."

"Have you ever taken a woman against her will?"

"What do you think?"

"I think a woman has little will where you are concerned," she said and sighed when he brushed his knuckles down her neck. " 'Tis a truth you have used to your advantage."

"Why did you not take the lads up on their offer?"

"I did not want to."

"I heard something about three hands length. 'Tis quite impressive—if one has to prove his worth by size."

"How long were you listening?"

He kept his fingers from forming to fists. "Long enough to wish to kill them."

She glanced up, surprise in her eyes. "Why?"

"Will they be back?"

She was silent for several seconds. "Mayhap."

"This night?"

She shrugged. Firelight gleamed in her eyes and danced across her ivory throat. Against his chest, he could feel her bosom rise and fall, and beneath his fingers, her skin felt as soft as heaven.

"I will sleep on the floor," he said.

"You're wounded," she protested.

"Are you suggesting we share a bed?"

She licked her lips. " 'Twould make Lady Madelaine ecstatic."

"And you?"

"I can always scream for help should the need arise."

"The need arose long ago," he said dryly and scowled as he turned toward the bed. "But I would not scream if I were you—for in this house they surely would only gather to watch."

Chapter 19

Dreams, warm and heady, soothed Isobel, and she luxuriated in them. Here, in the haven of her imaginings, she felt safe and whole. 'Twas a place she had oft visited, a place where she was loved and cherished, protected and revered. A place that she dare not speak of aloud. But she would enjoy it while she could. So she smiled in her sleep and hugged her pillow closer. It was warm and firm and rippled with . . .

She opened her eyes with a start.

Gilmour MacGowan stared over his shoulder at her. "Shall I scream for help?" he asked.

She realized that her arm was hooked low around his hard waist, and one knee was pressed up between his thighs.

The door burst open. Isobel snatched herself to the far side of the bed, and Polly, smiling from ear to ear, popped into the room, brandishing a tray.

"Good morningtide. Don't the two of you look cozy. Didn't even have time to remove your gown, aye? Well, that's the way of it. Leastways, you got the rogue naked, aye?" She chuckled and scurried forward. "That's it. Sit up now. 'Tis time to break the fast. Although it looks as if the fast has been broke good and proper, huh?" She giggled and plopped herself down on the bed beside Gilmour. "Ummm," she said, and reaching out, stroked Gilmour's bare chest.

Isobel curled her lip and reached for Polly's hair, but in that instant lucidness visited her. Yanking her hand back, she sprang to her feet.

Polly started wildly. "Is something amiss, Isabella?"

"Nay. Nay," she said and spinning about on one heel, fled the room. The floor felt cool against her bare feet as she rushed on, hurrying down the hall until she reached Madelaine's door. Although it seemed against the house rules, she rapped twice.

"Enter."

Madelaine sat upright in her broad four poster, her green eyes still sleepy and her dark hair tousled.

"I have to leave." The words left Isobel's lips before she had a moment to calm them.

"Belva," Madelaine said. "Up so soon? I thought surely you would sleep late." She smiled and smoothed the blankets over her bent knees. "Or stay abed late at the least."

"Nay. I must away."

"Sit and . . ." Madelaine gave a small sigh, then smiled. "Have a seat and let us talk about it."

"Nay, I . . ." Isobel began, but in that instant the blankets moved while Madelaine remained still. A moment later a booted foot appeared from beneath the blankets. It was extremely large. She took a deep breath. "I must go now." The blankets rustled. "Immediately."

Madelaine sighed and shifted her gaze to the blankets, which she lifted slightly. "Very nice," she said, "but I fear our Belva needs my attention more than you do just now."

O'Banyon's head emerged from beneath the covers, massive as a bullock. "She could join us if she's a mind."

"Aye," Madelaine agreed. "But I think the lass had more than enough in her bed last night. Go break the fast, lad," she said. "I'll join you shortly."

He rose from the bed, completely naked but for his boots, which rose nearly to his knees. Isobel kept her gaze resolutely on Madelaine, who patted the man's bulging behind. Nor did she miss what bulged on his opposite side.

The door opened and closed.

"What's this about leaving now?" Madelaine asked.

"I must," Isobel repeated.

"Was the rogue so frightening, then?"

"This has nothing to do with MacGowan."

"Truly?"

"Aye, 'tis simply . . ." The blankets stirred again. Isobel stared at the shifting blankets and Madelaine shrugged.

"I get lonely. Now, why must you leave?"

Isobel rushed her gaze to Madelaine's sleepy eyes. "I must return to Evermyst."

"Whyever for?"

"I feel I am needed there. I fear for Lady Anora's safety."

"Why?"

"I had . . . dreams."

Madelaine idly moved the blankets aside to stroke her hand down a broad, male shoulder.

Isobel cleared her throat. "Dreams of Lady Anora in trouble."

"Truly? 'Tis not the sort of dream I expected to visit you after last night."

"We became very close while I stayed at Evermyst."

"He is a bonny lad, and quite taken with you if—"

"I refer to Lady Anora and I."

"Oh."

"And I need to leave alone, me lady."

Madelaine's surprise was evident. "May I ask why?"

Because she could not be near the rogue another second without giving herself to the wild impulses that tore at her. But that was not a worthy reason, and none she cared to share. "In truth, me lady, I am not atall certain of the rogue's intent. He . . ." She searched madly for some kind of reasoning that would make sense. "When first he came to the Red Lion, he accompanied the Munro."

"Aye, so you have said. Innes Munro, Laird of the Munros. How large is he, exactly?"

"He is a barbarian."

Madelaine raised her brows. "Even better."

"More than once he threatened me sis . . . me lady's peace. Why now would a MacGowan befriend him unless he plans some evil against his brother?"

"I know not," admitted Madelaine and lifted her gaze to a point behind Isobel's left shoulder. "Why might that be, *Monsieur* Rogue?"

Isobel jerked about just in time to see Gilmour shrug. "Truth to tell, the Munro is a most likable drinking companion."

"The Munro is a bastard!" Isobel spat the words, surprising herself as much as any by her vehemence.

MacGowan scowled. He was, she saw, dressed in a tunic and his ridiculously ineffective plaid. "What harm has he done you, lass?"

She shifted her eyes quickly away. Madelaine did not know of her kinship with Anora; she did not know that the Munros had accused Isobel's mother of witch-craft. Did not know, in fact, that it was the Munros who had caused her death, and who might very well cause her own should they learn that twins had been born to the lady of Evermyst.

"Isobel," he said and took a quick step forward. "Did he force himself on you?"

"Nay!" She was desperate to keep him at bay, for she could not think when he was near. "Nay," she re-peated and turned toward Madelaine. "Me lady, though you have done much for me already, I would ask a bit more. Might I beg a few supplies to make me journey the faster?"

"You hope to travel alone into the far north?"

"Aye—"

"Nay," Gilmour interrupted. "Not alone."

Isobel tried to argue, but within an hour's time they were mounted on matching gray steeds.

"Me thanks again, me lady," Isobel said.

Madelaine smiled. She was dressed to perfection in an ivory gown that showed her bosom to high advan-tage with her hair swept up and away from her face. "I would ask one request," she said and stepping forward, spoke softly. "When you return the steeds I will expect a full report on the rogue's performance."

Isobel widened her eyes and shot a glance toward MacGowan, who was packing supplies in black leather bags behind the high cantle of his borrowed saddle. "I have no intention of—"

"Neither does the sun intend to rise each morning in the east," Madelaine said. "And yet it does."

"Me lady," Isobel began, but Madelaine interrupted with a lift of her hand.

"Be happy that I am not demanding that you share the bounty. I but ask for a report. And to know if I am right about his secret."

Isobel glanced toward Gilmour again. He was just mounting, swinging one leg over the steed's croup, and revealing sun darkened muscles halfway up his thigh. "What secret?" she asked, though her throat had gone dry.

"If I told you, 'twould not be a secret," Madelaine said and smiling enigmatically, sent them on their way.

They rode in silence for a long while. Near noon, they rested their steeds for a spell and shared a bit of the fine white bread that Madelaine had sent with them.

"I would beg one question."

Isobel glanced up. They sat on the bank of a rustling burn, and while the silence between them had been wearing, she feared that any conversation would be more so. Indeed, being in the same universe with him was tiring.

"Do you truly think I plan some evil against me brother, or were you merely using that as an excuse to be rid of me?"

Isobel fiddled with her wooden mug and refused to

look at him. "You've given me no explanation for keeping company with the Munro."

"On the contrary—"

"Other than the fact that he is a good drinking companion," she said.

He nodded once. "And so, the jump to believing I intend me own brother harm. And what harm, I wonder?" he added. "Abduction? Murder?"

She said nothing.

"Why, Isobel? Why would I do it?"

"I do not know."

"Then I would ask what you believe."

She shrugged, trying to seem casual. "Mayhap you are jealous."

"Jealous. Of what?"

"Of your elder brother."

"Ramsay?" he said and laughed. It sounded forced.

"I forget," she said. "The great rogue of the rogues has no one of whom he is jealous. For he has all he could want." Silence settled over the glen, broken only by the soft rush of water nearby. "Except his brother's inheritance, his brother's . . ." She smiled faintly, remembering. "Allure."

"Allure? Ramsay?"

"One can see his soul in his very eyes," she said. "Depth there is and kindness. Still, there was a time I thought Anora daft for loving him. Until . . ."

"Continue."

" 'Tis naught," she said and prepared to rise. "We had best press on."

He caught her wrist. "Until what?"

She caught his gaze. "Until he kissed me."

"He kissed you!"

Her heart lurched in her chest for the intensity of his tone, but she calmed herself. "Aye, he kissed me," she said. "Indeed, I offered more once upon a time."

"Nay!" The sound seemed to come from the depths of his soul, but 'twas surely only his vanity that was hurting.

"Aye, I did indeed," she said.

"Was he such a magnificent lover then?"

"I would not know," she said, "for he sent me away. It seems he wished for no one but me sister."

His grip on her arm relaxed somewhat. "So he did not have you?"

"He is an honorable man."

"Shall I be jealous of that too then?"

"Nay. Not you," she said, and though she tried to sound sardonic, she could not quite manage it while remembering the night just past.

"Only his inheritance?"

"And his bride, of course." She had not meant to say the words, but they slipped out unbidden.

"Anora?"

"You have admitted to being tempted."

His voice rose. "I am attracted to her, thus you think I would see Ramsay gone so that I could have her for meself?"

"We should go," she said again, but he held her firm.

"After all we have endured together, you still think such of me? That I would harm me brother to hold his wife?"

"Where Anora goes, so goes Evermyst," she said, holding desperately to her beliefs lest she fall like a feather beneath his charms. "Mayhap 'tis the lofty keep that you covet. You would not be the first. Indeed, the Munro thought to have it by taking me sister and—"

"You would compare me with Innes Munro?"

"There are likenesses."

"I did not know you lusted so for the man."

"I do not lust after—"

"But you do for me."

"Nay, I—"

"You admitted as much, lass. Do you disremember?"

"I . . ." She searched for an explanation, but his closeness was boggling, and he grinned, seeming to read her mind. "I was merely attempting to make you feel better," she said.

His grin widened. "Shall I prove you a liar?" He drew her closer.

"Nay!" she said, and pulled away. He released his grip and she calmed her voice. "Mayhap you care not for me sister's well being, but I do."

She mounted rapidly, then turned her steed away. For a moment she hoped he might let the matter pass, but she was wrong.

"Who has mistreated you so that you would distrust me as you do, Isobel?"

"Why do you ask, MacGowan? Would you defend me honor?"

"Who has mistreated you?" he asked again.

Their gazes caught and held, but she turned away. "I am not me sister," she said. "Indeed, I spent much of me own youth in Madelaine's household, and there is none more likely to teach a lass to be unafraid of the pleasures of the flesh."

"So you enjoyed her lads, did you?"

She shifted her eyes away. "Who would not?"

"Then why did you not accept their offer last night?"

"Do I not still have the freedom to say no if it pleases me?"

"So you were merely not interested at that time."

"That is so."

"You lie, Bel. When you left me you were wet with longing."

She could not look at him. "You flatter yourself," she said and felt heat rise up her neck to her ears.

He leaned closer, nudging his gray to the side so that his knee brushed against hers. "Nay lass, you flatter me. Each time you tremble, each time you sigh—and yet I am made to beg for the merest touch. Why is that, lass, when you want my touch so?"

"I do not."

"Aye, you do, but you are frightened. So I ask again, who has wounded you?"

"I have not been wounded."

"Aye, you—" he began, then paused. She turned rapidly toward him, thinking there was some evil on the road ahead, but his eyes were for her alone.

"What is it?" she asked.

"Men have not mistreated you?" he asked.

"Nay. Not until you," she said, but he barely acknowledged the gibe.

" 'Tis the answer then," he said.

"The answer to what?"

"Why you turn me aside. 'Tis not pain that you fear, but pleasure."

Her breath stopped in her chest. "What foolishness do you spew now? Why would anyone be afraid of pleasure?" She turned to stare woodenly between her mount's ears. Even so she could feel his gaze, hot as sunlight on her face.

"I do not know, Isobel," he said. "But I wish to."

"This I tell you; I am not afraid of anything you—" she began, but when she met his eyes, she saw they were dark and earnest. No humor showed there, only interest and concern and the unwanted darkness of compassion. "We waste time," she said, and setting her heels to her mount, pressed frantically toward Evermyst.

Chapter 20

The inn where they stopped had none of the amenities of the Red Lion. The food smelled suspect, the ale was sour, and the common room was dirtier than the Lion's front stoop. Thus they drank heavily spiced wine and sat in silence as Gilmour tried to understand the mystery that was Isobel.

In the tallow candlelight, she looked tense and uncertain. Why? What troubles bothered her? he wondered, and watched her avoid his gaze until she was unable to ignore him any longer.

"What is it you want?" she said finally.

"I was simply thinking that it was good of Lady Madelaine to lend us coin for an inn. If we are frugal, we shall have enough for this night and the next."

"Nay," she argued. "Tonight will require most of our sum."

"Not if we share a room."

She stared at him. "This night will require most of our sum," she repeated.

" 'Tis a rough area, Bel. Surely you've no wish to spend the night with other travelers rather than taking advantage of me protection?"

"That is me wish exactly," she said and stirred her wooden ladle about in her stew. It smelled strongly of onions, yet the scent could not quite hide the idea that the mutton had seen a number of days before meeting the broth.

Gilmour settled his shoulder against the wall to his right and studied her.

"Tell me, lass, who is it that fostered you in your early years?"

She abandoned her ladle with something of a start. "Why do you ask?"

He shrugged as if the topic was of no great interest to him. "I but wish to pass the time. I dare not eat the food, so I wonder, when Meara took you from your mother's arms, to whom did she send you?"

"I don't remember them," she said and pushing her stew aside, took a drink of wine.

"Then where did you spend your youth?"

"Wherever I wished. Then, as now, I had no wish to stay in one place for any great length of time."

"Even after finding your sister?"

Her gaze flickered to him and away. " 'Twas time to be off, is all."

"But surely you could not have simply come and gone when you were a wee lass. Someone must have cared for you. Did they live close to Evermyst?"

"Nay," she said and drank again.

"Who were they?"

"No one of import."

"You jest," he said. "Surely those who nurtured you in your early years are important."

"As I told you, I do not remember them."

"Was it a man and wife? Were they nobles? They must have had names at the least?"

"It matters naught," she insisted and fidgeted with her mug.

"Of course—"

"They died!" she said, then drew a slow breath. "Of a fever . . . and not so far from this place."

"Oh. I am sorry."

"There is no need. I can no longer even recall their faces."

"How old were you when they found their graves?"

She cleared her throat and drank again. "Five years, mayhap. I am unsure. I was only told that I was . . ." She stopped again.

He watched her. She was small and fragile, yet there was a rare strength to her, like that of a finely crafted rapier. "A bonny lass?" he guessed, imagining her youth. "Bright as a bauble? Sharp as a dirk?"

She glanced quickly up, and in her eyes there was some indefinable emotion that cut his breath from his throat even before she spoke. "Dollag said only that I was very small." She paused, fidgeting again. "Not worth a sliver."

Gilmour froze as the bright image faded to nothingness in his mind. "Dollag?" he asked.

Her fine lips were slightly pursed, and one hand lay curled into itself upon the rough tabletop, but she spoke casually. "She took me in after the Holiers' deaths."

"The Holiers? So they had names after all?"

" 'Tis only what Dollag called them—the Holiers Than Thous. The villagers called *her* Limp About Dollag. One leg was not right. 'Twas quite painful for her, I believe. Mayhap that had some bearing on her temperament."

Reaching casually for the wine bottle, Gilmour filled her mug. "She was unkind," he said.

She took another sip from her mug and lowered her gaze. "When I was a wee lass I thought the Holiers had asked Dollag to take me, and I wondered . . ." She paused.

"What?" he asked and tried to sound unrushed.

" 'Tis growing late. I should find me bed."

"Only the fleas await you," Gilmour said and smiled, hoping to disarm her. "What is it you wondered?"

She glanced toward the door, then back at him. "I wondered what I had done to make them despise me so."

His stomach lurched. "Enough to send you to Dollag?" he asked.

She didn't answer, but remained perfectly still, as if the slightest movement might weaken her defenses somehow. And in that moment he realized the strength it took for her to put her memories to words. To open the wounds for him to see.

"This I tell you, Bel," he said, his voice low and certain, "they could not have despised you."

She smiled a little, but the expression was as fragile as hoarfrost, never reaching her eyes. "Maybe they did not," she agreed. "Dollag hated them. So perhaps they were kindly folk after all."

It seemed almost that in that moment she was a child again, tiny, defenseless. No bigger than Ramsay's wee Mary, wanting naught more than to be loved and cherished. It made him want desperately to pull her into his arms, to defy the idea that she could have spent her young years in loneliness. To promise that forever and always she would be safe—but he was not quite that foolish.

"They had no other children?" he asked, his tone idle, his fingers tight on his mug.

"I pray not." The words came very fast.

Gilmour snapped his gaze to her, hoping she would explain without prodding, but she did not. "Why do you pray, Isobel?"

"I but jest," she said, but her tone was tight. "They had no other children. I am certain of it."

If the truth be told, he wished to hear no more. Indeed, all he wanted was to take her into his embrace, to stroke her hair and kiss away the horrors of her past. But he could not fix them if he did not understand them. "You were very young," he said. "How can you be certain the Holiers had no other wee ones?"

"They did not!" she snapped and her hand shook, jostling the contents of her mug. Lifting it, she drained the thing, then peered inside. "She lied. I am certain of it," she whispered.

His gut twisted with premonition, but he kept his voice carefully steady. "Lied about what?"

"The baby." She whispered the words like a wee helpless lass, too frightened to speak aloud. She swallowed and glanced furtively up at him as her fingers twisted about the empty mug. "Dollag said there was a baby, but it was even smaller than I. Worth naught, thus she used it for the fire."

He dared not move, lest he frighten away the horrible truth.

"So I had best behave," she breathed. Her voice had taken on a childish lisp and her eyes were as bright as river-swept stones. "For the winters were cold and wood was hard to come—"

"Bloody hell!" Gilmour's stool clattered to the floor as he jerked to his feet. Isobel started and faces turned, but he cared not, for he could no longer remain apart from her. She reared back as if struck, but he gathered her into his arms and pulled her against the refuge of his chest. Above her silken head, he closed his eyes and struggled for calm.

"Is she dead?" he rasped.

She was trembling. It took her a moment to respond, and when she did her voice was uncertain, as though she were lost. "Wh-what?"

Not a soul spoke and in that moment he realized that every eye was focused on them. Even the innkeeper had emerged from the kitchen to stare, so Gilmour bent, and slipping his arm behind her knees, lifted her against his chest. Turning on his heel, he passed by the proprietor and in a hushed voice said simply, "Me wife and I shall be sharing a room, alone."

He realized upon reaching the hallway that he didn't know which room was unoccupied, but she felt like a doll of rags in his arms and more than anything in life he needed a place to kiss her, to hold her, to comfort her.

The second door stood open. He turned inside and finding it empty, closed the portal with his foot, then strode across the room to sit on the bed. She remained unmoving upon his lap, curled against his chest like a wounded kitten, and he took a steadying breath, trying to calm himself.

Slowly, gently, he ran his hand along the waves of

her hair. It fell soft and endless down her narrow back, but he failed to notice her delicate curves, for in his mind was a tiny girl with tears in her eyes and fear in her heart. Fear for herself. Aye. But fear for another, too, for it seemed that she was terrified for a babe that may never have existed.

His fingers tightened in her hair, but he loosened them with an effort and stroked again. She felt small and soft and heavenly in his arms. " 'Tis not your fault, lass," he whispered. "No matter what happened, there is naught you could have done."

"She was not always cruel." The words were so soft, he had to lean closer to hear. "She did not take me shell."

"Shell?"

She went on as if she hadn't heard him. "And once upon a sunny day she limped down to the market and brought me back an orange." Her fingers curled into his tunic, and she cuddled closer as if wanting to hide. " 'Twas a magnificent thing, it was. I feared for a time that she meant to tease me with it, but nay . . ." Her voice was filled with wonder. "She gave it to me to keep for me own. I thought mayhap that she must not detest me so. 'Tis a strange truth," she said and paused as if lost in her thoughts, "that a moment of kindness only makes the stripes the worse."

He gritted his teeth and damned the woman to hell, but he kept stroking her gently.

"She oft couldn't sleep . . . because of her leg." She drew her own limbs closer to her chest, curling into herself. "If I was awake I was swifter than she, but . . ."

His teeth ached. He unclenched his jaw, forcing

himself to relax a smidgen. "She struck you whilst you slept?"

"There were times when I hid in the woods, but it was so dark." Her voice dropped away. "And cold. And once the lads from the village found me."

His hand trembled, but he forced it down her hair once again. He felt her whisper against his chest, as though she were afraid someone else would hear her secrets.

"Mayhap I was no bigger than a sliver, but I had seen what Hamish had done with the butcher's daughter, and I had learned to be cautious," she said and shivered.

Time ticked along on creaky feet. Gilmour waited for calm, but it did not come. Still, he waited.

"I hid well. Deep in the bracken, where they would not find me, but I had forgot about his hound. I could hear it coming for me through the ferns, and close on its footfalls was Hamish. Mayhap I should have stayed hid away, but I remembered the butcher's daughter and at the last moment I sprang from hiding. He was there, looming over me like the devil himself with the other lads behind him."

Silence settled in. Gilmour's heart thumped against his ribs like a heavy drum as he waited for her to speak again.

"Tell me, Isobel." He closed his eyes for a moment, calling up strength. "Did he harm you?"

"He reached for me. Like a bear he was, with hands like giant paws. I felt it swipe across me chest even as I leapt and knew his finger had caught in me pendant, but at that moment, I cared not, for 'twas me shell or me life." She burrowed deeper against Gilmour. "Me chain broke and I fell backward. 'Twas then that he laughed, for he thought he had me, but I was quick as a mouse, and I scrambled away before he could call his lads. Still . . ." She sighed and curled her fingers absently against the simple bodice of her gown. "I miss me wee silvery shell."

"The one given to you by your mother?"

Again, she didn't seem to hear him, but kept her hand loosely against her chest. "There were times when I would imagine that I was the daughter of a great lady. 'Twas she who had given me the tiny pendant, of course, because she cherished me so. Still, I dared not try to get it back," she whispered.

The bastard! Gilmour stroked her hair once again, careful to keep the sweep of his hand steady. "You are safe now," he said, but the damned words sounded weak and ineffective to his own ears. "All is well."

"Aye." Her fingers loosened a bit. "Aye, I am no longer a weakling child and Hamish is far away."

"Where?" he asked, and forced his hand to return to its soothing course down her satiny hair.

She sighed. He eased her off his lap and onto the mattress. She did not look up, but curled against the coverlet as if she were spent.

"Isobel," he murmured and brushed the hair back from her elvish face. "Where did you live with Dollag?"

"Glencroe," she said and winced as if struck. " 'Tis not so very close."

But close enough to bring back such haunting horrors. "You are safe, lassie," he said. "None will harm you."

"I can use a sling," she said, "and a knife."

"I remember, Isobel," he said and smoothed his palm down her arm. It felt as lax as a child's beneath his hand. "You are a strong woman."

"Gordon of the Mill did not think so."

He truly did not wish to hear any more, for his blood felt hot, but he was not a violent man. Nay, he was a lover, and he would soothe her. "Gordon was a fool," he said.

"Aye." Her lips twitched into a small smile, but she did not open her eyes. "A fool he was, for he thought he could pay Dollag and I would lie with him."

Neither was he a cursing man, but a foul word slipped out and for a moment he could do nothing but remain motionless and wait for the rage to pass.

Her eyes opened wearily. "I escaped, MacGowan."

"Aye." He swallowed hard and kept his hands to himself now lest she feel them tremble. "That you did."

"And I will not go back, for I am safe now."

"You are safe, Isobel."

Her eyes fell closed again. "And mayhap . . ." For a moment he thought she had fallen asleep, for she was quiet for a long while, and when she finally spoke her voice was so soft that he could barely hear her. "Mayhap 'tis best the babe died, for she was not as strong as I," she whispered.

He waited in silence a long while. Waited for her to speak again. She did not. Waited for the anger to pass. It did not.

So he watched her as she slept, not fitful or restless, but soundly, like a wee small babe who trusted him.

Finally he rose, but when he stepped away he found that his strides were short and tense, his fists still clenched.

• He paced the room, glancing now and then at the small still figure on the bed. He was a lover, he reminded him. Not a violent man. He was a lover.

He ground his teeth as he reached for the door latch. Aye, he was a lover—but there were few things he loved more than justice.

Chapter 21

Isobel awoke slowly. Her mouth felt dry and her body limp. Light seeped from the narrow window behind her and memories returned slowly to her—words she had spoken, truths she had spilled.

MacGowan. Where was he? she wondered and sitting up, turned to find him watching her. He sat upon an oaken trunk not far from the bed, his fine body bent forward, his elbows on his knees. As she watched, he straightened slowly, his gaze solemn and unwavering.

Her throat tightened nervously.

"About last night," she began and cleared her throat. "I fear the wine did not agree with me. Indeed, mayhap it was spoiled and the spices but hid its quality, for it quite addled me brain."

He still watched her, his notorious smile noticeably absent. "Did it?"

"Aye."

He looked tired, she thought, yet relaxed somehow. The sleeves of his tunic were rolled up, exposing his lower arms. Veins swelled from his browned skin, weaving double paths toward his broad elbows. Quiet strength exuded from him and for a moment she wanted nothing more than to slip into his arms and be held by that strength. But she would not, for weakness was one thing she could ill afford.

" 'Twas most likely the wine and fatigue," she said. "Conspiring against me."

"You were tired," he agreed.

"Aye, and I fear me imaginings got the better of me."

He leaned back, resting his weight against the wall behind him, but still he did not speak. She cleared her throat.

"I . . . me apologies," she said.

"For what?"

She forced a laugh and flipped a hand at him as though he were silly to ask. "For the blathering. I am not usually so foolish. But what with the attack and the escape and Lady Madelaine . . . perhaps one cannot blame me mind for taking flight and . . ." She almost could not force out the words, though she was not sure why. "And imagining such a *ridiculous* past, making up names and whatnot. Truth to be told, I can barely remember me youth, it was that nondescript. Serene really with—"

"Isobel." His voice was solemn and steady. She took a breath and hoped to hell he believed her lies more readily than he believed her truths.

"Aye?"

"Dollag is dead."

She sat bolt upright, her heart lurching in her chest. "How do you know this?"

"I made a journey last night."

"To Glencroe?" she asked, but now she could see that his shoes were atypically muddy and his plaid stained.

"Aye." He nodded soberly. "To meet with Dollag."

"And she is . . ." Her heart lurched again. "Did you—"

"I was not the one who killed her."

Her breath stopped in her throat and her lips moved but she found no words for several seconds. Then, "I never imagined you were."

He scowled as if he'd assumed too much, then continued. "She died some years back." His fists tightened, then loosened, as if by the greatest of control. "Painfully, I am told."

"Oh. I . . . I am—"

"Don't say you are sorry!" He jerked to his feet and she started, frightened by the action. "Do not say it, Isobel."

She nodded once and watched him.

"I spoke to those who knew her. They remembered you, also. A wee ragged lass, they said. You were there for some five years or more and then gone. They knew not where, though they said they tried to find out if—"

"Who tried?"

"I believe she was called Dulcie of the Craigs."

"Dulcie," she said, remembering against her will. "She was kind to me."

"Kind?" His fists ground together again and he paced. "She said you oft had bruises and that you seemed forever hungry."

" 'Twas a time she gave me a pigeon pie all for me own," she said and smiled.

"A pie!" he growled. "She knew you were being beaten by Dollag. Indeed, she feared that the hag might have killed you and disposed of your body, and yet she did nothing."

Isobel felt breathless and pale.

"Is that the 'kindness' you endured all those—"

"How?" she asked.

"What?"

"Did Dulcie say how she thought Dollag might have gotten rid of me body?"

He scowled. "Nay, she . . ." he began, then paused and took a deep breath as he realized her thoughts. "There was no babe."

"What?"

"The Holiers, who fostered you, had no babe after you, and Dollag was never seen with a bairn."

Hot relief flooded her. "She lied, then."

"Aye, there was no babe killed by Dollag, Isobel. No one for you to protect."

"She lied," Bel repeated.

"Aye," he said and watched her with eyes dark with emotion, "but 'twas hardly her greatest sin."

"Nay," she agreed and lifting her gaze to his, forced a laugh and tried to shake off his sympathy. "She stank, too. Like a—"

"Hamish sends his apologies."

She felt the blood drain from her face. "Hamish?"

He flexed his hands and she noticed now that his knuckles were bruised and that the wound above his ear had been reopened.

"You saw Hamish?"

"Aye. He begs your forgiveness for his sins against you and wishes you naught but good."

"You challenged him," she whispered.

"Why do you think so?"

"Hamish was cruel. Cruel and bold and strong as a bull."

"Mayhap he was not so strong as he thought," Gilmour said and paced again, his strides restless. "Mayhap he was only bold when he tormented wee lassies."

"Did you fight him?"

"Of course not," he said, and scowled. "I thought you knew, I am a lover, not a fighter. Hamish was quite reasonable when I explained things."

"Explained things," she said. "To Hamish."

"Aye," he said and flexed his fists. He almost didn't wince.

She watched the movement. "Why did you fight him?"

"I told you—"

"You battled with him," she interrupted and scowled, trying to understand. "And since you are still walking, I shall assume that you won. I but wonder why."

A muscle danced in Gilmour's jaw and he turned restlessly away. "We had a difference of opinion."

Her throat felt tight, but she forced out words. "About what?"

"About how wee lassies should be treated." He tightened his fingers on the shutter beside the window before turning to her. "He gave me this for you," he said and held out his closed fist, palm up.

Her gaze caught on his hand. Strong, yet elegant somehow, it was bruised, abraded across the knuckles. She swallowed. Her eyes burned and though she knew better than to try to speak, the words came.

"What is it?" she asked, keeping her hands closed tight by her sides.

He said nothing, but reaching for her wrist, drew it upward and turned it. She opened it, breathlessly, and without a word, he dropped a tiny silver shell into her palm.

Her throat closed up and her eyes burned.

"I'm sorry Isobel," he murmured.

She tried to swallow, but she couldn't.

"Don't cry, lass."

"I don't cry."

"Bel," he said and took a step toward her, but a thousand emotions scorched her soul. She turned and fled the room.

Gilmour followed her, racing down the steps in hot pursuit. The door slammed in his face, but he grasped the handle and prepared to yank it open when the innkeeper yelled.

"Ay!" he barked. "You wouldn't be thinking of leaving without paying, would you now?"

Gilmour slowed his breathing and opened his sporran.

By the time he reached the stable, Isobel was pulling up the girth on her mount. "Where are you bound?" he asked.

"To Evermyst," she said.

"Could it not wait until after we break our fast?"

"Nay," she said and when she turned he could see that she had strung the silver shell onto a rough piece of hemp and hung it about her neck. "Anora is in danger."

"Is she?" he said. "Or is it you who are in danger?"

"Me?" Her eyes looked bright and haunted, but she laughed. "Nay. Of course not."

"So you are not afraid."

Unbuckling the horse's head collar, she fitted the bit

to the animal's mouth and scowled at him. "Afraid of what? I am no longer a helpless lass, but—"

"Afraid of being loved."

"Loved?" She barked a wild laugh as she mounted. "Is that how you secure your conquests, MacGowan, by making them confuse love and lust?"

"Mayhap," he said and caught her reins just as surely as he caught her gaze with his own. "Mayhap that is why I have had so many lovers, aye, Isobel? Because they mistake emotion for nothing more than physical desire."

"Mayhap," she said, but the word was a whisper.

"But you are not confused," he added, "for you understand love perfectly."

For a moment she failed to speak, but finally she yanked the reins from his hand and pivoted away.

They spent that night in a nunnery. The accommodations were spartan, but satisfactory. Gilmour slept fitfully and rose with the sun. He assured himself that he was not worried that Isobel would leave without him. Still, his stomach settled at the sight of her, and soon they were off again.

Sometime after noon the clouds banked up in the west and rain began blowing into their faces. Seeing a crofter's cottage from a hilltop, they headed toward that refuge only to find that the cottage was no more than a ramshackle wall of tumbled stone. Nevertheless, with the rain worsening, they prepared to spend the night there. They made a small peat fire, then shared a bit of the provisions they had brought with them. Reaching across the flame, Gilmour handed her a chunk of stone-ground bread and for a moment their fingers brushed.

Isobel snapped her hand back, nearly dropping the bread in the fire.

Gilmour settled his back against the lone wall and perused her. "Tell me, Bel," he said finally, "what do you recall of the Holiers who fostered you?"

She darted her gaze to his. "Hoping to hear another sad tale, MacGowan?" she asked.

"Hardly that; I merely pass the time."

" 'Tis good," she said, "for the Holiers were naught but kind to me."

"So you remember them well?"

The memories were faint, not more than shadows and light that played across her mind with wisps of quiet voices. But she remembered the laughter. Aye, that she remembered well.

"Her name was Dearling," Bel said finally.

"Dearling." She could feel his gaze on her. "I've not heard that name before."

"Aye well, 'tis what Da called her."

"And what did your da call *you*, Bel?"

She shrugged. "I imagine he called me by me . . ." she began, but memories were crowding in, threatening.

"What is it?"

" 'Tis naught," she said, striving for nonchalance, but she could still feel his gaze on his face.

"Have you remembered something?"

"Nay."

Quiet stretched out around them, and it was into that silence that Gilmour spoke.

"Your da," he said, "he called you Dearling too, did he not?"

She shot her gaze to his.

"Of course he would," he said and leaned onto one elbow, still watching her. "For Dearling was not a name at all, but an endearment. He cherished you."

Pain gnawed slowly at her chest, but she ignored it. "Tell me, MacGowan, why do you glory in dredging up such memories?"

"Fond memories should not hurt," he said as if surprised.

"Then why—" she began, but stopped herself abruptly. "Nay, they do not hurt," she agreed. "I merely asked why you care to shuffle about in them."

" 'Tis simply intriguing to learn what events shaped a soul. Are you not curious about me own growing up years?"

"Nay."

"Well, then," he said and sighed, "we'll simply have to entertain ourselves with your memories, won't we?"

She should have learned by now that no matter how innocuous his statements there was always a catch with him.

"So he called you Dearling," he said, "and how did he spend his days? Was he a landlord or a merchant or—?"

"He was a leatherwright." She fell silent for a moment as memories crowded in. "Even Dollag had no ill to say of his craftsmanship."

"So he was a fair craftsman?"

"Beyond fair," she said and though she would hate to admit it, a hint of forgotten pride crept into her voice. "Upon their bed was the hide of a ram that he had tanned. 'Twas soft and thick, and when I was afraid they would . . ."

Silence again, heavy and deep, broken only by the crackle of their fire.

"What did they do, Isobel?"

She caught his gaze, then shifted her eyes away. "I would sleep between them at times."

" 'Twas a large bed?"

"No larger than most, I suppose."

"It must have been close quarters then lying between them."

"Aye. Close and warm."

"And safe."

She said nothing.

"And sometimes your mother would stroke your hair and tell you what a bonny lass you were."

Memories crowded in.

"And when the storms raged outside, mayhap your da would tell you wildling tales to put your mind at rest."

"He would sing to drown out the sound of the thunder. And Mum would laugh and cover me ears and say that his singing was surely worse . . ."

She swallowed hard. They were gone. She was alone, and she did not mind, for it had made her strong.

The fire crackled and hissed when a few wayward drops struck burning embers.

"Tell me, lass . . ." MacGowan's voice was as deep as the night. "Since the time when you were a wee lass, has there been a time when you were touched?"

"Aye, of course there—"

"Not in anger," he said. "Nor in passing."

"Lady Madelaine was always generous with her—"

"Neither do I speak of passion," he said. "But of touch freely given, with nothing to be gained."

" 'Tis none of your—"

"How long has it been," he asked, "since you trusted?"

It seemed as if her heart were thrumming in her very throat. "Because I do not trust *you*, MacGowan, does not mean that I do not trust others," she said.

He watched her in silence.

She swallowed and hurried her gaze back to the flame. "When trust is warranted, I trust."

"Do you?"

"Aye."

"Then what have I done to shun your trust, Isobel?"

She stared at him, and he was beautiful, his eyes solemn, his hands mesmerizing, and his body so alluring every fiber in her body begged for his attention.

"You are afraid of me, Isobel," he murmured. "Afraid that if I touch you again you'll be unable to live without it. Afraid that once you have lain with me you'll die without me in your bed."

She laughed. "You are vain beyond words."

"Mayhap." He smiled, then, without warning, he leaned close. She held her breath as his lips touched hers and she trembled to her very soul. "But I am also right," he whispered and rising to his feet, left her alone.

Chapter 22

Dreams plagued Isobel that night. Dreams of dark places and cruel laughter. Dreams of gentle hands and loving words. Dreams of Anora. She awoke with a start, breathing hard and afraid.

"What is it?" Gilmour asked, but she could not explain.

Anora was in trouble, that much she knew and 'twas for that reason that she turned to hurry home. The miles rushed beneath the hooves of their borrowed horses, until finally, just as the sun dropped behind the horizon, they saw Evermyst's turrets rise high above the crashing waters of the firth below.

Fatigued and worried, Isobel pressed her mount up the precipitous climb that led to the keep's outer curtain. Pulling the hood of her borrowed cape up over her hair, she stopped before the portcullis.

"Who goes there?" called the gate keeper.

" 'Tis I," Bel said, making her voice soft and mild. "Lady Anora's maid servant and—"

"Lady Anora?" The gate keeper raised his lantern and peered through the circle of light in their direction. "Is she with you then?"

Gilmour pressed his mount closer to the iron grill. "Is the lady not safely inside the keep, Hal?"

"Laird Gilmour, is that you?"

"Aye. 'Tis." His voice was impatient. "And what of Lady Anora?"

"Have you not heard? The lady and—"

"Quiet," warned another voice. "Do you want the whole of Scotland to know our worries? Raise the portcullis. They'll learn the truth soon enough."

It seemed to take forever for the iron bound gate to rise.

"The truth?" Gilmour ducked under the gate, rode ahead and straightened, his face intense in the gathering darkness. "What truth do you speak of, Thomas? Where is the Lady Anora?"

"We do not know, me laird. She has not yet returned, but Laird Lachlan searches for them even now."

"Them?"

"Laird Ramsay had accompanied her. They traveled the burn alone, but they never reached their destination. 'Twas some days hence that the boat was found. Empty it was, and overturned."

"And the babe? What of her?"

"The babe?"

"Wee Mary," Gilmour said, his tone strained. "Did she journey with them?"

"Nay, me laird. She was left behind with her nursemaid."

"And Lachlan? How long has it been since he left this keep?"

"Two days, me laird. He and half the warriors of Evermyst have gone to search for them, but I fear . . ." He paused.

Gilmour straightened. "What is it you fear, Thomas?"

The old gatekeeper shook his gnarled head. "The burn is bedeviled with falls and snags. I fear they may not be found."

"Lachlan is on the search. If there is aught to be found, he will find it. But do not despair, for Ramsay is too stubborn to die easily. He will return, as will your lady. Fear not, Thomas. Keep your vigil and your prayers and all will be well," he said and turning his mount, he rode up the slope to the inner curtain.

Isobel followed, her heart tapping hard against her ribs, her fingers clenched on the reins as she rode through the next gate and into the cobbled courtyard toward the hall. So her premonitions had been right: Anora was in trouble. But—

"Lassie!"

Bel jerked her attention toward the broad doors of the hall. "Meara," she gasped and slipping from her mount's back, ran to the frail old woman who leaned upon her cane beside the stairs. "Tell me, have you heard aught from her?"

Meara of the Fold shook her head, though that simple movement seemed almost more than her fragile body could withstand. "Nay, lass. I am sorry. It seems forever since she has been gone and not a word to soothe me. But what of you? Have you had no forewarning? No—"

It was at that moment that the door opened and another woman rushed down the stairs toward them, a babe hugged to her bosom.

"Me wee lass! You have returned," rasped the newcomer and grabbing Isobel with her free arm, pulled her close.

Isobel extracted herself carefully, feeling Gilmour's gaze on her back. "Aye, Helena. I am returned," she said and touched her niece's back, just to make sure she was real, that she, at least, was safe. "But what is this dreadful news?"

"Lady Anora," Helena began, her broad face worried as Mary turned to stare at them with sky wide eyes. "She has gone and not returned. I fear—"

"Keep your fears to yourself, Stout Helena," Meara ordered. "We've enough of our own."

"How is the babe faring?" Gilmour asked, stepping forward.

Mary gazed at him with shell round eyes, then lifted her arms in a solemn request. He took her without a second's hesitation, drawing her against the strength of his chest. Stroking her back, Mour closed his eyes for a moment and whispered something to the child. And the babe, at the tender age of less than a year, dropped her head against his shoulder with an audible sigh.

Isobel could not help but stare, for despite everything—the babe's tragic past, the rogue's recent arrival, and the turmoil that surrounded them—Mary trusted him. Indeed, if the child's expression was true, she adored him.

Absolute silence filled the place as every woman stared until Gilmour glanced about him with a scowl. "Is something amiss?"

Helena swiped away a tear and Meara cleared her throat.

"Duncan." Her tone was brusque. "Where is that lad? Duncan!" she yelled and a giant young man appeared.

"Maid Isobel," he said, wiping ale from his lips with the back of an enormous hand. "You have returned."

"Aye," she agreed and smiled. "You are well, Tree?"

He bobbed his head shyly, not quite able to meet her eyes. "I won the wrestling match last—"

"Aye, that's all well and good," Meara interrupted. "But the lass and the rogue are weary. See to their mounts, Duncan. And Helena . . ."

The old cook stiffened at the other's imperious tone.

"Well . . ." groused Meara, pausing as she glanced up at the other. "I suspect you are tired in your old age. I'll get another to fetch their meals."

"I am not so withered as you," Helena said. "And certainly not too weary to see that these two be fed. Come hither," she insisted and hurried back up the stairs she had just descended.

The meal arrived in a matter of minutes, but while Gilmour ate in the great hall with the child upon his lap, Isobel dined in the kitchens where the other servants ate.

As for Meara, she tottered about the far side of the long, rough-hewn table and leaned upon her cane beside Isobel. "Is she well?" Her voice was scratchy and low, and when Isobel lifted her gaze, she saw the deep worry in her ancient eyes.

"I pray so," Bel murmured.

"What's this?" Meara's voice rose slightly. "Do you say that you are uncertain of the welfare of your own—?"

Isobel glanced at a passing servant. Meara fell silent, then creaked down to sit beside the maid on the trestle.

"Tell me what you know," insisted the old woman.

"I dreamed I was drowning," Isobel began.

"Drowning!" Meara's bent fingers clutched frantically at Bel's sleeve. "Where?"

"I meself was in a shallow burn when the fears took me."

"And you think it was Anora that was in peril."

"Aye. Of that much I am certain."

"But you could not tell where she was?"

"Nay. Only that she found the surface and escaped whatever evil held her."

"And now?"

Isobel shook her head, trying to see through the shadows. "I do not know, but I feel she is well."

"Then why has she not returned to us?"

"Because she cannot. Something or someone keeps her away."

"Someone?" Meara's voice was low. "Who?"

Isobel's mind rushed along. "I do not know."

Meara narrowed her rheumy eyes. "But you suspect."

Bel did not answer, but shifted her gaze toward the door, remembering the feelings that had overwhelmed her. Remembering the impressions of Mac-Gowan.

"You think someone in this keep wishes her ill?"

"I cannot be sure."

"Nay." Meara shook her head. "It cannot be. There is not a Fraser who does not love his lady."

"Nay. Not a Fraser."

Meara drew back as if slapped. "You are wrong," she said. "Her husband cherishes her like none other. He was meant to be hers for all time. The prophesy foretold him; it could not have been wrong. He would not harm—" She stopped abruptly. "You do not mean it is Ramsay who wishes her ill."

"Nay, but when the fear took me, I felt MacGowan's presence."

"Laird Gilmour?" Meara hissed.

Isobel merely nodded.

The old woman watched her closely. "Tell me, Isobel, why do you think this?"

"Mayhap it is not Anora that the brigand wishes to harm," she whispered. "Mayhap, 'tis Laird Ramsay he hopes to be rid of."

"You think Laird Gilmour would harm his own brother?"

" 'Tis a horrid sin, but one that has been done since the beginning of time," she murmured.

"But why do you suspect him?"

"When first I saw him he was in Henshaw with the Munro."

Meara remained silent as if waiting.

" 'Twas shortly after that I felt as if I was drowning."

Still the old woman said nothing, but stared at her with unblinking eyes.

"Why would he be with the Munro unless he were planning some evil against the Frasers?" Isobel asked.

"Do you forget that a peace has been forged between the clans?"

"Nay, I do not forget," hissed Isobel, "but might it not be that Gilmour means to shatter this peace, to be rid of his brother so that he can have Anora for his own?"

The ancient brows rose in surprise. "You think it is our lady and not Evermyst that he covets?"

"He has long adored her."

"Has he?"

Isobel fidgeted a mite under the woman's withering gaze. "Have you not noticed how his eyes follow her when she is near?"

"Nay," Meara said, "I have not, but mayhap I have not been watching this rogue as closely as you have."

Isobel drew herself up. "Mayhap I do not trust him so easily as some just because he is bonny and charming."

Meara's brows rose, creasing a million additional wrinkles into her dried apple face. "Is that why you suspect him, Isobel? Because you lust for him?"

"I do not lust for—"

"Whyever not?"

Isobel searched for words but found none and the old woman chuckled.

Bel pursed her lips. "Just because I was not raised as a noble does not mean that I have no morals, old woman."

"Of course not," said Meara and stilled her laughter. "Me apologies," she said. "I see that you have no feelings for Laird Gilmour. After all, as a Fraser lass, you too must follow the prophesy."

"What?"

"The prophesy. Surely you have heard it," Meara scolded. "You cannot blame me for thinking the rogue of the rogues might possess the necessary attributes. Kindness, cunning, power—"

"MacGowan?"

"You think not, lass?"

"Nay," she breathed, her lungs too tight in her chest. The old woman shrugged, but her eyes were ungodly bright as she watched Bel. "Mayhap you are right. Still, glad I am that you are back where you belong, and glad that you have brought this news of your sister. But what shall we do now? Have your gifts given you any idea where we might search for her?"

Isobel scowled, trying to keep up to the old woman's flitting thoughts. "Lachlan searches for her even as we speak, does he not?"

"Aye, he and three score of Evermyst's finest warriors."

"Then there is no more to be done. Leastways, not unless I have some idea where to look. Until then I will remain here, for here is where I feel her the strongest."

"Aye," Meara agreed quietly and rose laboriously to her feet. "Aye, stay here, lassie." Cupping Isobel's cheek, she stared deeply into her eyes. "Here is where you were born to be. It does me old heart good to see your face, even if it be half hidden by rags once again."

Isobel smiled. " 'Tis good to return."

Meara nodded. "Aye. And do not fret, 'twill not be much longer before you can take your rightful place amongst your people. Mark me words. I too see things," she declared and grinned toothlessly. "As for this night, I've given instructions to ready Lady Anora's chambers for you. Go there and await her return. God willing, she will need you soon."

It was not much later that Isobel made her way down Evermyst's narrow hallways to Anora's chamber. The door creaked open and she stepped inside. A single candle had been left to flicker in the sconce beside the door. Anora's four-poster bed remained as it always had, its broken foot post tilting slightly. A faded tapestry adorned the far wall and behind that tapestry was a hidden door through which Isobel had traveled more than once. During the Frasers' trouble with the Munros, Senga had been quite an active ghost. Isobel smiled to herself. There had been advantages to being Evermyst's shade. After all, ghosts were basically left alone, while flesh and blood was subject to all sorts of emotional upheaval.

Isobel quickly turned her thoughts aside. She was not some idle maid to worry over a bonny man's smile; she had come here for a reason. Shutting her mind to all but Anora, she drew in the memories, feeling the feelings, but there was no danger that she could sense. Anora was safe. She must be. Isobel stepped farther inside. 'Twas then that she noticed the tub that steamed full of water in the far corner. Since Anora's wedding, Laird Ramsay had overseen some renovations at Evermyst. The walls had been shored up, a new well had been dug, and the plumbing had been altered so that water could be pumped to every floor. Tonight, this once, she would take advantage of that improvement, even though she was naught but a servant to the Fraser clan.

Pushing her hood back, Isobel removed her cape, then slipped out of her overskirt. Pulling her chemise over her head, she dropped it to the floor with the rest of her garments. It felt marvelous to let down her hair, then tilt her head back and ease her fingers across her scalp. The water felt better yet, rising up her shins, then higher as she sank into the warm depths and leaned back against the smooth wood, reveling in the steam.

All would be well. Anora was safe. Whoever had threatened her had been thwarted. The sisters would be reunited, and mayhap this time Isobel would stay. MacGowan had been entirely wrong; she was not afraid of being cherished. Nor had her unexpected bond with Anora frightened her away. Neither was she afraid of Gilmour. True, he was handsome, and aye, he possessed a smile that challenged the light of the sun, but he was hardly the first to smile her way, and it was unlikely to send her scurrying for cover. In fact, she was not averse to admitting that memories of him brought a flush of pleasure. He had touched her like none other, had made her feel things that she had not felt before.

Reaching for the soap, she dunked it beneath the water and smoothed it over her shoulder. He had kissed her there, she remembered. And there. She closed her eyes and ran the bar, sweet with the smell of lavender, across her breasts. Her nipples peaked, but she doubted that it was because of the draft of cool air that curled through the chambers. Nay, during her time at Evermyst, she had become accustomed to those eerie currents of air that seemed to come from nowhere.

Evermyst, after all, was haunted. Isobel smiled a little, remembering. It was fear of Senga's ghost that had sent the Munro slithering from this keep. No one need know that Isobel herself could be as ghostly as the next lass when the need arose.

Superstition was for fools and cowards, and she had not survived by being either. Nay, she had survived by her wit, by knowing the truth and using it to her best advantage.

She slipped the scented bar along her collarbone

and remembered Gilmour's touch there. She could admit the truth: it was thoughts of him that made her shiver. But he had only moved her physically. She did not long for him. Indeed, she didn't even like him. Regardless how ridiculous Meara thought her suspicions were, she had no proof that it was not he who caused Anora's disappearance, and if that was found to be true, she would hardly be brokenhearted, for he had elicited naught in her but a base response. Naught but animal instincts, and regardless what the noble class believed, human nature was little changed from animal nature. Just then her fingers skimmed the silver shell that hung from her neck. She closed her eyes, remembering how he had looked when he'd handed it to her.

Why had he done that? What did he hope to earn by retrieving it for her? Surely it was not simply out of kindness. If she had learned anything from Dollag, it was to be cautious, to trust no one. And that knowledge had thus far kept her safe.

So he had retrieved the shell in hopes of gaining her trust and gaining her gratitude. After all, he'd made it no secret that he desired her. Skimming the soap downward, she left a frothy trail of white between her breasts, then eased lower, over the dark honey hair and down between her thighs.

He had touched her there, too. Remembering his kisses, she spread her legs the slightest degree and let her head fall back as she slipped her hand lower still.

"Bel."

Isobel slapped her arms across her chest and turned her head to peer frantically into the corner by the door.

Gilmour stood there, his arms crossed against his chest as he stared at her. "I but wondered," he said, his grin flashing in the candlelight, "might you be needing some assistance?"

Chapter 23

Isobel's cheeks felt hot, and her head strangely dizzy. "What are you doing here?"

Gilmour eased away from the wall, moving with that cat-like elegance that was his alone. "I did not realize these were your chambers."

"Then why were you slinking about like a fevered weasel?"

He smiled, but whether it was because of her words or his view, was uncertain. "So you are saying these *are* your rooms then, Isobel?"

She narrowed her eyes. "What do you want, MacGowan?"

He brightened his smile, and between her legs, she felt the effect.

"Besides that which is obvious?" he asked.

She lifted her chin and did her best to calm her pulse. "Why are you here?"

"Originally I came to see your sister's chambers. To try to guess what might have befallen her and Ramsay."

"And have you discovered anything?"

"Aye, something quite interesting," he said and

leaned one hip against the nearby wall as he stared at her. Her breathing rushed along, though she did her best to calm it. "But I fear your presence here has driven me original intent quite out of me mind."

"I've oft thought you were out of your mind."

The dimple in his right cheek deepened. Her mouth went dry.

But he sobered in a moment, still watching her. "Where is Anora, Bel?"

Isobel drew a deep breath and told herself to be wise, careful, calculating. Or at least, to keep breathing. "You think I know?"

He watched her, his ungodly long lashes heavy over his narrowed eyes. "You are so bonny. There are times when I believe you can do no wrong."

His words caused a shiver to tremble through her, but she forced herself to remain lucid. "You are right, MacGowan. 'Tis a saint, I am."

" 'Tis what I thought of your sister when first I saw her unconscious on MacGowan land. Surely a lass of such beauty could do no harm, I thought."

"Does your brother know how you adore his wife?"

"Does he know that you covet her place in the world?"

Isobel raised her brows as a dozen wild thoughts scurried through her mind. "Might it be that you believe I mean to be rid of me own sister in order to gain her home?" she asked.

"I overheard Meara and you in the kitchen."

The words fell flatly into the silence and her mind spun, trying to recall exactly what she'd said. "Did you, now?" she asked and thought her tone was impressively steady.

"And I wonder how it is that Meara thinks you will soon take your rightful place."

The old woman's words rushed back to her. "I, too, wonder," she said. "But you must have some idea, or you would not be here."

" 'Tis not necessarily true." Leaving the wall, he paced nearer. "Where are they, Isobel?"

" 'Twas the very question I hoped to ask you, Mac-Gowan."

"Me?" Lifting a mound of linens from where they hung on the tub's rim, he seated himself. Although his expression remained cool, his nostrils flared like those of a blooded stallion's. "Are you accusing me of me brother's disappearance?"

"Why were you with the Munro?" She tried to pretend she wasn't naked, that he wasn't within touch, and that, despite everything, her body didn't thrum for him.

"Ahh, that again. I had almost forgot. But of course, you thought from the beginning that I had evil intent, did you not?" Reaching out, he brushed a strand of hair from her face. She shivered, and for a moment, his fingers hovered near her cheek, but he pulled his hand back and watched her in silence.

She stilled her tremor, then raised her chin a notch. "You haven't answered me question," she said.

"Nor have you answered mine. Where are they?"

She felt a flicker of fear skitter through her. After all, he was not only a man, nearly twice her size and strength, but he was also a MacGowan—and although she may be among her own people, most of them saw her as nothing more than a servant. But she had not survived a score of years by being paralyzed by fear.

'Twas always best to take the initiative, to be in control. And almost anywhere was safer than here in the confines of this bath. Thus, it was time to leave. Forcing her arms to unbend, she reached nervously for the rim of the tub and eased herself to her feet. His gaze followed her. That much she knew, though she refused to look at him.

"I tell you, MacGowan," she said, trying to distract him from her unveiled exodus. "I have no evil plans against me sister."

Water coursed down her body as she stepped with false boldness from the tub. But she had forgotten that he held her towel, and she turned now, fighting panic.

"In truth, lass," he said, his gaze hot as it raised to her eyes. "I long to . . . believe you."

"But you cannot, for I am lowly born and surely covet me sister's lofty station?" she asked and reaching out, grasped the towel. He held a corner and rose languidly, as if pulled to his feet by her movement. They stood now, face to face with little between them but that silly towel.

"Is it the truth?" he asked and stepped forward a half pace. "Is Evermyst your desire?"

"Nay," she said and felt his nearness like a potent tonic, burning through her system like fire. "Is it yours?"

"You wish to know me own desire?" he asked and skimmed his gaze down her naked body. She trembled beneath his perusal and when he tugged at the towel, she had no strength to keep it in her grasp. In fact, she barely managed a response.

"Aye," she said.

"Then I'll tell you true, sweet Bel." He leaned toward her so that she felt the whisper of his words against her cheek. " 'Tis not cold stones piled one atop another that I covet. 'Tis something much warmer." He reached out. She closed her eyes in a hopeless attempt to remain aloof, to withstand the feel of his fingers, but he only slipped the towel about her back, then pulled her slightly closer with the linen slung against her shoulder blades. "And softer." It seemed like an eternity before his knuckles brushed her breast. She drew in a hard breath, but he was only wrapping the towel about her torso. "But mayhap if I did not already have a place of stone and mortar to shelter me, I would feel differently."

"So that's it, then? You think I must want me sister's keep because I have nowhere else to make me home?"

" 'Tis possible," he murmured and trailed the back of his fingers along the edge of the towel.

"I do not covet what is me sister's," she said. "Indeed, it seems that being the lady of Evermyst has brought her little but sorrow."

"Sorrow? Surely she had all that her position could secure for her."

"Aye, a ragged clan that clamors for attention and a father who would all but sell her to the highest bidder."

Gilmour raised his brows at her. "She was promised to another before me brother?"

"She was bartered about like a shorn sheep, Mac-Gowan. She was used and discarded by the laird of Tytherleigh. Even so, our noble father thought the good laird would make her a fine match. But Tytherleigh had his eye on another, thus she was promised to Laird Grier of Winbourne, until Father learned of that one's penniless state. It was surely not enough that he was a good man who cared for her, for Munro's eldest son still wanted her. It mattered little that he was cruel and deceitful.

"Me sister had no one to turn to, no one who would challenge the laird of the Myst. Nay," she said. "I do not covet what is me sister's."

He raised his brows. "Not even her husband, me brother with the soulful eyes?"

So he remembered her words. The realization sent emotion singing through her system, but she stilled such foolishness. After all, he was accusing her of heinous crimes. Surely even a hound would not be attracted in such a circumstance. She turned away, putting distance between them. "Do you think I hoped to be rid of Anora so that I might have a chance at winning your brother's affections?"

"The thought has crossed me mind."

She laughed aloud. "And what would make me think that a man like your brother would want the likes of me?" she asked and turned by the bed to watch him.

Emotion flickered in his eyes, but what it was, she was not quite sure. "Did you?"

"Did I what?"

"Did you hope to win Ramsay's affection?" There was something in his tone. Anger perhaps, but more. Jealousy? Could it be? Her heart skittered along on its dangerous course. "Did you?" he repeated and stepped forward to grasp her arms.

Their gazes clashed.

"I would not harm me sister," she vowed. "Not if all the world were laid at me feet."

His grip loosened slightly. "Not even for one who could fulfill the prophecy?"

She remembered Meara's words with a start. "You do not have the attributes, MacGowan."

His lips parted in surprise. "I meant me brother."

"Oh. Nay. Of course not!" she snapped and jerked out of his grip. "I had naught to do with their disappearance, whether you believe me or nay."

"Then why are you not worried?"

"You think I am not?"

"You are here," he said, "bathing in the chambers they shared. Preparing to sleep without a care. You showed not the least bit of surprise that they were gone."

She said nothing, but turned her gaze fretfully to the bed.

"Why were you not surprised, Bel?" he asked.

"Because I already believed that she was in trouble."

He stood still, scowling. "How?"

Her mind raced. Obviously he had not heard the entirety of her conversation with Meara, or he would realize her sporadic ability to feel her sister's thoughts. And that was good, for more than one woman had lost her life for what men perceived to be witchcraft.

"I knew because you were with the Munro, the very man who threatened me sister's existence. Why else but to plan some evil against her?"

"The Munros and the Frasers are at peace," he said, his tone rife with frustration.

" 'Tis no reason to befriend him."

"And so you think that I must be planning some evil plot? You could not believe such lunacy."

"Why is it lunacy?" she asked. "Because you are a MacGowan? Because you are the rogue of the rogues? Because you have glided through your life without a care? Might it not be that you could not bear the fact that 'twas your brother, and not you, who won Anora's hand?"

"Mayhap I did not want her hand," he said and took a step toward her.

She swallowed hard. "Then mayhap you could not bear the fact that your brother won the whole of her."

He grinned and tilted his head in concession. "The whole of her is tempting," he admitted and reaching out, brushed a lock of hair from Isobel's face. "Why were you not surprised that she was gone?"

She pushed his hand aside. "I told you, because I already knew you had executed some plan against her."

His hand had not gone far. In fact, he brushed the flat surface of his nails across her chin, then ever so slowly drew them along the edge of one collarbone. "Have I?"

"Aye."

He slipped two fingers gently into the tiny dell at the base of her throat. She felt her pulse thrum against them.

"And what is it I have done, bonny Bel?" he asked and slipped his fingers ever so slowly downward.

"I do not know. But you have failed!" she said and jerked away.

He didn't try to follow, but watched her every move. "I have?"

She swallowed, steadying her nerves and trying desperately to determine what was going through his mind. "I . . . I pray so."

"If I have plotted and failed, where are they, Isobel?"

She was trembling like a feeble lambkin and hated herself for it. "I would not tell you if I knew."

"Because you do not trust me."

"Aye! 'Twould be foolish of me, since you are the one who put her in danger at the outset."

"I did no such thing, and in your heart you know it."

"I do not."

"Then why did you kiss me?"

"I did not—"

"Why did you touch me? Why did you beg for me—"

"I *never* begged!" she gasped.

His smile was slow. "You do not think I harmed your sister," he said. "You but use the possibility as a shield against me."

"I've no idea what you mean, MacGowan."

" 'Tis yourself you do not trust, lass," he said and slipped his arm about her waist.

She jerked away. "The truth is this, MacGowan. 'Tis only meself I *do* trust, and none other."

"Or so it has been for so long that you cannot bear the thought of letting another get close?"

"And why would I, MacGowan, when you are but awaiting a chance to accuse me of me own sister's murder!"

"Murder!" His face went pale. "Tell me 'tis not so."

She felt as if the air had been knocked from her lungs. "Could it be that you truly believe this, MacGowan?" she said. "Could you truly believe that I am to blame for her disappearance?"

He ground his hands into fists and turned away. "In truth, I do not know what to believe."

"And so you have decided to believe that I am a murderer."

He glanced toward her, his eyes troubled. "Why were you not surprised that she was gone?"

"Have I not explained that already?"

"Nay, for you could not have believed that I would harm her!"

"So you can believe the worst of me, but I cannot possibly do the same of you, is that the way of it?"

He scowled. "You twist me words."

"You twist your own words, MacGowan. The truth is, you do not trust me. Indeed, you believe I have murdered me only sister, and yet you would bed me."

He said nothing and she laughed. The sound was harsh against the masonry walls.

"Strange, is it not," she said, "that such a man would think himself above suspicion?"

"Bel—"

"Get out," she said and her voice was steady now.

"Tell me—"

"Get out!" she repeated.

For a moment she thought he would refuse, but finally he turned on his heel and left her.

Chapter 24

❧◦◦◦◦◦❧

It was true, Gilmour thought, and took another quaff from his horn mug. He did not trust her and yet he wanted her.

"More ale, me laird?"

What exactly *did* that say about his moral integrity?

"Me laird?"

"What's that?" He lifted his head and looked at Ailis. She was buxom, giving, available, and had been ever since he'd met her some months before. And although she sometimes smelled like the goats she herded, he had oft appreciated her charms. "Forgive me. Did you say something?"

"I asked if you wished for more ale."

"Oh. Me thanks, but nay," he said and returned his glare to his mug. Damn that Isobel. It wasn't as if she trusted *him*. Hardly that. And yet she wanted him, too. Maybe.

"Your mind is far away this night."

He glanced up, caught Ailis's smile and soothed his own scowl. He was getting as crotchety as Lachlan and as introspective as Ramsay. "Me apologies," he said. "But there is a good deal to ponder."

"Aye," she agreed. "I too worry about your brother and his wife."

"Do you?"

"Aye. She is me departed husband's distant cousin, you know, and Ramsay . . ." She didn't sigh exactly, but her bosom lifted slightly as if she entertained lurid thoughts. "Your brother is a extraordinary man."

Extraordinary! Gilmour almost snorted. He'd heard quite enough of Ramsay's fine qualities for one night, thank you, and—

"And a gentle man," she added, her tone dreamy.

Gilmour slammed his foolish jealousy to a halt. Gentle? Was she implying that she and Ramsay had some special bond?

"What do you think has befallen them?"

She shook her head. "I do not know, but . . ."

"But what?"

" 'Tis naught," she said and turned as if to leave.

Gilmour caught her arm. "Please, Ailis, if you know anything that might shed light on this matter, I would much appreciate it."

She glanced about. "I fear this is not the place to speak of such things."

Surprise smote him. Did she really have some knowledge that she might share? "Where, then?"

"I have a cottage in the village."

He remained still for a moment, his mind racing along with his pulse. "Very well," he agreed.

She smiled, then straightening, hurried away.

Gilmour did not rise immediately. He finished his ale instead and finally, when he saw that Ailis was no longer in the great hall, he too departed.

It was not difficult finding her house, and when he knocked, she answered promptly.

"Laird Gilmour." Her tone was somewhat breathy, her dark hair down about her shoulders. "Come in."

He did so. Her cottage was a humble place, tidy, lighted by a single candle.

"Would you like some ale?"

"Nay. Me thanks."

"Mead, mayhap?"

"I would hear what you know of me brother's disappearance," he said and she nodded gravely.

"Aye. Of course," she agreed and wrung her hands. "Let me just say at the outset that I wish to cause no trouble. I merely strive to do what is right."

He said nothing, only watching her.

" 'Tis Anora," she said finally. "She never wished to marry."

He tried to figure some connection between her words and their present conversation. Nothing came to mind. "What's that?"

She glanced at her hands. "She was . . . afeared of men."

Betrayed, Isobel had said.

"Indeed, before her marriage, I thought . . ." she began, but stopped as if embarrassed.

"What is it you thought?"

"Remember please that I have naught but the highest regard for Lady Anora."

He would have assumed as much if she didn't insist on him believing that very thing, but now he wondered. "Of course," he said and nodded his encouragement.

She wrung her hands again. "Since Isobel's arrival at Evermyst, they spent much of their time together." He waited, saying nothing as she watched him closely.

"They were . . . companions," she said, as if in explanation.

" 'Tis only natural, I suppose, since—"

" 'Tis nothing natural about it."

Her meaning dawned on him with a start. "Do you mean to say Lady Anora is . . . attracted to women?"

"It gives me no joy to say these things, me laird, but with your brother's disappearance . . ." She shrugged as if pained. "The truth is, she and Isobel were oft closeted away together. And once upon a time, late at night when I went to the river . . . I found them together."

He felt as if his eyes might very well pop from his head. "Together . . . ?" he asked, his imagination running wild.

"Aye, me laird."

"And were they doing something . . ." He shook his head slowly, trying to remain lucid . . . "unseemly?"

She leaned closer. "They were . . . swimming."

"Naked?"

"What?" She reared back slightly as if surprised.

He cleared his throat and tried to calm his wayward thoughts. His imagination was running wild and seemed to be taking his wick with it. "Were they unclothed?"

"Nay."

He almost sighed with disappointment. The Fraser twins . . . swimming naked. Ahhh.

"But they wore only their shifts, and 'tis surely not normal to spend such time in the water. So I . . ." She paused. "I am shamed to admit it, me laird, but I hid behind the bracken and listened while they talked."

"And what did you learn?"

She remained silent for several seconds, then, "They are sisters," she whispered. "Twins."

He continued to wait, but realized finally that this was the extent of her secret knowledge. "I fear I do not see the connection between their possible kinship and me brother's—"

"Do you not understand?" she hissed. "They . . ." Shifting her gaze, she scanned the walls as if they might well have ears then added, "They were lovers in the womb."

His brows shot into his hairline. Now this *was* news.

"Have you not heard that 'tis the way with twins? They mate while yet unborn," she insisted. "Their lady mother knew this. She knew, and so she separated them. But somehow, by hook or by crook, they found each other and wished to renew . . . their bond."

Gilmour struggled to consider her words. "But if such is the case, why did Anora wed me brother atall?"

"Your pardon, me laird," Ailis said and smiled a little, "but the MacGowan name carries some power even here in the far north. And too, your brother's arrival saved Anora from wedding the Munro, or any other of the swains who came to Evermyst in an attempt to claim her hand."

"So you think she married Ramsay to gain her own ends."

"As I said, me laird, I have naught but the highest regard for me lady, but now Laird Ramsay is missing and I . . ." Her voice broke and a whimper of dismay escaped her pretty lips. "I do not trust this Isobel and I fear—" She sniffled and he moved forward to console her. She melted into his arms. "I fear she has gotten rid of Ramsay so that she can be reunited with her sister."

"There now," Gilmour said and stroked her hair. "You needn't fear, lass, for if the truth be told, I think some wee trouble has befallen me brother and his wife and that they will be home posthaste."

"But if that is so, why would Isobel return now just when Ramsay has disappeared?"

"Tell me, Ailis," he said, his mind spinning, "have you told others about your suspicions?"

She gazed into his eyes and shook her head.

"Have you shared your belief that they are sisters?"

She tightened her arms about his waist and pressed her face against his shoulder.

"Ailis?"

"Nay," she said, "I feared I could trust no one but you."

"Then you needn't worry, lass. For I am certain 'tis only fear for your lady that makes you believe such things. She seemed happy with me brother, did she not?"

"Aye," she agreed hopefully and glanced up again. "She did, and you are right, I am sure, for who would not be happy in the arms of one of the famous rogues?"

He smiled. There were few things on earth that he enjoyed more than flattery. Isobel never flattered him. In fact, she spent a good deal of time confronting him with his faults and the rest of their time driving him insane. She was opinionated and sharp witted. He had never like opinionated, sharp-witted women, so why couldn't he get her out of his mind? Could Ailis be right? Might the girl be attracted to women? But she had trembled beneath his hands. Had it been revulsion? Nay, he could not yearn for a woman who did not yearn back. And despite everything, he did yearn. Just the memory of her in the burn hardened—

"The brothers MacGowan have indeed been the answer to our prayers here at Evermyst," she whispered. "Peaceful and powerful, cunning and kind, loving and . . ." She paused, looking him straight in the eye. "Beloved."

He smiled. " 'Tis kind of you to—" he began, but just then she rose up on her toes and kissed him.

Placing his hands gently on Ailis's arms, he eased back. "It is not that I do not wish to stay," he said. "But I fear I must return to the keep."

"And disappoint your desire? There is none at the castle who can give you what I can," she said and kissed him again.

"I am sorry," he said and caught her hands in his own. "But I fear I must leave."

It was not a simple task to fight his way out of her cottage, but finally he succeeded. The great hall was dark when he reached it, but Gilmour made his way past the sleeping hounds and servants without lighting a candle and slipped up the stairs toward the bed chamber he had once shared with Lachlan. The castle seemed strangely quiet and a cool draft wafted up from the hall. He glance behind to see if the door had been opened.

"Most remain longer."

Gilmour started at the words and jerked about, but

the speaker was only Meara, leaning on her gnarled staff as she gazed at him with bird bright eyes from the top of the stairs.

"What say you?" he asked.

"Most remain longer at the widow's house," she said. "Why did you not?"

He raised his brows. "What makes you think I was with the widow?"

She scowled, drawing her overgrown eyebrows together in a wrinkled line. "What is it that makes you think me a fool?"

He reached the top step and gazed down at her. "I would call you many things Meara of the Fold," he said. "Fool would not be amongst them."

"Why such a swift return?" she repeated.

The top of her grizzled head barely reached the cat-eyed sporran that hung from his shoulder, but there was a force to her and a crackling intellect that warned one and all to watch his step.

"Tell me, old woman, what do you think happened to me brother?" he asked.

"You think I know?"

"I think you know a good deal."

"So mayhap I have plotted some evil against him?"

"How would Isobel rise to her rightful place?"

It was her turn to start in surprise. Then she nodded down the narrow hallway. "Come," she said and waddled off.

Taking a square, iron-bound lantern from a peg on the wall, she pushed open a door and stepped inside. Gilmour followed. The old woman raised the light and its mellow glow flickered off oiled portraits, gleaming from one to another until Meara stopped in front of a vast, gilded painting. The woman portrayed there was young and bonny. Her hair was the color of summer wheat and her lips bowed up in a winsome expression, but it was her eyes that captivated him. They were Isobel's eyes, and yet they were not.

"Anora?" he asked.

"Nay," said the old woman. " 'Twas Lady Senga, their grandmother."

He thought for a moment. "So you had some loyalty to this Senga," he said, "and now her estranged granddaughter has returned, looking so like her kinswoman that you cannot bear to see her act the servant. But how, I wonder, do you plan to elevate her station?"

"You listened in on our words," she said.

"How?" he asked, ignoring her accusation.

"You think I would sacrifice Anora so that her ragged sister might take her place as lady of this hall?"

He shrugged and followed the course of the wall, glancing at the portraits there. "Mayhap you feel some guilt for your part in Isobel's past."

"There is blame aplenty." She sounded weary, and when he glanced her way he saw that she had taken a seat not far from a half-finished tapestry. The loom stood silent and waiting.

"You regret your actions?" he asked, turning toward her.

"I regret idiocy."

He raised his brows.

"Superstition!" she spat. "Fear! They make fools of men."

"But not of women?"

She shrugged, looking weary and ungodly old. "Often enough they make martyrs of women."

Something cramped in his gut. "So 'tis best that Isobel was sacrificed."

She scowled at him. "Isobel was not born to be a sacrificial lamb. Isobel was born to survive."

"And to take Anora's place when that lady falls?"

She creaked with surprising speed to her feet. "There was a moment when I thought you had some intelligence, MacGowan. Try not to dissuade me now. Why did you return so speedily from the widow's cottage?"

He watched her as he milled Ailis's words about in his mind. "Why did your lady wed me brother?"

She seemed surprised by his question. "Have you not heard the prophesy?"

"Aye. It just so happens that I care little for the tales of old wives."

"So that's what the prophesy is to you? Naught but a tale spun by idle tongues?"

He lifted an appeasing palm and she snorted. "Mayhap I was entirely wrong about you, lad."

"In what regard?"

"Mayhap you are not in the least bit cunning."

"And mayhap you could answer one simple question put before you, old woman," he said and stepped toward her. "Why did she marry me brother?"

"Because she could not live without him."

Gilmour stopped in his tracks some six feet from her. Meara glared up at him.

"How so?" he asked.

"She was not complete without him."

"So she found Ramsay . . . appealing?"

The old woman tilted her head like an aging crow. "Appealing?"

"She was . . . attracted to him."

Meara snorted. "Hell lad, I was attracted . . ." she began and stopped abruptly. "What did the widow tell you?"

Gilmour cleared his throat and Meara cackled a laugh.

"So that's what she says to lure bonny lads into her bed these days? That the woman he truly desires will never desire him?"

"I know not what you speak of."

"I speak of Ailis's lies," she croaked and pointed her staff at him with vengeance. "She knows not that the lassies be born of the same womb, thus she must think of another way to spill suspicion on them. But I never thought that a MacGowan would believe . . ." She paused again, eyeing him like a hungry raven. "Did you couple with her or nay, lad?"

The question took him back a pace. " 'Tis none of your concern."

"All that concerns me lassies concerns me," she rasped. "So tell . . . But wait. You were not gone long enough, not if your reputation was honestly earned."

He folded his arms across his chest and glared at her. Never in the past had his reputation irritated him more. In truth, it did nothing but bedevil him these days. "After all your years upon this earth, you must surely know that rumors are rarely true."

The old woman's eyes brightened even more. "What are you saying, lad?"

"Only that you should not believe all you hear."

Not for a moment did her arrow sharp gaze leave his face, and then she mumbled something. Something he could not quite hear.

"What say you?" he asked, canting his head.

She grinned toothlessly. "Aye, it takes power to do what you have done. And surely with your bonny looks, you are sorely tested." She nodded and chuckled. "Aye. You are lovable. But of the other . . ." Her voice drifted away.

"What are you mumbling about, old one?" he asked, but she merely shuffled toward the door.

"Time will tell," she muttered. "Time and circumstances."

Chapter 25

Gilmour stood on the grassy slope beside Evermyst's towering heights. Isobel had left the keep in a creaking dray sometime earlier, had accompanied Stout Helena and wee Mary, escorted by Tree down the tortuous trail toward the village. But upon reaching the level plain below, the women had dismounted with the babe and foraged out upon the warm, sun-dappled grassland in an apparent search for wild herbs.

Who was Isobel, really? Gone were the bright garments she had worn in Henshaw. Once again she was garbed in a weathered gown and sloppy coif, but it made little difference, for he had seen beyond her ragged clothing to the woman beneath.

From directly above them, he watched her bend and pluck up some unknown plant, watched Helena set wee Mary on the ground not far away. Dressed in a cherry red shift, the child sat upon the turf and gazed into the sun as Helena presented her with a flower. She giggled and smiled, displaying tiny, bright teeth. The sight soothed his soul somehow. Still, questions nagged at him. Where were Anora

317

and Ramsay, and what did Isobel know of their disappearance?

He had always believed that she cared for her sister. But if such was the case, why did she not mourn? Why did she not worry? There was no way for her to be certain of Anora's whereabouts unless she herself had ordained them.

Scowling, Gilmour raised his gaze as he caught a flash of movement on the road that wound from the south toward Evermyst. At this distance he could not tell who it was, someone on horseback perhaps.

Minutes ticked by. The traveler came closer. It was two horses. Gilmour straightened, his heart beating faster. Could it be Ramsay and Anora? But nay. He saw now that only one horse was ridden, and that by a tiny person, too small to be Anora.

Francois! He recognized his steed suddenly and saw Stout Helena straighten as she shielded her eyes to gaze in the direction of the road. Isobel turned, paused, then rushed up the hill toward the rider.

In that instant, Mour realized the traveler was Claude, mounted astride Francois, and following behind was Isobel's mare. Gilmour laughed out loud and prepared to descend the rocky stairs toward them, but in that instant a cool draft of air swept over him. It shivered up his spine, raising the hair at the back of his neck. He turned with stiff premonition to scan the figures far below, but all seemed well. Isobel was already reaching for Claude's hand. Helena was making her way through the heather toward the newcomer, and wee Mary . . . Like a blow to his throat, his breath stopped. Mary was gone. Disappeared! But nay, there she was.

Thrilled by her newfound freedom, she had followed a butterfly's course and pulled herself to her feet at the edge of the rushing water of the firth.

Terror gripped him even as he bellowed her name.

Everything seemed strangely slow, after that. He saw Mary look up, saw Isobel glance toward him, then away. He heard her shriek the baby's name in sheer terror, but even as she bolted toward the child, it seemed as if her movements were mired in time.

Wee Mary started violently, and then, like a mug set atremble, she tumbled backward, striking her bottom on the edge of the cliff, then rolling inexorably toward the water.

Mour saw the waves splash skyward, white and frothy. He heard Isobel's scream echo Helena's, but the child was already gone beneath the restless waters, being swept relentlessly downstream. Sunlight glinted golden off the tip of a wave. Isobel raced on, but the water's edge was a lifetime away. Directly below him, Gilmour thought he saw a flash of red. In an instant he was at the cliff's edge, and for a heartbeat he remained. And then he was falling, tumbling hopelessly toward the sea. The water struck him like a stone wall, then closed around him, sucking him in. He couldn't breathe. Couldn't think. Panic clawed at his gut, but off to his left a streak of red caught his eye.

Mary! Her memory tore aside the terror, and he turned, fighting his way through the tumultuous waters.

There! Red again. He tried to pull himself toward it. But suddenly it was gone. He turned about, trying to find her, but frothy water was everywhere, stinging his throat, burning his lungs.

Air! He needed air, but in his mind's eye he saw the

child's limp form. He heard the weeping, felt the despair. Desperate, he turned again, and there, not two rods away, he saw a flash of color.

Clawing through the water, he pulled himself toward it. Gone. Gone again, and his lungs were bursting. But there it was again! He reached out, and his hand closed around something, but the current crashed against him. A burst of pain blasted at his shoulder. Agony crushed his chest.

He could think of nothing but air now. Where was it? Up. But where was up? Frantic, he tore through the water. But there was no hope. Only pain. Only white, burning pain swirling around him, blasting his mind and pulling him down into the screaming abyss.

Gilmour thrashed into awareness, trying to reach the surface, his lungs burning.

"MacGowan! Lie still."

He jerked again, reeling in hopelessness, but reality settled slowly around him. He was no longer beneath the waves. No longer dying. He took a deep breath. The air burned his lungs, but it was air and not the aching brine.

He turned and realized that he was lying in Evermyst's infirmary.

"MacGowan." Isobel's voice was quieter now, but her face, when he focused on it, was as pale as death. Memories stormed back; Mary beneath the waves, her tiny body pummeled just beyond his grasp.

"Mary—" The name tore at his throat. Terror ripped at his heart. "Did you find her?"

Isobel stared at him. Her face seemed bleached of all color but for the stark blue of her eyes.

"Nay." He shook his head, disavowing her sorrow. "Nay!" he groaned and closing his eyes, swept his arm across his face, shutting out the world.

"MacGowan." He felt her hands on his arm, but he pushed her away, not able to look into her face.

"Leave me be," he ordered, but she touched his arm again.

"MacGowan, wee Mary is well."

The world seemed to halt around him. He tried a careful breath, then slowly opened his eyes. They stung, as did his throat.

"She is well," Isobel repeated. " 'Twas you who saved her."

He searched for words, for belief, but nothing came for a moment.

"Do you lie?" he asked.

"Nay."

He tried to reach for her, but his arm did not move and he glanced down, distracted.

"Healer said . . ." Isobel began, then grimaced, making the teardrop glitter in a shaft of light that fell through the high, narrow window. "Healer said it had been yanked out of place."

He scowled, first at the bandage that bound his arm to his chest, then at her.

"Your arm," she said. " 'Twas not in its socket. But she says it will mend well."

Memories blurred in his mind. Water, terror, pain, but nothing of bearing wee Mary to shore.

"It took Tree some time to pry your fingers from her clothing." She cleared her throat. "It seems they had locked in the fabric before you fell unconscious."

He shook his head. "I didn't reach shore."

"Nay, but you had reached the surface and were easy to find. While Mary . . ." Her mouth twitched and her next words were barely audible. "I could not get to her."

He realized suddenly that she was wet, her gown hanging heavy and damp from her narrow shoulders. It made her look all the more fragile. "You should remove those garments," he said and felt strangely heavy himself, as though he were still weighed down by the water. As though his mind was working with unusual slowness.

She said nothing.

He scowled. "You are certain she is well?"

"Aye."

He remained silent for a moment. "Was it you who saved me?"

"I was not strong enough. Tree pulled you out." She cleared her throat. "You brought Mary with you . . . though you were not awake."

"Why aren't you with her now?"

She wrung her hands. "I wish to know why—"

" 'Tis enough now." A harsh voice cut her off, and Gilmour raised his gaze. The movement made his head swim, but he focused on the familiar face of Evermyst's physician. "Rest now, me laird," she said. " 'Tis bad enough that we have lost your brother."

"Why do you—" Isobel began, but Healer stopped her.

"Quit now, girl," she insisted. "Can you not see the debt we owe Laird Gilmour?"

He watched Isobel as she backed away from him. She said nothing, only stared for a moment longer, n turned and slipped from the room.

* * *

"Isobel."

Bel turned at the sound of her name, but did not remove her hands from the dough she was kneading. Two days had passed since MacGowan had saved Mary. She hadn't seen either of them since. Indeed, she had said little more to Claude, who had slept almost continuously since her arrival. "What is it, Meara?"

"Laird Gilmour is in need of an ale."

Isobel shifted her gaze to a nearby maid who was just swinging a steaming pot away from the fire.

"Clarinda," she said. "Might you—"

"Clarinda is busy," Meara said. " 'Tis you who must fetch it for him."

"The bread needs—"

"I care not what the bread needs," Meara interrupted. " 'Tis your task to do. After all, he saved your lady's child. The least you can do is bring him a mug to quench his thirst before he sleeps."

Something akin to fear curled in Isobel's stomach, but she raised her chin and looked the old woman in the eye. "I do not take orders from you, Meara of the Fold."

The old woman's grizzled brows rose as if shot from a cannon. "Don't you now, lassie?"

"Nay," she said and returned her gaze to her dough. "I do not. Take him the ale yourself if you're so convinced with his needs."

The old woman was silent for a moment, then, "So you are ready to declare yourself?"

"What's that?" Isobel glanced up sharply.

"I, too, think it is time for you to take your rightful place. Clarinda can be the first to know."

Clarinda was just lifting a round bottomed pot from the glowing embers and turned her reddened face toward them. "What is it I should know?"

Meara turned her gaze slowly from Isobel to the maid. "The truth is this, lass—"

"I shall take him the ale," Isobel said.

Meara smiled. "There's a good lass," she crooned. "You'll find him in the infirmary. And take wee Mary from him so he can sleep."

Isobel made her way slowly down the darkened hall toward the sick room. Her bread needed attention, and though Clarinda was good enough with soups and the like she was far from adept at baking. Bel should be back in the kitchen where she belonged.

Candlelight spilled from the open door of the infirmary, but the glow did not quite meet the far wall.

Isobel's feet slowed even more as she approached her destination. Damn Meara. The old woman was hardly the lady of the keep. In fact, Isobel thought, her stomach churning, if she wished, she could leave this very night. Could flee Evermyst and never return. Not because she was afraid, as others suggested. Nay, 'twas because . . .

Voices murmured from the infirmary, stopping her thoughts.

"You are well?" Claude spoke just above a whisper. So she had left her bed to find the man who had given her a name.

"Aye, lassie," Mour said. "I only lie here to gain sympathy from the maids. And to spend time with wee Mary, of course. Do I not look pitiable?"

Aye, he was pitiable—not a champion at all, but a vain rogue, Bel told herself and stepped level with the doorway, intending to finish her task and be gone. But one glance into the room and she halted, frozen in the dimness of the empty hallway.

Inside the narrow chamber, candlelight shone in a golden circle around the bed, and in the center of that circle sat MacGowan. His hair glimmered like dark honey upon his bare shoulders and below that, where his arm was trussed to his chest by white bandage, his muscles rippled in rows across his abdomen. But even that sight was not the one which stopped Isobel's breath in her throat. Nay, it was the tenderness of his expression that seized her.

Propped upon his arm, Mary lay motionless, gazing with sleepy adoration into his eyes. Her tiny, bowed lips were slightly parted and one perfect hand was curled into the bandage that crossed his chest.

As for wee Plums, she stood cautiously back from him, her fingers wrapped tight in the folds of her rumpled gown.

"You should be abed, Claude, me love," MacGowan said, but the girl shook her head.

"I . . ." Her words faltered. ". . . feared . . ."

"There now, lass. There is no need to fear," Mour soothed, but Claude spoke again, her voice broken, her right hand crunching her much-abused skirt.

"I thought I had k-killed you."

"Killed me? Nay!"

"I thought . . ." There was a long painful pause. "When I care . . . die . . ." She labored for breath through her terror and in the hallway Isobel squeezed her eyes shut, feeling the girl's ravaged thoughts burning to her own soul. ". . . I arrived and . . . couldn't see you . . . waves . . ."

Her words were no longer discernible, but were lost in her breathy panic.

"Hush, now," Mour soothed. " 'Tis silly, you're being. I am not dead, wee lass, nor will I be anytime soon, God willing."

A few stuttered breaths could be heard, but nothing else.

"Be calm now. All is well."

"You fell . . . so far."

"Nay," he denied, and reaching past Mary, took her hand in his own. "Nay, lass, 'twas hardly a drop atall." Gently, he tugged her forward until she nearly touched his bed. "Little more than a wee step into a bath, really. Maid Isobel does as much for sport."

"She . . . won't speak to me."

"Isobel?"

The girl nodded. "She knows it is me fault that—"

"Nay, she thinks no such thing. She is worried, is all."

Claude shook her head, but he squeezed her hand and drew her closer still. "Here now, I've a few things to tell you, Claude, and these things you will believe, for I will not be lying to you. You had nothing to do with me dive into the firth, heroic though it was. 'Twas Mary here who decided to take a swim. I but tried to fetch her out. And here we are, both safe and hale. 'Tis not your fault and Isobel knows this as well as I."

Silence settled over the chamber for several moments. Claude punished her faded gown with her free hand.

"You left," she murmured.

It took him a moment to respond, to catch up to her thoughts. "I know, lass," he said. "But I would have returned to Henshaw when I could. You should not have come so far alone. There are many evils between here and the Red Lion's front door."

"Francois came back."

"Of course he did, lass, for he remembered your kindness. But you should have remained where it is safe."

"He is fleet."

" 'Tis true," Mour agreed, "and he would have kept you safe if he could, but what if brigands came upon you whilst you slept? Then you would have been caught afoot, and I dare not think what might have befallen you."

The world seemed utterly silent before the girl spoke again, just barely above a whisper. "You asked me to care for him. And I knew . . ."

Isobel squeezed her eyes closed against the words, for she already knew the truth. The girl had *not* slept. Nay, she had left all she knew, had risked her life and remained astride for days on end just to be near—

"I knew Francois could not live without you," Claude whispered and in that moment the horn spilled from Isobel's hand and crashed to the floor at her feet.

Mary jerked. Claude started, and Gilmour raised his smoldering gaze to Bel's.

"Isobel," he breathed. "Is something amiss?"

She tried to speak, but her throat burned and her eyes stung, and in the end there was nothing she could do but wrap her fist about her silver shell and flee back to the safety of the kitchens.

Chapter 26

~~~ᐧᗐᗹᑇ~~~

Gilmour awoke some time later. It felt cool in the room and dank. Shifting slightly, he realized wee Mary still lay in his arms. Claude had left sometime before, her brown eyes wide, but her brow untroubled.

Near his bed, the candle flickered in a wayward draft. Perhaps it was Senga, he thought, and smiled as he stroked Mary's golden locks. She was safe. Isobel was well. Even Claude had arrived unscathed. Thus, all was right, for Ramsay would not return to find that those he cherished had been lost.

He *would* return. Gilmour was certain of it. Ramsay was too surly, too obstinate to be lost forever. And then there was the matter of Anora. Not while he lived would Ram allow evil to befall his bride. Therefore, Gilmour simply had to make certain all they held dear still prospered upon their return.

He closed his eyes for an instant, trying to find assurance in the babe's closeness. Wee Mary was safe, he repeated, but as the thought passed through his mind, she wriggled closer as if chilled.

Gilmour snuggled the child against him. The small

328

infirmary, which usually seemed so warm, felt strangely cool just now, and surely a draft would do the babe no good. He'd best return her to her own bed. Carefully scooping the wee cherub onto his hale arm, Gilmour rose to his feet and stepped into the hallway.

Despite his thoughts to the contrary, it was not yet late. Companionable voices sounded from the great hall, and though he was not usually the sort to avoid an ale and a good yarn, he did so now, turning down a dim hallway toward the nursery.

Stepping through that doorway, he bent carefully and placed the bairn into her cradle before drawing the woolens up around her. He prepared to leave then, but in that instant the babe opened her eyes with a startled cry. Dropping to his knees, he rocked the tiny bed back and forth and sang to her in Gaelic. The tiny body relaxed, the sleepy eyes fell closed, but for several moments Mour could not leave. Instead, he crouched over her and whispered a prayer of safety for this night and always.

"Laird MacGowan."

Startled, Gilmour looked toward Helena.

"What be you doing here?" she whispered.

"Wee Mary sleeps," he said, keeping his voice low as he rose somewhat sheepishly to his feet. "I thought it best to return her here."

"But you should not have left your own bed. I came to fetch her. And when I found her gone—" She lifted a quivering hand to her vast bosom as words failed her.

"All is well, Helena. Fear not."

"Aye," she said and nodded quickly as she shuffled forward to huddle over the cradle for an elongated moment. "All is well because of you." She glanced up, her faded eyes filled with tears. "And for that I owe you an endless debt."

"You owe me nothing."

" 'Twas me own folly that . . ." For a moment she could not go on. " 'Twas me own fault that she was endangered."

"It'll do no good to dwell on it."

"So it is true," she whispered and stared at him, her eyes wide with fear.

"What is true?"

"You are as your brother," she said, and lifting her overskirt, buried her face in the soiled folds to sob.

Gilmour stared at her in perplexity.

"There now," he soothed uneasily. "What is amiss?"

"Do you not see?" she asked, glancing up. " 'Tis the prophesy come true again. Always I knew you were loving and beloved. One glance at your bonny smile told me true." She sniffled as she stared at him. "But now I fear you have the other attributes, as well."

"Other—"

"Peace and power and cunning and kindness," she said. "You possess them all, me laird."

Smiling, he reached out to wipe a tear from the old woman's plump cheek. "I am flattered, but I do not understand why you would find such an idea distressing. Surely this would be a good—"

"Do you not understand?" she asked, her voice anguished. "You have become our champion."

He tried to discern her meaning, but gave up with a shake of his head.

"Another hero to save Evermyst," she explained impatiently. "Another hero to wed a Fraser bride. And though I cherish Isobel, I cannot bear to lose . . ." She collapsed into tears again, scrunching her skirt against her reddened face.

"Helena, calm yourself," he soothed. "Whatever are you talking about?"

"I know the truth," she stuttered.

Gilmour wished he could say as much. "You do?"

She nodded miserably. "Wee Isobel," Helena whispered, her voice strained from crying. "She is me lady's sister true born."

"Ah." Was there anyone at Evermyst who didn't know the truth? "So you know that, do you?"

"Aye. I am not so foolish as old Meara thinks."

He smiled fondly. "Indeed not, but why does this make you so unhappy?"

"Isobel has been sent to us here at Evermyst," she said as if everything was ultimately obvious. "And you to wed her."

In truth, he couldn't have been more surprised if she had told him he'd been send to draw the sun into the sky each morning, and no less sure of his ability to achieve that end. "I?" he asked, spreading a hand across his chest. "I was sent to wed Isobel?"

"Of course. 'Tis clear that you long for her."

"If that were true, why would this concern you?"

"Because she has been sent to replace her sister, and you to replace your brother now that they are . . ." Words failed her and Mour grasped her arm in one hand.

"Helena," he said, "hear me now. Me brother is not dead. Neither is his bride." Fear curdled his stomach, but he could not believe, *would* not believe, that they were gone forever. They were the brother rogues; naught could defeat him. But even as the thought passed through his mind he said a silent prayer. "Ramsay is alive," he said, tightening his grip on her arm. "And he shall soon return with his bride."

"Do you think so?" she whispered, glancing up through watery eyes.

"Aye," he said, "and when they do, they shall find that all is well here at Evermyst."

"But—"

He tightened his grip. "All must be well," he said and fought down the desperation in his voice. "Thus I need you to care for wee Mary."

"But I have f-failed."

"You have not failed," he said. "And you shall not. Now brace yourself woman, for Evermyst cannot survive without you."

She sniffled and straightened slightly. "You are kind, me laird."

"And bonny, too," he said and grinned. "But don't let it set you crying again or you'll wake the babe."

Helena chuckled sloppily and in the hallway Isobel blanched. It could not be true, she thought in a panic. He had not been sent to fulfill the prophesy. She was not a true Fraser and she did not want him, did not need—

She heard his footsteps approach, and stepped rapidly into a shadowed doorway. Fool! Surely she would be found, for he would walk right past her on his return to the infirmary.

It took only a moment, however, to realize that she was wrong. That he had gone in the opposite direction.

Scowling, she peeked out from behind the stone wall to watch his retreating back. Where was he going at this late hour? Could it be that he was planning some mischief even now? Could it be that he only saved the babe so that they would trust him all the more?

He was cunning, after all. Even Stout Helena admitted that. And mayhap that was his ploy, to win the hearts of the people and take his brother's place here at lofty Evermyst. Mayhap he even planned to do just as Helena had suggested—to take Bel for a bride so that the castle would be rightfully his. But it would not work.

Stepping from her hiding place, Isobel padded silently down the hallway behind Mour, and when she saw that he did not turn aside either for the great hall or the kitchens, she hurried her steps. It was only a few minutes until she peeked around a corner and found him standing at the door to the master chamber, the very chamber where she had tried to rest only minutes before. He raised his hand as if to knock, then drew his fist back to his side, and turned away.

Isobel ducked rapidly out of sight, but there was no need, for in a moment she heard the sound of her door being opened.

He was entering her chambers.

How dare he go inside uninvited! Then she remembered that less than a full hour before she had sneaked down to the infirmary to spy on him. It was not that she was drawn to him, of course. Nor that the sight of him with wee Mary made her heart ache. Nay, she had no deep feelings for either him or the babe. 'Twas simply that she needed to observe him in secret in order to determine his true motives. But he had been fast asleep. His sable lashes had fallen closed and his hair, soft as the babe's, had curled about the corded strength of his throat. The feather that always adorned his single braid lay beside Mary's parted lips and fluttered softly with each quiet sigh. But it was the sight of the babe's hand atop his arm that had held Isobel hidden there for long minutes. Each perfect, ivory digit was spread upon the dark muscle near his elbow, and as she watched, it seemed almost that the babe had placed her hand there just so to feel the strength of him, to feel the safety, to know that despite every evil that threatened her world, he was there to keep her well.

But wee Mary was only a babe, and did not know that often those who profess to care for you are those who wound you the worst. She had yet to learn not to trust. But perhaps, with this man near she would not have to—

Nay. Isobel halted the thought. Fools trusted and fools died, and she was not a fool.

And what the devil was MacGowan still doing in Anora's chamber? Though large by comparison, the rooms were hardly so immense that it would take him this long to—

A quiet gasp escaped her lips. Could it be that he had found the secret passage that wended through the rock to the firth? Or perhaps he had always known about it. Perhaps he was even now making his way toward the boat that waited on the water far below. But to what end?

Quietly leaving her hiding place, she pattered carefully down the hall and pressed her spine against the wall beside the bedchamber door. Not a whisper of sound did she hear. When the silence continued, she glanced inside. The room was dark, quiet, empty, but beside the bed . . . might there be a glimmer of light?

Stepping quietly into the room, she saw that the tapestry that adorned the wall had been pressed aside and the tiny door behind it had been left ajar.

It seemed she had little choice but to step through that portal and into the dark passageway. Little choice but to trip quietly through the blackness, fingers skimming the rough stone as she wended her way toward the heart of the mountain.

Why would he go to the boat? Where did he wish to be, and how did he plan to coerce the oarsman into following his directives? After all, the boat was meant to be used for emergencies only. Unless MacGowan planned some evil against the guard. Unless . . .

Her thoughts stopped abruptly, for in that instant, her fingers met thinnest air. The wall had disappeared. She stumbled to a halt, catching herself, and finding that that very wall continued only inches away. And yet, as she felt breathlessly about, she found that it was not the wall after all, but a door of sorts, made of the same stone that the hallway was carved from. Pushing her hand cautiously into the opening, she moved it slightly. It swung wide without a sound. She drew a careful breath, said a prayer, and stepped silently through.

The passage was narrow on the other side. Although she could see nothing, she could feel the closeness without even reaching out to the walls beside her. She moved more slowly now, down and inward, her heart thrumming in her chest.

It seemed like an eternity before she saw the glimmer of light to her right. She stopped, listening. Still, she could hear naught but the sound of her own breath in the darkness. Thus she moved, slowly, ever so slowly until she came to a gray rectangle that outlined an opening in the rock. No sound disturbed her, so she turned and peered into the chamber. It was dark but for a pale, distant light shining from behind a wall. A trunk stood near the door, but otherwise it was empty. Taking a deep breath, she stepped into the chamber.

A dark form reared over her. She shrieked, jumping backward and knocking the door closed. The shadow swore and stumbled to a halt.

"Bugger it!"

"MacGowan?" Her voice quavered on his name as she pressed her back against the rough wood of the portal behind her.

"What the devil are you doing here?"

Anger swelled up on the wings of her fright. "That is me own question to ask," she said. "What were you doing in me sister's chambers?"

Even in the dim light, she could see that his brows were pulled low over his eyes.

"I wished to talk to you," he said. "But I found the light rather disturbing."

"What light?"

"The one that shone from behind the tapestry."

"The hidden door was open?"

"Nay."

"Then 'tis not possible that you could have seen a light."

"One would tend to agree," he admitted. "Unless Senga has a penchant for making mischief. I brought no light with me, and yet the candle glowed in this chamber."

She stared at him. Was he joking or did he believe in

shades? And if he believed, how much foolishness would he believe about herself and her sister? "Why are you here?"

"At Evermyst, or at—"

"Here," she interrupted. "In this chamber. And how did you find it? I have lived at Evermyst for some time and never knew of its presence."

He shrugged. "As I said, there was a light. Why are you here?"

Good question. "When I . . . returned to me sister's chamber I saw that the passage had been breached."

"But you did not know by whom?"

She carefully kept from fidgeting. "Nay. How could I?"

He grinned a little, his teeth as white as the bandage that crossed his bare chest. "You were following me."

"And why would I do that, MacGowan?"

"Because you are in love with me."

"I am not."

"Aye, lass, you are," he said and stepped toward her. "But you are afraid to admit it."

She managed a laugh. It was not very convincing, but it was the best she could do under the circumstances. "You have forever thought much too highly of yourself, MacGowan."

"Mayhap," he acquiesced and took a few deliberate steps around her, as if examining her from the side. "But perhaps not so highly as *you* think of me."

"You, me laird, are deluded."

"Why were you following me?"

"I was not—"

"Why did you come to the infirmary?"

She felt her face redden. "How did you know—" She halted, catching herself, but his brows were already raised.

"I was awake," he said, then grinned with evil happiness. "Or was there another time? Tell me, sweet Bel, did you come back to watch me whilst I slept?"

"Nay," she said and he laughed.

"Why not admit it?"

"Because it is not true."

"I haven't even told you what to admit yet."

"But I know it will be false."

"You wonder about me," he said. "You wonder if I am as good as I think am."

She said nothing.

"The truth is this, lass," he said, his expression almost sober. "No one is as good as I think I am."

Her lips parted in surprise but he continued on.

"The truth is this, Bel; luck was with me when wee Mary fell. Naught else, for as you know I am not a powerful swimmer."

"Modesty?" she asked. "From you, MacGowan?"

He snorted. "Far from it. I simply have no wish for you to believe some nonsensical prophesy that was spoken long before our time."

"I am not Helena, who believes—" She saw the trap, but it was already too late. His delighted grin told her as much.

"You heard?" he asked. "You were listening to me conversation with the woman."

"Nay, I—"

"You were hiding in the hall," he countered, "eavesdropping as I spoke in the nursery."

"You're daft."

"Why did you come, Bel? Could it be that you could stay away no longer?" He took a step forward. "Could it be that you dream of me in your lonely bed and came to search for me?" He touched her cheek, and she swatted his hand away.

"I was not eavesdropping. I only came to check on the babe."

"I dream of you, also," he said. "But I will not let you believe that which is not true."

"Then you are admitting that you are a daft cad who—"

"I am saying that we were not sent to replace Ramsay and Anora. Nor were we sent to fulfill some foolish prophesy."

"I never thought so," she said.

" 'Tis good," he said. "For when you give yourself to me, I do not want to think 'tis because of some misguided belief."

She tried to think of some scathing rejoinder, but for the life of her, she couldn't. In fact, when she looked into his eyes, it was all she could do to continue to breathe.

"Tell me, Bel," he murmured, lifting his hand to her cheek again. "Is it time?"

Desire curled like wood smoke through her, and though she ordered her feet to move, they would not.

"Are you ready?" he asked and kissed her. "I ask, for I must warn you: once you give yourself to me, I shall never let you go."

Panic washed over her. Breaking away, she reached for the door. She jerked the latch, but nothing happened. Breathing hard, she tried again, but it was no use.

They were locked in.

Chapter 27

Isobel turned, her heart pounding. "Is this how you manage to deflower all your scores of virtuous maids?"

Gilmour didn't move, but stood watching her as if perplexed. "Are you saying we are locked in?"

"Do you pretend to be surprised?"

His brows rose with his grin, which lifted one corner of his tantalizing mouth. "You think I planned this?"

She rattled the latch. "How else would it have become locked?"

"Mayhap it was Senga's doing. Or else 'twas you what locked the door."

"What?"

"You want me, Bel, but you are afraid to admit it. Mayhap this is your way of having me while yet denying your desire."

"You are surely daft!"

"And you are afraid. But I will not hurt you."

"I am not afraid of you."

"Then come hither."

"Just because I am not afraid does not mean that I will lie with you."

He laughed. "And just because I can, does not mean that I will."

She scowled.

"Come away from the door. Do you know where we are?"

She glanced about. "In the heart of the mountain."

"I believe 'twas your mother's secret chambers."

"What? Why?"

Turning, he paced to the nearby trunk, then crouched to lift something from the ironbound box. The contents were flat and draped with blue velvet. The fabric fell away, and Isobel saw that it had covered a portrait.

Gilmour lifted it into the light so she could see the painting of a young girl. Her gown was an emerald hue, her hair bright as gold, and in her eyes there was happiness.

"Anora," she sighed, taking the portrait.

But Gilmour shook his head. "Look again, lass."

She scowled at him, then turned her gaze back to the portrait. It was then that she saw the tiny silver shell that hung from her wee neck.

" 'Tis me," she breathed.

"Aye."

"But the Holiers did not have the funds to commission—"

" 'Twas your mother," Mour said. "She knew your whereabouts and made sure of your safety."

"How do you know?"

"Because she cherished you, lass, and she commissioned this portrait to remember you by."

Isobel's eyes stung. " 'Twas guilt for sending me away."

" 'Twas love, Isobel, whether you can admit it or nay."

"Then why did she not . . ."

"Rescue you?" he asked.

She nodded against her will. As she stared at the small girl in the portrait, she could not help but remember the years that followed. Years of terror and hunger and dark hopelessness. If ever there was a child that needed rescuing, it had been she. And perhaps she still did.

"Evermyst was in turmoil," he said, his voice soft. "The Munros were hammering at its very door, and your mother . . . it must not have been much later when she died."

Isobel's stomach twisted. "All the trouble she went through to make certain her daughters were not accused of witchcraft, only to be accused of that very thing herself."

"I am sorry, Bel," he said.

She raised her chin. "Nay. There is naught—"

"Do not say it, lass," he interrupted, his soft tone full of emotion. "Do not deny the pain. You should have been cherished. You should have been held close and had the treasures of Evermyst for your own."

"What treasures?" she asked and forcing a laugh, bent to reach into the ancient trunk. A second velvet bound portrait came away in her hand. "A pair of paintings of lassies torn apart at birth?" she asked, but just then the velvet slipped away to reveal the portrait beneath. The oil was not of Isobel, but of a fair-haired lad. He was approximately the same age as the girl in the other frame, but where her mouth bore a whimsical smile, his was turned down beneath eyes of blue intensity. And about his neck hung a silver shell.

Isobel caught her breath even as Gilmour moved closer.

"Did your mother bear a son?"

She shook her head, her fingers tingling. "Nay," she whispered. "She would not have given up a lad." She shook her head, feeling dizzy. "Nay, she would have wanted a son."

The stone chamber fell silent. "Is that what you think, Isobel? That she gave you up because she did not want you?"

"Nay." She yanked her gaze from the portrait and shook her head. "Of course not. 'Twas because she could not keep me safe. This I know."

"Aye, you know it with your mind," Gilmour said. "But what of your heart?"

Her heart wanted to weep, to cry for the tiny girl in the emerald gown. "Me heart is well," she said and placed the portrait back in the trunk to rise.

"She cherished you, Bel," he repeated.

She stood, feeling restless. "And how do you know that, MacGowan?"

He rose and towered over her. "Because I know you."

She felt the blood drain from her face.

"Who is there who could resist loving you?"

"There are a few," she said, her throat tight.

"Dollag?" he asked.

She turned away. "To name one."

"She was evil, Isobel. Warped by pain and circumstances. It does not mean you are unlovable."

"Unlovable?" She laughed. "I never thought I was."

"Didn't you?"

"Nay," she said, but it was difficult to force out that simple denial.

"So you have felt the touch of love?"

"Of course."

"By whom?"

" 'Tis none of your affair, MacGowan."

"By whom, Bel?"

Her mind scrambled. "Me sister loves me."

"Aye." He nodded. "That she does, lass. And yet you fled."

"I did not."

"Then why did you leave Evermyst—this place you might have called home?"

"I grew weary of the sameness of the days."

"And thus you left the only person who cherished you or whom you cherished in return?"

It was difficult to breathe. "I do not know what you speak of."

"Don't you?" he asked and stepped closer. "What is the real reason for your departure?"

She felt trapped, terrified. "Leave me be, Mac-Gowan. You are forever baiting me. Perhaps you are the reason I left."

"Aye." He nodded. "Meself and Anora. The two who love you."

She gasped a breath and fell back a pace as if struck, but he did not follow her.

"What did you think, Bel? That I spend me days pursuing every lass I meet?"

"Aye. You are the rogue," she whispered.

"Even a rogue must meet his match," he said and reached for her.

She stumbled out of his embrace, breathing hard. "Nay."

"Believe what you will of others," he said. "But know this. If you will have me, I will not fail you. Not today or for all time. I will cherish only—"

"Nay! Quit your lies! I do not wish to hear them."

"Isobel—" He reached for her again, but she slapped his hand away. "There is no need to fear," he said and stepped closer.

"I do not love you," she said, and he stopped where he stood. "Nor shall I. Not today or ever."

"Do not say things you will regret, lass."

"Regret?" She laughed. "I will tell you what I regret, MacGowan. I regret ever meeting you. I regret every moment we have spent together, for I know the truth."

He stood very still, his face expressionless. "And what is the truth, lass?"

"You have no caring for others. 'Tis all a farce, for 'tis you who has taken me sister and plans to reign over Evermyst."

He said nothing for several seconds. "Is that truly what you believe?"

She could barely breathe, could not possibly think. "Aye," she whispered.

"Me apologies, then," he said and bowing at the waist, turned toward the door. For a moment the latch resisted, but the tendons in his wrist tightened and the door sprang open, listing on one leather hinge as he strode away.

The air left Isobel's lungs in a rush. She felt sick to her stomach, dizzy in her head, and suddenly the room seemed too small, stifling. She rushed out of it, but she could not bear to see him, could not return to Evermyst. She pivoted to the right, down toward the water's edge. She would find solace there, peace.

It was as dark as death in the passageway, but she did not care. She had to escape, get away, forget.

But from the end of the hall she heard a noise. The guard. She slowed her course. It was as dark as sin down here. Not a lantern was lit, for even though the passage was well hidden, they would not risk a light. Pausing, she listened, but all she heard was the lap of waves against the roots of Evermyst. Then, when she strained her ears, she could hear the guard's quiet breaths. He slept, so she crouched low beneath the stone arch and passed on silent feet before him, around the curve of rock and out into the open.

Moonlight fell softly on the face of the water, gilding the waves. She took a deep breath of night air and found her way around the steep roots of Evermyst. Not far from the escape route was her favored spot in all the world. The place where she and Anora had oft gone together. 'Twas there that her feet took her now, winding down the side of Evermyst until she came to a quiet inlet. Nearly surrounded by the mountain's towering heights, the water here was still and hidden. Here it was quiet, soothing, and it dawned on her suddenly that she should have found her way here sooner, should have found this place where memories of Anora lived so strong. She would sit a while and let the images come to her—but in that instant she heard a noise. It was only the slightest crackle of sound, and yet she froze, fear skittering wildly up her spine as she turned.

"Isobel," said a voice. "You have come."

Her heart hammered against her ribs. "Who goes there?"

For a moment not a soul moved, and then, from the deepest shadows, a figure stepped forth.

Chapter 28

❧ ◦ ◦ ◦ ❧

I sobel reared back. "Laird Winbourne?" she breathed.

"Aye." Moonlight flashed across his smile. "You've given me quite a chase, lass."

"Chase?" she asked, then suddenly, she knew. It had been he who had snatched her the first time. Why? Why? her mind screamed. But there was no time to consider that; there was only time to escape. She pivoted away, but hands closed around her. She tried to scream, but her mouth was covered, and suddenly she was being carried. Wrestling madly, she tried to get away, but already she could feel the cut of hemp against her wrists as her arms were bound behind her back. Cloth pressed across her mouth and nose, threatening to smother her. She moaned against the pressure and the fabric slipped lower, closing up her mouth as it was pulled tight behind her head.

Through the rush of blood in her ears she heard voices, and then they were moving, marching toward the sea.

Why? Panic filled her and she struggled all the harder. The earth rocked beneath her, and it took several seconds to realize that she was in a boat. Already they were moving, rowing rapidly toward an unknown destination. There was nothing she could do. Indeed, she could barely breathe. And so she lay, unmoving, waiting, worrying until a lifetime later the hull of the boat scraped against earth.

They dragged her out of the vessel and a short time later she found herself in the depths of a woods.

Set upon her feet, she burst away from her captors. Stumbling on the uneven turf, she shambled to a halt as she glanced wildly around her. But no new terror met her gaze.

"There is no need to fear." Winbourne's voice was soft. She shifted her eyes rapidly in his direction. "I'll remove your gag if you promise to be a good lass."

She crushed her panic with all her might, until it was a dull roar in her ears. Then she nodded. Striding over to her, he turned her away from him then worked at the knot.

"It's damnably tight isn't it? My poor lass," he murmured and finally the fabric slipped away.

She spun toward him. "Why?" The word sounded garbled, barely audible for the pain in her throat.

"Do not try to talk yet, my Bel. Not until you've soothed your throat. Finn, fetch the poor lass some mead."

She ignored the words. " 'Twas you who took me before," she accused.

He nodded. "I admit that it was my lads. I left them in Henshaw to do the task, for I could ill afford to be connected to your abduction. Indeed, I worried that MacGowan had seen me with them at the Duke's Inn and would suspect something, but apparently I had other things to worry on. It seems that if I wish a task well done, I'd best see to it myself. Here," he said, taking a horn from Finn. Even in the darkness she recognized the man's lean, wolfish form. "Drink this." He nudged it toward her mouth. She turned away. "Come now, lass," Winbourne crooned. "I've no intention of harming you. You have my solemn vow."

"Then what is your intent?"

"Drink and I will tell you."

She did so, her gaze never leaving his face.

He smiled like a doting uncle. "There's a good lass. Now, where shall I start?"

"Why have you brought me here?"

He lifted one hand as if to apologize. "To become my bride."

Her knees buckled, but he caught her and held her until her legs steadied. "Here, drink more."

"You jest," she croaked.

"Nay, lass, I do not."

"Why me?"

He smiled again. "Such modesty is becoming, but surely you know that you are bonny."

"I think there would be other bonny maids willing to marry you."

"Perhaps because of my station, you think I could take any woman to wife," he said and paced slowly before her. She followed him with her gaze. "But you would be mistaken, Isobel. Indeed, I asked for your sister's hand long ago."

"Anor—" she began, then stopped abruptly on a sharp intake of breath. "I have no sister."

He laughed. "Aye you do," he argued gently. "A twin, in fact. I've known for some time. Indeed, I spent a few nights with the maid named Ailis. I fear she has no particular love for you, lass. Something about mating in the womb."

Isobel shook her head, but even she wasn't sure if she still denied kinship or if it was a gesture of her confusion.

"But I do not particularly care what you and your sister did in the womb. Some years ago, I made a bid for Anora's hand in marriage. I was willing to give her time. After all, rumor has it that she was hard used in her youth. I thought that mayhap her hauteur was really naught more than fear of men. But she had no trouble with MacGowan, it seems."

She shook her head again, and he laughed as if amused by her confusion.

" 'Tis simply this, lass," he said. "I am the fourth son of an old man who has squandered his fortune, so I was left to my own defenses. Evermyst would make a fine port with a goodly profit if managed correctly. Long I have wanted it for my own, but the lady of the keep would not accept me. Still, I did not give up. Even after her marriage, I thought there might be hope. I considered getting rid of her pesky husband and wooing her again, but she seems strangely attached to him. It would not work," he said and sighed. "Thus, you must be lady of the keep, and you must be my bride."

She felt her stomach curdle. "And what of Anora?"

"Come now, lass," he crooned. "You know what must happen to Anora."

She felt faint, weak, terrified.

"Indeed, the widow Ailis thought you had considered it yourself."

"Considered what?"

"How best to be rid of her."

Isobel tried to shake her head, but it seemed as if the world was spinning around her.

"You can admit the truth, lass. I will not hold it against you. You hoped to be the lady of Evermyst. Indeed, with your sad childhood, how could you not long for that power? The moment I met you, I knew there was something strange about you. Something . . ." He paused, watching her askance. "Something . . . familiar, and yet not so. It took me some time to learn the truth. You are the lady's twin. So tell me lass, are you the saintly one or the evil one?"

She shook her head, fighting down the panic and he laughed.

"It matters naught, for your new life will begin soon."

Fear skittered like icy water down her spine.

"Sleep now. I have matters to attend to."

"What do you mean?" Her voice quavered. "Where's Anora?" she cried, but he was already out of sight and she was being pulled away.

The night was endless. Tied to a tree in abject darkness, she slept in fitful starts and horrible wakenings. Dawn came like gray dishwater, washing over the land.

Footsteps startled her. She jerked her head up and Winbourne was there again.

"My apologies for your poor accommodations," he said and going behind her, undid her knots. "But I dared not let you go free lest you ruin our lives forever."

She stood painfully. Her knees threatened to spill

her to the ground, but she kept upright by dint of will-power alone. "I will not marry you." Her voice was harsh, low.

He smiled indulgently. "I fear you have no choice, lass."

"There is always a choice."

He scowled. "What say—" he began, but a sound stopped his words. "Ahh. They have arrived."

Premonition jerked Isobel upright. Three horses stepped into the firelight.

Anora rode before one of the baron's men. Her cheek was bruised, her hair filthy and disheveled, but she was alive, hale. She turned her head and caught Isobel's gaze.

"Blakeley. Where are the others?" asked Winbourne.

The guard stepped from his mount, and Isobel noticed that one of his eyes was swollen shut. "There was some trouble."

"What kind of trouble?"

"Baron and Kirk are dead."

Winbourne swore with vengeance. "And Mac-Gowan?"

"Dead also."

Isobel jerked, but even from this distance, she could feel her sister's emotions. There was terror there. Terror and aching fatigue, but not hopelessness.

"Dead?" said Winbourne. "Who killed him?"

"Kirk."

"Where is the body?"

Blakeley scowled. "It was lost . . . in the river. I had no time to retrieve it. You said to bring the woman here as soon as we could take her."

Winbourne paced closer, dragging Isobel along.

"Aye, you were to bring her here as proof, lest you muck up the job like you did on the river."

"I have her now."

"So you do. But it took the lot of you to find her, and half of you to misdirect those who search for her. You've seen no sign of Laird Lachlan and his men?"

"Nay. They are far gone, heading south after Owen. They'll not catch him."

"Good," said Winbourne and turned. "Lady Anora," he said. "You've given my men some trouble."

Her face was ungodly pale, but her chin was lifted. "Why have you done this?"

"I would tell you, your ladyship, but I fear there is no time. For you were to be dead long ago.

"Finn." From somewhere behind Isobel, Finn stepped forward. "Cut her throat," he said. "But have a care with the gown. We'll need it for my bride."

Finn strode across the turf and grabbed Anora's bound wrists.

Panic burst in Isobel like a flood.

"He's not dead!" she gasped.

The guard jerked. Finn froze, and Winbourne turned slowly toward her.

"What's that?" he asked.

"Anora's husband," she said. "He's not dead."

The baron narrowed his eyes. "And how would you know that, my love?"

"Isobel!" Anora's voice rang in the stillness. "Please—" she began, but Isobel cut her off, her gaze never leaving Winbourne.

"You were right," she rasped. "She is me sister. Me twin." Her legs were shaking. "And I can . . . read her thoughts."

The guard fell back a pace.

Even Winbourne seemed to falter. "You are a witch?" he asked.

"I can read her thoughts," she repeated. "And he is not dead."

"Blakeley?" said Winbourne, turning.

The guard licked his lips and squinted through his good eye. "The rogue was grievous wounded when we left him."

"But not dead."

"Jackdaw battled him."

"And you did not assist?" Winbourne growled.

"I was to return here—"

"He will give himself up for her!" Isobel interrupted.

Winbourne turned toward her. "What's that?"

"If you do not harm her, Laird Ramsay will give himself up for her."

"He is dead," Anora argued. "I know it."

The baron stared at her for a moment, then smiled. "So he yet lives and you would give your life for him."

"Nay," Anora rasped, but Isobel spoke simultaneously.

"If you keep her safe until his arrival, you will have him."

Winbourne turned toward her, his expression bright. "So you have seen the wisdom of my plan?"

"Aye," she said and swallowed her bile. "But you cannot kill her yet."

Silence lay like poison on the camp before the baron spoke again.

"Very well. Finn, tie the lady yonder so that her husband will see her when—"

"I tell you he is dead by now!" interrupted the guard, but Winbourne turned to Anora, boring his gaze into hers.

"Nay," he said finally. "He is not dead, but he soon shall be."

He gave orders rapidly. In minutes, Anora was tied to a tree. Isobel was positioned nearby. The night fell over them like a dark tide as Winbourne sent his guards into the woods.

Minutes dragged by like hours. Terror grated at Isobel. The night seemed to darken. Fatigue wore at her, but suddenly a scream broke the silence.

Isobel jerked. Footsteps whipped through the darkness. Winbourne wrenched his sword from its sheath as a guard galloped into camp, dropped his sword from bloody fingers, and toppled slowly to the ground.

It was Roy, but his eyes were glazed and his hands lifeless.

"Finn!" Winbourne commanded, and the brigand smiled as he pressed his sword to Anora's throat. "MacGowan!" called the baron. "If you do not want to see her dead, you will come in unarmed."

Not a sound answered him. Seconds sliced away.

"Very well then," Winbourne yelled and glancing toward Finn, raised his arm.

"Halt!" shouted a voice.

Isobel held her breath as a wraith-like figure stepped from the shadows.

Winbourne smiled. "So you have—" His words stopped as he squinted into the darkness. Firelight glinted off the other's golden hair. "You're not her husband."

Gilmour MacGowan smiled grimly. His bandage

was gone, and his hands were empty. "And lucky you are that I am not," he said, still approaching the fire. "For me brother is not so forgiving as meself."

"What the devil are you doing here?"

"Let the women go, Grier."

"Guards!" he yelled.

A brigand leapt from the shadows. Moonlight glimmered off his sword as it sliced toward Gilmour.

Isobel screamed. Mour ducked and came up with Roy's sword in his hand. He swung and the guard shrieked. In one fluid motion, Gilmour turned toward Winbourne.

Winbourne stood frozen. "She'll die!" he warned.

Finn grasped his sword in both hands in preparation, but a sound whistled through the darkness and suddenly Finn was stumbling backward. His weapon fell to the earth as he raised his hands uselessly to the Maiden's blade in his throat.

A shadow stepped from the blackness.

"Ramsay!" Anora moaned and he came, knife held before him in a bloody fist.

Riders leapt from the darkness. Gilmour swiped and ducked. Isobel screamed in fear. Ramsay sliced through Anora's bonds, dragging her into the darkness, and Mour was alone, fighting off the brigands who streamed toward him. He was surrounded now, but suddenly a cry tore through the night.

The earth trembled beneath thundering hooves and a score of horsemen leapt into the fray.

"Brother!" Lachlan yelled, and suddenly the tide was turned.

The brigands fell aside as the men of Evermyst rained down upon them. Through the melee, Isobel saw Winbourne fly toward her. In an instant, she felt his hand in her hair and a second later she saw Gilmour.

"One step closer, MacGowan and she dies." The words hissed by her ear, and she felt the tip of his blade press into her neck.

"Let her go." Gilmour's voice was low and steady. "Let her go, Winbourne and you'll not die this day."

The knife left her throat for a moment. Her hands burst free. But her hair was wrapped hard and fast in his fingers, and pain pricked her neck again as she was pulled backward.

"Drop your sword!" Winbourne hissed, "or she'll die this instant."

Gilmour stopped. Winbourne pressed the blade more aggressively to her throat. She squeezed her eyes shut, but even so, she knew the moment Gilmour dropped his weapon.

"Follow us and she's as good as dead, MacGowan," Winbourne said, and suddenly she was being dragged through the woods. She hung back, digging in her heels, but he crashed his fist against her skull. Fire exploded in her head. She reeled as he lifted her into his arms. They jolted through the darkness. She tried to struggle, but her limbs were weak, the world was hazy, and suddenly it was swaying.

A boat. They were back on a boat.

"Nay!" Isobel cried and struggled for the gunnel, gripping the edge with clawed fingers. Winbourne struck her again. She reeled sideways, but heard a roar of fury, and saw Gilmour launch from the shore. He struck Winbourne's shoulder, and they toppled into the black waters.

"MacGowan!" Isobel wrenched upright, but they had already sunk out of sight. The water boiled white and rabid. A knife streaked above the waves and she screamed as the men broke the surface. Winbourne stabbed at Mour but MacGowan caught the other's wrist, immobilizing it inches from his chest, and then they were under again, scrapping and flailing.

Gripping the gunnel, Isobel tried to peer into the depths, but she could see nothing. Muffled cries echoed from the camp, but not a sound was heard from the water.

Terror drowned Isobel. She could wait no longer. Drawing a deep breath, she dived beneath the waves. Water closed over her head. Blackness greeted her, but there was something to her right. She streamed toward it. Fabric met her fingers, but the body was limp. With a lung bursting effort, she pedaled toward the surface.

"MacGowan! MacGowan!" she sobbed and turned the body over.

The baron of Winbourne lay limp on the water's surface.

Sobbing, she turned, her gaze skimming the water. Nothing. She took a deep breath, but in that instant Winbourne's arm streaked around her neck.

She screamed, but the sound was warbled for she was already sinking beneath the waves. Lungs burning, she jabbed him with her elbow. Pain sliced her arm, but of a sudden he was ripped away from her. She spun around and there was Gilmour.

Winbourne raised his hand. The blade flashed in the moonlight. Screaming, Isobel slammed her fist against his skull. The knife veered sideways and in that second, Gilmour caught it and drove it downward. There was a gasping hiss of agony, and then Winbourne sank slowly beneath the waves.

Isobel watched him go. It took her a moment to realize that Gilmour had gone down with him.

Screaming his name, she launched forward and dragged him back up to the surface. He was like lead in her hands, but she pulled him toward shore.

"MacGowan!" she rasped. "MacGowan!"

He didn't answer, but lolled in the water.

Tears streamed hot and unnoticed down her cheeks. "Nay!" she screamed, but he did not move. "You cannot die now, Mour! You cannot die."

The world seemed utterly silent. Then, "Why . . . is that . . . Bel?"

The words were barely audible, forced from lips that were all but immobile.

"MacGowan?" she rasped.

He coughed, breathing hard. "Why . . . can't I . . . die now?"

"You're alive," she breathed and he lifted one hand weakly to her cheek.

"I would have been . . . true to you, Isobel. That . . . I swear." Letting his hand fall into the water, he dropped his head to the side.

"Nay! Nay! MacGowan!" she wailed, and wrapping her arm about him, pulled him up against her body. "You cannot die! You cannot. Not now that I know the truth."

"What . . . truth?" he whispered and she cupped a shaking palm against his cheek.

Her voice quavered. "You are powerful and peaceable, and cunning and kind."

His eyes opened slowly and he winced. "But am I . . ." He coughed. "Beloved?"

Panic filled her, the panic of a lifetime alone. And as she hesitated, he slipped quietly beneath the waves.

"Aye!" she cried and sobbing, dragged him back up. "Aye! You are beloved."

"Then . . ." He coughed again. "You will marry me?"

She trembled. How could she bear to love and lose? How could she touch, then live out her days without it? How—

Gilmour sighed and slumped into the water.

"I'll marry you!" she shrieked and pulled his head up. But his eyes remained closed.

"MacGowan, wake up!" she sobbed.

Nothing, not the slightest movement, nor a breath of air.

"MacGowan! You cannot die, now," she whispered, "for you owe me a wedding night."

He moaned and opened his eyes slowly. "Did you say wedding night, lass?"

"Aye," she said, sobbing and laughing all at once as she pressed him toward the shore.

"Very well, then. One wedding night . . . for the Lady Bel," he said, and crawling onto dry land, promptly passed out.

Chapter 29

A throng filled the great hall of Evermyst.

Gilmour's sister Shona stood near the corner, laughing with her cousins as their children played nearby. They were a noisy lot, but for Sara's wee Maggie, who sat out of the way, stroking a hound that looked like a wolf and whispering earnestly to Claude.

Not far away Gilmour's parents mingled with a host of old friends and new. But it was to Isobel that Mour's attention always strayed.

She was there, in the center of the hall, as radiant as the sunrise, as beautiful as spring.

They were wed, truly and forever. Gilmour tried to adjust to the realization, but it took some doing, for his heart could hardly believe his good fortune.

"Mour."

He jerked back to the conversation at hand. "What's that?"

Ramsay grinned. He and Anora had nearly drowned when they'd first been attacked by Winbourne's men, but they had managed to escape, only to be caught again. It was during the ensuing battle that he had been wounded, but since then he'd spent a good deal of time abed. Rarely had his wife left his side, and that time seemed to have done much to improve both his health and his disposition. "I said, 'twas a fine wedding."

"Ahh." Mour nodded. Where was she now? Oh yes, she was speaking to the Munro, he realized, and scowled. He had spent too much time apart from her during his recovery. It had taken weeks for his arm to heal, for he'd dislocated it again, and recuperation had given him too much time to think, to dream about the night to come.

"I am glad you could attend," Lachlan said.

Gilmour jerked his attention back to his brothers and they laughed.

"He seems a bit distracted, does he not, brother?" Lachlan asked.

"Aye, he does that," Ramsay agreed. "Not so glib on this night of nights."

"Nor so cocky as usual."

The Munro was laughing as he lowered his head toward Isobel. Gilmour's finger twitched.

"Mayhap our wee brother is nervous," Ramsay suggested.

"Nervous?" Gilmour said with a start. "Why would I be?"

They chuckled again and Gilmour grinned. "Ahh well, we cannot all be so worldly wise as you, Ram."

" 'Tis true," Ramsay agreed.

"Nor as lucky as you," Mour added and turned his smile on Lachlan.

"Lucky?" Lachlan grumbled, already on the defensive.

"Aye," Gilmour said, all innocence. "I heard that you were saved by another from sure death."

"Humm." Lachlan shifted his gaze around the hall. "The warrior who led us to the battle," he said, and found the lad called Hunter standing alone near the door. "He is not much to look at."

It was true. He was neither tall nor particularly brawny, but there was a soberness to him, a reticence that warned of caution.

" 'Tis said he carried you unconscious from the firth to the keep," Gilmour added.

"Aye," Lachlan admitted, "although I would have been fine on me own, mind."

"Of course," Ramsay agreed.

"Aye." Gilmour concurred. "Still, 'twas good of him to carry an ingrate like you all that way."

Lachlan looked taken aback. "Who here is an ingrate?" he asked. "I thanked him." He scowled. "A bloody lot of good it did, though. He will barely say three words in return."

"Ahh well. Maybe that's because . . ." Gilmour shrugged. "He's a woman."

A moment of silence was observed. Then, "What?" Lachlan snapped.

Gilmour turned his gaze to his bride again, then back to his brother. "The warrior. Your champion. He's a woman," he said and strode off to greet his guests.

"I am glad you came," Isobel said, and the Munro grunted.

"You thought I would not?"

"I admit that I have thought some evil against you."

His brows scrunched over his narrow eyes.

"When I saw you at the inn with MacGow . . . with me husband, I thought that you planned some trouble."

He tensed. "But now you know better?"

"He would not tell me your purpose there."

"Aye, well that is best, for I'd hate to kill him on his wedding day."

"Perhaps *you* could tell us then, Laird Munro."

He turned at the sound of a woman's voice, then widened his eyes at the sight of Lady Madelaine. "Who are you?"

The lady raised her brows at him. "I am someone who knows bad manners when she sees them."

He scowled, immediately offended. "You are uncommonly outspoken for a woman with no protector at hand."

"And you are uncommonly large for . . . anything."

"Aye. I am," he snarled and squeezed his hands to fists.

Isobel tensed.

Madelaine smiled. "Everywhere?" she asked.

"Lady Mad—" Isobel gasped, but Madelaine turned a haughty expression on the girl.

"I understand that your new position at Evermyst allows you some rein," said Madelaine. "But run along now, Belva. Innes and I have things to discuss."

Isobel stepped closer. " 'Tis a fragile peace that exists between the Frasers and the Munros," she murmured. "I would not have you—"

"Do you know his secret yet?" Madelaine interrupted.

"What?"

"Your husband's secret. Do you know it yet?"

"Mour's?"

The lady's brows raised again. "Do you have another husband?"

"Nay, I—"

"Do not fret." Madelaine smiled knowingly as she placed a hand on the Munro's massive arm. "You will find out soon enough," she said and glanced toward the women, who hurried to escort Isobel to her wedding bed.

"Ho, the rogue of the rogues!" shouted the crowd, and hoisted the bridegroom into the air.

A hundred voices echoed through the keep as lascivious suggestions were shouted and Gilmour was borne from the great hall and up the stairs to his chambers. The chambers he would share with Isobel.

Gilmour's throat felt strangely dry. In truth, the past month was a blur in his mind. Somehow the battle at the firth had been won, even though he'd made a dozen mistakes. He should have recognized Winbourne's men at the Duke's Inn. He should have realized the evil in the man. He should have questioned Ailis and known that she had told Winbourne Isobel's true identity. The two of them would bother Bel no more, for the baron was dead and Ailis had left the village, but he could have avoided much hardship if his wits had been sharper.

"To Gilmour!" someone bellowed.

A host of cheers followed as he was jostled down a narrow hallway. They were almost there.

"And to his lady!" someone else yelled. "Who will surely benefit from his years of practice this night."

There were loud guffaws as he was tipped toward the floor. The mob was well into their cups and Gilmour had to scramble to gain his feet.

"Perhaps we should stay," yelled another, "and see the deed done right."

Gilmour grinned and raised a hand. "I would dearly love to assist you in your quest for knowledge," he said, "but I fear there are some things that must be learned on one's own." He cleared his throat, and his hand was somewhat unsteady against the door latch. "Good night to you, lads."

Well wishes were bellowed amidst a bevy of foolish suggestions, but as Gilmour opened the door, the crowd began to disperse.

He stepped inside. The room was dim. A single candle flickered by the window, casting its golden glow upon the woman in the bed.

"Good eventide," she said, her voice low.

Gilmour managed to shut the door. "Good eventide," he answered, and remained by the portal. "They, ahh . . ." He nodded toward the hallway from whence he had just come. "The lads thought mayhap we should spend this night together."

"Did they?" Her hair had been loosed about her ivory shoulders. Candlelight gilded the soft waves and cast a pink hue to her cheeks. Or perhaps it was a blush.

He moved a step closer.

" 'Twas a fine wedding," he said, although in truth he barely remembered it. He had almost lost her, but he would not be so careless again.

"Aye. 'Twas," she agreed.

"I was surprised Lady Madelaine made the journey to share in the festivities."

"I fear she has plans for the Munro."

"About the Munro . . ." He cleared his throat. "The thought has occurred to me that if I had been honest with you from the start, mayhap we could have avoided some hardship."

"Honest?" she asked.

"About me reasons for being with him at the Lion. Mayhap if I had shared the truth you could have trusted me sooner."

"Nay," she said and glanced at her hands on the coverlet. "For I could not let meself trust." She paused for a moment as she fiddled with the blanket. "I could not let meself be like all the others who swooned for you, and ye . . ." She shrugged. "From the first I longed for you, but I dared not let you know. I tried to believe that you were involved in Anora's disappearance. Indeed, I felt a MacGowan was there when she nearly drowned. But it was Ramsay, and I suspect I would have known that if I'd let meself. I tried to believe you were selfish and superstitious and—"

"Vain," he finished.

"You *are* vain," she countered and he grinned.

"Mayhap I owe the Munro me thanks," he said. "After all, it was he who led me to your door."

"And all because he wished to learn to woo a maid."

"You knew our reasons all along?" he asked, stepping toward her.

"Nay," she said. "I just found out this night. Rhone told me."

He stared at her, perplexed.

"The warrior," she explained. "I believe you call him Hunter. On a night some weeks back, I asked him to find out what evil you and Munro were plotting."

" 'Twas Hunter you met with by the Mill?"

"You followed me?"

There was a note of outrage in her voice, so he grinned, hoping to disarm her. Tonight would be a poor time for an argument.

"I had to," he explained. "For I feared you were planning a tryst."

"Perhaps I was," she said, and he smiled. "There *have* been men who adored me in the past, even if I have not had so many conquests as you."

The smile dropped from Mour's face. "About that," he said, and took another step toward the bed. She looked like a wee angel just sent from heaven, for she wore naught but a voluminous white gown. It lay loose at the shoulders, with the open ties falling with casual greed across her bonny breasts. His throat felt dry. He should have told her the truth long ago. "Isobel, there have been many women who—"

"You needn't tell me the number," she said softly, but her voice was a bit forlorn. "So long as I am the last."

He seated himself on the edge of the bed, facing her. "You will be the last, Bel, that I swear. But—"

"Then that is enough."

"Nay. I must say this, so that you know." He cleared his throat and looked into her eyes. "There have been many women who were—"

She kissed him. Heat suffused him, rattling his wits, and he pulled back quickly, lest he lose his nerve.

"Bel," he said. "I am untried."

Her mouth opened, but no words came, and her lips remained parted for a moment. "What's that?"

He winced as he drew her hand into his. "The truth is this, lass," he said and stroked her wrist. "Never have I bedded a woman."

Some sound escaped her throat. He wasn't certain what it was, exactly.

"But the tales of . . ." she began.

He shrugged. "Just tales, I fear. I have always admired women—many woman—and they seem to be . . . rather fond of me, but there was never one who . . ." He lost all words for an instant. "Who I wished to live out me days with."

"You're a virgin!"

" 'Tis not as bad as all that," he said, taken aback. "I realize the groom is expected to have a bit of experience. But I truly doubt if I am incapable of learning the—"

She wrapped her fingers in his doublet and kissed him again. Desire roared through him. With a groan, he pressed her back upon the pillows.

Her fingers were busy on his buttons, and in a moment his doublet lay open. He moaned at the feel of her hand against his chest, then gently suckled her bottom lip. She trembled, and in an instant his brooch was undone from his tartan.

He kissed her throat, her shoulder, the tiny v where her pulse beat like thunder.

She groaned, but her hands had already slipped to his belt.

Slowly, reverently, he slid his palm down her shoulder, scooping the gown away from her pearlescent flesh and kissing every satiny inch revealed. Dear heavens, she was perfect. He slipped one finger along the edge of her gown, then followed the ribbon down, down, over her nipple.

It was that which most fascinated him. That nipple, just below the fabric. So close. He leaned in and gently kissed it.

She gasped as her hands tightened against his belt.

"Dammit, MacGowan." She yanked at his buckle. "Are you going to help me with this thing, or am I going to have to find someone with more experience?"

He growled, lowered his hands to his belt, and ripped it away.

His plaid was gone in a second. Her hands felt hot and nervous as they grasped his tunic. Their gazes met as she pulled it up, skimming the fabric along his abdomen, up his chest, over his head. And then he was naked.

He leaned toward her, aching with need, but she pressed a hand to his chest and pushed him back as she ran her gaze down his hard muscled form.

"What do you want now, Bel?" he asked, his voice deep and low.

"Me?" She moved her gaze slowly up his rippled torso. "I want what all women want," she whispered. "I want Mour."

Epilogue

❦

Christmas day came again to the high castle. Children laughed, parents feasted, and young men battled and wooed. But finally the day came to an end.

Silence fell over Evermyst. The hounds made circles in the rushes on the floor of the great hall, then settled down to rest. In the stables, the horses snorted, blowing frosty air into the night and then resting their hind legs as they nodded over their hay. High above the crashing surf, in the rooms below the turrets, the MacGowan rogues cuddled with their brides. And in the nursery where Mary sucked her thumb and Claude slept without a care, Senga hummed a soundless tune.

Aye, she had done well. She had brought Anora together with her bonny laird, and she had led sweet Gilmour down the dark passage to the secret chamber she herself had cherished long ago. Then young Isobel had met him there. Stubborn, she was, as stubborn as her mother, but in the end it had all worked out for the best. For they were happy. Aye, they were content.

There was only one left now for her to help. Just one, Senga thought, and smiled as she planned.

Dear Reader,

Are you ready for the historical romance that *New York Times* bestselling author Lisa Kleypas calls "the most enthralling reading experience I've had in years"? Then don't miss Adele Ashworth's SOMEONE IRRESISTIBLE, the first Avon Treasure from this Rita Award-winning writer. It's London—the place to be in 1851. Mimi Marsh has adored the brilliant and dashing Nathan Price in secret for years . . . but now their passion is about to burst forth.

Karen Kendall's contemporary romance debut, SOMETHING ABOUT CECILY, marked her as an author to watch. Now she's back with TO CATCH A KISS. It's just as delicious, as sensuous, as delightful as her debut. Tony Sinclair gives the phrase "To Protect and Serve" a whole different meaning when he's hired to bodyguard Jazz Taylor. She's in no mood to be followed around, but soon gets very used to having Tony's very delectable form in her life.

If you want a bold, dramatic love story set in England, don't miss Taylor Chase's HEART OF NIGHT. Lady Claire Darren is a woman who'd do anything for love . . . including entice Sir Adrian Thorne into her arms. He says he wants nothing to do with her—and then he kisses her . . .

Maureen McKade's love stories are just plain unforgettable, and HIS UNEXPECTED WIFE is her best yet. When high-spirited Annie Trevelyan leaves the mountains of Colorado to seek fame and fortune, her meddling father sends sexy Colin McBride hot on her trail. Soon, Colin has marriage on his mind.

One final note, if you're seeking a book that will make you laugh and cry from one of the genre's most beloved authors, don't miss ANOTHER SUMMER by Georgia Bockoven. *New York Times* bestselling author Catherine Coulter says, "Bockoven is magic! Don't miss ANOTHER SUMMER."

Until next month, enjoy!

Lucia Macro

Lucia Macro
Executive Editor

REL 1101

Avon Romances—
the best in exceptional authors
and unforgettable novels!

THE LAWMAN'S SURRENDER   by Debra Mullins
0-380-80775-0/ $5.99 US/ $7.99 Can

HIS FORBIDDEN KISS   by Margaret Moore
0-380-81335-1/ $5.99 US/ $7.99 Can

HIGHLAND ROGUES: by Lois Greiman
THE FRASER BRIDE
0-380-81540-0/ $5.99 US/ $7.99 Can

ELUSIVE PASSION   by Kathryn Smith
0-380-81610-5/ $5.99 US/ $7.99 Can

THE MACKENZIES: ZACH   by Ana Leigh
0-380-81103-0/ $5.99 US/ $7.99 Can

THE WARRIOR'S DAMSEL   by Denise Hampton
0-380-81546-X/ $5.99 US/ $7.99 Can

HIS BETROTHED   by Gayle Callen
0-380-81377-7/ $5.99 US/ $7.99 Can

THE RENEGADES: RAFE   by Genell Dellin
0-380-81849-3/ $5.99 US/ $7.99 Can

WARCLOUD'S PASSION   by Karen Kay
0-380-80342-9/ $5.99 US/ $7.99 Can

ROGUE'S HONOR   by Brenda Hiatt
0-380-81777-2/ $5.99 US/ $7.99 Can

A MATTER OF SCANDAL   by Suzanne Enoch
0-380-81850-7/ $5.99 US/ $7.99 Can

AN UNLIKELY LADY   by Rachelle Morgan
0-380-80922-2/ $5.99 US/ $7.99 Can

Available wherever books are sold or please call 1-800-331-3761
to order.   ROM 0801